MADE FROM SAPPHIRE

By Gerry Hines

To Joey Gallagher

ISBN-13: 978-1516963607
ISBN-10: 1516963601
BISAC: Fiction / Occult & Supernatural

~1st Movement: Capriccio~
Allegretto

.:Carnelian Kinship:.

~Opus 1~

"Today is just one more step that leads to the journey of your life, son. No looking back now; just focus on your future, aim high, and keep pushing forward. Don't let anything get in your way. Go out there and learn what it means to be a man."

Such were the words of my dad on the day of my high school graduation. His go-get-'em speech may have been an earful of mushy, clichéd enthusiasm, but I was glad to hear it nonetheless. If only I had known at the time just how important clichéd enthusiasm is for staying on your feet in the years beyond the lockers, cafeteria lunches, homecoming games, and annoying hall monitors, I would've done more than take my father's words with a grain of salt.

In simpler terms, I had no idea that the real world could be so harsh, demanding, and at times, ridiculous.

While in high school, I had the notion that hard work today means great rewards tomorrow. If I just wake up every morning, go to school, study hard, graduate, go to college, and get a degree, then my life would be easy, right? So that's what I strove for. I spent my high school years behind the books rather than out terrorizing the neighborhoods with "those damn teenagers" who stayed up all night and slept in class all day. After four long years of textbooks and the turmoil of never-ending high school drama, I finally made it to college.

The college kids…a population in and of itself. The jobs we hold are as reliable as bubblegum glue. The cars we drive raise middle fingers on the highway when they get stuck in first gear. We find that the stacks of bills and debt we unknowingly bury ourselves in are rivaled only by the stacks of empty pizza boxes from a night we would rather forget. Over time, we trade out the essences of "breakfast," "lunch," and "dinner" and replace them with anything that could be microwavable or handed out a drive-thru window. Nutritional choices take the backseat as more convenient choices lead the way.

While I attended my first year at Elm Valley College, I inevitably fell into the rut of being a stereotypical college student. Not like I was complaining, though. I was perfectly happy with being a regular college student. A round of applause for being a normal guy with the dream of growing up to be a normal guy.

It's just fine being normal, I would always think. *I don't want to be super special or anything. Besides, if I'm not normal, then I'd be weird.*

My brother Jacob is four years older than I am. He spent nearly a full year in college and would fill my head with all kinds of crazy stories about his time there. I remember him always telling me that college is a thousand times better than high school, and when I finally experienced it for myself, I could confidently say he was right. College didn't have the underlying sense of confinement that I felt in high school. There's a greater feeling of freedom than in high school because there *really is* a lot more freedom. Unfortunately for Jacob, his freedom came to an end when he landed himself in jail while attending a rather shady party to celebrate the upcoming final exams. I won't go into detail about the infamous event, so let's just say that Jacob pushed the limits of his freedom a little too far when he combined alcohol and bottle rockets with a busy four-way intersection in the downtown area. Ever since that incident, his interest in college faded and rotted away.

My oldest brother, Sal, who is six years older than me, never went to college. He jumped straight into the Army as soon as he wrapped his fingers around his diploma. His motto was "Less books, more bullets," and the thought of going to school after school was more daunting to him than the thought of looking up and seeing a rainstorm of napalm falling at his face. Whatever floats your boat, I guess. However, Sal has performed honorably while enlisted, and I'm happy for him. When I was a kid, he would always talk about being a soldier, so it's good to see him living out his dream.

Just weeks before my second year of college, it was safe to say that I was going a different route than my two older brothers. I had tunnel vision when I looked at my future degree; nothing was going to prevent me from being the ideal normal guy I had always imagined myself being.

3

Easier said than done, I soon found out. My steadfast determination was put to the test in late August when the sound of my cell phone tore me out of my peaceful sleep. Groggily and clumsily, I struggled to clutch my phone with the limp arm I was sleeping on, wondering who could possibly want to talk to me at four in the morning. My eyes strained to focus on the name of the incoming caller.

It's Aaron? I thought muddily. *Oh great, this ought to be good.*

Aaron was my friend whom I'd met early in our first year of college. He was a cool guy, but I swear he had a few screws loose. There was just something a little odd about him. I considered just ignoring his call, but was mildly curious as to why he was calling me at such a miserable hour. Perhaps he butt-dialed me, or something.

"Hello?" I answered in a croaky voice.

"Hey, Mike!" Aaron replied, sounding surprisingly energetic. "I'm sorry if I woke you up, but dude, you have to hear this!"

"What?" I asked, trying to force the consciousness into my brain. "Is everything okay?"

"You have to come downtown right now!" he exclaimed. "The library is on fire!"

I immediately jolted awake. The library was where I worked.

"Are you serious?" I asked, dumbfounded. "You mean where I work?"

"I'm dead serious, man!" I could hear ruckus in the background. "It's totally engulfed! There's no hope for this place, man!"

"Hold on!" I said. "I'm coming right now!"

I quickly slipped on a pair of dirty socks, grabbed my wallet and keys, and I was out the door of my apartment in record time. Jumping into my car, I didn't even take the time to check my mirrors as I backed out of the parking spot with the pedal to the metal. After slamming the transmission into drive, I squealed the tires as I took off, not wanting to waste a single second of time.

4

I can't believe this is happening! I thought. *That was a great job. Now I have to find another before my rent is due. All of this just in time for school, how wonderful.*

The streets were empty, as most people were still asleep. I felt as if I was dreaming and was hoping to wake up at any moment during my short drive to the library. As I grew closer and saw the orange glow from a distance, the realization began to settle in. My life was about to get very interesting very quickly, and I could only hope that I was prepared for it.

When I turned onto the street and saw the flames for myself, the sensation was utterly surreal. I gripped the steering wheel tightly as I slowly crept forward through the small crowd of people who had been lured out by the burning glow and wails of the emergency response vehicles. Streams of water from at least four fire trucks were hissing violently in an attempt to douse the mighty flames. The library was just as Aaron had described...totally engulfed.

My attention was broken away from the giant bonfire of literature by someone flagging me down by the side of the road. The light from the flames was enough to turn the surrounding area into day, and I was able to recognize the person as Aaron with his pudgy face and stocky build. I turned into a parking lot shared by several small stores and parked crookedly next to Aaron's bright yellow truck, which was also parked crooked. As soon as I opened my door, Aaron came rushing over.

"Isn't this wicked?" he shouted, sounding a little more entertained than necessary. "Come on, this way!"

He took off running toward the burning library, and I followed closely behind.

"What the hell happened?" I asked while we were running.

"I don't know," he replied, stopping a little ways before the nearest fire truck. "I was driving past the area a couple blocks down when I noticed the light, so I decided to check it out."

"What were you doing out at this time?" I asked curiously. "Don't you know what time it is?"

"Never mind what I was doing," he told me abruptly.

5

I quickly dismissed Aaron's rude and strange response. The sight of my workplace looking like a solar flare was so entrancing that I really couldn't care about anything else at the time. Tomorrow, it was back to the unemployment lines.

"Man, look at that place burn," I muttered. "I can feel the heat all the way back here."

"It's all those books," said Aaron. "I bet that's what helped it catch easily."

"Yeah," I replied. "This sucks, man! I'm out of a job now."

"Are you sure?" Aaron asked. "You might want to wait for a phone call from your boss, or something like that."

"Dude, take a look at the place!" I said, pointing at the library. "I'm pretty positive that I won't be coming into work tomorrow."

"Yeah, that's really too bad," said Aaron. "You have that apartment to pay for."

"I know," I groaned. "Luckily I just paid this month's rent, so that gives me a little more time to find another job."

"What'll happen if you can't?" Aaron asked. "Would you have to move back in with your parents?"

"I don't know," I shrugged. "Probably, but I really don't want to. They live too far away from the college."

Aaron turned away from me for a few seconds and looked at the burning building.

"Well, I'd let you stay with me for a little while," he said, "but I don't think that'd work out, you know?"

"Nah, don't worry about it," I told him. "If it comes down to it, then I'll just have to move back in with Mom and Dad."

"They wouldn't mind?" Aaron asked.

I shook my head.

"Not if I explain the situation," I said. "This was kinda out of my control, so they shouldn't have much of a problem with it. I'd have to find another job as quickly as I could, though, and getting to college would be...difficult."

"Hey! You two need to back up!"

6

A fireman had noticed Aaron and I standing a few feet away from the fire truck.

"Sorry," I apologized to him, "but could I ask how this started? I work here."

"The cause of the fire has not yet been determined," the fireman replied, "now I need to ask you to back away at least twenty more yards."

"That far away?" Aaron asked.

"This isn't a show," the fireman replied irritably, "so please *back away!*"

Without saying a word, the two of us turned and walked away. Before we had even checked to see if we had gone twenty yards, we stopped walking and glanced back at the burning library.

"I think I should get going," I muttered. "I'm tired and need some time to think crap over."

"Okay," said Aaron. "What are you doing tomorrow?"

"You mean today, right?"

"Well, technically," he said. "I still consider it to be today until I go to bed and wake up, not when it's midnight."

"I don't know, dude," I sighed. "I'll probably be looking for work, I guess. If I find some time, I'll let you know."

"Alright, man," said Aaron, clasping my shoulder. "Take it easy."

As Aaron walked back to his truck, I stood in place for a moment, taking one last look at the library. It wasn't as if I had any special feelings for the place itself, but the fact that it was my workplace gave it a unique sort of sentimental value, and seeing it turn to ash and smoke was somewhat depressing. Compared to my other jobs in the past, the library was by far the best because it was easy and laid-back. No doubt it definitely beat pushing cheap food across a counter to annoying, whiny customers.

My drive back to the apartment was just as quiet as it was on my way to meet Aaron, but it felt much quieter. The excitement was over, so all I wanted to do was sleep at this point. As I climbed up the stairs to the second floor of the apartment building, I couldn't help but smile.

At least I don't have to go to work tomorrow, I thought. *This'll make a pretty cool story to tell everyone, too.*

I climbed back into bed, yawning heavily and thinking about the day ahead. My goal now was to get another job before the semester started, which was only a couple of weeks away. Doing so wasn't going to be easy, especially due to the economic recession, but I was up for the challenge. Whenever I thought things were getting tough, I always thought about my brother Sal in the Army. He was across the seas, risking his life in foreign countries so I could be here right now, taking on whatever petty problems I had to deal with.

Waking up several hours later didn't seem to pass the time much, but I was able to spring out of bed with confidence beneath my feet. Today was a new beginning, and I felt ready to take it on, starting with a big breakfast to kick it off with.

Okay, so maybe the really big bowl of cereal I made for myself wasn't exactly the glorified breakfast of champions, but it was satisfying at best. As the mass of milk-soaked whole grain settled into my stomach, I hopped into the shower to wash away the sands of yesterday and then proceeded to bury my face in my laptop to partake in the mundane pastime of job hunting.

No fast food this time, I told myself. *I took an oath never to do that again. I'll lose my mind if I ever have to hear another beeping fryer telling me to pull the fries up.*

As I searched the local listings, I read the descriptions of any job titles with words I didn't need to look up in a dictionary. If the name of the job was difficult to read, it was probably difficult to perform.

Let's see here. "Information Processor" doesn't seem like my kind of thing. "Quantitative Analyst"? What the heck is that? Whatever it is, I'm gonna pass.

I was quickly becoming aware that most of the jobs in the area were for managers, required some level of experience or degree, or were just out of my territory. Feeling a little flustered, the thoughts of greasy fryers and burger assembly lines kept me going. The days of hanging out the drive-thru

8

window to hand a milkshake to someone in a car five feet away were over, and I was *never* going back!

"*Senior Architect,*" "*Lead Software Developer,*" "*Client Marketing and Sales Executive.*" *Give me a break, people! I'm not even old enough to buy a beer yet, let alone be a senior executive or whatever these are.*

With a disgruntled groan, I closed my laptop and leaned back in my chair, rubbing my eyes. Internet job sites never seem to be of any help to someone who hasn't been working for over half of their life already. I ruffled my hair and took a second to think things over. Maybe it was time for another strategy.

Plan B was simple: if I couldn't find a job from home, then I'd have to get out there and look the old-fashioned way. There really wasn't any need for me to just sit at home and wait for a phone call saying that I was out of work. I quickly got dressed in semiformal clothes in case I needed to do any sudden interviews, grabbed my keys, and headed out the door. Hopefully, I could go around town and find a place with a big sign that blatantly said, "Help wanted."

I cruised around town for nearly ten minutes, taking the time to carefully look at each and every window for the telltale sign. This didn't seem like a very reliable method, but I was feeling particularly lucky today, despite the fact that my old job had literally gone up in smoke.

After a few more minutes of aimless driving, the seeds of hope seemed to grow into a blooming tree as I passed through the parking lot in front of Harbert's Groceries. In the window was the large sign I was looking for. I whipped into a parking spot close to the front of the store, strutted through the automatic doors with confidence and pride, and abruptly confronted the first clerk I saw. He appeared pretty bored as he leaned on his cash register, so I figured I'd give him something to do.

"Excuse me," I said to him, "I'm here for the job offering."

"You'll need to speak to the manager," he told me. His eyes were glassy, as if he was about to fall asleep. "Wait here, I'll go get him for you."

9

I watched the clerk walk off as I stood by the drinking fountain, amazed that I had already found a potential job. If everything went well, I'd be able to pay the bills on time with little hassle. When I glanced around the store, I noticed a familiar face lazily bagging groceries for a small line of customers. His name was Lawrence, and he was one of Aaron's other friends. I didn't know him very well but had seen him around the campus. Just another college kid locked into the lifestyle of low-paid people attempting to make a name for himself.

Time began to creep past, and I was growing a little impatient, as there was still no sign of the manager. Shoppers wandered around the store in their search for milk, bread, or whatever it was they needed. While I watched them going about their business, the reassuring thought of store customers being far more tolerable than restaurant customers kept me from running away from this job opportunity like a scared little child, or so I hoped.

The clerk I talked to returned with a tall, lanky man with large glasses and a bushy mustache. He walked over to me as the clerk stood back behind the register, and I perked myself up for the presentation.

"Hello," the tall man greeted, "you wanted to speak with me?"

"Yes, I'm here to ask about the job opening."

"Ah, yes," he replied. "I'm Bill Straussford, the manager. Right this way, please."

I followed Mr. Straussford across the store to the back where he led me into his office. The room was small and packed with filing cabinets. Stacks of paper were everywhere, and I found it hard to even walk into the room without knocking something over. Boxes were lined up and stacked against the wall, and there was barely enough room for the two of us. For a manager's office, it was pretty unorganized, even borderline messy. Mr. Straussford sat down behind his desk and used his entire arm to push everything to one side and clear an opening big enough to write on a piece of paper.

"Take a seat," he told me. He sounded a little unenthused.

I looked around for a chair.

There's no chair in here, I thought. *Is this some sort of test?*

"Sir, I don't see a chair," I replied, trying not to sound confused. Confidence is an important factor in a job interview.

"Hmm, just pull up a box and use that," he told me. It was hard to tell if he was trying to be funny at all.

I grabbed a nearby tote box and slid it across the floor to position it in front of Mr. Straussford's desk. Taking a seat on top of it, I tried not to feel as awkward as possible, sitting up straight. Maybe if I pretended it was a stool, it wouldn't be so bad. Mr. Straussford cleared his throat obnoxiously and straightened his large glasses.

"So, what's your name?" he asked me uninterestedly.

"Michael," I replied.

"Okay, Michael, have you ever worked for a Harbert's Groceries?"

"No, sir," I replied.

Mr. Straussford gazed at me through his glasses for a few seconds before opening a drawer in a nearby filing cabinet. He sorted through a tight collection of folders and papers, took out an application, and handed it to me across his desk with a pen and clipboard.

"Go ahead and fill that out for me," he said.

While I was quickly filling out the application, I couldn't help but feel a little triumphant. This job was in the bag, I could feel it. At this rate, it would be like I was never unemployed after losing my last job. I signed the dotted line at the bottom of the page and gladly handed it back to Mr. Straussford. He scanned over it, then filed it in another drawer.

"All I need you to do now is fill out some more paperwork," he told me, digging out some more papers from four different filing cabinets. How he knew exactly where everything was baffled me.

With the exception of a few things to fill out, the paperwork consisted mainly of checkboxes and signatures. I easily completed the forms, but being hunched over a clipboard

11

while sitting on a tote for an extended period of time was tiring. After the last box was checked and the last signature inked, I handed the papers back to Mr. Straussford. He scanned through everything quickly, set them down on his desk, and looked at me with the first smile I had seen that man crack.

"Alright, looks good," he told me. "Welcome aboard."

He and I both stood up and shook hands.

"Thank you sir," I replied.

That's all I had to do? That was a million times easier than I thought it would be. No way did this all happen so easily!

"I'll give you a call to inform you of a follow-up meeting," he said. "You'll need to bring your driver's license or ID card next time. After that, you'll be all set."

"Okay," I said, "thank you, Mr. Straussford."

I strutted out of the manager's office feeling light as a feather. There was no need to worry about my bills or rent now. Mr. Straussford seemed all too eager to hire me, although I didn't think I made *that* great of a first impression. Whatever the case, I had no complaints.

I approached the automatic doors with my hands pressed together out in front of me, then pulled them apart as I pretended to open the doors like Moses parting the Red Sea. Yeah, I was feeling cocky, but wouldn't you be if you were in my shoes just then?

Before I could make it back to my car, I felt a vibration in my pocket. Reaching inside, I removed my phone and checked the caller ID with Aaron's name on the screen.

"What's up?" I answered.

"Not much, man," said Aaron. "How goes the job hunt?"

"It couldn't go any better," I boasted. "I just got hired at Harbert's Groceries!"

"You don't say," said Aaron with a chuckle. "That was quick."

"I practically walked in, asked the manager about the job, and he gave it to me," I said, unlocking my car with the remote. "All in about forty-five minutes."

"Nice, nice," he said. "My buddy Lawrence works there."

"Yeah, I saw him," I replied, sitting down in the driver's seat.

"Well, that's cool," said Aaron. "What are you doing right now? I was seein' if you wanted me to come to your place so we can chill and stuff."

"Sure thing," I said. "I'm heading home right now if you want to meet me there in about twenty."

"Alright, man," he replied, "peace out."

"Later."

I started up my car and immediately put one of my favorite CDs in the player. My ride home was celebrated by jamming out with what I like to refer to as my "victory music." Exactly what that is, I'll leave it up to your imagination.

Propelled by excitement, I flew up to my apartment two stairs at a time, feeling like a king entering his castle as I unlocked the door and marched proudly inside. However, being nothing more than a lowly college kid in his apartment, all I could do was grab a granola bar, hop on the couch, and flip through the TV while I waited for Aaron to show up.

"Are you finding it difficult to find work in today's job market?" said one commercial that just came on.

"Nope," I replied, changing the channel with a smirk.

A few minutes passed before I heard a knock on the door. I opened it and greeted Aaron by pounding fists.

"Hey," I said.

"What's up?" he said, stepping inside. "Man, it's hard to believe how easily you got another job. I wish it was that simple for me. I was unemployed for almost three months after I got laid off."

"I'm just as surprised as you," I said as I walked back over to the couch and sat down. "The manager was a little strange, and I wasn't sure if he liked me very much at first."

"Strange, huh?" Aaron took a seat on the other end of the couch. "How was he strange?"

"I don't know," I said. "He acted really bored, or like he didn't want to talk to anyone."

13

Aaron acknowledged it with a nod. "But whatever, right?" He grinned.

"Yeah, I'm just glad to have a job," I replied. "I can deal with a weird boss knowing how easily he hired me. The interview was really short."

"Maybe he just wanted to hire a tool," said Aaron. "He probably didn't see much in you, so he figured you could just clean up after his other employees."

What's that supposed to mean? I thought.

"Oh, thanks," I replied, feeling a little irritated.

"I'm just sayin'," he said. "You gotta watch out. Some of these employers are underhanded like that. Did you read the fine print on everything you signed?"

"Well, not all of it," I muttered. "Some of it was just a bunch of legal stuff that I've seen before."

"You need to make sure you didn't sign something weird," Aaron warned. "Are you sure you didn't see anything about receiving a lower pay because you're going to be the guy who keeps the coffee flowing, or the bag boy's assistant, or the weekend backup custodian?"

"I doubt it'll be anything like that," I told him. "Do you really think I'd make that bad of an impression?"

Aaron quickly examined my clothes, then rubbed his chin.

"Your clothes don't look too bad, so it probably wasn't something superficial."

"So, you're implying that I *did* make a bad impression," I said.

Aaron could be really annoying sometimes, and this was turning out to be one of those times. I crumpled up the wrapper for the granola bar I had just eaten and let it fall to the floor.

"Well, it's possible that he just didn't like you," he said conclusively. "You said he seemed bored. Was he like that the entire time?"

"Up until the end when I shook his hand," I said.

"Yeah, I don't think he likes you," said Aaron.

"We'll see," I replied. "All that matters is I got the job. Let's order pizza in memory of the library. I'm hungry."

"Ah, yes, the library," said Aaron. "I'll eat to that. Hey, do you think anyone has ever roasted marshmallows over a flaming building?"

Why would anyone want to? You come up with the weirdest things.

"Um, I wouldn't doubt it," I replied passively as I looked up the several pizza parlors saved in my phone's contacts. "Where do you want to order from?"

"Forelli's is having a special," said Aaron. "If you buy two large pizzas, any number of toppings, you get a free medium pizza with any number of toppings."

"Really? That's pretty cool," I said, "but I don't think we'll need that much."

"We'll have leftovers," Aaron suggested. "Why not, man? Isn't this your lucky day? I think that deserves something special."

I thought about it for a moment. What harm would it do to just go all out this once? Besides, pizza makes awesome leftovers.

"Yeah, why not?" I agreed, selecting Forelli's from my contact list.

~Opus 2~

Working at Harbert's Groceries wasn't the best way to earn a buck, but it didn't give me much to complain about. I typically had to do stocking and bagging, which are tasks usually expected for the new guy to do. On the brighter side, I was becoming more acquainted with Lawrence. As soon as he found out that I was friends with Aaron, we immediately kicked it off. He seemed like a really cool guy from what I could tell, although his work ethics were kinda lacking. In other words, he was a little slow to get things done.

The final days of summer break quickly came and went, and my second year at Elm Valley College began before I knew it. When I woke up on the first morning of class, I took a deep breath as I braced myself for the year ahead. All I had to do was pretty much the same thing I had done the previous year, and then I'd be officially dubbed as a college graduate. This was going to be a breeze!

Don't get the wrong impression, though. I wasn't exactly excited to be back in school. No offense to those people who love to learn, but I was just there for my degree.

Let's get this over with, I thought as I walked out to my car with my backpack filled with heavy textbooks. *Just don't screw it up.*

I glanced over my schedule while sitting in my car in the campus parking lot. First class of the day—psychology. That was just what I needed first thing in the morning; learning what my parents did to make me so screwed up. At least I was somewhat interested in psychology, so I wouldn't have to worry about being bored as well as sleepy in the morning.

The campus was full of students as I made my way across the grounds. I noticed a few familiar faces but nobody I really associated with. They were all just other students I went to class with. My goal in college wasn't to make friends, though. Being in a classroom full of people I didn't know never bothered me at all, and I never took priority in striking up a conversation with the person sitting next to me.

16

When I approached the building that my psychology class was in, I pulled the door open and held it for the people behind me. A couple of them looked depressed as they walked up, cracking a small, courteous smile as thanks when they passed by. They appeared just as thrilled as I was to be going back to school.

I stopped in front of one of the classrooms and read the number next to the door. Checking my schedule one more time, I made sure that I was in the right place, stuffed my schedule in my pocket, then walked in. The seats were slowly filling up as I quickly scanned for a place to sit and saw that the back of the room had some empty spots left. Seizing the opportunity, I grabbed a chair in the last row and sat down with a small sense of satisfaction. Sitting in the back was always my thing, don't question it.

There was still some time left before class started, so I decided to do a last minute inventory check. Not like it would've helped me much to see that I had left my book back at my apartment while sitting in class, but it still gave me something to do. As I was going through my stuff, someone sat down in the seat next to me. When I looked at who it was, I was a little surprised. Lucky me, it was a cute Asian girl.

She looked at me and smiled.

"Hi," she said sweetly.

So, naturally, I smiled back.

"Hi," I replied. "Back in school already. Where'd the summer go?"

The girl chuckled.

"Yeah, really," she said. "Thanks for reminding me."

"I'd better remind you now before the first test comes up," I said, playing along, "otherwise you'd get a nasty surprise."

"Yeah, I guess you're right," she said. "My name's Miyuki, by the way."

"Miyuki?"

That's an interesting name, I thought.

"I've never heard that name before," I replied.

"It's a common Japanese name," she told me. "I have a lot of Japanese ancestry."

"That's pretty cool," I said. "I'm Michael, but everyone calls me Mike."

"Well, it's good to meet you, Mike," said Miyuki happily. "Here's hoping to a good year!"

"I hope so," I told her. "I could definitely go for another good year in college."

"Oh, this isn't your first year?" she asked.

"It's my second," I said.

"This is my first time in college," she said, fiddling with her pencil.

"Really? Did you graduate high school this year?"

"Yup," she replied.

"College was pretty exciting for me when I started," I said. "Are you nervous?"

"Um, a little," she said. "Fear of the unknown and all that. People tend to be kinda scared of things they aren't familiar with."

"I know what you mean," I said. "You'll get used to it fast, I think. It's a lot like high school, but without the feeling of being a prisoner."

"I can't really say I know what it's like being a prisoner," said Miyuki, smiling, "but if college is better than high school, I'm all for it."

The instructor walked into the classroom just as the bell rang. Either she had really good timing, or it was just coincidence. I recognized her from last year as Mrs. Flynn, although I never had a class with her. The limp she walked with was unmistakable, and her light, curly hair made it possible to spot her from a mile away. A few students were still coming into the room as she took a seat behind her desk and smiled as she looked around at the fresh faces she'd be teaching. Minutes later, after everyone was positioned, she stood up to address the class, and the dull sound of conversations transitioned into the snapping and clicking of pens, pencils, and binders.

18

"Hello everyone," Mrs. Flynn announced. "Welcome to the new school year! I'm Mrs. Flynn, your psychology instructor for this course."

My mind wandered a little bit as the instructor talked. It was the same discussion that every single teacher gives on the first day. She explained the class rules, gave an overview of what material we'd be covering, explained the procedures, and so on and so forth. After nearly an entire period of this, Mrs. Flynn wrote something on the board for us to write down. I flipped open my notebook, put my pencil to the paper, and felt the familiar snap of graphite.

"Gah, really?" I muttered, looking at the broken pencil tip.

Miyuki had noticed and immediately dug into her book bag. She took out a small pencil sharpener and handed it to me.

"Thanks," I said courteously, taking it from her. I sharpened my pencil, blew away the shavings and dust, then proceeded to jot down what was written on the board.

The bell rang to signify the end of the first class, and some people were already out of the room before I could finish putting my things away. After standing up, I turned to Miyuki.

"It was nice meeting you," I said.

"Same to you," she said sweetly. "What class do you have next?"

"Communications," I replied, taking my schedule out from my pocket.

"I have music theory," she told me.

"Oh," I said, "I didn't realize music had a theory."

"Apparently it does," she said with a smile.

"Hmm, alright." I put my notebook into my backpack. "Maybe I'll see ya around."

"Yeah, maybe," she said. "Bye."

We walked out of the classroom and headed in different directions.

My communications class was in the room I had used for my public speaking class the previous year, located only a short distance from my psychology class inside the same building. Mr. Holden, the instructor, was the same as well. He was a very entertaining person and made his classes interesting, so I was looking forward to another good course with him.

Miyuki, huh? I thought to myself while walking. *Let's see if I can get her phone number by the end of the month.*

I wore a discreet grin on my face on the way to my second class until a bulletin board caught my attention. Deciding to check it out and see if anything cool was coming up, I stopped and examined what flyers and announcements were posted. One of them was for an upcoming gig at a nearby venue called the Boney Feather, and it mentioned local bands and other live entertainment.

This flyer says it's tonight, starting at seven, I thought. *I don't have to work tonight so maybe I'll go to that. Who knows, it might be interesting.*

Using the back of my class schedule, I wrote down the name of the venue and address.

"Hey, Mike!"

I looked to see who was calling me and saw Aaron walking up. He was with a short black guy who appeared to be our age.

"Hey, man, what's up?" I said to Aaron.

"This is Chad," said Aaron, introducing the short black guy. "He was in my class just now."

"How's it goin'?" said Chad, shaking my hand.

"Good," I replied. "Nice meeting you."

"My dad works for the fire department," Chad told me. "He was there on the night when the library burned down."

"Oh, really?" I said, suddenly becoming very interested. "I used to work there before that happened."

"That's what Aaron said," said Chad. "When the firemen searched the place afterwards, my dad found this book. Aaron said you might be interested since you used to work at the library."

Chad reached into his bag and took out a large book, which he handed to me. Normally, someone wouldn't have thought anything special about it; it appeared to be just an old book. However, considering the fact that it was inside a building completely destroyed by fire, it was strikingly odd that the book was totally unharmed.

"There's no sign of fire damage at all," I said, checking the entire exterior. I quickly flipped through all the pages, noticing that it showed no unusual wear. Other than being a little dirty from the ashes, it was in pretty good shape.

"We started talking about the library fire," said Aaron, "and that was when he showed me the book."

"It was found underneath a bunch of smoldering wreckage, my dad said," Chad told me. "He couldn't believe that it was unharmed, so he asked the library director if he could take it home and give it to me."

"That's crazy," I said in awe, looking through the pages more slowly.

There was a lot of weird stuff written in it, and while some of it was printed, most appeared to be handwritten. Strange pictures and symbols were on nearly every page, indicating some sort of odd, religious context. I also noticed that it was in at least four different languages, including English.

The book consisted of what appeared to be over three hundred pages made from different types of paper, as if it had been pieced together from multiple writings. If that was the case, then it had been assembled very well with evenly trimmed pages and a nice binding.

"What kind of a book is this?" I asked. "It looks pretty strange."

"I'm not really sure," Chad replied. "I really can't understand any of it. I don't even think it has a title. You can have it if you want. I don't really have a use for it."

Initially, I considered taking it, but then I thought about having one more book to carry around. The weight from my textbooks was already enough.

"I don't have much use for it, neither," I said. "Thanks anyway."

"Okay, that's cool," said Chad, taking the book back. "Thought I'd ask."

"Funny how we ran into you just now," Aaron told me. "We were saying how you'd probably want to see it."

"Yeah, I can't believe it survived the fire," I said. "I mean, you saw the library, Aaron. That fire was massive."

"The world's a strange place," said Aaron with a smile. "Well, my next class is on the other side of the campus. I'll catch you guys later."

"Nice meeting you, Mike," said Chad.

"Same here," I replied.

When I walked into my communications class, Mr. Holden was already seated at his desk, having a conversation with a couple of students in the front row. I noticed some empty seats in the back of the room and headed straight for them. The remaining chairs filled up rather quickly as I sat and waited for class to start. A guy with a shaved head took the seat next to me, and I saw that his arm had a large, intricately detailed tattoo of a banana split. We both greeted each other with a simple nod.

A banana split tattoo. What bet did he have to lose to get that?

By the time the bell rang, every seat in the room was occupied. I looked around at the full class, thinking I had to know at least one person in this room with so many students, but was surprised when I realized that wasn't the case. If I was planning on striking up a conversation with someone in this class, it would have to be with baldy-banana-split dude, and he didn't look very willing to talk with anyone.

"Well, we have a full house as you can see," said Mr. Holden happily once class had started. "I didn't think I was this popular. I'm Mr. Holden, and this is communications. In this class, we talk about how and why people communicate through conversation, art, and media, among other ways. This will only be a basic class that briefly touches on all the various aspects of communication."

Another thing I had noticed about college is that some of the classes seemed pretty unusual or out of the blue. I had never heard of a communications class before, and I had no idea that there was an actual study of communication. I had to learn some things that were pretty useless to me during my pursuit of the almighty degree, and I would just have to suck it up and accept the fact that I was going to learn something I'd probably never apply. Despite being in my second year, I still didn't

22

know what I wanted to major in. I had switched from business to math, mainly because I was good at math, but my career pathway was still open-ended, so it was hard to determine what knowledge could be classified as "useless" or "important" at this point. With that being the case, I figured I should just learn whatever I could. Knowledge is power and all that jazz.

My attention was directed back to the banana split tattoo. It was almost photorealistic, possibly even mesmerizing. The longer I looked at it, the more I wondered *why*? Just why?

An hour eventually passed as I halfway paid attention to the instructor's recycled first-day speech, and I forced myself not to be taken in by the bald guy's mysterious ink job. Once dismissed, I looked at my schedule to find out where my last class of the day was, which was located in a different building.

The sun was hot and the air was dry as I journeyed to the next building. Having a campus with multiple buildings annoyed me because I would have to go out in the cold and the snow during the winter. Rain wasn't much better, and sitting in class while dripping wet made me uncomfortable. Luckily, it was a warm and sunny day that Monday, so I didn't have to worry about anything other than bees. Someone had once told me that the flowers planted around campus were more attractive to bees than other flowers. I wasn't sure if that was true and honestly didn't care.

Each building has seating areas in various places for the students to sit, relax, enjoy a quick read, or squeeze in a little extra studying between classes. Most of the areas looked pretty comfortable, but I never took the time to use any of them. As I was walking by one of them, I noticed Chad sitting there, thumbing through the mysterious book he had shown me, so I decided to say something to him.

"Chad," I said as I approached him, "how's it going?"

"Oh, what's up, Mike?" he said with a big smile. "You got a class 'round here?"

"Yeah, U.S. history," I replied.

"Hey, me too!" He shut the book and stuffed it back into his bag. "Mr. Weechik, right?"

I checked my schedule really quick.

"That's the one," I said.

"Well, what do ya know, it looks like we're classmates," he said, shaking my hand.

This Chad guy's pretty friendly. I don't think we'll have much trouble getting along.

"I saw you were checking out that weird book," I said. "Find anything out?"

"Not really," he shrugged. "I just think it looks interesting. The more I look at it, the more I'm convinced that it's put together from other books or something."

"Well, the library used to receive donated books," I told him, "and some of them looked old. I've filed and organized a lot of weird things while working there, so something like yours isn't completely new to me. But I have to admit that I've never seen one quite like that one."

"Books come in all shapes and sizes," said Chad, "but this one's special because it's the only thing that survived the fire."

"Wait," I said curiously, "you said the *only* thing that survived?"

"That's what my dad said," said Chad. "Everything in that library that could catch on fire did just that. Everything but the book. All of the other books, the building, all of it. It's one hundred percent ash, except for anything metal, stone, and this book."

"That's really strange," I said. "So the fire department couldn't do anything about it?"

"My dad said it was like they weren't even doing anything," said Chad. "The fire just burned and burned."

I was lost for words. Not knowing what else to say, I looked at my phone to see what time it was. Class was going to begin shortly, and although I didn't care if I was a little late, the subject was begging to be changed.

"I think I'm going to class now," I said. "We only have a couple more minutes."

"Yeah, let's go." Chad stood up and slung his book bag over his shoulder with an eager look on his face. "U.S. history time. It's one of my favorite subjects, ya know?"

"Oh really?" I said. "Maybe you can help me out if I have trouble."

"Sure, sure," Chad replied eagerly. "I love history, so ask me if you have any questions."

I chatted with Chad all the way to our class. He told me how he became a history tutor in high school after his teacher caught him giving away answers during a quiz. When he explained that he just *had* to help other students with history because he loved the subject so much, the teacher appointed him as a tutor due to his excellent grades in the class. He also said that other students used to help him in other classes (because apparently history was the only thing he was good at), so he saw it as a good opportunity to return the favor.

"I've known Aaron since high school," Chad told me as we waited for class to start. "I got to know him a little bit when I helped him with history, but we ain't very close. He graduated a year before me, so I didn't see him after that."

"I met him last year when we started college," I said. "We hang out every now and then. All of my friends from high school either didn't go to college or went to a different one."

"Aw man, for real?" said Chad.

"Yeah, it's crappy," I said, "but hey, what can you do?"

"Right, right."

When Mr. Weechik started the class, it was obvious that it was going to be the same discussion as in the other two classes I had had that day. Even so, Chad was in his zone, listening intently to every word the instructor said. Nothing against Chad; he seemed like a really nice guy, but I hoped he was being truthful about the whole loving to teach history thing. I hated history.

The bell rang, signifying my release from school for Monday. I walked back to my car, feeling good about my first day back. Everything was off to a good start so far, so I just had to make sure that everything stayed good. I'd heard stories of people who were well on their way to completing college, but carelessness steered them off track and they ended up in unforeseen messes. However, I was keeping my eye on the prize.

Before going back to my apartment, I wanted to swing by somewhere and pick up some lunch in the drive-thru. I ordered some chicken sandwiches and onion rings, which I was craving for whatever reason. The smell was tantalizing as it filled my car, and I couldn't wait to get home and eat.

At my apartment, I sat down at the table with my food and books in front of me. Mrs. Flynn had us write down what the first psychology assignment was, so I figured I would get started on it. There was still plenty of time left before the show at the Boney Feather. With a sandwich in one hand, I opened my psychology textbook and began reading the first section of Chapter One, eating as I went along. I didn't know very much about the mind and brain, but everything was making sense to me so far. After finishing my first chicken sandwich, I unwrapped my next one and continued through the chapter.

The assignment was to answer the questions in the section review. I flipped open my notebook and wiped off my greasy fingers so they wouldn't slide off the pencil as I wrote. I started off strong, answering the questions quickly and confidently, but as I made it a quarter of the way through the assignment, I began to slow down.

There's a lot of information in this first chapter, I thought as I continually flipped back and forth to find the answers. *If I would've known it'd take this long, I would've ordered more food.*

Completing the questions eventually took over an hour and wore me out more than I had expected. For the first assignment of the year, it was rather difficult. As I closed my books with a sigh of relief, I wondered if the other students had difficulty as well and that it wasn't just me.

I left for the Boney Feather later that evening with the directions scribbled down on a small notepad. Before I'd left, a quick check on a map website was necessary to find out how to get there. Living in Elm Valley for only a year, a lot of places were still a little unfamiliar to me.

Finding the venue proved easy, but finding a place to park was more challenging. A flood of people had shown up, and after driving around the block for a parking spot, it was apparent that I was in for a walk.

A small crowd of college students led the way to the larger crowd congregating in front of the venue. As I stood in line and peered over the people shorter than me, I noticed they were checking IDs at the entrance. When it came time to show my driver's license to the person doing the checking, he used a black marker to draw an X on my hand to show that I couldn't buy alcohol. I was only twenty until the fourth of next May, after all. Handing the man ten dollars for admittance, he gestured me inside.

As soon as I was through the doors, I took a quick look around to see exactly what kind of place it was. Along the outside were tables and chairs, and a bar was located on either side. In the middle was a large lower section with more tables and chairs, and the back wall housed the stage where equipment was being set up.

The venue was filling up fast, so I ventured into the lower middle section to look for a good place to sit. A small table decently close to the stage was unclaimed, so I made it mine. Once I was seated, I looked around some more to see if I knew anybody there. Aside from some people I only knew by their faces, there was no one I recognized.

Up on stage, the tech crew was still setting up for the show. Right in the middle of them was a girl practicing a bass guitar. She had shiny, black hair that was pulled back into a ponytail with a purple ribbon, and her long bangs covered nearly one side of her face. A large, silver ornament hung from her necklace, but I couldn't see exactly what it was from where I was sitting.

Strangely, she seemed totally oblivious to the tech crew trying to set things up around her. Cords kept getting caught around her feet as they moved equipment around. When asked to move, she would walk a few steps to the side and stop, never once taking her concentration away from her bass playing. She looked so engrossed in what she was doing that I was actually waiting for someone to plug her bass into an amp so I could hear her.

I took another look around, and when I realized that the seating around me was nearly full, I locked eyes with another

27

girl…a beautiful girl with brown hair and stunning green eyes. She instantly approached me and stood next to the chair across the table from me.

"Do you mind if I sit here?" she asked hopefully.

Please do, I thought.

"Go ahead," I offered.

"Thanks," she replied, taking a seat. "I was beginning to think there were no more places to sit."

When she placed her purse on the table, I noticed a black X on her hand.

"Is this your first time here?" I asked her. The noise from the growing crowd was increasing so I had to raise my voice a little.

The girl smiled and nodded.

"I'm new around here," she said, fidgeting.

"Oh yeah?" I said. "Are you going to college here?"

She smiled and nodded again.

"It's my first year," she told me, playing with her hair.

I could tell she was shy just by looking at her. This was her first day at college, so it was understandable that she'd be a little nervous.

"I'm Mike," I said, extending my hand across the table.

"My name's Hayley," she replied, shaking my hand.

"This is my second year here," I told her, "so if you have any questions or anything just let me know."

"Okay," said Hayley bashfully. I could see her face turning red, and it was almost too cute to watch.

"So," I said, attempting to make her more comfortable by getting to know her more, "did you come here with friends?"

"No," she replied timidly with a small smile. "It's just me."

I had to hand it to her for coming here by herself. She was probably trying to break out of her shell by getting more socially involved, which isn't very easy for some people.

The lights dimmed and I turned my attention to the stage. Everything was set up and ready to go, but the girl with the bass guitar was still standing up there. She had stopped practicing and was just gazing out into the audience with an

28

expressionless face. For a moment I thought she was going to announce the start of the show, but a young man walked from offstage and took the microphone from its stand.

"Hello Elm Valleeeeeey!" he announced enthusiastically, invoking a roar from the audience. "Welcome to this year's annual variety show here at the Boney Feather!"

Another roar from the audience followed.

"How many Elm Valley College students are in the audience tonight?" he asked.

I should've been prepared for it, but the following response probably rattled the liquor bottles on their shelves.

"We have some entertainment lined up for you this evening," the announcer continued. "First on the list is a local rock group some of you may be familiar with. This is their last performance, as the band's members have stated it's time for each of them to go their own way. They've worked hard for this final night, so let's show them our appreciation. Give it up for Triangular Lockjaw!"

Wait, what did he say the band was called? I know somebody used a random word generator for that.

As the members of Triangular Lockjaw came into position onstage, it was soon apparent that the black-haired girl was part of the band when she plugged her bass into an amp. The other members took a moment to quickly tune their instruments and made sure everything was ready to go.

The first note ran me over like a freight train, and I suddenly felt as if I was at a real rock concert. For a college band, Triangular Lockjaw sounded impressive, and I eventually found myself getting sucked into the music by the end of the first song. When the song ended, I joined in with the loud applause that I felt the band fully deserved. When I looked over at Hayley, she smiled and looked away.

With her large necklace ornament swinging, the girl on bass practically assaulted her instrument. At times, she shredded faster than the guitarists. The purple ribbon in her hair fluttered behind her as she rocked out at full force; quite a surprising sight due to her relatively small size. There were a few moments when I was afraid she'd rip that bass guitar in half, but I figured that'd actually be pretty cool to see.

The band performed five songs altogether, each one being more than good. I had a hard time believing that they were breaking up. Each member was very talented, and I suspected that they were moving on for a better cause, or whatever it is bands break up for. I had to see if I could buy a CD from them by the end of the night.

"Thank you all so much," said the lead singer after the last song. "We really appreciate all the support that so many of you have given Triangular Lockjaw. I hope you all have a good evening."

That's it? No introduction of the band members? No explanation as to why you're breaking up? No CD reminder?

The rest of the acts for the remaining evening weren't quite as entertaining as the first. Essentially, the entire event was a talent show and most of the acts had nothing to do with music. Some people performed short skits while others showed their strange and unique talents, but putting the most energetic act first was a bad idea. As half of the audience proceeded to get drunk as the entertainment value dwindled, I figured it would be a good time to try and hit up the girl across the table from me some more.

"What do you think of the shows?" I asked her.

"They're good," Hayley replied.

"You're not bored, are you?"

"No, I'm having a good time," she said, playing with her hair again. "Are you having a good time?"

"Yeah," I said. "I really liked that first band the most, though."

"I liked the skit about the restaurant," she said. "I thought it was pretty funny. 'I said I wanted *fried* rice!'"

"'Sir, we won't deep fry battered grain.'"

We both laughed at our cheap reenactment of the skit just as the next act was coming on. The announcement was made, saying that it was going to be the last act of the evening, so I looked at my phone to see what time it was. Almost eleven.

I guess every talent show isn't complete without a juggling act, and that's just what the last act was. As the performer threw sharp knives and heavy objects, I wondered how many people in the audience secretly wanted to see something tragic happen. Despite any possible dark fantasies going on in the crowd, the juggler successfully pulled off his show with no injuries. When the curtains closed and the lights came back on, everyone slowly headed for the exit. I stood up and stretched, feeling something pop in my back.

"Well, that was nice," said Hayley.

"It was, but I think sleep sounds nicer," I said with a grin.

Hayley smiled and looked at the floor. There was something irresistibly cute about how she did that.

It took some time to get outside since there were so many people in the venue. I didn't go to the previous year's show because I didn't know about it, so I had no idea that it attracted such a large audience. I took a deep breath of fresh air once I was outside, and it felt so nice compared to the stuffy building.

"It was nice meeting you," Hayley told me. "Mike, right?"

I nodded.

"Nice meeting you too, Hayley," I replied. "Maybe I'll see you around."

Hayley smiled shyly and blushed a little.

"Maybe," she said. "Bye."

"Bye."

Now some of you may be thinking that I'm a moron for just letting her walk away like that. Like I said before, I wasn't in college to meet people. There was a degree I had to focus on and I had no intentions of going out of my way to get involved in much else. The fact that I let Hayley walk away that night was proof of my determination.

Little did I realize at the time that even the most steadfast determination can waver if not kept in check.

~Opus 3~

I'm proud to say that the first week of school went very well. My biology class was a three-hour lab session from 12:40 in the afternoon to 3:40, and it was a pretty lousy time of day for such a long session. Fortunately, both Aaron and Lawrence were in that same class, so I at least had some people to keep me company.

As for Miyuki, she was also in my math class first thing in the morning on the days I didn't have psychology. I saw her in my classes more times a week than anyone else I associated with, and I quickly found out that she was one of the more pleasant people to talk with.

"Do you like watermelon?" she asked me in math one day.

I tapped my eraser against the table as I thought of my answer.

"It's alright," I responded. "I'm not too big on watermelon unless it's a hot day, then it can be pretty refreshing."

"I love watermelon," Miyuki told me. "I could eat it every day."

"I don't like the seeds," I said. "Someone told me a long time ago that they'll grow in my stomach and it freaked me out."

Miyuki giggled as she completed writing down an equation.

"You know that's not true, right?" she said.

"Yeah, I know that now," I said. "My oldest brother, Sal, told me that when we were kids just to terrorize me."

"Oh, so it's his fault you don't like watermelon," said Miyuki with a smile. "Is that what you're saying?"

"It *is* his fault," I said accusingly. "He ruined the ways of the melon for me."

Everything school-related was going great for me so far, so what about work, you ask? The answer is simple: work was work. After being at Harbert's Groceries for over half a month, I was beginning to see that Lawrence was an intelligent fellow...he was just slow...at *everything*. I found myself repressing my irritation toward him since he was such a smart and cool guy, but I would often wonder just how long I could keep it up. It's important to note that I normally wouldn't have a problem with my coworkers being slow, but a lot of the tasks appointed to me were two-man jobs, and Lawrence was often man number two. Therefore, when it took him a long time to do something, it took me a long time to get it done.

Come on, Lawrence, I would think as I watched him mosey along. *What's so hard about just moving faster? It's that simple. Just move faster, man.*

Mr. Straussford had given Lawrence and me the task of checking expiration dates on the perishables one evening. Doing so was fairly simple, yet boring and time-consuming. We had to make sure all of the goods in the entire store were checked within a certain amount of time, or Mr. Straussford would give us an earful about efficiency and good workmanship and all that.

"Alright, Lawrence, let's do this *quickly*," I said, hinting subtly about his slowness.

He gave me a look of readiness and willingness that easily concealed his below-standard rate of operation.

"Sure thing, let's jump on it." That's what he would always say.

We started on separate ends of the market and worked our way toward the middle. As I was going through the refrigerated items, I realized that someone hadn't rotated them while stocking. The older items were supposed to go in front so they'd be picked by the customers first and used before they expired. However, the items were out of order, and this made it more difficult to check the dates because I had to look at every single date instead of assuming the items in the back were good. Still, I persisted without complaints.

The more items I checked throughout the store, the more I realized that everything wasn't properly rotated, and this wasn't the first time this had happened. My irritation meter was beginning to rise, as I knew this lack of organization was slowing down my progress. This wouldn't have been much of a problem in the long run, but Mr. Straussford just had to show up and make things worse.

"Michael," he said, looking at me over his glasses, "are you still checking for expiration dates?"

"Yes," I replied.

He stared at me with the same uninterested stare as the first time I had met him.

"Well, I'm going to need you to work a little faster around here, okay?" he told me.

"I'm doing the best I can," I said defensively, "but the items aren't rotated and it's slowing me down."

"I believe that I often place *you* in charge of stocking the shelves," said Mr. Straussford sternly.

"I'm not the only one who stocks," I said, holding back my growing anger. Was my boss blaming me for something I didn't do? I didn't need this.

"Well, I'm still going to need you to finish checking these dates faster," he said. "You've been at it for a while now and I would like to go home sooner."

"Go tell that to Lawrence," I said irritably. "I always have to make sure he's keeping up with me."

"It's not your job to worry about what everyone else is doing," said Mr. Straussford. "That's my job, so just do *your* job and we won't need to have this discussion again. I need efficiency in my store."

What's his damn problem? I thought angrily as Mr. Straussford walked away. *I'm doing my job, so why can't he see that? I can't wait to get out of here tonight.*

I happily clocked out of work that night after Lawrence and I had removed all of the goods that had reached their dates. Something was giving me the impression that Mr. Straussford just didn't like me, just as Aaron had said. This wasn't the first time at Harbert's Groceries that I had been accused of being inadequate for someone else's lack of work.

"Did Mr. Straussford say anything to you while we were checking dates?" I asked Lawrence on our way out.

"No," he replied. "Why, did he say something to you?"

34

You have to be kidding. You're the slowest guy here and you don't get scolded, but I do?

"He basically told me that I wasn't doing a good job," I muttered.

"Oh, don't let it get to you, man," Lawrence assured. "You just need to learn how things go around here, and that takes some time."

"But I was doing good," I argued. "I think he just likes getting on my case."

"Just keep working hard, bro," said Lawrence. "You're a good worker, and it'll just take some time for the boss to see that. I'm sure of that."

"Thanks," I said, unlocking my car with the remote. "Have a good night, Lawrence."

"Are you still going with us this weekend?"

"That's what I'm planning on," I said as I got into my car. "It sounds like a great time."

"Alright, later."

Aaron had been planning a camping trip with his friends for a while and invited me to come with. It was to celebrate his birthday early, which was in the second half of September. I quickly accepted since I wasn't scheduled to work that weekend. We were going to a remote place out of state, and Aaron had said it's a really nice area for camping because you're all alone out in the woods. Camping was fun for me but I had only gone on trips with my family, so a trip with friends sounded a lot more exciting.

I made it to my apartment and immediately shed my work clothes, feeling like a man with a new skin as I changed into something more comfortable. My plan was to study for my upcoming communications quiz, but I wasn't feeling up to it. The conversation with Mr. Straussford was still bothering me, so I heated up some leftover Chinese food and took out my frustration with some online zombie killing. That quiz wasn't for a couple more days, so I would just study for it tomorrow.

The next morning, I felt better about what happened at work, but was tired from staying up all night playing games. I had met some other players online and was annihilating zombies, so I couldn't just ditch them in the middle of it just for being tired. It's a common predicament for any seasoned gamer, so I had prepared for a rough morning.

Reluctantly slumping out of bed, I trudged into the kitchen to find something quick to eat. Without really caring about what I wanted for breakfast, the little jar of nacho cheese dip in the fridge looked like a reliable choice. Combined with some salsa and corn chips microwaved to above room temperature, a quick meal of simple nachos would suffice.

On my way to psychology class, I stopped by a coffee vending machine for a little boost. Coffee wasn't typically my thing, but it helped on mornings such as this. I took a seat in one of the chairs nearby and sipped the freshly brewed, bitter elixir of American fuel. Sugar and cream never found their place in my cup because I figured the bitter taste helped wake me up more, so I just tried my best not to grimace after every gulp.

As I began to feel the effects of the caffeine slowly kick in, Aaron walked up and took a seat next to me.

"You're still coming, right?" he asked.

It took me a second to figure out what he was talking about.

"You mean the camping trip?" I said. "Yeah, I've been looking forward to it all week."

"Great, so here's the plan."

He took out a road map and spread it out across the table in front of us, using his finger to show me the route.

"On Saturday morning, we'll meet in the college's north parking lot at ten," he said. "We'll travel eastbound and jump on the highway here, heading south...."

After tracing the entire route, he folded up the map and put it back in his bag.

"The entire drive will take about two and a half hours, considering that we don't stop," he told me. "I'm telling everyone to bring water for themselves."

"Do we have a driver?" I asked.

"My buddy Jorge is taking his SUV," said Aaron. "It'll be him, you, me, Lawrence, and Chad."

"Chad's coming?" I asked. "I didn't know he'd be interested."

"I asked him, and he really liked the idea," said Aaron as he stood up. "I'm off to class now, so I'll see you later."

"You're going already?" I checked my phone. "We still have ten minutes."

"Yeah," he replied, walking off.

I continually sipped my coffee in an attempt to finish it before class started. With only about a minute to spare, I took the last gulp of bitter brew and tossed the cup into the trash on my way to the classroom. Mrs. Flynn, who was limping along right behind me, always somehow entered the room just as the bell was ringing, so I theorized I was going to be on time as long as I was in front of her. When the bell went off just seconds after I walked through the classroom door, I snickered to myself, knowing that my theory was correct.

I wonder if slowing her down in the hallway could offset the bell's timing, I thought. *Or maybe she'd just run me over.*

I stopped in front of the instructor's desk to drop off my assignment from last class. I felt more confident about this assignment because it was a multiple choice worksheet rather than a review out of the book. Out of all my classes I had this semester, psychology was the only one giving me problems.

"Good morning," Miyuki pleasantly greeted as I sat down next to her.

"Hey," I replied.

"I noticed you came in just on time," she said.

"Yeah, I know," I said, "but Mrs. Flynn was behind me so I knew I was fine."

"Nice." Miyuki chuckled. "I think she probably has OCD or something with being on time."

"She has what?" I asked.

"OCD," said Miyuki. "Obsessive-compulsive disorder."

"What's that?" I asked curiously.

Miyuki just smirked.

"We'll learn about it eventually," she replied.

In my peripheral vision, I saw the light, curly poof of hair position itself in front of the class, so I waited for what Mrs.

Flynn had to say. She had a stack of papers in her hand as she got the students' attention.

"Good morning, everyone," she said, holding the papers in the air for the class to see. "I have your assignment from last class graded, so I'll hand these back for everyone to look at."

"I had a hard time with that one," I remarked to Miyuki as the instructor walked around.

"Really?" she said. "It didn't give me much trouble, actually. What part did you have trouble with?"

"Trying to remember what each part of the brain did," I replied. "I had to keep looking it up."

"Do you think there's something wrong with your hippocampus?" she asked me with a grin.

"My what?" I had to think for a second. "That's the short-term memory thing. Hey, wait a minute!"

Miyuki laughed, and I had to just laugh along with her at myself for being a victim of her wit. Mrs. Flynn placed my graded assignment in front of me, and I felt a lurch in my stomach. The horrible grade written in red ink at the top of the paper was enough to make my insides churn.

"Aw, that's too bad," said Miyuki, looking at my score.

"Even the benefits of multiple choice questions didn't help," I said disappointedly as I looked everything over.

Miyuki received her paper with a nice "32/35" on it. A quick calculation in my head brought her score to a little over ninety percent.

"You answered a question correctly that I got wrong," she told me, trying to make me feel better. Her sympathy was touching, but hardly necessary.

"It's fine," I said coolly. "This only brings my class grade down to about a seventy percent."

"But isn't a failing grade in college anything below a C?" Miyuki asked, sounding slightly concerned. "Anything below a seventy?"

"Yeah," I replied, "but I'm not sunk yet. I still have the rest of the semester to get my grade up. The first test is next Monday, so I'll just study for it."

"Now that you all have your papers back," said Mrs. Flynn to the class, "we can begin discussing any questions you may have."

Needless to say, I had plenty of questions. Most of the class period was spent answering questions, and I did my best to cram everything into my memory. As Mrs. Flynn explained everything to me, I strained my brain to fit everything together, but there were still some things that were a little fuzzy to me.

When the questions had all been asked, the class was told that we'd be picking up the pace. Each assignment from that point on would consist of three to four sections at a time instead of just one. This was tragic news to me to say the least, and I was desperately hoping that the material would only become easier.

Our next assignment would mark the end of the first chapter in the psychology textbook. Before getting started on the homework, I flipped ahead to see what Chapter Two was all about. To my dismay, I couldn't understand any of it.

Nothing special happened in my communications class that day. The bald guy's banana split tattoo continued to be the subject of my curiosity as he sat next to me every day in that class. Sometimes, I felt the urge to sit somewhere else, or at least on the other side of him, just to put an end to the nagging sense of disbelief that someone would put such a picture permanently on his skin. Was there some deep, inspirational purpose behind it? I did not know.

Mr. Holden lectured the entire period, and all I had to do was take notes. Lecture was my favorite way to learn material, and listening to someone talk was easier for me than reading. On top of that, communications was fairly simple to me. I smelled an easy A in this class.

I was walking to the next building for history when I saw Chad coming from a different direction. He gave me a big smile when I walked up to him.

"Hey, what's up, Mike?" he greeted.

"Not much," I said. "So, I heard you're going on that trip with us."

"Yeah, definitely," he replied enthusiastically. "I've never gone camping and Aaron asked me if I was interested, so I took his offer."

"I think it's gonna be awesome," I said. "We'll be out in the woods with nobody around to bother us."

"Yeah, yeah," he said. "Too bad we don't have any women coming along, eh?"

"Right, I know," I chuckled. "It should still be pretty cool, though."

"Us men ain't afraid to get dirty!" said Chad. "We can live in the wild with no problem!"

"We'll catch our own food if we have to!" I said boldly. "Then skin it and cook it over a campfire!"

The two of us laughed as we joked around on our way to class. I could tell this trip was going to be a lot of fun.

"Oh man, that's too much," said Chad, trying to calm down from laughing. "To be honest, though, it really would be nice having some women come with us."

"That's true, but I still can't wait for this weekend," I said. "Girls or not, I'm going to have a great time."

Everyone appeared to be getting pumped up for the camping trip, myself included. The time just wouldn't go by fast enough while Chad and I attended history that day. However, time was about to go a lot slower for me that evening when I had to go into work.

The very moment I clocked in for my shift, Mr. Straussford approached me. When I saw him, I thought he was going to tell me I had to clock in faster or something. However, he told me something much different than I had expected.

"I'm putting you on checkout," he told me.

Sweet, I thought, *no heavy lifting today! Working register in a store can't be nearly as bad as register in fast food.*

"Okay," I said.

"Go to checkout four," he said. "Nancy will show you how to work the register."

Nancy was an elderly lady who had been working there for years. I walked over to checkout four where Nancy was standing, and she smiled as I came up to her and stood behind the register. A customer showed up just in time for her to walk me through everything. This wasn't my first time using a cash register, but it was a little different from one at a restaurant. Still, I was able to learn it pretty quickly.

"You look like you know what you're doing," said Nancy. "Do you think you can handle it on your own now?"

"Yeah, I think I've got it," I replied confidently. "Thanks."

"Just ask someone if you need help," she said. "I'm going to take my break."

As I checked out customer after customer with no problems, a feeling of relaxation swept over me. This was one of the easiest ways I had ever dealt with customers. I didn't have to take their orders because everything was just handed to me, scanned, and bagged. Not to mention that working the conveyor belt was oddly amusing. Despite all that, I assumed that it could get really mind numbing after working all day. Simple tasks lead to bored minds, I guess.

A little old woman was purchasing a few household items, so I proceeded to check her out as normal. When I told her the price, she reached into her purse and pulled out a card.

"I'm going to use this," she said.

"Just swipe it on that machine and follow the onscreen directions," I told her. "Will it be credit or debit?"

Without answering, she swiped her card and the transaction didn't follow through.

"Ma'am, you need to tell me if you'll be using credit or debit before you swipe," I said.

The little old woman looked at me questioningly.

"I already used my card," she said.

"It didn't work," I said, "because I need to select credit or debit."

"How do I do that?" she asked, looking at the card swipe machine.

"You tell me," I said patiently.

She looked taken aback, giving me an angry glare.

"There's no reason to be rude, young man," she said shortly.

What? I think she misunderstood me.

"No, I mean you have to tell me if you want to use credit or debit," I explained.

"I don't know what you're talking about," she replied irritably. The veins in her skinny neck were beginning to stick out. "I never had to do this at other stores."

Oh boy, I thought despairingly. *Did she take too much medication today, or what?*

The line was growing longer, and I hated keeping people waiting. I glanced at the other registers and realized that I was the only checkout lane open. Wasn't Nancy done with her break yet?

"Some stores have different computers," I told the old woman, upholding my calmness. "Either they have you swipe your card first, then select your payment type, or they —"

"I just swiped my card!" she croaked. "I just told you that!"

My blood pressure began to rise, so I heaved a deep breath to cool myself down. Just as I was about to explain it to her in agonizing detail, Mr. Straussford popped in out of nowhere.

"Is there a problem, ma'am?" he said courteously.

"This young man needs to learn his manners!" she spat, pointing a crooked finger at me.

Oh, you did not just say that, lady, I thought, clenching my fist.

"Go help Martha with the inventory check, Michael," Mr. Straussford told me. I could tell by his voice that he was very displeased. "I'll take over here."

Without a word, I stormed out of the checkout to the back of the store, getting more agitated with every step. Even after being polite while trying to explain something so simple, that old lady was going to cause me to get written up. She was the impolite one, not me. Not only that, I had been left on checkout completely by myself. Sure, I was quick to learn how to do it, but that's no reason to just abandon me right away.

"Hi, Michael," said Martha when I entered the back of the store. "How was working register?"

"It was fine," I muttered, "then this old lady yelled at me for being rude when I wasn't. Now Mr. Straussford's pissed because *she's* pissed, and *I'm* pissed...."

"Those kinds of things happen." Martha shrugged. "There's not much you can do about it."

"I thought working register in a store would be better than in a restaurant," I vented, "but noooope. Anyway, I was told to help you with inventory."

Martha looked at her clipboard, then at the boxes of supplies.

"Well, I'm actually almost done," she said. "If you can just take over for me, then I can get back to checkout. Was it busy up there?"

"A little," I said.

"Then I'll just leave this to you." She handed me the clipboard and pen. "You seem to know how to do it."

"Okay," I mumbled.

The rest of the evening presented no more hassles. I was back to doing work behind the scenes as usual, only everything felt a little gray and dull. Preventing myself from being discouraged was something I was used to, and I just had to keep my mind off of the old lady with her crooked, accusing finger. As the night came to a close, I had mostly cooled off.

I was about to clock out when Mr. Straussford approached me again. The speech was about to come down on me, and I was prepared for whatever he had to say.

"I need to talk to you, Michael," he said firmly.

I didn't say anything, but just looked at him.

"We've been having some trouble with you around here," he said, "and I believe it's time for that to change."

"Okay," I replied obediently.

"That's why I feel it would be best if you don't come in to work tomorrow," he told me.

I furrowed my eyebrows and stared at Mr. Straussford.

"Are you suspending me?" I asked. "I didn't do anything wrong today. I tried to tell that lady what she needed to do and she got mad at me."

"Yes, yes," he said, ignoring what I said, "she told me all about it."

"She told you wrong!" I argued. "There was a misunderstanding!"

"It's always a misunderstanding, isn't it?" he replied arrogantly. "You're the one who misunderstood anything, Michael. You're not suspended. You're fired."

My teeth and fists clenched tightly as Mr. Straussford stared at me over the top of his glasses. I felt my lip quiver as a thousand things to say to his face built up in my throat. With a level of self-control I had never experienced before, not a single one of those things escaped from my mouth as I clocked out and walked away.

I sat out in my car, not bothering to even start it. Instead, I just stewed in disbelief over what had just happened. Part of it didn't seem real, but I knew that it was as real as it could be. I had just been fired. Fired from the lucky job that was so easy to find when I had lost my previous job at the library. Now I was unemployed, and once again it wasn't my fault.

"Rrrrgh!" I grabbed my steering wheel as tightly as I could and growled angrily. Everything that I wanted to say to Mr. Straussford came out as one forceful noise. As soon as my lungs were empty, I caught my breath, started my car, and drove back to my apartment.

When I made it home, I tore off my work clothes and slammed them into the trash, ridding myself of the oppressive establishment's attire once and for all. Dressed in nothing but my boxers, I removed a loaf of bread from the cupboard, took out a few slices, angrily packed them into a single solid ball, jumped on the couch, turned on the TV, and ravenously consumed the bread ball. I really had no idea as to why I wanted to eat a ball of bread at that time, but it sure made me feel a lot better.

I'm really screwed, I thought. *How am I going to find another job so soon? Just because it was easy last time doesn't mean it'll be that way again.*

The rest of the night was spent trying to cool down, but there was a limit as to how much I could just ignore being fired.

This was the first time I had ever been told those words, and it's a lot harsher than most people may realize.

~Opus 4~

"Jorge's late," said Aaron on the Saturday morning of the camping trip. He, Chad, Lawrence, and I were waiting for Jorge in Elm Valley College's north parking lot. He was our ride, so we weren't going very far without him. Aaron had already texted, called, and left a voice message on Jorge's phone, but there was still no word back from him.

"Try calling him again," I said.

"I doubt it'll do any good," Aaron replied, taking out his phone. He put the receiver to his ear for a few seconds, then hung up. "It went straight to voicemail again. Why doesn't he have his phone on? He knows we're waiting for him."

"He might be sleeping," said Chad. "I had to wait for a ride from my buddy once, and I ended up waiting for an hour and a half because he was sleeping."

"That's pretty bad." Lawrence chuckled.

"Oh man, tell me about it," said Chad. "I was stranded at a doctor's office, and those places ain't fun. I don't like going to the doctor...gives me the creeps, ya know?"

"The doctor's office?" I couldn't imagine being stuck there for over an hour. "That's, like, only one of the worst places to be."

"Technically, it's one of the best places," Lawrence chimed in. "If anything happens to you, you're in the right place."

"Yeah, I guess." Chad shrugged.

"But wouldn't a hospital be better?" I added. "If you had a heart attack at a doctor's office, they wouldn't be able to do much, would they?"

"Hmm, I don't know," said Lawrence. "They might have some kind of resuscitation equipment at the doctor's, but I don't think it'd be the same level of equipment a hospital would have."

"At least you'd be surround by trained personnel," I said. "That's better than collapsing at a floral shop or something."

46

"It's almost ten-thirty," Aaron told us. "We were all supposed to be here at ten. What do you guys want to do?"

"Let's just wait some more," said Lawrence. "People are late all the time, and I don't want to just call off the trip."

"Does that sound good to everyone?" Aaron asked. "Group consensus."

Everyone had been looking forward to this trip for a while and we weren't willing to give up on Jorge so easily. We all agreed to keep waiting with the hopes that he'd call back soon. I had spent the previous night looking for my hiking boots and getting things packed. In addition, I really needed a leisurely vacation to get my mind off of my quarrel with Mr. Straussford. Job searching had been unsuccessful this time around, and I was feeling stressed out from it.

We passed the time by sitting and talking in the bed of Aaron's yellow truck. The college was quiet that morning, although a few students were arriving for the handful of classes offered on Saturdays. Sunday was the only day of the week when the campus was completely empty.

The air was a little chilly on that mid-September morning, but the rising sun quickly started to warm everything up comfortably. My windbreaker sufficiently kept the breezes off of my skin. If the weather forecast was correct, I'd be able to spend the rest of the day in a T-shirt.

"This place we're going to," said Lawrence to Aaron, "what's it like?"

"Secluded," Aaron replied. "We don't have to worry about other people being around. It might be a long walk through the woods from where we park."

"That makes it even better," I said enthusiastically. "I like walking through the woods."

Aaron suddenly stood up in the back of his truck and peered across the parking lot. We all turned to see what he was looking at and saw someone walking toward us. I couldn't make out who it was, but Aaron quickly recognized him.

"Jorge!" Aaron called, waving his arms to flag the person down.

I had never met Jorge before, but I recognized his face from my chemistry class. He was a tall Hispanic with movie star looks and a wardrobe to match. Just having this guy in the same room could lower your own sex appeal.

"What are you doing over here?" he asked. "Was I supposed to meet in this parking lot?"

Aaron rolled his eyes and looked at Jorge with disbelief.

"I told everyone to meet in the north lot." Aaron replied smoothly. "Why didn't you answer your phone? I tried calling you."

Jorge slapped his forehead and laughed.

"I'm sorry," he said. "I thought the parking lot over there was the north one. And something's wrong with my phone. It doesn't work anymore. I think it might have a bad battery like every other smartphone I've ever dealt with."

"At least you showed up." Aaron sighed. "Everyone, Jorge. Jorge…this is Mike, Lawrence, and Chad."

"I'm sorry, everyone," Jorge apologized again. "I'll drive around so you don't have to carry your stuff."

"I don't mind walking to the car," Chad told him. "We'll be walking a lot anyway, so I don't think it matters."

"Yeah, let's just head over to the other parking lot now," said Aaron, jumping down from his truck's bed.

I retrieved my duffel bag from my car and followed Jorge with everyone to the south parking lot. The hike across the campus was sort of like a warm-up for the woods, and I was able to test the weight of my luggage. Not feeling weighed down by my duffel bag when I reached Jorge's SUV, I was confident that I hadn't over-packed. After all, this was only going to be an overnighter and didn't require a lot of supplies.

"Nice ride, man," Chad told Jorge as we approached the SUV.

"I won it in a drawing," Jorge replied as he unlocked it with the remote. "It's not even two years old."

"Wow, nice," I complimented. "I wish I could win a car. I'd probably sell it for the money of course…I could use it about now…."

"What did you have to do to win it?" Chad asked.

Jorge opened the back of the SUV and moved around some things that looked like tents.

"I filled out a paper and put it in a box at the mall," he said. "Half a month later, I got a phone call. That's all there was to it."

"I know what I'm doing the next time I go to the mall," said Aaron.

We placed our belongings in the back of the SUV and climbed into the seats. Lawrence, Chad, and I decided that since Aaron had planned this trip for us, he deserved to ride in front. Even with the five of us packed into the vehicle, there was still plenty of room inside. Before taking off, Jorge opened his center console and took out a stack of DVDs.

"I have a DVD player if you guys want to watch a movie," he said, handing the movies back.

I looked through the stack of DVDs with Chad and Lawrence. They were all good choices, but there was something very unique about them.

"I've heard of all these movies, Jorge," said Lawrence, "but all of these are the Spanish versions. I don't understand Spanish, bro."

"Yeah, my family's mostly Mexican," Jorge explained. "They should all have English subtitles."

"I don't like to read movies," I said. "Anyone else can watch them if they want."

Chad and Lawrence both looked at each other with unconvinced expressions.

"I think we'll pass on the movies," said Chad politely, handing the stack to Jorge. "Thanks for the offer."

As we were pulling out of the parking lot, Aaron unfolded his large map and looked it over. The paper took up more than half of the front of the vehicle, resting over Jorge's arm as he was driving. With a look that implied frustration, he watched Aaron fumble with the map sprawled across the dashboard.

"Aaron," he said, "why do you have that big map?"

"To see where we're going," said Aaron. "You don't want us to get lost, do you?"

"I can't drive with that thing all over the place," Jorge told him. "Why didn't you write down the directions?"

"I memorized the directions," said Aaron, concentrating on the map. "I just need a visual to go by."

"Then you didn't memorize the directions," said Jorge, shoving the map off of himself. "Fold that thing up, man. I can only see out half of the windshield."

"Get on the interstate," Aaron told him, folding up the map. "We need to take it south."

Jorge's SUV rode smoothly and had a comfortable interior. I leaned my head back and prepared myself for a long, relaxing ride. The interstate was a little quiet when we merged onto it, as most people who work in the mornings had the day off. Jorge turned on the radio with the volume down at a soothing level.

"What kind of music do you guys want to listen to?" he asked.

"Can you turn on country?" Lawrence asked.

"Anything but that," said Jorge. "Country is forbidden in my vehicle."

"Aw, come on," said Lawrence. "That's cold."

"I'm just playin', man," said Jorge with a grin. He flipped through the stations until the first country song came on.

"Not this station," Lawrence told him. "Go to 97.5."

"How can you tell the difference between country songs?" Aaron joked. "They all sound the same."

"There's a difference," said Lawrence. "If you listen to it as much as I have, you'll be able to tell. That goes true for all types of music. The listeners of a particular type of music can pick out different things, such as what era the song is from, what subgenre it falls into—"

"Well, yeah, that's how it is with a lot of things," said Aaron, interrupting what sounded like a potential speech that nobody wanted to hear.

I wasn't fond of country, so I just gazed out the window while I attempted to tune out the music. My dad used to listen to country a lot, and it was his way of getting some alone time without needing to say anything. If he wanted to build a fence without anyone pestering him, he'd take the stereo out in the yard with his favorite country CD and get all the alone time he needed. He was also the only person I knew who used music as a form of punishment when his children misbehaved. For that reason, I'm pretty sure my taste for country music has forever been shot and buried in the mud.

During the trip, Aaron entertained himself with some portable video games. My portable game system had been dropped in a puddle, so I no longer had the pleasure of video games while on the road. Chad seemed interested in what Aaron was doing, so he was leaning forward to watch.

"What game you got?" he asked Aaron.

"It's *Ultimate Food Poisoning*," said Aaron, not taking his eyes off the screen.

Where does he get these games? I thought.

"That sounds weird," I said. "What do you have to do?"

"It's like those restaurant games where you make the food and serve the customers," Aaron explained, "except you have to sabotage the food."

There was a moment of silence.

"Is it any fun?" Chad asked.

"Dude, what *doesn't* sound fun about sabotage?" Aaron answered.

"I don't play restaurant games," said Chad, "but this one sounds alright."

"You get extra points depending on how you sabotage the orders," Aaron continued, all while keeping an eye on the game. "Putting glass shards in someone's food is more diabolical than spraying the food with window cleaner, so it earns you more points. However, you have to try to remain inconspicuous, otherwise you'll get busted and have to start the level over. Giving the customer an illness has a higher success rate than physically harming them directly. You really need to strategize."

I see where you're coming from, but let's be honest. This is one of the most bizarre concepts I've ever heard.

"Hey, navigator," said Jorge, "I need you to navigate for me. Our exit's coming up, right?"

Aaron paused his game and took out the map again.

"Let me see it," Lawrence offered. "Jorge needs to drive."

"No, I got it," Aaron dismissed. "I won't unfold it all the way."

As Aaron tried to find our location on the map without unfolding the entire thing, Jorge was taking the off-ramp at our exit. I peered out the windshield and saw a traffic light coming up.

"Which way?" Jorge asked, creeping up to the light.

"Uh, hold on," said Aaron, flipping through the map. "Right, I think."

"You think?" said Jorge skeptically.

"Go right," Aaron repeated, folding the map back up. "There's a place we can stop at."

"Yeah, let's make a pit stop," I said.

We stopped at a gas station next to the bypass and climbed out of the SUV. The convenience store was about to be raided by five guys who'd been on the road for over an hour. As soon as I walked through the door, the cold air conditioning made me shudder in my windbreaker.

"Why do they have the air on full blast?" I muttered to Lawrence. "It's not really hot outside at all."

"Maybe it's on an automatic timer," said Lawrence, "or the thermostat could be in a warmer room."

"Or maybe the owner is an Eskimo," I said.

My first priority was to use the restroom. Just like most convenient store restrooms, this one was not without its signature puddles, missing tiles from the walls and floor, the flickering fluorescent light that added a strobe effect to the room, and the one working urinal that was about two inches too high. Jorge had beaten me to the toilet, so I was stuck with the urinal. Standing on my tiptoes, I could only wonder what towering beast this contraption was meant for.

My second priority was to find something cheap to eat, and I was in the right place for that. Now without an income, my spending limits were greatly reduced. I browsed the shelves for my meager options and settled for a bag of mini muffins. They contained grains, dried fruits, and nuts, so I guessed they were okay. Added with a bottle of orange juice, it seemed somewhat well-rounded to me.

The second half of our drive was more boring than the first. Jorge had his mp3 player on shuffle while plugged into the stereo to provide a constant stream of tunes. He listened to a lot of strange music, and not just the stuff in Spanish. Chad was napping next to me, and I wished I could do the same. Sleeping in a moving vehicle always made me sick.

The more we drove, the more the landscape changed. Thicker woods were encroaching us from all sides as we headed down winding back roads that grew narrower and more rugged with each mile. I just hoped that Aaron knew where he was taking us.

At long last, Aaron showed Jorge the dirt path leading into the woods. This was the final turn of the driving portion of our trip. More than two miles through the trees and wilderness, the path opened into a small clearing where we parked the SUV. I climbed out of the vehicle and stretched, taking in the fresh, clean air.

"This is it," Aaron announced.

"Where do we have to go from here?" Chad asked.

"We just pick a direction," said Aaron.

"Can we really go wherever we want?" Lawrence asked, looking all around. "It's all available?"

"That's right," said Aaron.

I looked in all directions, seeing nothing but woods. This really was a secluded place, just as Aaron had said. Jorge opened the back of his SUV so we could grab everything. I strapped on my duffel bag and made sure the laces on my hiking boots were secure.

"I brought lots of mosquito repellant," said Chad, handing a can to everyone. "There's more where that came from if anyone needs it."

"I think this is enough," I said. "Thanks, man."

A thick cloud of repellant filled the small clearing as we applied generous amounts of the spray to our bodies. Jorge grabbed the two tents from the SUV, took one last look to see if everyone had everything, and locked it up. Once everyone was all set, we simply picked a random direction and started walking. To ensure we wouldn't get lost, Aaron took out his compass to help keep track of where we were going.

Our plan was to go deep into the woods on foot. The ground was fairly dry with little mud, perfect for hiking. We had no trails to follow, relying on Aaron as our guide. He supposedly had been camping in the area several times before and was familiar with it, so I just hoped he was right.

Nearly an hour into our adventure, we stopped to take a small break. Aaron took a deep breath through his nose and let it out with a content look on his face.

"There's something soothing about the desolate smell of earth when you're out in the woods," he said.

"Yeah, yeah, I hear ya," Chad agreed. "It's refreshing."

"It's so quiet and peaceful," said Jorge, setting the tents down. "Well done, Aaron. I'd say this is a good area."

I looked at Lawrence tagging behind a little. He was breathing hard and sweating when he caught up to us.

"Hey, you okay?" I asked him.

"Yeah, I'm fine," he said, wiping the sweat off his face. "Just a little tired."

"Do you need help carrying anything?" Jorge offered.

"No, don't worry about me," Lawrence assured, leaning against a tree. "I just don't get out too much."

"Sitting inside every day in front of the computer is starting to catch up to you, isn't it?" Aaron mocked.

"I don't sit in front of the computer every day," said Lawrence defensively.

"How much farther do you want to go, Aaron?" I asked. "We've walked pretty far already, don't you think?"

Aaron scanned the surroundings.

"We should look for a better place to set up camp," he said. "As soon as we find a good spot, we can stop. We shouldn't have to travel much longer."

Lawrence opened his backpack, took out a canteen, and gulped down some water. He put the canteen back into his bag and gave us a smile.

"Alright, man," he said, "let's jump on it."

There was a nice, big, flat area we stumbled upon, so we decided to set up camp there. We checked around for any poison ivy or dangerous animals living nearby, and pitched both tents when everything looked clear. I had a great time setting up as we talked and joked around, and before I knew it, camp was set up.

Scouting for firewood in an untouched, wooded area was easy work among five people. I stacked up as many sticks and branches as I could carry, making four trips by myself. By the time everyone had finished searching for wood, we had a big pile that appeared sufficient for the one night we'd be spending outside.

We spent the daylight hours exploring around our campsite and chatting about random topics. I had a tree climbing contest with Jorge to see who could climb to the top of a tree the fastest, but I lost when I pulled myself onto a branch that broke off. Thanks to my quick reflexes, I made like a spider monkey and grabbed onto a lower branch before meeting the ground.

Chad found a snake hiding under a pile of leaves by stepping on it. His shouting caught my attention, and I looked to see him scuffle backward and trip over a root sticking up. When I hurried over to help him up, I noticed something slither between my feet, and I couldn't help but laugh when I saw how small it was.

"It's just a little snake, Chad," I snickered.

"I don't care if it was a *little* snake," he said. "It was a snake, and that's all that matters to me, man."

After a long day of romping around in the wilderness, the skies began to darken as the sun set behind the thick cluster of trees that spread for miles in all directions. We headed back to the camp and attempted to start our fire, which proved to be a little more challenging than we had assumed. With our hands dirty, our heads light from blowing on dying flames, and our eyes burning from waves of smoke that didn't want to give way to fire, the pile of sticks finally caught and stayed lit. Everyone took their own chair and gathered around the fire, ready for an enjoyable evening.

"So, Lawrence," said Aaron after the sun had completely set, "have you heard from Megan at all today?"

"Nope," Lawrence replied, skewering another wiener onto a stick. "She's probably studying."

"All day?" said Aaron. "I don't know, man. That sounds a little fishy to me."

Lawrence shrugged and stuck the hotdog over the fire.

"Who's Megan?" Chad asked, munching on some chips.

"This girl I met in my public speaking class," said Lawrence. "I've been trying to get with her."

"Does she seem interested?" Chad asked. "That is, if you don't mind me asking."

"I don't know," Lawrence sighed. "She keeps making excuses not to do stuff outside of class, so I guess not."

"Oh well, it happens," said Chad. "I tried talking to this girl I went to high school with. Her name was Lexi, and it seemed like everything was going good, ya know? We were hanging out and stuff, everything was cool, and I thought I'd ask her out one day. Turned out she already had a boyfriend from a different school. Now why wouldn't she tell me that instead of actin' all interested and stuff? Man, I tell ya...."

"That happened to me one time," said Jorge, "but it was worse. I knew this girl who acted like she wanted to be with me. Instead, she was just using me to get her ex back."

There was collective groan among the group. I was lucky enough to never have something like that happen to me, but I could still imagine how bad it could be.

"Don't you hate stories like that?" said Aaron.

"To make it even worse," said Jorge, grinning, "it actually worked. Her ex threatened to stab me...literally *stab* me!" He chuckled ironically at the thought. "The next day, they were back together."

There was a brief moment of silence during which everyone just shook their heads.

56

"So, Mike," said Aaron, "what about you? Have you been talking to that Asian chick I always see you with at school?"

"Oh, Miyuki?" I said. "Yeah, we talk all the time. I have two classes with her."

"Have you thought about asking her out?" Jorge asked.

She is a really nice person, I thought, *and cute, too.*

"I haven't really thought about it, actually," I replied truthfully. "I mean, she's really nice to talk to and stuff."

"What do you guys talk about?" Lawrence asked me.

"Just whatever," I said. "Sometimes she'll start up a random conversation about...whatever."

"Does she have a boyfriend?" Jorge asked. "That's important to know."

I tried to remember her ever saying something about having a boyfriend, but nothing came to mind.

"Not that I know of," I said.

"Go for it!" Aaron told me. "What's stopping you?"

"Yeah, man," said Chad, "you might just land a girlfriend."

"I don't know, guys," I said. "She seems like a really nice person, but I don't want to put my classes at risk."

"Oh no, don't say that!" Aaron groaned. "What kind of a man are you?"

"Hey, I know it's a crappy decision," I said, "but I have to think about what's really important, and that's my degree. Once I get that, I'll be free to date as many girls as I want, but for now—"

"Come on, dude," Aaron persisted, "grow a pair and live for the moment! Carpe diem!"

"Whatever," I muttered, standing up. "Where's that poking stick? I'm gonna stir the fire a little."

Jorge handed me the sturdy stick, and I moved the logs around in the fire so they'd burn better. I placed some more wood on top of the fire and took a seat after the flames picked back up.

We continued roasting hotdogs and marshmallows through the night. I had some canned sardines to share with everyone, but they all turned down my offer. My family was big on eating sardines, so I grew up to love them and didn't care about what other people thought.

After a while, we got on the subject of the library. Everyone had heard about it by now, but it still found its way into conversations on occasion. I wasn't very fond of talking about it, though, since it reminded me of how I was still unemployed. As my mind drifted down that route, I forced myself not to think about it right now and have a good time.

"My dad says they suspect arson," said Chad, "but they can't find any evidence."

"Yeah, like someone would want to burn down a library," said Aaron sarcastically. "I don't think that's what happened."

"Speaking of which, I'll be right back." Chad stood up and walked over to his tent. He searched around inside for a little bit, then returned with something in his hand. When he came back into the light of the fire, I saw that he was holding that weird book.

"You're still carrying that thing around?" Aaron asked him.

"Just for this trip," Chad replied, gripping the book. "I was doing some research the other day, and I think this book is something called a grimoire."

"Did you say it's a grimoire?" Lawrence asked, sounding deeply interested.

Chad nodded.

"What's a...grim war?" I asked.

Chad looked a little skeptical to explain. I could see the hesitant expression on his face in the orange light from the campfire.

"A grimoire is a book of magic," said Lawrence. "They contain instructions for magic spells, incantations, summoning, and the like."

"Hmm." Aaron raised one eyebrow.

A feeling of uneasiness sank into me. I wasn't necessarily a believer of magic, but that kind of thing made me uncomfortable.

"I don't know about that, Chad," I said. "I've always steered clear of occult stuff."

"I'm just sayin'," said Chad, flipping through the pages, "that's what it looks like to me. I don't know if it's true, though."

"I don't believe in magic and the supernatural," said Aaron. "Science, through and through. Big Bang, Darwinism...that's what I stick with."

I smelled a heated and controversial debate in the works, so I quickly changed the subject.

"The fire's going down again," I announced. "We should go get more wood."

"Who's going to find some more wood?" Jorge asked openly.

"Let's play a game to see who goes," Lawrence suggested. "The loser needs to go fetch."

"We'll play rock-toilet-bazooka," said Aaron.

"What the hell is rock-toilet-bazooka?" Chad asked.

"It's like rock-paper-scissors with different things to choose from," said Aaron. As he explained, he showed the bizarre gestures to represent toilet and bazooka (and they are bizarre). "Bazooka bombs rock; rock clogs toilet; toilet...uh, beats bazooka. It splashes water on it, I guess. Everyone got it?"

"Uh, I think so," said Jorge. "Let's do it."

Lawrence seemed quite humored by the game's logic.

"Toilet beats bazooka, huh?" He chuckled.

"We'll do a tournament," said Aaron. "Losers of each round will face each other to see who the bigger loser is. I'll go first against Chad."

Trying to remember the bizarre gestures and what beat what was all part of the fun. The final round was me against Chad, and I ended up being the loser.

"My rock beat your toilet!" he cheered loudly.

"Aw," I groaned. "I lost."

"Find some good logs, okay?" Aaron mocked.

"Don't bring back any wet ones," Jorge sneered.

"Yeah, yeah," I muttered, grabbing a flashlight. "I'll be back."

As I walked away, I continued to face the barrage of mocking from the guys. However, it was just harmless fun and didn't bother me at all.

I scanned all over for anything that looked like good fuel for the fire, and I realized that it was going to be a lot harder than anticipated. Most of the wood had been gathered from earlier, and I found myself venturing out farther and farther. Eventually, I was unable to see the light from the campfire, and the guys' voices were only faintly heard.

More than five minutes later, I had found a decent amount of wood, but I decided to look for a little longer. The surrounding area was completely dark, and the sound of animals came from all around me. Suddenly, a nearby scurrying sound made me jump a little, and I spun around to see what it was. Shining my flashlight in the direction of the sound, I caught a glimpse of a deer scampering away. Feeling a little stupid for having a deer scare me, I resumed my search.

The sound of leaves and twigs crunched beneath my feet, so I stopped to see if there was anything I could take. I took one more step, then felt something snag my leg. Before I knew what was happening, my foot was dragged out from underneath me, causing me to fall and hit the ground hard. The flashlight and wood I was carrying flew out of my grasp as I felt myself flying into the air. No more than three seconds later, I was dangling upside down, suspended in the air in total darkness.

I'm dead! An anaconda got me! My friends are gonna find my bones in the morning!

Not much time had passed before I realized that whatever had grabbed my leg wasn't alive. The wave of panic subsided, giving me the chance to assess the situation. I looked down (which was up from my perspective) at the ground and saw the flashlight. When I followed the beam of light, I saw something that looked like a bunch of large rocks inside a net resting on the ground nearby. Straining my abs to pull myself up, I felt what was wrapped around my leg.

A rope, I thought. *I'm in a freaking trap!*

Rope climbing was one of my favorite activities when I was in gym class, but I never imagined that it would come in handy. I struggled to pull myself upright and proceeded to climb the rope. When I reached the top, I climbed up onto the branch I was hanging from and noticed a pulley firmly attached to it. Whoever built this trap really knew what they were doing. Sitting on the branch, I untied my leg, climbed back down the tree, gathered everything I had dropped, and trudged back to the campsite.

"There you are," said Chad when I returned. "What took you so long?"

"I got caught," I said scruffily, dumping the wood haphazardly on the ground.

Everyone looked at me awkwardly as I took my seat in front of the fire.

"You got caught doing what?" Aaron asked curiously.

"I got caught in a trap!" I told him. "Someone rigged a trap out in the woods! I had to escape from it."

Aaron suddenly busted out with laughter. Everyone else seemed to ignore him as they stared at me with their mouths open.

"A trap?" Lawrence looked thoughtful. "That's odd."

"What kind of a trap?" Chad asked.

"The kind that uses a rope and a weight to pull you into the air," I explained. "Just like how you see in the movies!"

"Dude, no, no," said Aaron through his laughter. "Oh, I'm so sorry, man. I'm so sorry...that's too funny!"

"It wasn't funny for me!" I replied indignantly. "I thought I was going to die for a second!"

One by one, everyone else started to laugh. At least *someone* found some enjoyment out of it, because I sure didn't. The part of my leg that was snagged by the rope was in pain, and I could have easily sprained my ankle. I was lucky to have come out of the situation relatively unharmed.

"Who would set a random trap like that out in the woods?" Aaron chuckled. "And what are the odds that you'd be its victim, Mike?"

"I have no idea," said Chad. "I'm just glad my rock beat Mike's toilet, or it could've been me gettin' caught!"

Before going to sleep that night, I was in the tent, checking myself for any injuries. There was a rope burn that left a red ring around my leg, but the skin wasn't broken. I had a scratched elbow and the area below the back of my neck felt bruised from hitting the ground, but that was about it.

Aaron and Jorge were sharing the same tent with me, and Lawrence and Chad were in the other one. I made myself comfortable inside my sleeping bag as Aaron was looking at his road map again. He must've had a strange obsession with cartography or geography.

"I still can't believe you got caught in a trap," he said amusedly, folding up the map. "That's priceless, man."

I grunted and rolled over, not wanting to hear any more of it.

"You have to admit, Mike," said Jorge, "something like that is pretty intriguing."

"It sucked," I said bluntly.

"So, other than the trap situation," said Jorge, "I think today was a great day, don't you think?"

"Of course," I replied. "I had an awesome day."

"Definitely," said Aaron. "Too bad we have to go home tomorrow."

Going home...there was a chance that my home wasn't going to be my home for much longer. Although it was true that I was having a blast with my friends, that still didn't change the fact that I was jobless. Rent was coming up, and I barely had enough money squirreled away to pay it. That was why I did my best to forget about being ensnared by a fiendish rope trap and have some fun while I could enjoy it.

~Opus 5~

In the middle of the expansive woods, Aaron stood atop the highest ground in the general area and observed every direction. His compass was out in front of him, and the puzzled look on his face was anything but assuring. When the navigator appears to be confused, it's almost never a good sign. We were supposed to be on our way back to Jorge's SUV, but the hike seemed to take a lot longer than the one from yesterday.

"Guys, I have some bad news," said Aaron coolly as he walked over to us. "We're lost."

"You're kidding," I groaned.

Chad scratched his head as Lawrence caught his breath against a tree. I looked over at Jorge, who was half scowling at Aaron.

"You were the navigator, Aaron," said Jorge. "This isn't navigating. This is failure."

"Does anyone have a GPS or map app on their phone?" I asked.

"I did," said Jorge, "but my phone doesn't work."

"That figures," I said. "The only phone that could've helped us right now is out of commission."

"Are you *positive* that we're lost?" Lawrence asked, having most of his breath back.

"I don't recognize these parts," Aaron replied. "I always check for benchmarks, but I don't see any of them."

"How can you find benchmarks in the woods?" Chad inquired, glancing around. "It's all trees and dirt!"

"I've hiked a lot," said Aaron. "I know what I'm doing."

"Apparently you don't," I muttered irritably. "I have a psychology test tomorrow that I have to study for! I can't afford to spend all day out here!"

"Did you bring your psychology stuff with you?" Aaron asked.

"No."

"And whose fault is that?" he said.

I tilted my head back and groaned at the sky. This couldn't be happening. *Why* did these things keep happening?

There was a small rock next to my foot, so I kicked it as hard as I could to vent some of my anger. The rock ricocheted off a tree and disappeared beneath the foliage.

Aaron pocketed the compass and pointed his finger.

"Let's go this way," he said.

"Are you suggesting a random direction?" Jorge asked through squinted eyes. "Did your decision include rational thought?"

"Hey," said Aaron defensively, "you guys just have to trust me. I know I steered us astray, but I won't do it again. We have to travel east, but I think we might've gone a little too far south."

Everyone exchanged glances and shrugs, and we silently followed Aaron. I couldn't say that I was very confident about the direction we were going in, but it was better than just standing around. There wasn't much we could do other than put what little trust we had left into Aaron's muddled sense of direction.

The farther we walked, the thicker the woods became. Most of the area was fairly easy to walk through, but this particular spot had a lot of plant growth. We marched through increasingly denser foliage, and the plants seemed to get taller and thornier with each step. Needless to say, the situation was looking a little grim. Minutes later, I had completely lost sight of everyone because I couldn't see through the plants.

"Man, this ain't the right way," said Chad as he plowed through a twisted bush. "This is some major shrubbery, dawg."

"Yeah, Aaron," I heard Lawrence say from behind, "let's turn back."

"We're probably almost through this," Aaron called from somewhere. "Keep pushing forward."

"I think these plants are gonna eat us," Chad mumbled. "There are leaves in my undershorts."

A vine came out of nowhere and slapped me across the face. I had absolutely no idea as to where it came from.

"This is so damn stupid!" I blurt angrily. "There'd better be no poison ivy or crap like that through here!"

"No guarantees," I heard Aaron say.

"Ticks are sucking my blood right now," Lawrence sniveled despairingly. "I know they are. There's no way we're not covered in ticks."

Oh, I hate ticks. I really, really do.

"Dude, shut up!" I demanded, crushing a thick layer of plants underneath me with a brutal stomp. "I don't wanna hear that!"

"Hopefully the bug spray is keeping them off," said Chad from somewhere. "Where the heck *is* everyone, anyway?"

"I'm here!" Aaron called from ahead.

"Here!" I called.

"Blah!" Lawrence spat from behind.

"Wait, everyone stop!" Aaron called.

I heard the rustling sounds cease as everyone stopped moving. Peering through the vines, twigs, leaves, and branches, I could barely make out where Aaron, Lawrence, and Chad were.

"Where's Jorge?" Aaron asked. "Does anyone know?"

"Jorge!" Chad called loudly.

"Up here!"

I looked up to see Jorge climbing up a tall tree. He waved to get our attention, and I could only wonder what he was doing way up there.

"The boy's a genius," Chad chuckled. "He's probably tryin' to get an aerial view."

"What do you see from up there?" Aaron called.

"Turn back!" Jorge replied. "It's all thick woods ahead of you!"

"Okay!" Aaron turned around and I could hear him coming back.

"What, that's it?" I said. "That's all you have to say, Aaron?"

"What do you want me to say, Mike?" he asked curtly.

"You were leading us the wrong way," Lawrence told him. "Not cool, bro."

Backtracking through the dense plant growth wasn't as easy as it sounds. The foliage was so thick that we had left hardly any trail while pushing through it. When we finally emerged, everyone looked rugged and disgruntled.

"We need to go around if we want to keep heading in that direction," Jorge told us when he caught up.

"Like how far around?" Aaron asked.

"I couldn't see, it was too far," said Jorge.

Aaron thought it over for a bit.

"We could do that," he said. "Group consensus."

"I don't care," I grunted.

"Whatever, man," said Chad. "I don't care."

Lawrence just shrugged and mumbled something.

"I think we should go this way," said Jorge, pointing. "It looked like it might be shorter."

"Then let's do it," Aaron replied.

The hike continued for what seemed like hours. After a while, I gave up on thinking about what direction we were heading in. Having the compass didn't do any good since nobody knew where the SUV was relative to our location, and we ended up walking in random directions. The sun moved farther and farther away from the center of the sky, but there was still no sign of the vehicle. I was beginning to fear that we might not make it back in time for me to take the test at all.

My fears were officially justifiable when the sky grew too dark for us to continue anymore. The group decided to stop searching and set up camp for another night. Fortunately, there was enough food and drinks to last, but none of that was going to prepare me for the psychology test in the morning. My grade in that class was going to be severely wrecked if I missed any tests, and it looked as if I would just have to suck it up and take the blow.

"First off, I wanna say I'm sorry," said Aaron once we had all gathered around the campfire. "I didn't plan on this."

Everyone was silent for a second, probably holding in what we really wanted to say to Aaron for getting us lost in the middle of nowhere.

"Don't worry about it," said Jorge, snapping a twig and tossing it into the fire. "Worse things have happened."

"Yeah," said Chad, "we didn't run into any bears, at least."

"I don't think many bears live around here," said Lawrence, "but I could be wrong."

"Hey, Mike," said Aaron, "wasn't your dad in some kind of wildlife committee? What do you know about bears?"

"I don't know," I replied.

"Look, I'm really sorry," Aaron said. "I know you have that test tomorrow, and I just want you to know that I would never dream of making you fail a class...."

Well, it looks like you will, I thought.

"...But if you knew you had a test, you should've brought your stuff with you on this trip or studied before we left."

I hate to admit it, but he has a point. I wasn't prepared for any unexpected problems like this.

"It's cool," I said. "I'm not blaming you for causing me to fail my test."

"Is it an important test?" Lawrence asked.

"Yeah," I said, "I'm not doing too good in psychology, and getting a zero on this test will hurt my grade a lot. I'll really need to bust my ass to make it through by the end of the semester."

"I'd help you out," said Chad, "but I don't know anything about psychology."

"Yeah, me too," said Aaron. "Chad, let me see your book."

"Why?" Chad asked.

"I wanna look at it," Aaron replied.

Aaron followed Chad to one of the tents and came back with the grimoire and a flashlight.

"I'm gonna do you a favor, Mike," said Aaron as he took a seat.

"And what would that be?" I asked skeptically.

"I don't really believe in this magic stuff," he told me, looking at the book's cover, "but I'm willing to give it a shot."

"Wait, what are you talking about?" Lawrence didn't seem very comfortable. "You're going to cast a spell?"

"I don't know." Aaron shrugged, flipping through the pages. "I might be able to find something to help Mike. It's the least I can do for getting him stranded out here when he has that test tomorrow."

"No, I'm fine," I assured. "You don't have to do anything...weird."

"Yeah," Lawrence agreed, "you shouldn't get involved with magic or anything. I've heard stories about people who did that stuff, and most of them don't end well. I don't want to be visited by Captain Howdy or some crazy hell-beast."

"Lawrence, don't be a baby, man," said Aaron. "Nothing might happen at all. They're just stories, and I think this kind of stuff is pretty cool, although I don't really believe in it."

"If you think it might not work," Lawrence argued, "then why try it at all?"

"I just wanna try it," Aaron replied. "If it makes you feel better, I'll look for something that doesn't require dead chickens or something."

"Would chicken nuggets work for a spell that requires a chicken sacrifice?" Jorge asked. When we all stared at him questioningly, he added, "I was just curious."

"You have an interesting point," said Chad. "I think voodoo might call for fresh blood, though."

"Yeah," said Jorge, "and the mechanical separation of chicken meat might not be personal enough to count as a worthy sacrifice."

"I'm not so sure about some of these fast food places anymore," I said. "Some of their food seems like it has a little black magic worked into it somewhere."

"Like how it's so delicious, yet so diabolical on your health," Chad joked.

"Here we go!" Aaron announced, looking at something in the grimoire. "I found something for you, Mike."

I walked over to see what Aaron was talking about. He used the flashlight to illuminate the page so I could read it. The words for the incantation were simple, but it sounded like they were for summoning something, which made me uneasy. I wasn't much of a believer in the supernatural, but I tended to steer clear of sketchy spells and occult rituals.

"What made you choose this one?" I asked Aaron.

"It's short, simple, in English, and doesn't require anything we don't have," he told me.

"No!" said Lawrence angrily. "Don't do anything stupid, guys."

Aaron ignored him and kept reading.

"All we need is a little of your blood," said Aaron.

"Not happening!" I replied.

"I'm kidding!" said Aaron. "It was a joke."

"Do you know what it does?" Chad asked. "You might want to make sure you know what it's for."

"Look," said Aaron, "it's probably just a bunch of garbage. I'm just trying to have a little fun, that's all."

"I thought you said you were trying to help me," I said.

"Well, that too," Aaron replied, getting a little aggravated.

"Come on, don't do this, Aaron," said Lawrence. "Do you think he should do this, Jorge?"

"I don't really care," said Jorge indifferently. "I'm a little interested, really."

"What do you say, Mike?" Aaron asked. "It's your decision."

The pressure was on. Part of me was hesitant to try anything to do with magic, another part was curious to see what would happen, yet another part didn't believe in any of it to begin with.

I sighed, thinking about what I would do.

"Screw it," I muttered. "Let's do it."

The spell required me to sit in a magic circle drawn on the ground using whatever method the caster desired; in this case, using a stick to draw in the dirt. The book provided a picture of the circle, which Aaron copied to the best of his ability. As I sat on the ground, feeling the ants crawl over my legs, Aaron recited the nonsensical gibberish scribbled in the book. Chad and Jorge watched intently while Lawrence proceeded to gnaw his fingernails down. In all honesty, he was the only person I'd ever met in real life to bite his nails when nervous. I didn't understand why he was freaking out so much. The spell we were using seemed far too easy for the common person to use and was probably taken out of some fairytale or written by somebody who was bored.

A summoning spell? There's no way, I thought. *Even if it does work, how is a summoned creature going to help me with psychology? Maybe we can conjure the ghost of Sigmund Freud. Hey, I remembered his name!*

I wasn't paying much attention to what Aaron was saying, and had little interest in the spell at all. By the time he had finished the invocation, I had already worked it out in my head that nothing was going to help me pass my test.

"Feel any different?" Aaron asked, looking down at me.

"I feel like I'm covered in bugs," I said flatly. "Can I get up now?"

Aaron quickly studied the page he was reading from.

"Uh, yeah," he said. "I think it's done."

I stood up, brushed the bugs off me, and looked around. Nothing looked different. Nothing felt different. Just as I had thought, magic was a hoax and nothing more.

"Anything strange at all?" Chad asked me.

"Nope," I replied, sitting down in my chair. "Everything seems normal."

"Did I do something wrong, or was it all just fake?" Aaron asked jokingly, acting like a classic detective. "Will anyone ever know?"

"I knew it wasn't real," said Jorge, snapping another twig and tossing it into the fire.

Aaron handed the book back to Chad, who looked slightly disappointed that his special book wasn't so special at all. He walked back to his tent to put the grimoire away and came back with a can. I couldn't make out what it was in the dim light, but it certainly looked like food.

"What's that?" I asked him.

"Beans and pork," he replied with a grin, "one of my favorites."

"You eat that crap?" said Aaron.

"Yes, I do," Chad told him.

"I like beans and pork, too," Lawrence added.

"Jorge," said Chad, "mind if I use your keychain can opener?"

"Sure thing."

Jorge tossed his keys over to Chad, who quickly opened his can of beans and pork. When he was done, he looked at Jorge's keyless entry remote for the SUV, taking sudden interest in it.

"Jorge," he said, "do you know what this red button on the remote is?"

"No, I never used it," Jorge replied.

"This is a panic button, dawg," Chad told him.

My jaw dropped. I looked at Jorge, who didn't appear as shocked or confused as I had anticipated.

"What's that?" Jorge asked.

"It sets off the car alarm!" said Chad excitedly. "If it's in range, we could find your SUV!"

"For real?" said Jorge. "Toss it here."

Chad tossed the keys back to Jorge. He examined the button with an amused grin.

"I didn't know they make something like that," he said.

"Press it!" I told him. "Everyone quiet!"

Jorge pressed the panic button, and we all held our breath as we listened for the alarm. Miraculously, a very faint sound could be heard through the trees.

"Does anyone hear that?" Chad whispered.

"Yeah," said Lawrence, pointing. "It's coming from that way."

Without a word, all of us jumped up and hurried in the direction of the sound. Aaron had the only flashlight, so we followed him through the dark woods, stumbling over logs, roots, and who knows what. As we were getting close, the sound suddenly disappeared.

"Hit it again, Jorge!" said Aaron.

The alarm came back on, and we continued running toward it. A surge of excitement rushed over me as I could see a blinking light through the trees ahead of us. Before we knew it, the woods opened into a clearing, and we were looking at the legendary SUV with our own eyes. We immediately erupted into cheering.

"Let's hurry up and tear down camp!" Aaron announced. "We're getting out of here!"

Perhaps it was because I was too overloaded with joy and jubilance at the time that I didn't consider the fact that we had been camping so close to the SUV. I also didn't consider the fact that Jorge's impaired sense of common technology nearly cost us another night sleeping like the natives. Instead, the honking and flashing lights from the SUV played out like a mini disco club in our half-delirious minds, causing us to put aside any ill thoughts of strangling either Aaron or Jorge. All was well.

~Opus 6~

Despite it being in the middle of the night and the fact that we were worn out from hiking all day, we managed to pack up and hit the road fairly quickly. Jorge gulped down an energy drink to help keep him awake while driving through the night. I didn't realize exactly how tired I was until I was settled into the SUV, thinking about the two-and-a-half-hour drive ahead of us. There was some comfort in knowing I'd be back in time to take my test, but I had no time to study for it. No way was I going to pull an all-nighter going over material that puts me to sleep during the day.

I wasn't sure when I fell asleep, but I remember waking up in the Elm Valley College parking lot after one in the morning. Perhaps I was too tired to have gotten carsick that time, which usually happens when I sleep in a moving vehicle. The five of us dragged ourselves out of the SUV and grabbed everything we had brought for the trip. We exchanged short farewells, then headed our separate ways. My duffel bag weighed me down twice as much as usual while I walked back to my car.

Sitting behind the wheel, I yawned deeply and ruffled my hair. My apartment wasn't too far away, and I could barely wait to collapse into bed. I stayed awake long enough to drive home and pass out, not worrying about the psychology test as I sank into the mattress.

The test didn't rear its ugly head until the alarm clock pulled me out of my deep sleep the next morning. I clumsily turned the alarm off and remained in bed, thinking it'd take a little while for me to drag myself to the bathroom to get ready for class. I rolled over and rubbed my eyes, thinking about how cold the room felt and how warm the blanket was....

My eyes popped open. Did I fall back asleep? How long was I out? I looked over at the clock, feeling like a total idiot that I only had ten minutes until class started. Happy Monday to me.

I scrambled around my apartment, grabbing everything I needed and crammed it all into my backpack. Taking a shower would've been nice before going to class, but that didn't look like an option. I'd spent all weekend in the woods without a shower. I applied an extra thick layer of deodorant and sprayed myself down with body spray before running out the door.

I arrived in class ten minutes late. Mrs. Flynn was sitting at her desk when I walked in, and she beckoned me over. Acting cool and collected, I casually took the test from her and sat down next to Miyuki in the back of the room. She looked up from her test to give me a small smile. That smile gave me just the boost I so desperately needed. I briefly thought about what everyone on the trip had said about asking her out, but this really wasn't the time.

Unfortunately, something such as a smile wasn't much help for the tired guy who didn't get a chance to study for his test. Needless to say, I didn't stumble through the test...I straight up fell flat on my face and failed to pick up the teeth that got knocked out of my mouth. There were questions asking about material I didn't even recognize. I might as well have taken a test for a class I never attended.

Miyuki finished before me, leaving me to suffer alone. My brain fizzled and smoked throughout the entire period, and I eventually surrendered on the last page, simply rewording the questions into statements for my answers. When I placed the battered test on Mrs. Flynn's desk, I walked out of the room feeling like a defeated man.

Communications class dragged by as Mr. Holden gave his lecture. I was tired and discouraged, wanting nothing more than to just go back to bed. We had time to work on our assignment by the end of class, so I merely flipped through the textbook brainlessly, deciding to work on it that night.

"Hey."

For a second, I didn't know where the voice was coming from. The big, bald guy with the banana split tattoo had actually said something to me.

"Yeah?" Perhaps I was a little too interested in what he possibly had to say.

"Do you have psychology with Mrs. Flynn?" he asked.

Of all the damn things to say to me for the first time, it had to be about that?

"Yeah," I replied, "I just came from that class."

"You took that test today, right? I have to take it tomorrow and was wondering if you could explain to me the differences between the various projective tests. The textbook talked about them, but it was hard to understand."

"Sorry, man," I muttered, "but I really don't know. I think I flunked that test big time."

"Oh," he replied. "I just noticed you always did well in this class, so I thought I'd ask you."

"Psychology is worse than learning another language for me," I told him solemnly. "I really can't grasp it at all. I'm better off in math or something like this class."

"Alright," he said. "Thanks anyway."

Now was a perfect time. I had to ask.

"I see you have a tattoo of a banana split," I found myself saying.

"Oh yeah," he said, grinning. "I had my first banana split a few years ago. Right after that, I thought I'd get a tattoo of one."

If there were any crickets in the vicinity, they would've been chirping just then.

"That's it?" I asked, dumbfounded.

"Yeah," he said smugly.

There's no way I'm leaving this room on that note, I thought.

"It's a really detailed picture," I said. "I'm Mike, by the way."

"Trent," he said. "Nice meeting you."

The bell rang a few seconds later. Another class down for the day, one more to go. Maybe I would be able to get some sleep in history and have Chad fill me in on anything I missed. As I headed to the other building, I expected to see him come up to me from somewhere and start talking to me about how lucky we were to find Jorge's SUV last night. He didn't seem like the type to brag, but I was about to give him a hundred kudos for the discovery of the panic button.

Strangely, Chad didn't show up at the start of class. History class was halfway over when I figured Chad's empty seat was going to remain empty for the entire period. Unable to go with my plan of sleeping and having Chad fill me in, I stared despairingly at the board as Mr. Weechik wrote down the timeline of events preceding the American Revolution. When he announced that a test was coming next week, it drove one last stake through my gut for the day before I headed back to my car.

The first thing I did once I made it back home was take a shower. By the time I was dressed, the thought of taking a nap wasn't quite as appealing for some reason. My stomach growled quietly, reminding me that I had skipped breakfast during my rush to class. There was some cereal and a little milk left, so I poured myself a bowl and placed it on the table. I threw the milk carton away, knowing that I'd have to find another job soon to do some grocery shopping.

A strange noise suddenly came from the living room before I could put the cereal box away. The best description I can give is it was like a really loud vent with a lot of air blowing through it. I walked out of the kitchen to see what it was, and my heart nearly jumped out of my mouth.

On the floor of my apartment's living room was a large circle. Almost instantly, I noticed that it resembled the one Aaron had drawn for me to sit in when we were lost in the woods. However, this circle was made with thick, black lines that seemed to burn into the carpet. A shadowy mist began to collect in midair directly above the magic circle and take shape as a person.

What's going on? I thought nervously.

The most bizarre thing I had ever seen was taking place right in front of me, and it scared me to death. At one point, I considered running out of my apartment, but it was happening too close to the door for me to make an escape. I was trapped like a rat.

The shadow condensed into an opaque mass as it took a perfect human shape in just under ten seconds. In an instant, the circle and mist were gone, and I was suddenly staring at a

76

tall, seductively beautiful woman with long, black hair and piercing yellow eyes. Her dark garments were otherworldly, appeared smoother than water, and flowed more elegantly than air. I had no idea how she arrived in my living room, and it was almost as if I had experienced a lapse in consciousness during her arrival. The woman herself appeared how something would look in a dream; a striking contrast against the hard, tangible real world she was standing in. She seemed a couple notches down from being a physical being.

"Michael," she called to me.

Her voice..., I thought. *It doesn't seem real.*

"W-what do you want?" I asked nervously.

"Do not be afraid," she said. There was no emotion in her words or on her face. "My name is Sapphira. I am a demon and you are my master."

A sense of panic quickly rushed through me.

"Demon!" I croaked, making a cross with my index fingers. "Go away! I cast you out! Out! *Away with you!*"

Sapphira suddenly appeared next to me. I lost my balance and stumbled to the ground, then attempted to army crawl out of the apartment. The demon appeared in front of me again, blocking my only way out.

"Do not be afraid," she repeated in the exact same way as before. "I will not hurt you, Michael. I am unable to inflict harm upon my master."

I scrambled to my feet and backed away from her until I was up against the wall.

"What do you mean I'm your master?" I asked shakily.

"I am here to serve you," she replied. Her yellow eyes could turn steam to ice, and they stared directly at me. "It is my duty to obey your every command and fulfill your every desire."

"N-not interested," I told her sharply. "I don't want anything to do with demons."

"There is no breaking the pact," she said, drifting closer. "I am to remain by your side until your flesh is dust."

Not what I wanted to hear. There was no way I wanted a demon following me around for the rest of my life.

"Ack!" I choked as Sapphira grew nearer. "Go away! Leave me be, demon!"

"As you wish," Sapphira replied obediently.

And just like that, she was gone. I looked around my apartment, feeling my heart pounding against my ribs. Glancing around me with a level of cautiousness bordering paranoia, I eased my way over to my bowl of cereal. The entire time I ate, my escape was constantly mapped out in my head if the demon happened to return. The spoon shook in my hand, making it harder for me to eat.

Stay calm. I'm not going anywhere unless she comes back. Until then, I'm going to hold my ground.

Another sudden sound and vibrating feeling made me practically jump out of my skin before I realized I had received a text message. I thrust my hand into my pocket and removed my phone. Aaron had sent me the text.

Wut up man? Wut u up to rite now?

I immediately replied to his text, typing frantically on my phone's little keypad. During times like this, I wished I had a keyboard on my phone instead of just a number pad.

Hurry get over here right now theres some freaky stuff happening and i really dont wanna b left alone!!!!

I hit the Send button, but my phone told me that the message had failed to send. I tried again, but the message wouldn't go through. My phone had good service, so there was no reason why it wasn't working. With all the stress I was already under, I was getting extremely irritated. Several failed attempts later, I gave up trying to reply to Aaron's text.

This stupid phone! I thought. *If only I had the money to buy a new one, I'd replace this piece of junk in a heartbeat.*

Tossing my bowl and spoon in the sink, I figured that leaving the apartment would be a good idea after all. There was really no other choice but to move in with my parents. Crap had hit the fan, and it took everything I had just to keep from having a nervous breakdown on the spot...if I wasn't already experiencing one.

As soon as I whirled around to leave the kitchen, another tall figure appeared out of thin air right in front of me, giving me a jolt that could've given me a heart attack. While I was catching my breath, there was no mistaking that the tall man in white robes wasn't an ordinary person. His ethereal appearance and presence were very similar to the demon's, yet there was a polar difference that could only be sensed by intuition.

"Hello, Michael," he said gently. "I didn't mean to frighten you."

The concept of speech seemed to leap out of my head and crawl down the garbage disposal as I stared up at the man's kind face. I opened my mouth to say something, only to realize that I had nothing to say at all.

"My name is Lemuel," he told me. "I am an angel sent to watch over the relationship between you and Sapphira."

My lips quivered as the only response I could muster fell out of my mouth.

"Okay."

Lemuel looked around my apartment for a brief moment before turning back to me.

"It seems Sapphira is not here," he said. "Would you mind calling for her, Michael?"

The last thing I wanted to do was go against the towering angel's words, and I ended up calling for Sapphira despite of my desire to never see her again.

"S-Sapphira?" I said meekly.

She appeared a few feet away from me without delay. I was both shocked and disturbed at how quickly she followed my command.

"Yes?" she said, staring at me the way a doll stares straight ahead.

"Let's have a seat, Michael," said Lemuel softly, gesturing toward the living room. His words were comforting and warm, and I was surprisingly eager to follow him. I took a seat on the couch with Sapphira as Lemuel sat down on my big beanbag. Seeing such a tall man sitting on a beanbag was pretty amusing, but I just couldn't bring myself to enjoy the humor.

"You need to realize that magic and the occult are very dangerous," Lemuel told me. "You and your friends took part in such an activity last night."

"Yeah," I replied, feeling a little embarrassed.

"The spell you performed was written over two-hundred years ago by an occultist who locked away a demon with magic. Anyone who performs the ritual shall set the demon free and have full command over it for the rest of his or her life. That person is you, Michael, and the demon is Sapphira."

This can't be happening. That stupid spell was real! I can't believe it!

"I don't want this!" I retorted. "Can't you reverse it?"

"I am sorry," Lemuel said, "but I was not assigned to such a task. I am only to watch over your relationship with Sapphira, provide guidance to you, and ensure that Sapphira does not act outside of her pact."

"Wait a minute," I said, "you mean you're like Sapphira's parole angel?"

"You could put it that way," he replied. "This is a very special, yet dangerous coalition between Earth, Heaven, and Hell. Keeping track of it at all times is of utmost importance. With that said, I need to explain the situation in full to you. Listen closely, Michael."

I leaned forward to hear everything that Lemuel was about to tell me. The situation I had gotten myself into was beyond twisted, and I wanted to make sure that I did everything correctly. No telling what would happen if I messed anything up with a demon.

"Your close relationship with a demon has opened many doors between you and the spiritual world," Lemuel told me. "At this very moment, spirits, demons, and angels are beginning to notice your relationship with Sapphira. You will need to remain cautious and alert."

"Oh," I muttered, "that's...just great...."

"Do not fret," Lemuel assured. "It will not be as you think. You may have unusual encounters, but your life will not be drastically changed nor affected as long as you remain cautious and alert. Not all spiritual happenings will present themselves to you, but there are many powerful and malevolent beings that will attempt to lead you astray or harm you in less subtle ways. Do you understand?"

"Uh, I think so," I said.

"Very good." Lemuel seemed pleased. "Enjoy this very unique gift you have been granted, Michael. Sapphira may be a demon, but she is incapable of harming you or anyone else unless you desire it. She will do anything you ask of her, as long as she is capable of doing so."

I looked over at Sapphira sitting next to me. She was a demon, but I had to admit that her beauty was breathtaking. Tall with long legs....

She'll do anything I ask of her....

"Thou shalt not commit adultery, Michael," said Lemuel.

"Huh? Yeah, I know," I replied quickly.

Lemuel smiled.

"I shall be going now," he said. "Farewell, and may you receive many blessings."

He instantly disappeared without a trace, leaving me on the couch with Sapphira. She looked at me with a blank expression that made me uncomfortable.

Ohhh man, I thought.

"What will you do now?" she asked me.

I felt like I had just swallowed a brick. I didn't know what I wanted to do! How was I supposed to be normal after what had just happened?

"I'm ordering pizza," I told her, taking out my phone. "I could really use some right about now...."

"Would you like me to retrieve it for you?" she asked.

"No, no," I replied abruptly, "I'll do it myself, actually."

Ordering pizza over the phone was something I was used to doing, but Sapphira watching me the entire time made it more than awkward, even nerve-racking. When the employee answered the phone, I had demons on my mind more than pizza.

81

"One large lover's meat," I said quickly. "I mean...large Meat Lover's. Thin crust...."

"Will that be for pick-up or delivery?"

I kinda didn't want to be in my apartment at that time. Some fresh air would probably do me good.

"Pick-up," I said.

When I hung up, Sapphira was still watching me closely with her freakish yellow eyes.

"Are you leaving?" she asked. Her voice had the life of a burnt charcoal briquette.

"Uh, yeah," I said.

"Shall I accompany you?" she asked.

"No," I said, "just, uh, stay here, okay? I'll be right back. Don't, like, kill anything...or possess anything...or anyone...."

"Understood."

Honestly, I felt more lost than a kid in a flea market. One second I was grieving over normal problems, and the next I was handed a demon with no instruction manual. How exactly does one handle a demon servant? Giving Sapphira orders was exceptionally strange for me, and it just didn't seem right...or safe.

There was still some time left before my order was ready as I sat in my car outside of the pizza restaurant. My head was buzzing with thoughts about what had just happened back at my apartment. Can you blame me for questioning my sanity? Put yourself in my shoes and think about it for a moment.

I took out my phone and attempted to text Aaron back and see what he was up to. There was no way I was going to tell him about my situation, though. Just having someone to communicate with would be better than stewing in my prospective insanity. Maybe he would want to hang out, although I was sure it wouldn't be at my place.

hey aaron whats up?

To my relief, the message actually sent. Maybe my phone understood it was two inches away from being thrown

82

out the window if it didn't cooperate with me. Not much later, I received a response from Aaron.

> i wanted to ask if you wanted to catch a movie with me lawrence and jorge but we r already at the theater

So much for that plan. I realized that Chad wasn't with them, indicating that he was probably sick since he hadn't been in class earlier that day. I considered contacting him to see what he was up to, but decided against it.

Time slowly ticked by, and I looked at the money in my hand to pay for the pizza as my order was getting closer to being done. I knew that I should have been saving as much money as possible, but I really didn't care at that point. I was still going to move in with my parents. Maybe I could just ask Sapphira to bury herself in the backyard and remain quiet for the rest of my life.

I headed back to my apartment with my pizza. Trudging up the stairs was difficult to do with the knowledge of having a demon waiting for me. Hopefully she wouldn't just pop up and scare me half to death again. I remained on my guard as I stepped through the door, but Sapphira was nowhere to be seen.

"Welcome back."

Just as I had dreaded, Sapphira suddenly appeared directly in front of me. Being able to successfully deter a heart attack and catch a pizza in midair at the same time was quite an achievement for me. I should get a fireplace just to reserve a spot over it for that trophy.

"I crafted a gift for you, my master," she said, handing me a little trinket.

I placed the pizza on the table and took the trinket from her, which was a finely crafted piece of shiny metal containing a large, beautiful, dark blue gem inside it. Personally, I was quite impressed at how nice it was and that it didn't look too girly.

"Uh, this is pretty cool," I said quietly, not sure how to respond.

"It is an amulet to protect you from lesser demons and spirits," Sapphira told me. "It is made from sapphire. That is your birthstone."

"I was born in May," I said. "I thought the birthstone for that month was emerald."

"There are many varying ideals behind the birthstones," said Sapphira. "I am referring to the birthstones according to the Zodiac."

"Ah." I held up the gem to the light and observed the refractions and prisms. "You know, I think I heard something recently that the astrological signs have changed...."

"I have received no such news," she said. "Do you accept my gift?"

"Uh, sure," I replied.

A strong presence emanated from Sapphira, and I watched in surprise as she suddenly appeared fully tangible, rather than ghostly and nonphysical. Other than her strange clothes and piercing yellow eyes, she now looked like an ordinary person.

"Our pact is now complete," she stated. "I thank you for welcoming me into your world, and I will do my best to carry out your wishes."

"Hey, wait a minute!" I said shortly. "What are you saying? I didn't agree to that!"

"You accepted my gift," she said, "therefore you have completed our pact."

"No, no, no," I groaned. "Why didn't you tell me this before?"

"My apologies," said Sapphira, bowing down to me. Seeing her do so made me feel uncomfortable. "I was not aware you had such a wish."

Looking at Sapphira made my eye twitch. I gripped the sapphire amulet tightly in my hand before slipping it into my pocket, walked over to the table to grab a slice of pizza, and stressfully gobbled it down. Strengthening my bond with Sapphira was the last thing I needed.

The sensation of someone looking at me tickled the back of my head, and I turned to find the demon staring at me like a motionless gargoyle as I ate. A shiver ran down my spine. Why did she always have to *stare* at me?

"Is there something you wish to ask of me?" she asked.

I carelessly dropped my pizza crust into the pizza box as I searched for the right words to say. If I was stuck being Sapphira's master for the rest of my life, then I was going to have to get used to ordering her around despite the fact that she was a demon. Preparing myself to speak, I took a deep breath and put forth my authoritative side.

"We need to lay down some rules," I told her. "Number one: don't stare at me like that."

Sapphira immediately turned her head, diverting her gaze from me.

"Er, you can still look at me," I said, "but just not for, like, extended periods of time. Number two: uh...don't let any living people know that you exist. I don't want that kind of attention. The media would never leave me alone. You got that?"

"Yes," she replied.

"Number three: don't appear right in front of my face. I hate it when you do that...it scares me, I'm not gonna lie. Number four: no killing or possessing people. I already told you that, but it applies for all the time."

I paused for a moment and tried to think of any other rules.

"Is that all?" she asked.

"Yeah, that's all for now," I said. "If I think of any others, I'll let you know."

"Understood," said Sapphira.

I stared at her, still trying to soak in what I had gotten myself into. She stared back at me...for about three seconds, then turned her head to the side again. Well, at the very least she was listening to me.

What now? I thought. I looked over at the large pizza sitting on the table.

"Uh...do you want some pizza?" I offered.

"I must humbly decline," she said. "Demons do not eat."

"Oh." I paused for a second. "Well, you're dismissed."

"Very well."

Sapphira vanished, but I still had a feeling that she was around. I looked at my phone to see what time it was and noticed that it was only one o'clock in the afternoon. So much had already happened that day, and the day was only half over. My communications class had that assignment I was going to do, but I definitely wasn't in the mood to work on it. The couch looked more inviting than usual, so playing video games and eating pizza all day seemed like a great idea. I felt as if I had deserved a long evening of doing absolutely nothing constructive. I placed my amulet on the nightstand in my bedroom and started up the game system in the living room.

Happy Monday to me.

~Opus 7~

If someone had placed a time-lapse camera in my living room, the resulting video would have been very pointless to watch. With the game controller in my hand and the pizza box sitting on the couch right next to me, I had no reason to move. Some people may think that sitting in one spot for more than six hours straight takes some sort of skill, but I assure you that it doesn't. Just the lack of ambition and a rugged-ass morning.

However, no matter how deeply immersed I became in the game, and no matter how much soothing comfort food I had within arm's reach, my thoughts were never free of the supernatural events that I had witnessed. I was beginning to think I would never be able to relax again. There really was no solace in having a demon around, slave or not. I was highly disturbed by the thought, and I will firmly stand my ground when saying that I had every right to be scared for my life.

Eventually, my ambition-less gaming binge ran out of gas. Seven o'clock had rolled around, and I had homework to do and a bathroom to visit. That would count as my break, and I planned on jumping right back into my lazy mode as soon as I completed my assignment. Communications was rather easy for me, and it'd be a good way to lasso my sanity before it packed its bags and called a taxi.

I started out strong on my assignment, answering questions quickly and elaborately. Shortly after the halfway point, though, I began to lose steam and felt a little tired. The day's events combined with my lack of sleep the previous night were making a powerful team. Still, I was determined to finish before calling it quits.

There were only a few questions left when I must have nodded off. Out of nowhere, a loud sound caught my attention and snapped me out of it, and I anxiously looked around to see what it was. Did Sapphira make that sound, or had I been visited by yet another inhuman entity? I held my breath, trying to listen as closely as possible.

Another banging sound shortly followed, and it seemed to come from the living room window. I couldn't see anything outside from where I was, so I slowly walked over to try and figure out what was making that noise. I stopped as I saw two hands reach up from the bottom of the window and attempt to pry the screen off from the outside. Someone was trying to break in! Grabbing a chair for a weapon, I waited for the burglar to show his face before bludgeoning him.

The screen came loose and fell outward. I advanced closer with the chair raised up high. When the person's face finally popped up, I was surprised to see it was a girl, which might have saved her from being bashed over the head. I thought it was Sapphira at first because of her long, black hair, but I quickly realized that it was someone else. The fact that she didn't look like a demon or spirit made me feel instantly calmer, albeit completely confused.

I kept the chair held up above me as the girl gave me a look that almost dared me to make the first move. All I could do was just stare at her as she stared back at me. For reasons that I can't explain, I actually let her climb through the window and stand in my apartment. Perhaps it was because I swore I had seen her somewhere before.

"You can put that down," she said firmly. "I won't bite if you don't provoke me."

I set the chair down, not taking my eyes off her.

"Who the hell are you?" I demanded. "Why did you climb through my window?"

"I had to see if you were home," she said.

"Then why didn't you just use the pager at the entrance?" I asked.

"Does it matter?" she asked. "Doors and windows are both holes in the wall, and I'm in here talking to you right now, which I would've been doing anyway if I'd come through the door."

Oh man, I thought cynically, *why am I having all of the most abnormal visitors today?*

That was when something in my memory clicked. This girl was the bassist for the band Triangular Lockjaw who had played at the Boney Feather on the first day of the semester. The large, silver ornament strung on her necklace was unmistakable.

88

"Hey, you're in that band," I said, suddenly taking slight interest in her. "I saw your last performance."

The girl simply raised her eyebrows and brushed aside the bangs that masked almost half of her face (which did absolutely nothing since they fell right back into place).

"So," she said, "you were there, huh?"

"Yeah," I replied, "you guys were great."

She looked at me in a mildly quizzical way and didn't seem to really acknowledge my compliment. Pulling my bludgeoning chair closer to herself, she casually took a seat in it.

"You can call me Raven," she said. "I'm allowed to tell you that much."

"*Raven*? Is that your real name?"

"Is *that* your real *face*?"

"Whoa, hold on," I said irritably, "there's no reason to get so defensive."

Raven looked subtly intrigued by my reaction. However, it was very hard to tell just what she was thinking. Just by looking at me, she was bombarding me with mixed messages. By this point, I only wanted to get her out of my hair as soon as possible.

"I'm Mike," I said, "so now that we know each other, you can tell me what you're doing here."

"I'm here for business reasons," she told me. "My boss wants to meet you."

"Your boss?" This was getting interesting. "Who do you work for?"

"We call her Miss Flamingo," said Raven. "I'm allowed to tell you that, too."

I had to cough to keep myself from laughing. My condolences to anybody going through life with a name such as "Flamingo."

"And what do you do?" I asked when I regained my composure.

"We're a research team, mostly," she said. "There's more to it than that, but you'll find out only if you let me take you to our lair."

Raven made it sound like she worked for an evil underground organization, and that turned me off to the idea of allowing her to lead me anywhere by myself.

"Not interested," I answered.

"You'll be rewarded with money," she bribed.

Is that so? You just said the magic word.

"Money?" I said. "What kind of money?"

Raven took a quick look around the apartment.

"Likely enough to pay rent for this place," she said.

Now she definitely had my attention. I had some feelings of hesitation, but it sounded as if a job offering had literally come in through the window. Maybe putting a little trust in this strange girl could do me some good, and it probably wouldn't hurt to just check it out. I could likely avoid moving back in with my parents. Giving it a brief thought, I reached my decision.

"I guess I could go," I said. "I have homework to finish, but it's easy and shouldn't take long. I'll do it later."

Raven cracked a small, satisfied smile.

"Great," she said. "You have a car, right?"

"Yeah."

"You can follow me there. It's not quite ten minutes away."

"Wait," I said, "we need to fix my screen."

She quickly stood up and climbed out through the window. I walked over and looked out to see her descend a long ladder all the way to ground, pick up the window screen out from the bushes, and climb back up to hand it to me.

"I'll see you outside," she told me before heading back down.

I fitted the screen back into the window, thinking about what crazy situation I was about to get myself into next. The last time I had agreed to something weird, my life suddenly changed forever. Hopefully, whatever normality was left would remain with me after going with Raven, and my desperation for a job led me to take my chances.

She was waiting for me next to a small electric car, which I could oddly enough see her driving. The vehicle practically demanded to be ridiculed, and I hoped that the future of alternative fuel would be drastically improved if I ever had to buy something like it. At least it had a backseat to make it slightly larger than what it could've been, but anyone bigger than a kid would probably be uncomfortable fitting in the back.

"Don't fall behind," she told me, getting into her miniature automobile.

I don't think that'll be a problem, I thought.

Raven took me in a direction away from Elm Valley. The night was approaching its full darkness, and I was almost concerned that a deer would run out in front of Raven and mangle her little car. I just couldn't get out of my mind how preposterous the vehicle looked as I followed behind it, and I figured that it couldn't be very crash-safe.

We drove for nearly ten minutes until Raven turned down a long private driveway that went straight into the woods. I wouldn't have been able to see the entrance if she wasn't leading the way. The dirt driveway took us deep into the woods to a cabin located in a secluded area. Although it was dark, I could make out more cars parked nearby. After stepping out of my car, I slipped on my hoodie to fend off the chilly breeze rustling through the trees. Raven silently beckoned me to follow her, and we walked up to the cabin along a stone pathway.

"Are there other people here?" I asked, looking at the other cars parked outside.

"There are; I was just talking to them on the phone," said Raven, "and don't say anything about the dangers of driving and talking on the phone because I'm just going to ignore it."

"I wasn't. I don't really care."

"You just might fit in here, you know that?" she said.

I'll decide if that's a good or bad thing after I see just what goes on in this cabin, I thought.

Raven opened the front door and I followed her inside, finding that the cabin had a very nice interior. As we walked through the living room, I figured that nothing appeared too out of the ordinary so far. It looked the way I'd expect a cabin to look, complete with a fireplace, bearskin rug, and a big moose head on the wall. I followed Raven upstairs to a closed door, which she knocked on.

"It's me," she called, "Raven."

A tall black guy opened the door, and he looked a lot like a rapper with his cornrows, gold chain necklace with large bling, and clean, white sneakers. He greeted us with a smile and let us into the room.

"Hey, Raven, you brought him," he said happily. "Good job!"

"Thanks, Cormorant," she said.

I looked around the room, which looked like a regular conference room with a large table in the middle. There were three more people in the room, and not a single person looked much older than me. One was a girl with glasses sitting at a desk with organized stacks of papers, working on a laptop. Another was a scrawny guy quietly seated in the corner, reading a book. The third person looked like a beefy wrestler and was standing next to a table loaded with refreshments. He was already pouring himself the second shot of gin in the four seconds I had been there. They all meagerly acknowledged my arrival before returning to what they were doing.

"Is Miss Flamingo still here?" Raven asked Cormorant.

"Yes," he replied, "she's right behind you."

I turned around and came face-to-face with a young woman standing in the doorway. She had dirty-blonde hair, was about five inches taller than me, and a cute face that was hardened into a firm countenance as she gave me a look of suspicion. I couldn't quite put my finger on it, but something just gave her an air of authority and leadership, and I quickly moved out of the way so she could come into the room.

"I have completed my assignment," Raven told her.

"Good job, Raven," she said as she swept past me. Her voice was solid and administrative. "You have completed your task desirably."

"Thank you," said Raven humbly.

Everyone gave Miss Flamingo's presence the same level of acknowledgement they had given me, so I suddenly didn't feel so bad. She was holding an envelope in her hand, which she handed to Raven. When Raven tucked it into her pocket without a word, I decided not to ask about it.

"You can sit down if you wish," Miss Flamingo told me.

I sat down in the seat nearest to the door. If anything crazy happened, I was prepared for a fast getaway. However, Cormorant stood by the door with his arms crossed, so I assumed he was the doorman and that I would have to go through him before leaving.

Miss Flamingo walked over to the refreshment table and poured herself a cup of coffee. The muscular guy took his final shot of gin (I think his fourth since I'd arrived) and clumsily leaned on the table, making it move and causing Miss Flamingo to spill some of her coffee.

"Kookaburra!" she snapped. "Please try to be more careful."

"Oh, my bad," he replied stiffly, wiping the spill with a napkin.

Sipping her coffee, Miss Flamingo took a seat at the far end of the table. I could smell an interview in the making.

"Welcome to our cabin," she told me in a business-like manner.

"Thank you," I replied. "My name is—"

"I have no need to know your name," she said abruptly. "You may address me as Miss Flamingo."

"Uh, alright."

"Would you like a drink?" she offered, gesturing toward the refreshment table that Kookaburra was leaning on. "Water? Tea? Coffee? Chocolate milk? Beer? Gin? Absinthe? Blood?"

"What was that last thing?" I asked quickly.

"Cow blood," said Miss Flamingo. "It's a nutrient-rich drink that's enjoyed in more tribal communities around the world."

"No, I'm not thirsty, thanks," I said, feeling a little queasy.

"Then let's get down to business," she said. "I've been watching you since the beginning of your term at Elm Valley College, and I believe you would be a fine part of our team."

"What do you mean?" I asked sternly. "You've been watching me?"

"Not personally," she said. "I have eyes and ears that do the work for me, such as Raven, and you weren't the only person of our interest. We've been keeping track of many people, and you're the only one who matches what we're looking for. Now our search is over."

That was somewhat discomforting to know. Raven had been spying on me? I could imagine her nestled in a tree outside of my apartment with a pair of binoculars.

"What do you do?" I asked. "None of you look like a professional or ordinary team."

"Watch your tone, man," Kookaburra warned, glaring at me.

"We're a supernatural inspection team," said Miss Flamingo, ignoring Kookaburra, "and I suspect you possess powerful ties to the paranormal."

I suddenly felt very unsettled as I realized that I had once again wandered into dangerous territory. As Miss Flamingo explained all this to me, it was odd to see everyone else just going about their business as if nobody around was talking about crazy stuff.

"What makes you say that?" I said, trying to play it off. "How do you know if I have ties to the paranormal?"

"Don't take me as a fool," said Miss Flamingo. "Now that you're sitting here in this room talking to me, I can tell that you are strongly associated with the spiritual world. You would be a good addition to our team, and I assure you that there's money in it for you."

She didn't know about Sapphira, did she? The fact that Miss Flamingo had invited me to a meeting right after I met Sapphira and Lemuel seemed like more than a coincidence.

This is bull, I thought. *I don't wanna get involved in this.*

"I'm not so sure," I said. "This all seems a little sketchy to me, and I'm not very comfortable with any of it."

Miss Flamingo sipped her coffee quietly.

"Suit yourself," she said. "There's the door."

Everyone in the room was watching me. I stood up and slowly walked over to the door, which Cormorant opened for me. The entire time, I kept telling myself to keep walking. There are plenty of other jobs out there. I might be able to find a good job before rent is due....

Not likely.

I stopped in front of the door and turned around, screaming at myself on the inside for even considering what I did next.

"If I worked for you, what would you have me do?" I asked Miss Flamingo.

"Oh, simple things," she replied. "I'd start you off with running errands, and you'd be paid per completed assignment."

"So I'd be your errand boy?" That sounded like a lowly position, and I wasn't sure if it'd be worth it in the end. "What would my hours be?"

"We meet here every Monday and Thursday at seven in the evening," she told me. "You will also be on call twenty-four-seven, except when you have class."

The gears in my brain were turning. Running errands sounded like something I could do, and Raven said that I could make enough money to keep my apartment. On top of that, being uncomfortable about the supernatural world wasn't a very good excuse, since I was already in over my head with a demon slave chained to my life. I was confident that I could keep Sapphira a secret from everyone, and she would probably even be able to help me with my work if I needed it.

"One more thing," I said. "What if I join your team, but decide to quit?"

"You may quit whenever you please," said Miss Flamingo. There was a frightening gleam in her eye that made my hair stand up. "I run a club here, not an official business. However, you will be sworn to secrecy for life. I know for a fact that you won't want to tell anyone about us."

I looked at everyone in the room, and they all were giving me the most serious look I'd ever seen outside of a funeral or prison. The silence was almost just as unsettling, and I had to break the tension fast.

"Alright," I said finally, "I'll join."

The tension in the room suddenly fell to the floor, but I still had an uneasiness lingering over my head like a spider dangling from the ceiling. Only time would tell what consequences, if any, I would soon be facing for agreeing to join this club.

"There we have it," said Miss Flamingo, although she didn't seem very excited or enthusiastic.

Everyone other than Miss Flamingo walked over and shook my hand, and I began to feel slightly more comfortable as each of them welcomed me into the club.

"I'm Oriole," said the girl with glasses. "I'm in charge of information organization, data entry, and research."

The big, beefy guy shook my hand next.

"Kookaburra." I could smell the alcohol on his breath as he gripped my hand tightly and painfully. "I get rid of unwanted spirits and demons."

"Call me Skylark," said the scrawny guy reading the book. "I work with Kookaburra to ward off spirits."

"As you know, I'm Cormorant," said the tall, rapper-looking guy. "I'm the club's vice president and Miss Flamingo's personal assistant."

"Welcome to the club," said Raven. "I do information gathering and miscellaneous stuff that secret agents are known for."

I'm afraid to know what stuff that could possibly be, I thought.

Miss Flamingo poured herself another cup of coffee and asked everyone to sit down around the table. After I took my seat, Miss Flamingo sipped her coffee and gazed across the table at me.

"The first thing we need to do," she said, "is assign you a club name. You will be referred to by your club name, and you will refer to everyone else here by their club names."

"Alright," I said, "but I noticed that everyone here is nicknamed after a bird. Do I have to have a bird name, too?"

"Yes," she said firmly, "that is the rule."

"Are you serious?" I muttered.

"Watch it," Kookaburra growled, giving me a dirty look.

"One thing that you will learn," said Miss Flamingo, "is that I am *always* serious."

I wanted to retaliate, but everyone's faces warned me to do otherwise, so I just shut my trap and listened to what was being said.

"Now, we need a name for the newcomer," said Miss Flamingo. "Any suggestions?"

"Pigeon!" Oriole blurted out.

"You always suggest that one," said Kookaburra. "Haven't you learned that nobody in this club will ever be named Pigeon?"

"I was just saying," said Oriole quietly.

"Owl?" Skylark suggested. "Or does he look smart enough?"

"Hmm, I don't know." Cormorant studied me. "That doesn't seem like a good name for him."

Wait, what did he mean by that?

"Dove, maybe," said Raven.

Everyone looked at me for a moment, then at each other...then back at me. That wasn't a good sign.

"Dove, huh?" said Oriole. "Yeah, that seems suitable...."

"I don't think so!" I said.

"Vulture seems fitting," said Cormorant. "Does anyone else think so?"

"Something like that," said Skylark.

"Maybe Vulture...or Buzzard," said Oriole.

"Yeah," said Raven, "either of those sounds nice."

Why are you guys suggesting such nasty birds to name me after? Do I look like a scavenger? Or...do I...?

"How about Phoenix?" I asked. "Can we use fictional birds? I think it sounds pretty cool."

"We already had a member named Phoenix," said Miss Flamingo. "No two names can be alike, so think of another."

"Well, Phoenix was a black guy," said Kookaburra, "so we can name this guy White Phoenix."

"That's just a stupid name for anything," said Raven curtly.

"Wait, what happened to Phoenix?" I asked.

There was a moment of silence. Miss Flamingo drummed the sides of her coffee cup.

"He passed away not too long ago," she told me. "That's why we needed a replacement."

"I'm sorry to hear that," I said. "What happened to him?"

"He had a stroke," said Oriole mournfully.

"Good guy," Cormorant murmured.

"Okay, let's keep focused," said Miss Flamingo.

"Well, I have a suggestion," I said. "I'm going to be an errand boy, so how about Roadrunner?"

There was more silence as everyone thought it over for a second.

"That sounds pretty good," said Oriole. "I think I like that."

"Roadrunner," said Raven with her eyes closed. "Hmm...Roadrunner."

"Yeah, I kinda like that," said Cormorant.

"Are you sure you don't want Dove?" Oriole asked me. "Or Pigeon?"

"Uh, no," I replied.

"Is everyone in favor of Roadrunner?" Cormorant asked. There was a murmur of agreement accompanied by nodding heads. "Well then, I think we've settled on Roadrunner, Miss Flamingo."

"Roadrunner it is," Miss Flamingo announced. "Oriole, bring Roadrunner an application and a copy of the contract."

Oriole quickly left the room and returned with the paperwork and a pen, which she placed on the table in front of me. The application was very similar to your average club admittance form, requiring my club name, address, phone number, etc. I quickly filled it out and moved on to the contract, which I closely examined for any suspicious entitlements. The contract basically explained that I had to attend every meeting, respond to every assigned duty, swear to secrecy, and follow orders. I signed the bottom of the contract with my club name, wrote down my class schedule, and handed the papers to Miss Flamingo.

"Meeting adjourned," was all she said.

Once I was outside, someone had turned on the lights in the driveway, allowing me to see everyone. Cormorant was walking next to me, so I figured I would say something to him.

"I have to admit," I said, "Miss Flamingo has a lot of faith that we won't tell people about our club."

"I know, I know," he replied, "but there's something you need to know about Miss Flamingo. She claims to be a psychic."

I looked at Cormorant skeptically.

"Is that so?" I said.

"That's what she says," he said. "None of us have ever seen her actually use her skills."

"So what?" Kookaburra added. "Everyone she chooses to work for her seems to fit the role perfectly, and it's almost as if she already knows that we'll do what she tells us. It's like she knows something about us…and it's hard to explain, but she just *makes* us do the things she wants us to do."

"I'm gonna be honest with you, man," said Cormorant quietly, looking around. "None of us here are really comfortable around that girl."

"Shh!" Oriole hushed nervously. "Careful, Cormorant."

"Then why do you guys stick around?" I asked.

"Because of the pay," he replied. "She always keeps her word, and she always makes sure we get plenty of money for what we do. I started working for her while looking for a part-time job on the side, but I was soon able to quit my real job because of how much she pays."

All of this promise of money sounded extremely enticing.

"How much money are we talking?" I asked curiously.

"Anywhere from several hundred to a couple grand a week," said Cormorant, "but it all depends on the assignments."

Before I could get over Cormorant's glorious answer, Kookaburra called me over to his car. When I walked over to see what he wanted, he pulled out a bottle of whiskey from his backseat and handed me a shot glass.

99

"This is to commemorate your induction," he said, filling my glass.

Admittedly, this wouldn't have been the first time I had any alcohol, despite being underage. However, I just wasn't in the mood at the time.

"No, I can't, man," I said. "I have to drive and I'm only twenty."

"I don't give a damn," said Kookaburra gruffly, pouring himself a shot. "Either drink it with me or I'll put it in you through a more unconventional method."

"It's true," said Skylark from afar. "He did it to me."

I looked at Kookaburra, noticing the no-nonsense look on his face, so I just sighed, toasted, and gulped the whiskey. It burned all the way down my throat and puffed out through my nose.

"See, that wasn't so bad." Kookaburra put the whiskey and shot glasses on the floor in the back of his car and covered them with a towel.

"So, do you guys use crossbows and stuff?" I asked him. "You fight supernatural stuff, right?"

Kookaburra looked at me like I was an idiot.

"What kind of a club do you think this is?" he asked irritably. "We don't hunt werewolves or slay vampires or track Bigfoot. Those guys aren't real. We deal with spirits and demons."

"You mean you do exorcisms?" I asked.

"Nah, not me, but Skylark is studying and practicing it. He's the demonologist. I don't mainly deal with that crap, just regular ghosts and spirits. They're not as dangerous. Just show up every Monday and Thursday and do your assignments. You'll learn what kind of stuff we do. It's nothing like the movies, though, so don't get your hopes up too high."

Kookaburra got into his car and took off with everyone else. I looked around and saw that I was the last one there, so I decided to leave right away. Being alone by that cabin was a little creepy.

While I was driving home, it occurred to me that I hadn't seen Miss Flamingo leave the cabin with everyone. Did that

100

mean she lived there? She apparently had a lot of money, and it made sense that she'd live in a big, secluded place like that.

At any rate, I had a job now, so naturally that made me happy. What didn't make me so happy was the fact that my job was centered around the very bizarre and unordinary. No matter what, I was still devoted mainly to my college work, and if anything weird got out of hand, I would immediately leave the club and try to forget all about it.

Miyuki was sitting at the corner table in the campus library with her nose buried in textbooks. I had asked her earlier if she wanted to meet me at the library to have a study session before I went to my biology lab. However, the real reason I wanted to go to the library wasn't to study. Perhaps it was because of the little talk about girls I'd had with the guys out in the woods, but there was something compelling me to get to know Miyuki more than I had been. Whatever the cause, I found myself meeting Miyuki in the library for something other than merely having a study buddy.

"Hi," she said with a smile when I approached the table.

"Hey," I replied, taking a seat. "What are you working on?"

"Music theory," she said. "It's kinda confusing, but I think I almost get it."

"Yeah, I can't help you much with that," I said. "I only just *listen* to music."

"After I started taking this class, I've been hearing music in a totally different way," she said. "I'm much more analytical now."

"Is that a good thing or a bad thing?" I asked.

"I think it's a good thing. Music is much more interesting for me, at least. So, how do you think you did on the psychology test yesterday?"

I grimaced at the thought of how that test ate me alive.

"Not so great," I sighed. "I was busy over the weekend and didn't have time to study for it."

"Oh, bummer," said Miyuki. "What did you have to do?"

"I went camping with my buddies and we got lost," I said. "We had to spend an extra day out in the woods."

"An entire day?" said Miyuki, wide-eyed.

"Yeah."

"That's terrible! How did you make it back?"

"Um, it's a long story, but we all made it back in one piece."

"I've never been camping," she said. "Is it fun?"

"It's a lot of fun," I said. "Just make sure you take everything you need."

During my conversation with Miyuki, I almost forgot that I was supposed to be studying. My English assignment was a short opinion report, but that required too much research and would distract me from the real reason I was there. There were some biology terms that needed to be reviewed, so I would just go over those.

"Do you know if any good movies are playing?" I asked.

Miyuki tapped her pencil on the table as she thought.

"I'm not sure," she said. "I haven't really kept track of the movies or anything. Do you know any?"

I shrugged. "I was just seeing if you knew any."

"I'm not a big moviegoer," she said.

Bah, she completely sidestepped me! Let's give it a different approach....

"You like music, right?" I said. "What about concerts?"

"Kinda," she said. "I really like orchestral and ensemble concerts, but there aren't any coming up in the area for a long time."

Her cell phone went off, and I immediately noticed the mushy pop love song for the ringtone. She quickly answered it with a bright smile that only brought rain to my side of the table.

"Hey, babe! Did you get my message?" she said flirtatiously. "I was checking if you picked those up for us.... You did? Oh, that's great! Yeah, I'm at the library studying with a classmate.... Are you gonna come pick me up? Okay, sounds good. I'll see you in a little bit. Love you!"

She hung up, wearing a happy face that can only be rivaled by those round, yellow smiley emoticons as she quickly packed up her books and folders.

"I'm sorry, but I have to cut this short," she told me. "My boyfriend's coming to get me in a few minutes to celebrate his birthday."

"Oh," I said flatly. "That's fine."

"We should do this again," she said, apparently not knowing that every one of her innocent words was like a flaming dagger through my body.

"Yeah, definitely. See ya later. Have fun."

"Bye!"

I stared down at the sheet filled with biology terms, trying to fully understand what had just happened, although I knew perfectly well. Oh well, it was a good thing that I didn't have any deep feelings for her. However, I was more disappointed that nothing seemed to be going right for the past few days. With a deep sigh, I packed my stuff and stood up.

Before I could walk away from the table, I noticed a girl who was looking at books on the shelves. I immediately recognized her as Hayley, the shy girl I had met at the Boney Feather. At that moment, something inside of me took initiative. Call it destiny, call it coincidence, call it rebound, but I called it opportunity. I still had two hours left before biology, and a little detour on my way to the exit wouldn't hurt anything.

"Hey, Hayley," I said as I walked over to her.

She looked at me with a confused expression for a second before she smiled.

"Oh! Hi, Mike!" she replied. "How are you?"

"Alright, I guess," I said. "I haven't seen you in a while."

"Yeah, I've been around," said Hayley, looking at the floor.

"I have to kill some time before my next class," I said, "so I'm just hanging out in the library. I don't feel like driving home and then coming back."

"I'm looking for a book to read," she said. "They have a lot here, so, you know...."

"You like to read?"

"Um, a little." Hayley looked around, and I could tell she was getting nervous. "Do you want to sit down somewhere? I mean, only if you want...."

"Yeah, let's find a table," I said.

We sat down at the nearest table. Hayley placed her bag on the chair next to her and flipped her brown hair. I knew she did that on purpose.

"Did you have classes today?" I asked her.

"Math and history," she said. "I just got done with them and don't have any for the rest of the day."

"I wish I could say the same," I said. "I still have biology lab. It's a three-hour class in the middle of the afternoon."

"Oh, that's no fun," she said.

"Man, it's torture," I said jokingly. "I'm glad I have my friends in it with me or I'd go insane."

Hayley giggled.

"Yeah, I know what you mean," she said.

"So, how are your classes going?" I asked. "Are you doing alright so far in your first year?"

"I'm doing alright," she said. "I don't think I'm doing *great* in any of my classes, but at least I know I'm passing. I had a psychology test yesterday that I think I did pretty well on."

"Is that so?" I said. "I have that class, too...."

"Yeah? How do you think you did on the test?"

I sighed, thinking that I had to explain the situation *again*.

"I flunked, I know it," I said dully. "Me and my friends were camping and got lost, so we had to spend the day I wanted for studying out in the woods."

To my surprise, Hayley started laughing.

"You had to stay out in the woods for a whole extra day?" she giggled.

"Uh, yeah."

"That's so funny! What did you do? How'd you get lost?"

"We couldn't find the SUV," I explained, "so we ended up walking all over trying to look for it. Our friend Aaron said he knew the area and where we were going, but he didn't know crap."

"Aw, that sounds like it'd be an epic adventure," said Hayley.

She can't be serious, I thought.

"Well, I guess it kinda was," I said. "One of our friends had to climb a tree to see where we were going."

"How'd you get out?" she asked interestedly, leaning a little closer.

"Panic button," I said. "We just followed the alarm."

"That's a good idea," she said. "So, did you feel like you were on one of those TV shows where the guy goes out in the wilderness and tries to survive?"

"No, it felt more like a mystery thriller to find out which one of us would strangle someone else first."

"I wish I could've seen it," said Hayley with a smile. "Did you tape any of it?"

"No," I said, "it didn't even cross my mind. Maybe next time we'll invite you, then you can enjoy getting lost."

"Um, I don't really like camping," she said. "It's not that I don't like nature. I just don't like getting dirty...or failing tests."

"Nobody likes failing tests," I muttered.

"I'm sorry about that," she said. "Did you really do that badly on it?"

"Yeah, I'm pretty sure it blew my grade to smithereens."

"Smithereens, huh?" She seemed contemplative. "That's gonna be my word of the day."

"Come again?"

"It means little pieces or fragments," she explained. "Did you know that most dictionaries only list that word as a plural because it almost never gets used in its singular form?"

"Really?" I said. "I really didn't know that."

"I'm gonna start using it in its singular form," she said, reaching into her bag and taking out a chocolate bar. "Would you like a smithereen of chocolate?"

"Yeah," I replied, reaching for the smithereen she broke off for me. "Thanks."

"Yup," she said.

As I savored the sweet, melting goodness, my phone vibrated to inform me of a text message. The caller ID said it was from an unknown number, so I curiously flipped it open to see who it was from and what they had to say.

It's Raven. You need to meet me at the gas station across from the laundromat downtown. Hurry up.

I just got hired yesterday and they're already giving me stuff to do? I thought. *More money for me, but the timing couldn't be worse.*

I didn't want to end my conversation with Hayley so soon, so I figured I'd see just how badly Raven needed me to meet up with her. When I saved Raven's number to my contact list, I quickly replied to her text.

Im in the middle of something so do you really really need me to go there?

The reply message took no more than ten seconds to get back to me.

YES!!!!

"Well, I have to get going," I told Hayley, putting my phone in my pocket.

"Did you get called in to work or something?" she asked.

"Um, something like that," I said, standing up.

"Here, take this," she said, handing me the chocolate bar.

"No thanks," I said. "It's yours."

"I want you to have it," she said. She stood up and literally placed it in my hand. "I'll see you later."

"Yeah," I said. "Later."

She grabbed her bag and swiftly left the library. I looked down at the chocolate bar that was still mostly wrapped.

That was odd, but whatever. Free food.

I went out to my car and put the chocolate in the cup holder. Hopefully, whatever Raven wanted wouldn't take more time than I had before biology. Unlike regular classes, it was mandatory to attend all lab sessions, so I couldn't afford to miss it.

Raven's tiny electric car was easily spotted as I pulled into the gas station. I parked next to her, and she was able to get out of her car and jump into my passenger seat before I knew where she even was.

"What are you doing?" I asked irritably.

"I'm giving you your first assignment," she said.

"Did you have to get in my car?"

"We can't discuss business in an open environment!" she hissed. "What we do is confidential. Remember that!"

"Then why did you choose to meet at a gas station?" I asked flatly.

Instead of answering my question, she looked all around to make sure it was safe to do whatever she was planning.

"Take this," she said quietly, handing me an envelope. "Follow the instructions and report back to the cabin."

I wanted to ask her what it was, but she jumped out of my car before I could open my mouth. Without a second to spare, she got into her battery-operated vehicle and drove away, leaving me alone to carry out my assignment.

"This is ridiculous," I muttered, tearing open the envelope.

I had been given $74.82 in cash, along with a printed list on a piece of paper. Reading the list, I immediately understood that my assignment was to go grocery shopping, and the instructions specifically mentioned I had to go to Harbert's Groceries.

Oh man, I told myself I was boycotting the place. I don't want to go back there.

After a moment of hesitation, I sucked it up and headed to Harbert's. There was little doubt in my mind that I could pick up everything on the list from somewhere else and nobody would tell the difference, but I didn't want to take any chances, especially on my first assignment. There was no telling where Miss Flamingo's "eyes and ears" were and if they were watching me. Honestly, that gave me the creeps. Besides, it wasn't my own money going to Mr. Straussford, so I had little to complain about.

The plan was to be in and out as quickly as possible. Sitting in my car in the parking lot, I studied the list and tried to remember where everything was, then calculated the fastest and shortest route through the store. With the money in my pocket and the list in my hand, I got out of my car and grabbed an abandoned shopping cart. This was going to redefine power shopping.

As soon as I barged in through the automatic doors and made a beeline for the ground coffee, I instantly noticed that something was wrong. Everything in the store had been moved and rearranged, so I no longer knew where anything was. Standing in the middle of the place I hated most, I realized that I would have to spend more time there than anticipated.

Don't stall! I told myself. *Keep moving!*

I read the overhead signs for every aisle quickly, then darted down the correct aisles and tossed the stuff into the cart without stopping. This seemed like an efficient plan until I reached the other side of the store and found out that I had missed a few things. Disgruntled and impatient, I had to comb over the store one more time before everything on the list was in my cart.

I hoped that nobody I used to work with was running the cash register as I headed to the checkout. When I scanned the different lanes, I was relieved to see that some new recruits had been hired. The line I stood in was run by some guy I had never seen before.

"That'll be $74.82," said the clerk after scanning everything I had.

Strangely, the total cost came to the exact amount of money in the envelope. Clearly, someone had shopped here way too many times. With all of the bags in the shopping cart, I hurried out of Harbert's Groceries back to my car. My first assignment for Miss Flamingo was going somewhat smoothly now, and all I had to do was take the groceries back to the cabin before biology.

While walking up to my car, I suddenly stopped dead in my tracks. Somebody was sitting in my front passenger seat. From where I was standing, it appeared to be Raven, although

I wasn't exactly sure. My car had been locked, so why would someone break into it just to sit there?

The person in the car turned to look at me, and I could see their yellow eyes piercing through the glass. There was only one person I knew with eyes like that, and I wasn't very excited to see her sitting in my car. Leaving the groceries in the cart, I unlocked the driver's door and confronted Sapphira.

"What are you doing here?" I asked irritably.

"I am checking up on you," Sapphira replied.

"I don't want anyone to see you!" I said, glancing around.

"I am not going against your orders," she said. "There is nobody here who will notice me. May I help you with the groceries?"

I groaned and ruffled my hair. Sapphira was worse than a little kid. Looking at the shopping cart, I just shrugged and figured I could take advantage of her being there.

"Go ahead," I muttered, getting in the car, "and put the cart in the corral when you're done. I used to hate retrieving stray carts in the parking lot when I worked here."

As I waited for Sapphira to place the groceries in the backseat, all I could do was hold my head and ask myself why I even bothered with her at all. I could easily order her to sit on the moon and let me live my life normally, but something unexplainable was compelling me to make use of her. Was there something about our pact that I was unaware of?

"All done," she said, taking a seat in my car again.

"Thank you," I said. "Hey, there's something I have to tell you."

"What is it?" she asked.

"I'm going to a cabin out in the woods a few miles from here," I told her. "Um, you should just stay away from that place. The people there claim to be demon hunters or something, and I don't want to take any chances with them finding you."

"Understood," said Sapphira.

"Alright, you're dismissed. Don't leave the apartment for the rest of the day."

The drive to the cabin wasn't very long, but it gave me plenty of time to think about Miss Flamingo's club. Everyone involved seemed decent enough. I didn't consider myself the most normal person in the world, but I was able to become a club member. That being the case, it helped with the possibility that I was working with moderately normal people, although something still didn't seem quite right. Perhaps the word "normal" didn't have a place anywhere within the entire situation.

The cabin looked much less ominous during the day. With a clear view of the surrounding woods, I realized that it was indeed a very nice area. I was sure it would look really nice once the trees would change into their autumn colors. Hopefully, the job of raking up the leaves around the cabin wouldn't be mine. There were a lot of trees with a lot of leaves.

I parked as close to the front door as possible to minimize the grocery-carrying distance. The door was unlocked, but I rang the doorbell and waited for someone to answer, since I didn't want to just walk right in. Some time passed, so I rang again. When there was still no answer, I tried knocking.

I don't think anyone's here, I thought. *I don't want to just leave the stuff outside.*

As I was texting Raven to ask her what I was supposed to do, the sound of footsteps could be heard coming from inside the cabin. The door quickly swung open and I came face-to-face with Miss Flamingo scowling at me.

"You need to inform me before you come here," she said demandingly. "You can't just show up like this."

"Sorry, I didn't know," I said. "I have the groceries Raven said you wanted me to pick up."

Miss Flamingo looked at me inquisitively.

"That was quick," she said. "I'm impressed."

"Thank you," I said. "I didn't want to spend too much time at the store. I have to get them out of my car."

"Bring everything to the meeting room upstairs," said Miss Flamingo before going back inside.

111

I removed the groceries from the backseat of my car and attempted to carry everything in one trip. With the bags in each hand, I waddled through the front door of the cabin as I struggled to keep my balance with so much weight on each arm. Most of the things I had to buy were canned, so that made the load much heavier. Miss Flamingo stood in the living room and watched me.

"You don't have to do it all in one trip," she said.

"No, I like to." It was difficult to talk without showing the amount of strain I was under. "It's quicker this way."

Going up the stairs wasn't as bad as I thought it would be, although I was feeling pretty worn out by the time I made it to the top. The bag handles were beginning to cut off the circulation in my hands. Turning the doorknob to get into the meeting room was a challenge in its own right, but I refused to set the bags down. When I finally made it inside the room, I put the bags on the large center table and heaved a sigh of relief as I flexed my fingers to get the blood flowing again.

Miss Flamingo walked in with a mug of warm tea. She seemed partly satisfied while wearing her little half-smile and lukewarm expression.

"Well done," she told me coldly. "I can do the rest from here."

"Have I completed my assignment?" I asked.

"That's up to you to figure out," she said.

I squinted my eyes at her.

"What's that mean?" I asked.

"If you believe to have completed your assignment, then report back to me," she said, taking a sip of tea.

"I'm...done with my assignment," I said hesitantly, wondering if I did it right.

"Good job, Roadrunner," she replied. "I have your payment."

She took an envelope with "Roadrunner" written on it out of her pocket and handed it to me. Before I opened it, I could feel the money inside.

This is it, I thought happily. *Everybody said she pays well. Let's see what kind of small fortune I've earned for this simple job.*

I reached into the envelope, removed the fairly thick wad of money, and felt my heart sink as I stared at the handful of one-dollar bills. Counting the stack, there were exactly twenty.

"Twenty bucks?" I said disappointedly.

"Is something wrong?" Miss Flamingo asked, looking at me as if she knew exactly what I was thinking.

"This isn't going to pay my rent!" I said disdainfully.

"You get paid per assignment," she told me coolly. "This was a small errand, so you get a small payment."

"Well, when am I gonna do big errands?" I asked impatiently. "I need more money than this!"

"If you're unhappy with the way I run things, then you're free to leave the club," she told me, taking another sip of tea.

I kept quiet, not wanting to make the situation worse. With nothing else better to do, I pocketed the money.

"Can I ask why you paid in ones?" I asked. "Can't I get a twenty or two tens?"

"I don't like to have too many one-dollar bills," she said. "You see, you're helpful to me in more ways than you think."

You're awfully smug about it, I thought.

There was an awkward silence. I expected Miss Flamingo to have something else to say, but she just stood there and sipped her tea some more. I wasn't positive if I could just leave, but I sure wanted to.

"Are you done here?" she asked.

"Uh, yeah," I said. "I should be going to class now."

"Take care," she said.

The chilly wind blew as I walked back to my car. I looked up at the sky, and there appeared to be a storm rolling in. Checking my phone's clock, I saw I still had plenty of time to make it back to the college before biology.

Miss Flamingo is so strange, I thought while driving. *She'd better start paying me better soon. I don't want to find out that everyone's been lying to me about the money.*

By the time I made it back on campus, the sky had grown dark and the wind was picking up. A few speckles of rain were hitting my windshield as I drove through the parking lot. Thunder rumbled in the distance as I walked briskly to the building to avoid getting caught in the rain. Luckily, I managed to enter the building just seconds before the heavy downpour arrived.

Aaron and Lawrence were already in the seating area where we usually would hang around before the lab session. I walked up and took a seat next to them. The shopping trip earlier had tired me out a little, and I was certainly not looking forward to class for three hours on a stormy afternoon.

"Did you hear about the storm coming in?" Aaron asked me.

"Yeah, I almost got caught in it," I said. "I barely beat the rain walking in here."

"The news said it's supposed to be pretty nasty," said Lawrence. "I was watching the radar and there's a lot of yellow and red coming this way."

"Let's hope the power goes out and they cancel class," said Aaron.

Before I could agree with Aaron, my phone went off. Raven had texted me again, and I was afraid to know what she possibly wanted this time. Whatever it was, it was going to have to wait until biology was over.

You forgot a can of green beans

Give me a break, I thought. *It probably fell out in my car, so I'll tell her I'll drop it off after class.*

I have class now so i'll drop it off after

"Who are you texting?" Aaron asked. "Your girlfriend?"

"No, definitely not," I said. "Hey, is there a vending machine around here? I think I'll grab a snack before class starts."

"I don't know." Lawrence shrugged. "I'm sure there's one around somewhere."

"Alright," I said, "I'll be back."

114

I took off down the hall, keeping my eyes peeled for a vending machine. There happened to be two around the corner, one with snacks and the other with drinks. An energy drink sounded both refreshing and energizing, so I reached for my wallet stuffed full of one-dollar bills from Miss Flamingo.

"I wouldn't use that machine," said a guy who was walking past. "It's notorious for stealing money."

"I'll take my chances," I said. "It has something I need."

The machine needed $1.50 for the drink, a cheap price for most energy drinks. When I inserted the first bill, it quickly pushed it back out. I smoothed out the bill and reinserted it. The machine took it that time. Feeling slightly accomplished, I inserted the second bill, which the machine also took. I pressed the button corresponding to the energy drink....

...And nothing happened. I pressed it again. Still nothing.

"Aw, dude. That sucks," said the guy. "I said it takes your money."

Vending machines are supposed to have a button for returning change, but it was broken off. Now it was clear that if I wanted my energy drink, I was going to have to put up a fight.

I banged the sides of the machine a few times. Nothing happened. I banged it even more viciously. There seemed to be some kind of mechanical movement going on inside that time, but then nothing. I grabbed both sides of the machine, locking it into a bear hug, then rocked it back and forth.

"Careful, dude," the guy warned. "More people die that way than you think. It, like, falls and crushes them. Splat."

Without heeding the guy's warning, I continued to rock the vending machine for a little longer. Suddenly, something inside began to move, and I stopped wrestling the machine to see what was going on. To my delight, it was actually working.

Heh, I wasn't gonna lose to this stupid machine, I thought triumphantly.

In that instant, a loud roar of thunder shook the building. The electricity went off for a couple of seconds before coming back on. I looked at the vending machine only to find that it had reset itself. Another dollar and fifty cents was required to get my drink.

"Aw, dude!" The guy was cracking up, practically in tears. "Dude, I'm sorry, but I wish I'd recorded that! I'd totally put that video on YouTube, man."

As the guy walked away laughing, all I could do was feel defeated. I scowled at the vending machine and wandered back to where Aaron and Lawrence were sitting.

"Hey, did you see that power outage?" Aaron asked me.

"Yup," I muttered, "sure did."

"Did you get anything?" Lawrence asked.

"No, the stupid machine took my money!" I said angrily. "I don't wanna talk about it, man...it sucked."

"What were you gonna get?" Aaron asked.

"An energy drink," I said, sinking into a seat.

"Aren't those bad for you?" said Aaron. "I hear about it all the time."

"Only if you drink a lot of them," said Lawrence. "Moderation is key."

"I was just going to have one," I said. "I get hyper if I drink too many. How much time left before class?"

"A few minutes," said Lawrence, checking the time.

"We should probably get going," I said.

"Sure thing, let's jump on it," said Lawrence, picking up his books.

I walked with Aaron and Lawrence to our biology class, feeling completely unenthusiastic about being there. Two dollars out of my tight budget had just been wasted for nothing, and I felt stupid for not listening to what that guy had said about the vending machine. My only hope was that Miss Flamingo had some better tasks for me and that she had a lot of them. Money stressed me out.

We waited in the classroom for Ms. Schwark to begin the lab. Outside, the storm was throwing a tantrum of heavy rain, strong winds, and plenty of thunder and lightning. I wished for another power outage big enough to cancel class, even if it meant that the lab session had to be moved to another day. However, that power outage never occurred, and I was stuck in the three-hour class doing various testing on plant cells. Lawrence had a great time with the testing, so Aaron and I let him do most of the work. Peering into a microscope just isn't something that I like to do for extended periods of time, no matter how strange the substance swimming around in the Petri dish happens to be.

About half an hour before the end of class, I received another nagging text from Raven. Miss Flamingo had plenty of other cans of green beans, so I couldn't understand why this one last can was so crucial. Could she be making a massive casserole, or something? Maybe it was just Raven, not Miss Flamingo, who was so desperate for the damn green beans. I texted back to say that class was almost over and that I would take care of it right away.

Ms. Schwark ended the session with a brief review over what we had learned in today's lab, and she informed us of what we'd be covering next week. I jotted down some notes that I thought would be important, helped clean the lab stations, packed up my supplies, and hurried out of the classroom before anyone could stop me or slow me down. The storm had mostly passed and been reduced to some scattered showers as I headed to my car, but at least I wasn't soaking wet. Sure enough, there was a can of green beans on the floor in the back of my car.

I sent Raven a text saying that I was on my way. Before I started the car, I noticed the chocolate bar from Hayley was still in my cup holder. When I unwrapped part of it, there was a piece of paper inside with the chocolate. Thinking that I'd won something, I quickly unfolded it to see what it said. To my surprise, all it had was Hayley's name and a phone number, and it was suddenly obvious why she wanted me to have the chocolate bar so badly.

That's pretty clever. I didn't even see her put this paper in here. It's no golden ticket, but it's just as good.

117

~Opus 9~

The rain and wind picked up again as I was on my way to the cabin, but I really didn't care at this point. Hayley had just made my day. Forget the stupid vending machine, the lousy shopping trip, the nagging texts from Raven, and the fact that Miyuki had led me on without letting me know she had a boyfriend. Things were starting to look up again, and I was pretty stoked.

As I was going up the long dirt driveway, I sent Raven a text message to let her know that I was about to arrive. Her car wasn't parked at the cabin, and I was beginning to wonder where she was. Not wanting to just walk up to the door again and have Miss Flamingo tear my head off, I waited until Raven sent a reply message a few seconds later that said to go right in.

I grabbed the can of green beans and jogged up the stone path to avoid being in the rain as much as possible. Lightning split the sky as I rang the doorbell, clutching the can tightly. The air was chilly but the rain made it downright cold, even for the time of year. Miss Flamingo opened the door moments later and invited me into the dry, warm living room.

"Here's the can," I said, handing it to her.

"Thank you," she replied. "I was beginning to think that you didn't get Raven's message."

"Wouldn't it be easier for you to just call me directly?" I asked. "And I could call you to let you know that I'm here so we don't have to go through Raven."

"Those are the rules," said Miss Flamingo firmly.

I couldn't understand why she was always so stubborn about her pointless rules. Maybe it was just a way to exercise her authority as the club leader.

"Do you live here?" I asked. "I'm just curious."

"Almost," she replied, walking into the kitchen.

"Uh...well, I'm done with my assignment," I called, "so I'll be on my way."

"Hold on." Miss Flamingo walked back to the living room and handed me another envelope with "Roadrunner" written on it. "Here's something for the extra effort."

118

"Thanks," I said, feeling a little better about driving all the way back out there.

When I was out in my car, I opened the envelope to find ten more one-dollar bills. It wasn't very much, but it would cover the gas I had used for the trip, so I actually felt slightly accomplished as I drove away from the cabin.

The storm was still going strong as I drove back to town. I had some soft tunes playing on the radio that seemed oddly appropriate at the time. Perhaps the lingering thought of Hayley's phone number put me in a softer mood even as the rain pelted the windshield and the lightning lit up the sky.

Regardless of the mood or music playing, nothing had prepared me for the wind knocking down a huge tree branch in the middle of the road in front of me. Without any time to react, I ran right over it with a hair-raising thudding and scraping sound.

"Just great," I mumbled, pulling off to the side of the road. "That sounded like it messed something up."

I put on my hazard lights and got out to inspect the damage on my car in the middle of the storm. There were no streetlights around, so I had to get the flashlight out of my trunk. The front bumper was a little scraped, but it was nothing too bad. None of the tires appeared punctured or flattened. My tailpipe seemed okay.

Not being able to find any severe damage, I dragged the branch off the road, got back into my car, and continued home. I had the radio turned off so I could listen for any unusual sounds coming from the car, but it was hard to hear much over the heavy rain.

No more than half a mile down the road, the gas gauge seemed a lot lower than it should have been. As I drove, I watched in disdain as the needle drooped lower and lower. When the inside of the car started to smell like gasoline, it was evident that something really lousy had happened.

I punctured my gas tank! I thought miserably. *At this rate, I'm not gonna even make it back to town!*

Inevitably, the car sputtered to its death and rolled to a halt. I rested my head on the steering wheel, fearing that I would have to walk over three miles down a backcountry road during a thunderstorm to get back to town. I thought about calling Aaron to ask if he could use his truck to tow my car and give me a ride, but my phone had died when I checked it. The battery had been on the fritz for a while and would sometimes lose its charge for no reason.

A pair of headlights came up from behind and reflected off my rearview mirror. Without giving it a second thought, I jumped out of my car and attempted to flag down the driver. When the car slowed down and pulled to the side of the road, I heaved a sigh of relief and hurried over to talk to the driver.

"Are you having car problems?" the middle-aged man asked.

"Yeah, I think I punctured my gas tank on a branch in the road," I explained. "I was wondering if I could get a quick ride into town."

"Sure, hop in the back," he said, sounding a little too happy to help.

"Oh, thanks a million," I said, climbing in the back seat.

There was a teenage girl sitting in the front, and I assumed her to be the man's daughter.

"Where are you headed?" the man asked me.

"The apartments on Windsor Street," I said.

"Did you call the towing service?" he asked.

"No, I have a friend with a big truck and some towing cables," I said. "Do you have a phone I could borrow so I could call him?"

"Sorry, but we don't have a phone," he said.

I leaned back in the seat and stared out the window. For some strange reason, I felt a little uncomfortable riding in that car. The girl in the front appeared to be sick or something, breathing hard and squirming around in her seat. I wanted to ask if she was alright, but that just didn't seem like a good idea.

"Is something wrong?" the man asked me.

"Huh? No, I'm fine," I replied. "I guess I'm just a little stressed out from the whole situation."

The girl seemed to be getting worse by the second, and I was growing increasingly uncomfortable. My uneasy feeling was hard to describe as it spread from my stomach to the tips of my fingers and toes. Something very weird was going on.

I don't like whatever's going on here, I thought. *These people just don't seem right. Maybe I'll have him take me to the edge of town, and I'll take my chances in the rain.*

Instinctively, I held onto the door handle in case I needed to bail from the car. The logical part of me felt that my uneasiness was irrational and that I just had a long day, but my intuition was saying that something was definitely wrong here. I began to feel slightly dizzy and disoriented, but I did my best to maintain myself.

After a few minutes, we approached the edge of town. The rain was still coming down, but I felt as if I had been in the car long enough.

"Hey, you can just let me out now," I told the driver. "I don't live far from here."

"Don't worry about it," he said. "You just stay put."

"No, really," I said. "You can let me out."

"I said I'll take you there," he said.

A negative energy started to resonate inside the car, completely engulfing me. The teenage girl was now writhing and groaning. She looked like she was about to throw up...or explode...or anything that I didn't want to witness. The man who was driving seemed to pay no attention to her.

Wait a minute, I thought. *What did Lemuel tell me? Something about having a stronger connection to the supernatural? What if these two are...ghosts or something?*

As soon as that thought crossed my mind, both the middle-aged man and the girl looked back at me. Their eyes felt like icy hands on my soul as the man slammed on the brakes. I knew I was a sitting duck, so I flung myself from the backseat before the car came to a complete stop. My elbow hit the wet pavement painfully, but I immediately got my footing.

"Get him, Marlene!" I heard the ghost man say.

"Yes, Father."

I believe there comes a time in everyone's life when it would be in their best interest to simply run like hell. Without looking back, I sprinted down the street. Maybe it's hardwired in every person's DNA that home is the first place to head to when seeking safety or shelter, because that was exactly where I was trying to go. There was no other plan or thinking behind it.

When I was in high school gym, we would have to run laps around the track. At the end of class, the gym instructor would randomly elect somebody to be "it" and chase everyone else. Anyone who was tagged would have to run extra laps, so it was a good incentive to move as fast as possible. That helped me a little during this current situation, except "it" was a freakishly deranged spirit chick who would probably do more than tag me if I was too slow.

A few blocks from the apartment, my foot snagged something on the sidewalk, and I fell on the cold, wet pavement. In a frantic shuffle to get back up, I noticed that the spirit girl was nowhere to be seen.

As I quickly collected my thoughts, a tall figure came up from behind and lifted me back to my feet. Through the rain, I saw that my helper was dressed in full camo army fatigues. For an instant, I thought I was looking at my oldest brother, Sal, for the first time since his last departure across the ocean almost two years ago. With a disheartening realization, the person in front of me turned out not to be my brother.

"Are you alright?" he asked me. His voice was deep and powerful, giving the impression that he had been through a lot more than I ever had.

"Yeah, thanks," I said.

"You need to be more careful," he told me. "It's dangerous out today."

Telling him my entire situation would make me sound like a lunatic, so I decided to give him only part of my story.

"My car broke down," I explained. "I hitched a ride from someone, but...."

"Would you like a ride back to your home?" he asked.

I glanced over my shoulder. There was still no sign of the spirits, and I didn't feel the uncomfortable sensations they were giving off. However, I thought it would be better to take the safe route.

"If you don't mind," I said.

"This way."

His motorcycle was parked on the side of the road nearby. Even in the stormy weather, I could see that it was a very nice ride. I knew that I was running for my life, but I couldn't believe that I didn't notice such an awesome motorcycle sitting so close.

The soldier (as I assumed he was) dropped me off in front of my apartment building. His bike rode like nothing I had ever felt before, and it was too bad that we couldn't talk about it over the sound of the motor and rain. The storm was going strong, and I didn't want to have him out in it for too long.

"Hey, thanks a lot, man," I said humbly. "It means a lot."

"You're welcome," he said. "You can call me Eli."

His words sounded kind, but he withheld a very strong and dignified persona. There was no telling what kind of tragedies he had experienced while stationed in whatever foreign country he was in.

"I'm Mike," I said.

"Watch out for yourself," he said. With a roar of his motorcycle, he took off.

I was dripping wet when I walked tiredly back into my apartment. Like a dog that had been staring out the window all day, Sapphira appeared and quickly welcomed me.

"Welcome home, Michael," she said.

"Ugh."

I trudged into my room and started to change into dry clothes. After everything that just happened, being dry was the first thing to make me feel much better. When I was in nothing but my boxers, Sapphira walked right in like it was nobody's business.

"Hey, what are you doing?" I asked. "I'm getting dressed."

"Excuse me," she said, "but this is important."

"What is it?"

"Something followed you here," she said, looking around.

I nervously glanced all around. The knowledge of some unseen thing watching me made my neck hairs stand on end.

"What do you mean?" I quickly threw some clothes on to avoid being naked if something crazy went down. "There's something here?"

"Yes," said Sapphira. "I can get rid of it if you wish."

"Of course I want you to!" I said, yanking a clean shirt down over my head. "Get it out of here!"

Sapphira walked over and opened my closet. There didn't appear to be anything strange in there, but she reached in and grabbed something I apparently couldn't see. Without even struggling, Sapphira pulled some kind of creature into our world for me to see, which turned out to be the spirit girl that had chased me.

"Holy crap!" I shouted in fright, jumping back. "It's...it's her!"

Sapphira was somehow holding the girl several inches away without physically touching her. As the girl writhed like a rabid animal and clawed in my direction, Sapphira calmly kept her subdued.

"I shall banish this human spirit from your presence," she told me.

"V-very nice, just do it!" I spat.

Using some incantation in what I suspected to be Latin, Sapphira banished the spirit from the apartment within seconds. The girl disappeared into thin air, and I was left wondering if it was over.

"She has been removed from this residence," said Sapphira.

"Alright," I said, calming down. "Thank you. Good work."

"I advise you to wear your sapphire amulet," she told me. "Having it nearby will prevent more encounters with malevolent spirits such as this one."

"So, that was just a regular ghost or something?" I asked.

"An intelligent human spirit," said Sapphira. "She has not crossed over and is wandering the Earth. They are normally

124

unable to inflict serious harm on the living, but your heightened connection with the spiritual realms has increased its danger to you."

I grabbed the sapphire amulet from my nightstand and stuffed it in my pocket; if carrying it around would ward off more encounters like that last one, I'd keep it glued to my chest if I had to.

A few minutes passed before I could get back into my correct mindset. My next priority was doing something about my car. With my phone plugged into the charger, I called Aaron to ask him about helping me with towing. He quickly agreed and showed up at my place shortly after to pick me up. The storm had mostly subsided, so we didn't have to worry about the rain.

"How the heck did you puncture your gas tank?" he asked while we were hooking up the towing cables.

"I ran over a branch that fell in the road," I said. "I couldn't find a puncture when I looked, but I guess that's what happened."

"Why didn't you just go around the branch?" he asked. "Or you could've moved it off the road first."

"I didn't have a choice!" I told him. "It fell down right in front of me. I didn't even have time to hit the brakes."

Aaron looked inside my car and noticed the chocolate bar from Hayley still sitting in the cup holder.

"Hey, can I have that chocolate bar?" he asked.

"No way, that's mine," I replied.

"Chocolate makes you feel better, you know," he said.

"Trust me," I said, "that chocolate bar in there made me feel a lot better. It almost makes up for everything that's happened today."

I had spent all night sending texts back and forth with Hayley, trying to get to know her a little more. I was surprised by a lot of the things she told me, from the activities she enjoyed to the foods she liked. Never in a hundred years would I have guessed that she loved baseball and super spicy Mexican food. She was a lot more interesting than I had anticipated, and as the conversation carried on into the late hours of the night, I found myself enjoying every minute of it.

The morning after I had punctured my gas tank and was chased by a psychopathic ghost girl, I received the news that school was canceled for the day. During yesterday's big thunderstorm, the main server for Elm Valley College's computing network was fried and would take a full day to recover. All of that had happened a little after I was done with biology, but better late than never, I suppose.

On the flip side, the storm had also ushered in the first major cold front of the season, causing temperatures to drop to an almost record low. The wintry chills were still far off, but the days of T-shirts and shorts were coming to an end for the year. I noticed this for myself when I awoke in a curled, shivering ball under my thin blanket. I wasn't ready to break out the comforter yet, but it was looking like I would have to soon.

After getting dressed, I remembered that I had to meet with the club tomorrow at the cabin. Aaron had towed my car back to the apartments last night, and it was sitting in the parking lot like a helpless boulder of metal. I had no idea how long it would be until I could get the tank fixed, especially on my budget, so I called Raven to inform her of the predicament.

"What do you mean you can't drive out tomorrow?" she said curtly over the phone. "Club meetings are mandatory!"

"My car has a gas leak!" I shot back. "You sound like it's my fault."

"Don't worry about it," she said. "Everything will be sorted out. This is gonna be three tens for a twenty in your advantage, just watch."

With that strange revelation, she hung up. I had absolutely no clue as to what she was talking about, but apparently I didn't have to worry about it. Maybe someone would give me a ride. Honestly, I really didn't know and I really didn't care.

I walked into the living room and my stomach let out a mighty growl. I was pretty much out of food and would have to somehow get a ride to the store. Just as I was trying to figure out my next course of action, Sapphira suddenly appeared and confronted me.

"Are you hungry?" she asked. "I can be of some help."

"Really?" I said, feeling a little ray of hope. "What can you do?"

"I can make something for you to eat," she said. "It won't be a problem."

"Yeah, but we're out of food," I said. "There's nothing to cook."

"It won't be a problem," she repeated.

Sapphira held her hand over the table, causing a small magic circle to appear on it. I watched in awe as something came up through the circle and quickly took the form of a sandwich. The magic circle vanished, leaving the photographically perfect sandwich resting on the table.

"That is for you," she told me.

"What? Are you for real?" I said. "There's no way I'm eating something that just came out of a hell portal!"

"You can be assured that it is safe," she said. "I believe you will find the flavor of this ham sandwich to be delicious."

"Nope," I said, shaking my head. "I'm not eating that. It's too weird."

"You can save it for later," she said. "This sandwich will never spoil."

"All the more reason for me to leave it alone," I muttered, reaching for my cell phone. "I'm gonna see what everyone is up to."

"What should I do with the sandwich?" Sapphira asked.

"Whatever. Just put it on a plate and set it in the fridge."

"Very well. However, there is no need to put it in the fridge because it will never—"

"In the fridge, please," I demanded.

"Very well."

The first person I took the privilege to send a text message to was Hayley. I wanted to see what she was doing for the day, but she said that she had already made plans to go shopping with her sister as soon as she found out school was canceled. Feeling a little disappointed, I contacted Aaron, Chad, and Lawrence to see what they were doing. We took some time to figure out what we could do on our day off, and we all decided to meet somewhere for breakfast and talk it over more in person.

I waited inside the apartment building's entryway with the sapphire amulet resting snuggly in my pocket while I kept a lookout for Aaron's bright yellow truck. When he arrived and picked me up, he took me to a local restaurant on the other side of town called Zoe Café where we met with Chad and Lawrence.

"I'm paying for you," Aaron told me. "Don't argue, just accept it. There's no way out, okay?"

"Uh, okay," I said. "Thanks a lot, man. What's the budget?"

"It's cool," he said. "Get what you want."

When the four of us were seated, I skimmed over the menu. This was my first time eating at Zoe Café, and I never even knew it existed in the first place.

"You guys don't know how happy I am that classes are canceled," said Chad with a big smile. "It's like a snow day, but better!"

"Too bad it didn't happen yesterday during biology," said Aaron. "That class is way too boring, and it sucks that it's three hours long."

"Yeah, I know," I said. "I was waiting for the power to go out the entire time."

"Why do you guys hate biology so much?" Lawrence asked.

"Because it sucks," Aaron mumbled. "Do you actually like it, Lawrence?"

"Well, yeah," said Lawrence. "I think it's interesting and kinda fun."

"What's that blip on my nerd-radar?" said Aaron, holding his cupped hands up to his ears. "Oh yeah, it's *Lawrence!*"

"What's that blip on my idiot-radar?" Lawrence mimicked irritably. "Oh yeah, it's *Aaron!*"

I held my menu up to shield against the shenanigans going on at our table. Besides, the pictures of the food all looked so good that I was too busy figuring out how best to fill the void in my stomach.

The waitress took our order, and I took full advantage of Aaron's offer by asking for the New York strip and potatoes. Despite the expensive price tag, Aaron looked somewhat satisfied that I so valiantly took his offer.

"I tried making a joke the other day," said Lawrence as we waited for our food, "but it didn't work."

"Was it a good joke?" Chad asked.

"If it didn't work, then it probably wasn't very good," said Aaron.

"Good jokes are pretty hard to make," said Lawrence. "I've tried, but nobody seems to get them."

"You're not a very funny person, though," I told him. "I guess some people are born to make jokes."

"A guy walks into a bar," said Chad, "and says, 'Ouch!'"

We all looked at Chad for a second. Lawrence started laughing and Aaron just grimaced. I, on the other hand, didn't get it.

"Chad, that was the stupidest thing I've ever heard," said Aaron.

"I thought it was pretty good," Lawrence grinned.

"I don't get it," I said. "Was that the entire joke?"

"If you didn't get it, then you're the luckiest one here," Aaron told me.

"Of course it's stupid," said Chad, "but that's why it's funny. It's stupid-funny."

Something suddenly crossed my mind, and I thought it would be a good time to say something. I had been meaning to ask Chad about it for a while, but never had a good chance.

"Hey, Chad," I said.

"What up, dawg?"

"You know that book you have?" I asked.

"Yeah," he said. "What about it?"

"I don't know," I said, thinking about how I wanted to say it. "Have you figured anything else out about it?"

"Hmm, not really," he said.

"Oh yeah, Mike," said Aaron, "how'd ya do on that test? Did my spell work?"

I immediately dismissed the thought of telling him what had really happened.

"Dude, I think I failed big time," I told him. "I was supposed to find out today, but class is canceled. I don't have psychology again until next Monday."

"I knew it was just a bunch of meaningless garbage scribbled down," said Aaron boastfully.

If only you knew. You have no idea what you got me into.

"That's disappointing," said Chad. "After all that stuff about it surviving the library fire, it's just another book."

Chad had initially offered to let me have the book, and I had considered asking him for it again. However, I didn't know if that was a very good idea. Staying away from that book seemed to be the most comfortable option for me. With my luck, some kind of beast might crawl out of it one night and strangle me in my sleep.

When the waitress brought our food, I felt my stomach rejoice at the sight of my order. Without a moment's hesitation, I grabbed my fork and dove into my meal. As the others had their little breakfast burritos and pancakes, I was carving into my steak and potatoes with the indulgence of a child eating a candy bar ice cream sandwich. In addition, whoever prepared my steak really knew what they were doing. So succulent...so tender....

"How's that steak?" Aaron asked me.

130

I took the time to finish chewing the delicious morsel in my mouth before answering.

"It's awesome, man," I replied. "This place makes a mean steak."

"Yeah, thanks for treating us, Aaron," said Lawrence.

"Yeah, thanks," said Chad.

"Wait," I said, looking at Aaron, "you're treating all of us?"

"That's right," said Aaron. "I didn't tell anyone, but I bought a lottery ticket a couple days ago. I won five hundred bucks."

"Whoa, cool!" said Lawrence.

"Ah, I wish I'd win that much," said Chad. "The lottery steals my money. I haven't won anything from lottery tickets at all."

"What're you gonna do with the rest of the money?" I asked Aaron.

"I don't know," he said. "Gas and stuff, probably. I don't want to blow it all at once."

"I've heard about people hitting the jackpot," said Lawrence. "A lot of people spend it all and end up going broke, so you have to be careful not to go crazy with the winnings."

"I'm not going broke," said Aaron confidently. "I'm hiding money away. I have a nice money cushion to fall on."

"Must be nice," I sighed. "I'm tight for cash."

"Did you ever find another job?" Lawrence asked. "It's not the same without you at Harbert's."

I didn't want to tell them everything about Miss Flamingo's club. By signing the contract, I was sworn to the club's secrecy. As long as I kept most of the details a secret, it would probably be safe to let people know about it.

"Yeah," I said, "on Monday I went to a job interview for a research organization and got hired."

"Right on," said Aaron.

"What kind of research do they do?" Lawrence asked.

"All kinds of things," I said. "I don't do any of the research, though. I just help out and stuff."

That didn't seem like I gave anything crucial away, I thought. *I didn't really lie, either.*

After Aaron paid for the bill, I leaned back in my seat while feeling totally satisfied with the first decent meal I had eaten since college started again. Despite how quickly I became full, I made sure to eat everything in front of me since there was no telling when my next full-sized meal would be. My only hope was that Miss Flamingo gave me an assignment that paid well sometime soon.

"So guys, what now?" Aaron asked, slipping his jacket on.

"I'm down for anything," said Chad.

"Yeah, I have until this evening to do whatever," said Lawrence.

"I want to swing by the grocery store at some point," I said. "I need to pick up some stuff."

"We can do that," said Aaron. "Who's down for a grocery adventure?"

Everyone shrugged in agreement, and we were on our way out of Zoe Café and to the grocery store. Lawrence offered to let everyone carpool with him, so we all piled into his car. I requested not to go to Harbert's Groceries, but it was too far to the next grocery store. No matter how hard I tried, I just couldn't escape Harbert's.

"You keep a clean car, man," Aaron told Lawrence.

"I try to," he replied. "People can eat in here. The seats are already stained anyway, so it really doesn't matter if anything spills. I'll just scrub it until it looks good enough."

"My car's a mess," I said. "I try to keep it kinda clean, but sometimes it just gets messy. Maybe I'll, like, vacuum it out before it gets too cold."

"There was this guy on the news I heard about," said Chad. "His car was so messy that he had mice living inside it, and he didn't even know."

"That's crazy, bro!" Lawrence laughed. "He was taking mice for a ride all that time and didn't know about it."

"Maybe you should get some traps, Mike," said Aaron.

"I don't have mice in my car!" I said. "My car's not that messy."

"How do you know?" Aaron asked. "You might wanna check."

"Dude, it's fine," I said.

The ride to the store took a little longer than I had expected. We weren't the only college students out taking advantage of the day off, and the resulting traffic was surprisingly heavy. Even the grocery store's parking lot was busy when we arrived.

"Man, it's a good thing I don't work today," said Lawrence, taking a look at all of the cars. "Why are there so many people shopping on a Wednesday morning?"

"What do you need to get?" Chad asked me.

"Just basic stuff," I said.

As we walked up to the store, Lawrence let me know about some of the sales going on.

"They're having sales on frozen meals, toilet paper, toothpaste, milk, and some other stuff," he said. "I can't remember everything."

"You just listed pretty much everything I need," I said happily. "Man, I came on a good day."

The moment we walked through the door, Aaron and Chad took off in opposite directions, indicating that we were going to spend time regrouping before leaving. I rubbed my wallet with my meager earnings inside, grabbed a shopping cart, and entered the realm of groceries.

For some reason, the store was full of people who appeared to be other college students. I recognized a handful of customers from around the campus, and I assumed that they were probably getting prepared for a long day of doing nothing.

Just as Lawrence had said, mostly everything I needed was on sale, so I was able to stock up on slightly more food than anticipated. Calculating the cost of everything in my head, I figured out the best way to stretch my budget. When everything was in my cart, I looked around for Aaron, Chad, and Lawrence. Being in Bill Straussford's nest made me

133

uncomfortable, so I just kept my head low as I glanced down each aisle.

Like a little kid chasing a ball into the street, Aaron suddenly ran out in front of my cart, causing me to stop abruptly to avoid running into him.

"Watch where you're going!" I said. "I almost ran right into you."

"Dude, check this out," he said softly, beckoning me to follow him.

"What?" I asked.

"Hotties in the bread aisle," he said. "Over there."

"So what?" I said.

Aaron looked taken aback by my response.

"What do you mean?" he asked. "You normally like it when I point chicks out to you."

"Yeah, whatever," I muttered. "Let's find Chad and Lawrence so we can get out of here."

"Hey, I know what's up," said Aaron, getting close and personal. "You're after that Asian girl, aren't you?"

"No," I said. "She has a boyfriend. Besides, I know a girl better than her, anyway."

"Oh, so it *is* a girl," he said, looking amused. "What's her name?"

"Hayley," I said, "and it's nothing serious."

"Hmm, if you say so." Aaron shrugged. "Are you done shopping? Let's go."

When I checked out, Chad was already waiting at the front of the store. Lawrence was buying something in a different checkout lane, and we had to wait for him to finish before we could leave. He was carrying a paper bag that looked pretty heavy.

"What'd you get?" I asked him.

"Cantaloupes," he said. "Everyone in my family loves them, so I thought I'd pick some up because they're on sale."

"You picked a paper bag," Aaron commented. "What, are you trying to be eco-friendly?"

"Plastic isn't biodegradable," Lawrence replied. "Think of all the good you could do if you replaced all of the plastic bags you use in a year with paper."

"Think of all of the trees you could save by switching to plastic," said Aaron.

"Oh man," I muttered to Chad. "I don't wanna hear another argument about environmental issues."

Chad just shrugged and smiled, apparently not wanting to partake in the discussion as well. Fortunately, Lawrence dismissed Aaron's contradicting opinion, and we were able to walk out of the grocery store quietly and on good terms with each other.

"Where do you guys wanna go next?" Lawrence asked, placing the cantaloupes in his trunk.

"I vote Mike's place," said Aaron. "We can get down on some games and stuff."

"Uh, sure," I said, putting my bags in the trunk. "I don't have a lot of food, so you'll all have to fend for yourselves."

"You just bought food, man," said Aaron.

"That's for me," I said. "I need to make all of that last as long as I can."

"That's cool, dawg," said Chad. "What I ate at the restaurant will do me good for a while."

"What about you, Lawrence?" Aaron asked.

"Yeah, I'll hang out with you guys," said Lawrence. "I'll take you back to your cars."

Lawrence drove us back to Zoe Café where Aaron and Chad had their cars parked. Afterward, everyone met back at my apartment. Hopefully, Sapphira wouldn't be around when my friends were there. Just to be safe, I quickly grabbed my stuff from Lawrence's trunk and darted up the stairs to beat everyone to my apartment.

"Sapphira!" I whispered.

"Welcome home, Michael," she said, standing in the middle of the living room.

"You need to hide!" I told her, hearing the guys coming down the hall. "My friends will be here!"

"Very well," she said, disappearing moments before Aaron appeared in the doorway.

"You sure looked like you were in a hurry," he said.

"Sometimes I just like to move fast," I lied.

"Yeah, you moved pretty fast," he said. "Hey, Jorge just texted me. He wants to know what we're up to. Would it be okay to have him come over?"

"Oh, sure," I said. "Ask him if he can bring any AA batteries for the game controllers. Mine are getting pretty low."

"You should get a controller charger," said Lawrence. "You'd save a ton of money if you don't buy batteries."

"The chargers are expensive," I said. "I need to weigh the cost of the charger with the cost of batteries I use on average. I'll probably buy a wired controller before I buy a charger."

"Wired controllers all the way!" said Lawrence. "I never have to worry about batteries and charging."

"No way," said Aaron. "Wireless is so much better. That's why phones aren't connected by wires anymore."

"Yeah, but I'm not gonna sit thirty feet away from my TV," said Lawrence.

"My dad bought a TV a couple years ago," said Chad. "It was ninety-something inches. I tell you what, it was huge! We could probably sit on the other side of a football field and still see it!"

"What could you possibly want with a TV that big?" I asked curiously. "I don't know how I'd get it inside a house."

"The thing is, we never got to use it," said Chad. "My dad got into an accident on the way home with it. Lost the TV and the receipt got destroyed, so he couldn't get a refund. Lost the truck, too...."

"Gah, I'd be pissed!" Aaron chortled, taking a seat on the couch.

"And it was Super Bowl weekend!" Chad added. "My dad gave away the old TV to our grandma, so we had to watch the game on a *really* old TV! He wanted to record the game, but the TV was so old that it wouldn't hook up to the digital recorder, and nobody in my family could remember how to use the VCR."

"Can we just play this game already?" said Aaron impatiently as he set up the video games. "Bunch of chatterboxes around here. Let's take down some zombies."

Half an hour of primitively entertaining zombie slaying passed before Jorge showed up with a pack of batteries, ensuring that the entertainment continued as long as our eyes, thumbs, and minds could endure. There's something deeply satisfying about partaking in a social game of virtual domination, reminiscent of a wolf pack taking down a meal. Senseless, harmless, barbaric, or any other way you want to look at it, you have to remember that it's a dude thing. We don't need to hunt for our food like we had to hundreds or thousands of years ago, but chasing down zombies with a controller in my hand and a grin on my face is a good indication that the hunt is still very much alive inside of us today.

After several hours, it was becoming apparent that another form of entertainment was in order. The zombie killing had grown old and we were getting tired of playing the same game, so it was time to switch it up.

"Do you have any other games?" Chad asked me. "Something that doesn't involve shooting zombies or shooting each other?"

"Uh, not really," I said. "Shooting things is what I do best. What do you guys wanna do?"

"I don't know," said Lawrence.

"I don't wanna shoot anything," said Aaron, going through my game selection. "I don't wanna strum on a plastic guitar, either. Didn't you have a racing game, Mike?"

"Yeah, I used to," I said. "The disc got scratched and it didn't play at all, so I threw it away."

"Dude, I can fix disc scratches," Aaron told me. "All you do is rub some toothpaste on the shiny side of the disc, but make sure it's actual paste and not the gel kind with sparkly stuff in it. Baking soda toothpaste is probably best. Then you put the disc face down in the toilet—"

"Are you serious?" I asked skeptically. "The toilet? For real?"

"No, listen to me," said Aaron. "Just give it a few flushes and—"

"No way!" I said. "That's disgusting, man."

"Wait, I think I've heard of this, Mike," said Jorge. "People have said that toothpaste really works."

"I'll sacrifice a game for the sake of not doing that," I muttered. "Can't I just clean the toothpaste off in the sink instead of the toilet?"

"Hey, I'm just telling you what I heard," said Aaron. "I've tried it, and it worked for me. That's all I gotta say."

I might want to check it out on the Internet first, I thought. *Until then, I'm not recommending it for anyone.*

"I have some movies in my SUV," Jorge suggested. "I can bring them up, and you all can see if you want to watch any."

"Are they all in Spanish?" Aaron asked.

"No," Jorge chuckled. "They're in English, I promise."

I looked around at everyone, and they all just shrugged.

"Sure, let's take a look at them," I told Jorge.

Jorge hurried out to his SUV and returned with a small stack of DVDs. All of us gathered around and went through the movies, slowly narrowing down our choices to two. With a flip of a coin, the final decision was made. The rest of the afternoon drifted away in a cinematic presentation.

Shortly after the movie was over, Lawrence said that he had to leave. Like a herd of sheep, everyone else decided it was time for them to go as well, and I was left in my apartment with Sapphira. She had done a good job of staying hidden, so I felt it was necessary to let her know that she had done well.

"Sapphira," I called shortly after the guys had left.

"Yes?" she said, appearing from thin air.

"They're gone now, so it's safe to come out," I told her. "You did good."

"Thank you," she replied modestly.

I walked back over to the couch and stretched out on it. The cushions were still warm from everybody sitting there. The television was on, but I wasn't really paying attention to it. My steak and potatoes breakfast had been replaced by the familiar void in my stomach, and I quickly made plans for my demon slave's next task.

"Hey, Sapphira," I said.

"Yes?"

"Can you make one of those frozen meals for me? They should be in the freezer."

"Which one do you want me to make?"

"I don't care. Choose one."

"As you wish."

I wonder if she knows how to do it, I thought. *Maybe I should show her how to use the oven so the place doesn't burn down.*

I walked into the kitchen where Sapphira was tearing open the box for the frozen meal. She did so with such little effort that it scared me a little bit. There was no telling just how strong she really was, despite her womanly appearance. When she noticed me standing there, her piercing yellow eyes turned to me.

"I'm making this one," she said, holding the box up for me to see that it was fried fish.

"That's fine," I said. "I wanted to ask if you know how to use the oven."

"Yes," she replied.

"And if you know how to follow the cooking directions."

"Yes," she repeated.

"Well then," I said, "uh, I guess I'll leave you to do that."

Since there was no school that day, I didn't have any additional homework that needed to be done. The short opinion report for my English class was almost done and due next week, and everything else was finished. While I sat in front of the TV and waited for my dinner to be cooked, I realized that the rest of the evening was going to be a boring one. My friends had left, the homework was done, and I had my daily dose of gaming. What was there left to do for the day? Not much, to be honest.

I surfed the web for a little bit, but that didn't hold my interest for very long. I never spent much time on social networking sites and people hardly ever sent me an email, so there wasn't very much to do on the Internet. However, I made sure to check Aaron's toothpaste strategy for scratched CDs, and I found that using baking soda toothpaste is very effective. Nothing was mentioned about using the toilet, however.

~Opus 11~

As I waited outside for Aaron to give me a ride to school the following morning, I stared at my miserable car resting in the same spot it had been in for two days. When I had checked the Internet for the price to repair a punctured gas tank, it ranged from pocket change to nearly how much my entire car is worth, depending on the extent of the damage. I was going to ask if Aaron could tow the car to a mechanic after school that day to get it evaluated.

That was when the flatbed tow truck arrived. I hadn't called anyone to have my car towed at seven-thirty in the morning, so I was a little distressed as the truck backed up to the front of my car and lowered its bed.

What the hell is going on? I thought, hurrying over to talk to the tow truck driver. *Did somebody call to have my car taken away?*

Before I could confront the driver, he was already out of the truck. Instead of somebody who looked like a mechanic or truck driver, this guy looked like your average rapper coming back from a concert. More interestingly, I knew who this guy was.

"Cormorant?" I said.

As soon as he saw me, a big smile spread across his face.

"Good morning, Roadrunner," he said, shaking my hand. "You're probably wondering what I'm doing with this tow truck, right?"

"Uh, yeah," I replied.

"Miss Flamingo has it all worked out, so don't worry," he said. "I'm gonna take your car back to the cabin to have it looked at and fixed up. A gas tank repair shouldn't be a problem."

"Really?" I said. "What do I have to pay?"

"I told you Miss Flamingo's taking care of it," said Cormorant, grabbing the winch and hooking it to the front of my car. "The club members look out for each other. If any of us needs anything, the others are always there to help out."

"Sounds like the mafia," I said bluntly.

141

"No, we're not anything like the mafia!" said Cormorant assuredly. "More like a family."

The mafia would say that, too, I thought.

"So, Cormorant," I said, "I thought you were second in command in the club. Why are you out here doing all the work?"

Cormorant activated the winch and my car was slowly pulled up onto the bed of the tow truck.

"I love working on cars," he replied with a grin.

"Really?" I said. "You don't look like the grease monkey type."

"Looks can be deceiving," he said modestly. "Anyway, someone will pick you up to take you to the meeting tonight, so be ready."

With the car firmly in place on the flatbed, Cormorant got back into the truck and headed off in the direction of the cabin. I watched my car leave the parking lot and disappear around the corner, and I could only hope that I wouldn't get screwed by having it sabotaged or scrapped for parts.

Aaron showed up minutes after my car was taken away. I wasn't in the mood to go back to school after having the day off, but at least my only classes were math and English. My goal was to finish any homework before seven o'clock when I had to meet with the club.

Surprisingly, Miyuki was absent from math that morning, making it the first class she had missed so far. Perhaps it was for the better, since talking to her would make me feel awkward after what had happened the other day in the library. I remembered what Jorge had said about the girl he tried to hook up with and found out she had a boyfriend. That same old story is probably told thousands of times a year. Why don't people wear flags or something to indicate that they're taken? Wouldn't it save a lot of people from a lot of grief?

Math class was a breeze for me that day. As Mr. Pardee explained the lesson, I was already working on the assignment out of the textbook and finished it fifteen minutes before class ended. With nothing else to do, I packed up and walked out of the room, taking my time moseying to where my English class would be.

A guy named Paxton attended the same English class with me, and he was also in my chemistry class along with Jorge. I wouldn't exactly call him my friend so much as an acquaintance, but at least he was somebody I could talk to during the hour-long period. He was almost ten years older than me, had a wife and three kids, and was just trying to make a better living by earning some sort of degree. His normal way of life was something I envied and strived for.

"How are you, Mike?" he asked as he took a seat next to me.

"Okay," I replied. "My car had to be towed away today, so a friend gave me a ride."

"That's too bad," he said. "Did you get into an accident?"

"I probably punctured my gas tank," I said.

"If you need a mechanic, my buddy can take a look at it," he said. "I might be able to get you a deal."

"That's alright," I said. "Somebody's already working on it for free."

"They won't rip you off, will they?" he said with a raised eyebrow.

"I hope not," I said with a forced chuckle.

I was looking forward to having an easy assignment to go along with my completed math homework, but that was far from the case. Mr. Baldwin had assigned us a three-page report about anything that had to do with literature. My short opinion report wasn't even complete yet, and now I had this dropped on me? Somebody must've known that my math homework had been too easy....

The room for English class was filled with computers at every seat. Figuring that it'd be best to get the previous report out of the way first, I plugged in my flash drive and got to work. With every keystroke, my mind was temporarily distracted from Miss Flamingo's club and the fact that they were poking around in my car. If I *did* get screwed, at least it wouldn't cost me anything up front.

I managed to finish the report, so I printed it off and handed it in, even though it wasn't due for another week. When class was over, I was still stranded at the college for another hour. Aaron had another class to attend, so he was unable to give me a ride home until he was done. You don't realize how much you depend on your car until a tree branch comes along and takes it from you.

I eventually found myself in the campus commons. This was the best place to get something to eat without leaving the college, but I just wanted to be somewhere livelier than the library. What seemed like a hundred students were gathered there for individual reasons, and I looked around for anyone I might have known. With a goofy sense of humor, fate had me run into them.

"Looking gloomy today, Roadrunner," said Raven. She was sitting at one of the tables with a bunch of papers and books spread out in front of her.

"Hi, Raven," I said unenthusiastically, taking a seat next to her for some reason. Maybe I was lonelier than I thought. "What are you working on?"

"I'm doing an overload," she said with her nose buried in a book.

"An overload?" Curiosity got the best of me.

"I'm expanding my cognitive capacity by trying to learn a lot of unrelated information at once," she explained, not looking up. "Do you want me to teach you how to do it?"

"Not really," I said.

"It's not easy," she continued. "I understand if you don't want to strain your brain."

"I didn't say I couldn't do it," I said. "I just don't want to."

"This kind of pruignition isn't for the weak," she said.

"Wait. What?"

Raven stopped scanning the textbook and looked at me with the one eye that wasn't obscured by her long bangs. There was a possibility that the other eye was looking at me too, but I really didn't know.

144

"What are you doing here?" she asked. "Did you forget how to get to the cabin? You'd best be there tonight."

"No, I didn't forget the location and the meeting," I grunted. "I'm waiting for my friend to get done with class. He's my ride home."

"I could give you a ride," said Raven, "but—"

"That's alright," I quickly replied.

"You didn't let me finish," she said. "I was saying I could give you a ride, but you'd have to prove yourself to me first."

I stared at Raven, trying to decipher the look on her face. "What's that mean?" I asked. "Prove myself to you?"

"It's a difficult task," she told me, "kinda like overload, but very different. I don't think you'd get it right the first few times. However, I'm lenient, so fret not."

"You're not making any sense," I said flatly.

She closed the textbook she'd been going through and rested her arms on it, giving me another enigmatic look.

"From what I've concluded so far, you are a bent straw and your manliness is a triple thick milkshake," she told me. "There aren't too many ways to fix that, but I'm sure it can be done."

I understood that she was serious, but that was about all I could understand. Call me cynical, but I thought she might have just insulted me.

"Whatever," I said. "You're saying that I'm weak?"

"Not necessarily weak," she said. "Just unpolished."

"How do you know?" I said, starting to feel angry. "You barely know me!"

"And *you* barely know *me!*" she replied. "Life's a learning experience, so let's learn about each other. We could be considered co-workers, right?"

"Uh, I guess."

"Then we'll have plenty of time to get to know each other," she said, and I could catch hints of eagerness in her tone. "If you show that you're worthy of my help, then I'll be happy to give you help."

I remembered what Cormorant had told me earlier and I decided to use it against Raven.

"But isn't the club supposed to be like a family?" I argued. "We help each other out because it's the right thing to do."

Instead of answering with some cryptic response, Raven just gave me a studious look. To my surprise (and confusion), a smile spread across her face. She leaned back in her seat and continued to look at me as if I was an impressive sculpture she had made.

"You're not too bad," she said. "Maybe I underestimated you."

I didn't know what to think. In any case, I found it hard to feel flattered by Raven's praise, even if it did make me feel slightly better. She packed up all of her papers and books and stood up. Without a word, she strutted off. Looking around the commons, I desperately wished for someone to fill me in on what had just happened. However, there really was no other explanation for it. Raven had happened, and that was all I needed to know.

There wasn't anything else I could think of doing, so I merely sat in the commons and thought about my second English report. Literature was a very wide subject to write a report about, but my deep disinterest in it was bound to make it a difficult task to complete. Maybe I could just do a biography on William Shakespeare. What English teacher doesn't like to read about Shakespeare? Tons of material about him can be found in any library and all over the Internet, so research should be easy.

Aaron finally finished his class and called me to ask where I was. He met me in the commons and I asked to have him take me straight home, even though he wanted to hang around town. I told him that I wasn't feeling like doing anything for the rest of the day, and he agreed to take me back to the apartment.

"Welcome home, Michael," Sapphira greeted as I walked through the door.

"Do you have to say that every time I come home?" I asked.

"I can say whatever you want me to say when you arrive," she said.

For a brief moment, she reminded me of my voicemail recording on my cell phone and how I could have it say whatever I wanted it to. However, it didn't feel right to use Sapphira the same way. That seemed a little too weird, although it would be pretty funny to have her say something ridiculous each time I came home.

"No, it's fine," I muttered, tossing my hoodie on a chair.

"Would you like me to cook your lunch?" she asked.

I unzipped my bag and placed my English materials on the table with the intention of working on it before the club meeting.

"That'd be great," I told her. "Make a frozen pizza."

"Which one do you request?"

"They're all the same, so it doesn't matter."

I was beginning to get used to ordering Sapphira around, but the fact that she was a demon still bothered me. I wasn't sure how long it would take me to be fully comfortable with having her around, if I *ever* would. Honestly, I still wanted her out of my life forever, but I figured I'd make the best out of it since I had no choice.

The pizza turned out to be as good as a frozen pizza can be, and I went straight to work on my English report after eating some. I pulled up some good websites on my laptop for research and was finding information faster than I had anticipated. With the rate I was going at, about a third of the report would be finished by the time I had to leave for the club meeting.

Unfortunately, my lack of essay skills eventually took the helm of my writing. Progress slowed down to a crawl, and I found myself getting both bored and frustrated. Researched information can be helpful, but it doesn't do any good if the researcher doesn't know how to put it all together. There was a certain kind of structure my report had to follow, and the blueprints for that structure were hard for me to apply.

Man, I don't wanna do this. Isn't there some easier way to get this done? Probably not, I suppose.

I considered having Sapphira do the essay for me, but I didn't want to take my chances. There was no telling what she would write, and taking credit for other people's actions was totally against my morals.

Time dragged by until it was almost time for someone from the club to pick me up. I saved what little bit I had typed, put my materials away, and got ready to leave.

"Are you leaving?" Sapphira asked.

"Yeah," I said. "I'll be back later. I don't know when."

"Understood."

Waiting outside for somebody to pick me up was never one of my favorite things to do. It would leave me wondering if the person was going to be late, or if something else popped up. This time, I didn't even know who was coming to get me. I had only assumed that it was someone from the club. Hopefully, I wouldn't get into a ghost car again, and I patted the amulet in my pocket to make sure that I had it with me. Even riding with Raven would be much better than with a murderous spirit.

When a car pulled up to the front of the apartment building, I was relieved that it was neither a ghost nor Raven. Kookaburra was my ride, and I hoped that he wasn't drunk or something. I got into his car and inconspicuously sniffed around for alcohol, but it didn't smell like there was any.

"Are you ready for this?" he asked me gruffly.

"Ready for what?" I asked.

"Anything," he replied. "This is your first meeting on the job, so you better realize that if something can happen, it just might tonight. That goes with every meeting."

"Is that a bad thing?" I asked.

"Sometimes," he said. "Stay sharp, and you might not get yourself killed."

"Seriously, it can't be that dangerous," I said.

Kookaburra let out a laugh that unsettled me a little.

"Can't say I didn't warn you, Roadrunner."

"So, what about my car?" I asked, ignoring his comment. "Is it getting repaired?"

"That's not my responsibility," he said bluntly. "Cormorant's the one who likes cars, so ask him. He's probably the one working on it."

I kept my mouth shut for the rest of the ride. Kookaburra apparently wasn't the social type, so I just let it be. Whatever danger he was talking about, I figured I'd have to see for myself to decide if it was as bad as he said. Just for comfort, I rubbed the amulet in my pocket again, knowing that crazy things had already happened to me before.

My car was sitting in front of the cabin when we arrived, and I was relieved to see that it was where I was told it would be. There were some bright lights set up around it, allowing Cormorant to see as he worked underneath my car. A lot of other machinery was nearby to make it look almost like an auto shop, and I was clueless as to where all of this equipment came from. Before going to the cabin with Kookaburra, I went straight over to Cormorant to see exactly what he was doing.

"Hey," I said.

Cormorant slid out from underneath my car to get a look at me.

"Roadrunner!" he said happily. "You made it. Did Kookaburra find your apartment alright?"

"I guess so," I said. "How's the repairs coming?"

"Well, the fuel tank had a hole torn in it, piece of junk," he told me, "but I'm goin' ahead and replacing the entire gas tank, vent hose, and fuel injector line. This won't be done until tomorrow."

"Oh," I said. "You don't have to do all that extra stuff."

"It gives me something to do," said Cormorant. "This stuff is like my hobby. I promise it'll be good as new when you get it back."

"How will I know when it'll be done?"

"I suppose somebody will let you know," he told me, sliding back underneath the car. "We'll drop it off at the apartments and it'll be like nothing even happened to it."

"Thanks," I said, trying my best to trust him. He seemed genuinely good-willed to me, but I was just playing it safe.

When I stepped inside the cabin, the girl with glasses and the scrawny guy were engaged in a game of chess in the living room. I remembered seeing them before and I attempted to think of their names without asking.

Uh, the girl with glasses .... I think she's Oriole. And the scrawny dude is Skylark. Yeah, that sounds right.

"Oh, it's Roadrunner!" said Oriole when she noticed me. "Hi!"

"Hey, welcome back," said Skylark.

"How are you two doing?" I asked as I walked over to them. I figured it would be best to get to know who I would be working with.

"Pretty good," said Oriole. "We're waiting for Miss Flamingo to start the meeting. Have a seat."

"Playing chess, huh?" I said.

"Yeah," Oriole replied. "Skylark's the only person I know who gives me a good challenge."

"Likewise," said Skylark, studying the board.

"Who's winning?" I asked.

"Hmm...it's pretty much even right now," said Oriole. "Would you like to play a game when we're finished?"

"No, that's alright," I said. "I'm not good with strategy stuff."

Skylark moved his rook to take one of Oriole's knights, in turn leaving his rook wide open for her to take with her bishop. However, she made a different move that I completely didn't understand, and I quickly realized that her level of strategy was probably way above mine.

I heard footsteps coming down the stairs, and I turned to see Miss Flamingo descending with her signature cup of tea or coffee. Oriole and Skylark barely took their attention from the game to look at their boss. Without a word, Miss Flamingo walked through the living room and out the front door. Moments later, she returned with Cormorant.

"The meeting will begin shortly," she said before trotting back upstairs.

Following Oriole's and Skylark's actions, I stood up and headed to the meeting room. Raven and Kookaburra were already there when we arrived. Everyone took a seat around the table and waited quietly for Miss Flamingo to begin the meeting.

"Welcome back, everyone," she said, looking at us with her powerful gaze. "First, I would like to announce that last week's incident at the Village Totem Motel has officially and completely been resolved. Oriole, do you have the documents?"

"Yes," said Oriole.

She stood up and grabbed a folder sitting on the computer desk, then handed it to Miss Flamingo before sitting back down at the table. Miss Flamingo flipped through the documents briefly before setting them aside.

"Very good," she said. "Let's try to avoid another incident like that one. We'll need to be much more careful. Isn't that right, Kookaburra?"

"Yes," Kookaburra muttered.

I had no idea what incident they were referring to, but I figured it was best to keep it that way. Besides, I had never even heard of the Village Totem Motel. Just how big of a region did this club cover?

The first twenty minutes of the meeting were spent discussing and reviewing past activities that I knew nothing about. All I could do was sit and listen, trying to pick up on as much as I could. Judging by the club's fluency and organization, it was safe to assume that there was a good level of legitimacy behind all of it. Miss Flamingo appeared to be a skilled leader who knew exactly what she was doing as she moved the meeting along.

"I would like to share the data for this month's financial expenditures," Miss Flamingo announced at one point. "Oriole, will you print out September's spreadsheet?"

"Yes," Oriole replied, taking a seat at the computer.

"Overall," said Miss Flamingo, "it was a very good month financially. Since you all have helped maintain the club's finances, you will all be receiving a bonus payment. That includes you, Roadrunner."

151

Everyone looked like they wanted to jump on top of the table and start dancing, but held in the urge. I, myself, was happy to hear that I'd be getting a bonus, although I wondered if everyone else knew how much it would be. Looking at their faces, I figured it had to be a favorable amount.

"Uh, Miss Flamingo?" said Oriole quietly from the computer.

"What is it?" Miss Flamingo asked.

"The printer's not printing," said Oriole. "I don't know what's wrong with it."

Miss Flamingo walked over to the computer to see what was wrong. After a minute or so, she called Skylark over to help.

"Is there ink in the printer?" Oriole asked.

"There should be," said Skylark, looking at the inside of the printer. "I changed the cartridges a couple days ago, so they should be plenty full."

"Roadrunner," said Miss Flamingo. "What do you know about printers?"

"Um...not very much." I shrugged.

"That piece of junk's been acting up for a while," said Kookaburra. "Maybe it finally broke."

Skylark spent several minutes checking the printer, testing the connection, and messing with the settings. When nothing seemed to work, he let out a sigh.

"I don't know," he said. "Kookaburra's probably right. An internal component must be worn out."

"I see," said Miss Flamingo. "Roadrunner."

"Yeah?" I said.

"I have a job for you." Miss Flamingo scribbled something down on a piece of paper. "Go to this address and bring back a new printer. When asked who it's for, tell them the name written down there."

I looked at the paper Miss Flamingo handed me. There was a rough sketch of a map, the address of the location, and the name Brian Balms.

"Wait," I said, "who's Brian Balms?"

"An alias," Miss Flamingo replied. "Now hurry."

152

"But I don't have a car," I said. "Cormorant, did you fix it already?"

"I said not until tomorrow," he told me.

"Skylark," said Miss Flamingo, "take Roadrunner to the emergency bicycle."

"This way," Skylark told me.

Emergency bicycle? I thought, looking at the map Miss Flamingo sketched for me. *I hope this place isn't too far away.*

I followed Skylark out to a shed by the side of the cabin. He unlocked the door and wheeled out a bicycle, and my jaw dropped when I saw it. The bike was bright pink with a flowery basket mounted to the front and colorful streamers coming out of the handlebars. There was even a cute little license plate on the back that had *FLAMNGO* on it. At least it had a battery-powered headlight on the front.

"Dude," I said softly, "what the hell is this?"

"Um, this is the emergency bicycle," said Skylark. "It's in case somebody doesn't have a vehicle."

"Can I just borrow your car?" I asked. "Like, really."

"Sorry, but no," said Skylark. "Miss Flamingo specified the emergency bicycle. Going against her orders...isn't a good idea."

I ruffled my hair, not believing what I was hearing.

"Can I at least take the basket off?" I asked.

"No can do," he told me.

"What? Why not?"

"I don't know, man," he said. "Uh, that's just the rule."

I thought it over for a little bit before coming to the conclusion that there wasn't anything to think about.

"Okay, then," I muttered. "I'll be back."

When I mounted the bike, I was surprised at how comfortable it actually was. Flipping on the headlight, I took off down the long dirt driveway. The bike rode very smoothly, and I wanted to kick myself for considering that it was probably better than any bike I ever had. At least it was getting dark, and people were less likely to notice the bike's unfavorable details.

I stopped for a moment at the end of the driveway to look over the map again, holding it in front of the little headlight to see it. After imprinting the directions into my memory, I stuffed the piece of paper in my jacket and headed off. Wherever this person lived, hopefully it was close by. Riding a bike in the dark always made me uncomfortable, and it'd be pretty tragic if another branch fell in front of me and I hit it at full speed. I wasn't wearing a helmet and couldn't remember if the state had a helmet law, but getting a ticket would be the least of my concerns whilst in midair over the handlebars, soaring into the dark unknown at the side of a forested road.

The first turnoff wasn't very far from the cabin at all. When I came to the second turnoff minutes later, I was starting to believe that it wouldn't be so bad after all. The third and final turnoff was only a little ways down as well. I made sure to check the address on every mailbox, and that was when I realized that my trip was going to be more of a long haul than I had hoped for. The address for the place I was looking for had a much higher number than the first few houses on that road.

Not that I was keeping track of the time, but it felt like thirty minutes had passed before I finally reached a house with the corresponding address. My small moment of rejoice was quick to pass when I unknowingly rode that atrocious bike into the middle of what appeared to be a party. An array of floodlights made the pink paint job glow brighter than everything around me, and I could feel the questioning stares of over twenty strangers. I got off the bike and walked with it up to the nearest person.

"Excuse me," I said coolly. "I'm sorry to interrupt, but I'm here to pick up a printer for...uh, Brian Balms."

The person I asked looked like a grizzly bear hunter, standing probably six-foot-six and wearing a thick vest over a flannel shirt. He was firmly holding a forty-ounce bottle of beer as he stared down at me, and I could only keep my fingers crossed that he'd help me out and not hogtie me in the backyard.

"You'll wanna speak to Claude," he told me with a gruff voice. He turned around and called out, "Claude! Hey, is Claude around here?"

"I think he's in the house," somebody called back.

"Go get 'im!" the big guy replied. "There's somebody talkin' about his printers."

Shortly after, the front door to the house opened and another big guy walked out. He approached me with a smile, and I couldn't help but think that the bike was making him laugh inside his head.

"Hello," he said in a friendly voice. "I'm Claude. Did you want to see me?"

"Yeah, I'm here to pick up a printer for Brian Balms," I said, trying to make the conversation go as quickly as possible.

"Ah, follow me," said Claude.

I propped the bike on its kickstand and followed Claude into his house. He led me into a room filled with computers and electronics, which were all still in their original packaging. Something felt a little shady about the whole thing.

"Brian Balms, you say?" said Claude, looking through everything.

"Yeah," I said.

Claude picked out one of the packaged printers and handed it to me. When I looked at the picture on the box, it appeared to be the same exact one in the cabin's meeting room.

"That's the one he always likes," he told me. "Is that all I can do for ya?"

"Yeah, this is it," I replied politely. "Thanks a lot."

"No problem," said Claude.

I walked out of the house with the printer and realized that there was no way I could fit it into the worthless, flowery basket on the bike. Getting it back to Miss Flamingo was going to be a challenge, and I didn't want to imagine what would happen if I dropped and broke it. After messing around to see what would be the easiest way to carry a printer on a bike, I propped the box up on my shoulder and held onto it with one arm, then kicked off and steered the bike with my other arm. I could hear people snickering at me the entire time.

I pedaled through the dark with the printer resting next to my head, feeling relieved that the transaction went so smoothly. The handlebar streamers flapped in the chilly wind, emphasizing how fast I was attempting to make it back to the cabin. My nose and ears were getting cold, and a nice cup of hot tea sounded really good about then.

The sight of the long dirt driveway was actually appealing for the first time. Making sure to first call Raven to let her know of my arrival, I headed down the driveway and met Skylark in front of the cabin.

"Hey, that was pretty fast for on a bike," he said.

"I just wanted to get out of there and be back here," I said flatly, getting off the bike. "My arm was getting sore from carrying this thing."

"Take the printer upstairs to the meeting room," he told me. "I can take the bicycle back to the shed."

The inside of the cabin felt warm and soothing as I carried the printer upstairs. When I barged into the room, I felt like an Olympic relay runner as I set the printer next to the computer.

"I finished my assignment," I said out loud.

"Well done," said Miss Flamingo, walking over to me. "Here's your payment."

I took the envelope, poured myself a cup of hot tea, and took a seat at the table. Everybody was still sitting in the same exact spot, and it was almost as if I had never left.

"What did I miss?" I asked.

"Nothing you would understand," said Miss Flamingo.

Well, that makes it easier for me, I guess, I thought, taking a relaxing sip of hot tea. I had never tasted anything so strange, but it warmed me up.

Skylark returned to the room and set up the printer. When it was all ready to go, Oriole printed out the monthly financial report and handed it to Miss Flamingo, who discussed the figures like a business CEO. Afterward, she summed up the meeting with more stuff I didn't fully understand, then moved on to the part we were all waiting for: passing out the bonus payments.

My bonus envelope felt significantly thicker and heavier than my previous payments, and I wondered how many ones were packed into it this time.

The meeting was adjourned, and everyone headed outside. I saw that Cormorant immediately resumed work on my car, adding to the prospect that he was truly a mechanic at heart.

I rode back to my apartment with Kookaburra. My two envelopes were in my jacket pocket, begging to be torn open to see how much money was in each. The first part of the trip was silent, but Kookaburra spoke up just as we were entering the town.

"So, Roadrunner," he said, "how did you enjoy the emergency bicycle?"

"The style was definitely not something I would choose," I said. "Other than that, I think it was nice. It rode really smoothly."

"That's the same thing we all said," said Kookaburra. "Except Oriole. She loves cutesy stuff like that."

"You all rode it before?" I asked.

"At least once," he said. "It's not called the emergency bicycle for nothing. Some of the weirdest experiences of my life were from the club's duties, and that bike comes in handy in the most unexpected ways. Miss Flamingo says it's special, and many of us have a hard time disagreeing with that."

"Can I ask you something?" I said. "Just who exactly is Miss Flamingo? She really doesn't seem like the average person to me. First of all, it's hard for me to take someone seriously who calls herself 'Flamingo.' Second, how does she get all of her money? I can't help thinking that she runs some sort of underground criminal organization."

"I'm gonna tell you one thing," said Kookaburra. "Don't try to figure Miss Flamingo out. All of us have come to the conclusion that she's very mysterious and we just leave it at that. Nobody knows much about her at all. Her real name, her age, where she actually lives...."

"Sounds shady to me," I muttered.

"When you get home," said Kookaburra, "take a look inside that bonus envelope, then you'll see why we all just keep our mouths shut and noses to ourselves."

157

When Kookaburra dropped me off, I walked up to my apartment, feeling the weight of the envelopes swinging in my pocket. A sense of excitement was building up inside me, and I was curious to see for myself why Miss Flamingo had such loyal workers.

"Welcome home, Michael."

"Hey."

"Is there anything you need?"

"No, you're dismissed."

"Very well."

I took a seat on the couch with the envelopes in my hand. The lighter envelope was for retrieving the printer, so I opened it first. I counted sixty dollars, surprisingly not in one-dollar bills, and felt somewhat content about that. Next was the big one. My fingers tore open the envelope as I held my breath.

Restraining myself from jumping with joy, I could hardly believe that I was holding seven crisp hundred-dollar bills. Although it was far from the small fortune I had believed it to be, I was not going to complain.

~2nd Movement: Serenade~
Rallentando

.:Ruby Entanglement:.

~Opus 12~

Once the routines were engraved into my brain, I soon found myself falling into the rut of college life. Into the first couple days of October, the realization had settled in that the semester wasn't anywhere close to the end, so the best thing to do was just flow with it. The students all marched along from class to class with the hopes that getting up at the crack of dawn to go somewhere they would rather not would someday pay off.

Despite my situation with Sapphira and the club, things were starting to get a little boring. Having Sapphira around was beginning to feel more like having a roommate, and nothing crazy had happened with the club so far. I really couldn't complain, though. Living a normal life was turning out to be much easier than expected, even though everything around me was begging for it to be weird.

My car drove much better after Cormorant had fixed it up. The first day I got it back, I quickly noticed that it was drastically improved. Cormorant told me that in addition to replacing the parts he had mentioned, he switched out a lot of old parts for new or better ones, including spark plugs, shocks, brake pads, belts, and even light bulbs, plus a lot of other car parts I wasn't familiar with. When I told him that he didn't have to do all of that, he said that he did half of it out of goodwill and half just for fun. The club funded all of it, so he didn't have to pay a dime. I only wondered if Miss Flamingo was okay with the added expenses.

It was Friday, and my only class was a three-hour chemistry lab, which was at the same time as my biology labs on Tuesdays. There's nothing quite as sobering as the idea of being in a room surrounded by substances that can explode or melt your skin off if someone mixes the wrong ingredients. In this environment, everyone is kind of on an unspoken mutual agreement that you'd best not screw up, or the classroom will be somewhere between a biohazard and ground zero.

Paxton, the only guy I talk to in my English class, was in the same chemistry class with me, although our conversations

160

in the lab were typically just a smile and a hand gesture. My lab partner was Jorge, who told me that he always had a knack for mixing explosive chemicals. I couldn't imagine Jorge being the type of person to construct homemade bombs in a garage or basement, but I really didn't care as long as he didn't make any at school. He told me that he used them to blow up tree stumps. Different people have different hobbies, I suppose.

"Hey, I still don't get this," said Jorge, staring at a worksheet I had filled out. "How'd you figure this one out?"

"It's easy," I explained. "See, the oxidation number of monatomic ions is the same as the ion charge."

"You sound like a dictionary," said Jorge. "There's a lot of numbers involved with all this. Numbers confuse me."

"I'm good with algebra and stuff," I said. "This comes pretty naturally to me."

"The Lewis structures are easier for me to work with," said Jorge. "I like to have visuals."

"But Lewis structures are used for showing the bonds between atoms," I said. "Right now we're dealing with electron transfers. We learned this last week, remember?"

For a second, Jorge looked like a kid who had his lollipop taken away, then he chuckled and scratched his head.

"Alright, I'll let you lead the lab session for today," he said.

"I can give you a quick review sometime," I told him, grabbing some test tubes. "Let's hurry up and mix some crap. We need to record these results."

Jorge and I worked diligently throughout the lab session. When there was less than an hour of class left, my phone suddenly vibrated quietly in my pocket. I discreetly checked it to see that I had received a text message from Hayley.

Hey what are you up to?

Making sure that nobody was watching, I quickly typed a response, keeping my phone down and out of sight. Jorge glanced at me curiously before resuming work.

Im in class right now. Whats up?

A few seconds passed before I received another text, not giving me enough time to get back to the assignment.

"I don't think you should be texting now," Jorge whispered when he saw me reach for my phone. "Mr. Youngren doesn't like it when people use phones in the lab."

"Nah, it'll be fine," I said.

I was happy to have Hayley to talk to, and I know it sounds clichéd, but there was something about her that was hard to describe. I had to upgrade my phone plan to include unlimited texting because of how much we talked, and Miss Flamingo's generous payments made covering the extra cost no problem.

I flipped open my phone and quickly read Hayley's message.

Sorry I didnt realize you were in class now. I was
just wondering if you had any plans tonight.

Suddenly, I had little interest in what we were currently doing in the lab. There was some chemistry going on that was far better than the ones in the test tubes. I wanted to keep the conversation going, but Mr. Youngren was walking around to check on the students, so I had no choice but to postpone the conversation.

Lets talk about it when class ends at 3:40

I snapped my phone shut and slipped it into my pocket moments before Mr. Youngren made his way to our lab station.

"How are you doing over here?" he asked.

"Pretty good," I replied.

Mr. Youngren held up our test tubes to inspect them.

"Everything looks good," he said. "You two seem to have a good understanding of today's lesson."

"Mike's been helping me out a lot," said Jorge. "I was a little confused, but I think I understand it better now."

"Good, good," said Mr. Youngren. "Let me know if you need me to go over anything for you."

"Right, I will," said Jorge. When Mr. Youngren had moved on to the next station, Jorge added, "Man, he almost caught you on your phone."

"Yeah, but I pulled it off." I snickered.

Jorge chuckled and shook his head.

"I hope you were having an important conversation," he said, "like trying to hook up with a girl or something."

"Actually," I said with a grin, "you're not too far off."

"Ah, very sly, my man," Jorge complimented. "Nice."

"I'm gonna talk to her after class," I said. "She wanted to know if I had plans tonight."

"There you go," said Jorge. "She pretty much made the move for you. I would've been texting underneath the table, too."

When the lab session was over, Jorge and I cleaned up our station as quickly as possible so I could talk to Hayley. I offered to help Jorge with anything he needed me to explain for class, but he insisted that I had an important mission to accomplish, then he headed off. After leaving the classroom, I sat down at the nearest seating area and called Hayley's phone.

"Hey," I said when she answered, "I just got done with chemistry."

"How was it?" she asked.

"Eh, it was boring, but it went alright," I said.

"That sounds like a typical class," she replied.

"Yeah...uh, I was seeing if you were, like, doing anything later on today."

"All I had planned was doing a little homework tonight," I said. "Other than that, I really didn't have anything going on. What, did you have something planned?"

"Um...no, not really," she said. "I just had some free time, that's all."

She's making this almost too easy, I thought.

"Well, do you have some money?" I asked. "I was thinking we could grab something to eat."

"Yeah, I have some spending money," she replied. "Where do you want to go?"

After a brief discussion over restaurants, the plan was made to meet Hayley at five o'clock at the Elm Valley Pancake House. They were having a special for all-you-can-eat pancakes. Not only were they known for the best pancakes in town, but with a serving of eggs and bacon at a low cost, I'd be more than happy to eat all I could.

I jumped into my car and headed home to get ready for my first date with Hayley. I considered it a date, and nobody was going to convince me otherwise. We'd been talking for nearly a month now, and this was going to be the first planned meeting outside of school. Unless I've been mistaken, I felt this had all the makings of a date.

Back at my apartment, I searched through my closet for something nice, but casual. My wardrobe was always a little on the minimalist side since I never wanted to haul around an unnecessary amount of clothes. I was the kid on Christmas morning who was never happy to unwrap a sweater. Now that I'm older, the harsh reality is that you have to dress to impress.

"Are you looking for something?" Sapphira asked as I was going through my closet. "I can assist you."

"I'm just looking for something to wear on my first date with Hayley," I said. "It shouldn't be too much trouble."

"Very well," said Sapphira before disappearing.

She didn't seem to have any interest that I'm going on a date, I thought. *I guess that's not too surprising. Why would a demon be interested in dating?*

I was able to put together a decent outfit fairly quickly. After a quick shower (I had missed yesterday's shower), I changed into the clothes I had set out. The shirt hadn't been worn in a few years, and I was surprised to see that it still fit fine. Adding a touch of body spray, I made sure I had the sapphire amulet in my pocket, slipped on my jacket, and headed out the door.

When I pulled into the parking lot at Elm Valley Pancake House, there were still almost fifteen minutes until I had to meet Hayley. Thinking I could sit back and relax for a little, I kept the radio on to kill the silence. As I scanned the radio stations, Hayley suddenly pulled up next to me.

"Hey, you're early," I said as we got out of our cars.

"Yeah, you too," she said with a smile.

When I saw her walk over, I could hear the cheers of a hundred guys in my head. Oh yeah...she looked good, there's no denying it, although I wanted to curse the chilly October weather for making her wear a coat and long pants.

"I don't know about *you*," I said, "but I'm ready for some all-you-can-eat pancakes."

"I would get that, but I might get full before they bring the second plate," she said, still smiling.

After we were seated, I already knew what I was going to order. Hayley looked over the menu, flipping back and forth between pages.

"Should I get something off the breakfast menu or the dinner menu?" she asked herself. "Breakfast for dinner is always fun."

"Would it be considered dinnertime now?" I asked. "It's only five."

"Um, I think," she said. "I know people who eat dinner around this time."

"Some people eat dinner a lot later, though," I said, "and they have lunch around three."

"I guess it depends on the person's or family's schedule," said Hayley. "If you wake up late and go to sleep late, then your meal times are gonna be adjusted."

"Well, I wake up early and go to sleep late," I said, "so does that mean I can eat whenever I want?"

"Or you could have an extra meal," said Hayley. "Like brunch or something."

"Is brunch really considered a meal?" I asked. "To me it seems like the redheaded stepchild of meals."

"What's that mean?" Hayley asked amusedly. "Like it's not a real meal?"

"Yeah, it's kinda like the reject," I said. "I hardly ever hear someone talk about brunch."

"I'm pretty sure it's a real meal," she said. "I could be wrong."

When the waiter came back to take our orders, Hayley asked for the veggie omelet combo and I asked for the all-you-can-eat pancakes with scrambled eggs and bacon. He brought my pancakes first so I could get a head start while I waited for the rest of the meal. I loaded the pancakes up with blueberry syrup and started down the road of infinite pancakes. Well, infinite in theory, that is.

"Those smell really good," said Hayley, looking at the stack of pancakes on my plate.

"They taste even better," I said. "You've never eaten here, have you?"

"No," she said. "I hear they have the best pancakes in town."

"Oh, absolutely," I replied. "They're supposed to go really good with the coffee they make here, but I don't drink coffee very often."

"I like coffee," said Hayley, "but I'm sensitive to caffeine. It makes me all squirrelly."

I ordered a second plate of pancakes, and the waiter brought it out along with the rest of the food we ordered. As soon as Hayley had her plate in front of her, she reached for the hot sauce and drizzled it all over her omelet and hash browns.

"Hot sauce on a veggie omelet?" I asked curiously.

"Yeah, it's so good," she said, cutting into the omelet with her fork.

"I've never seen anyone put hot stuff on an omelet before," I said.

"Really? Some people put jalapenos in theirs," she told me. "I've had them in an omelet before, and it was pretty good. It was some kind of southwestern or Mexican breakfast."

"You like really spicy stuff, don't you?" I said.

"Oh, I love it!" she replied. "The hotter, the better. I used to have a habanero hot sauce that I'd put on just about anything. I could use it to claim food by splashing some on it, then nobody else would want to touch it."

166

"I'm sure it was pretty effective," I said. "I probably wouldn't touch something doused in habanero sauce."

"It's hot, but so good," she said. "This omelet's really good, too. It's stuffed with a ton of veggies, just how I like it. Next time, I'll have to try the pancakes."

I ordered one more round of pancakes, feeling the bulge in my stomach begin to grow. My first date with Hayley was going well so far, and it seemed like she was having a pretty good time. Getting together today was actually her idea, so it was up to me not to disappoint her. When my last plate of pancakes arrived, I took my knife and cut the stack in half.

"Here, you can have half," I told Hayley.

"I can? Are you sure?"

"Of course. You said you wanted to try them, so here you go."

Her eyes lit up a little bit as I slid her half of the pancakes onto her plate.

"Thank you, Mike!" she said happily. She buttered them up, poured on some syrup, and took a bite. "Wow, they're really good."

"I told you," I said.

"I think they *would* go good with coffee," she said. "I'm not gonna have any coffee today, though."

"Maybe next time," I said.

"Yeah, definitely."

After we finished eating, we sat around and talked some more. We talked about the high schools we went to, and it sounded as if her school was a lot bigger than mine. I graduated with a class of about ninety students; Hayley had nearly two hundred. I wasn't sure if I would have liked to have that many people in my class, even though there are schools with way more students than that.

I glanced at the time and noticed it was almost seven o'clock, but I wasn't ready to call it a night yet.

"It's almost seven now," I said. "What time do you have to be back?"

"I don't know," she said. "Anytime, really."

Perfect.

167

"Do you have anything else you wanna do?" I asked.

"Hmm...like what?" she asked.

"We could see a movie or something," I suggested.

"I don't know what's playing," she said.

"We can swing by the theater and take a look," I said. "Students get a fifty percent discount. You can't beat that."

"Yeah, we can do that," she said. "I haven't been to the movies in a long time."

"Alright, sounds like a deal," I said, standing up. "If you want, you can ride with me and I can bring you back here to your car later."

"Are you sure?" Hayley asked, slipping her coat on. "It's not out of your way?"

Dropping Hayley off at her car after the theater would actually be pretty far out of my way, but that wasn't important right now.

"I'm offering to give you a ride," I said. "That should be a good sign that going out of my way isn't a problem."

Hayley smiled somewhat bashfully.

"Okay," she said, "thanks."

We paid for our food at the counter and went outside to my car. Luckily, my car happened to be cleaner than usual. I heard something in psychology that said a person's car can say a lot about that person. Hopefully, Hayley wouldn't get the impression that I was a neat freak.

"What kind of music do you want to listen to?" I asked.

"Do you have any country?" she asked. "I'm kinda in the mood for some country for some reason."

You and Lawrence both, I thought.

"I don't have any country CDs, but I have the radio," I said.

It took some time to find a country station since I didn't know any. I remembered how Lawrence wanted to listen to country on our camping trip, so I considered it practice for this occasion with Hayley. Her perfume began to waft around in my car, acting as a constant distraction against the music. Whatever fragrance it was, I personally liked it more than most perfumes

I'd smelled. Some of them seem to seep up into my brain and light it on fire, but Hayley's was actually pleasant.

The movie theater was usually packed on Friday nights, so I had to park around the corner. Hayley and I stood in front of the list of movies playing to figure out what we wanted to see before going inside.

Please not the romantic comedy, I thought. *Please not the romantic comedy. Please not the romantic comedy....*

"I know you might not want to," said Hayley, pointing one out, "but I kinda want to see that one."

Of course, the romantic comedy.

I wasn't going to put up a fuss. I had prepared myself for this. Hayley wanted to see the romantic comedy, so that's what I was going to do. We walked inside and stood in line at the ticket booth until it was our turn to order.

"I'm sorry, that one's sold out," the guy told me.

Relieved, I turned to Hayley with a sympathetic look.

"Oh," she said. "Well...uh...."

"Is there another one you'd want to see?" I asked her.

"Well...that was really the only one I wanted to see," she said. "You can choose one since I almost had you sit through a romantic comedy."

"No, it's alright," I said. "If you don't want to see a movie, we can do something else."

"I don't care."

"Let's go do something else," I said encouragingly. "We can always come back on a less crowded day, or when some more movies come out."

We walked out of the movie theater as I thought of something else to do with Hayley. I was determined not to let this night end on a sour note, but coming up with ideas was harder than I had anticipated.

"If you can think of anything, just let me know," I said.

"Let's walk around the town," she said.

"Really?" I said. "That's what you want to do?"

"Why not?" she said with a smile. "I'm still new around here. I wanna see the town some more."

"We don't have to walk if you don't want to," I said. "We can drive around."

"There's no fun in that," she said. "I like to walk. It's exercise and just feels more personal than looking at everything from the inside of a car."

"Alright, let's do it," I said.

I could never imagine myself going for a leisurely stroll just for the sake of strolling. However, having a gorgeous girl by my side made it all worthwhile. I wasn't much more familiar with this side of town than Hayley, so I was unable to show her around as much as I would have liked.

After walking for what felt like five miles, we went back to my car so I could drop Hayley off at Elm Valley Pancake House. During the ride, we talked more about whatever random topics came to mind, so I was able to keep the country music turned down.

"Thanks for hanging out with me today," said Hayley as I pulled up next to her car. "I had a good time."

"Yeah, thanks for inviting me," I said. "We'll have to do this again."

"Definitely," she replied with a smile. "Bye."

"Have a good night, Hayley."

"You too, Mike."

I hardly remember the ride home. All I know is that I clearly had something else on my mind. My first date with Hayley was a success, and I had already paved the way for a second date. Everything seemed to be going perfectly, and I felt on top of the world until I got back to my apartment and remembered I still had my English homework to do.

~Opus 13~

I took my seat at the table in the club meeting room with everyone else, waiting for Miss Flamingo to begin the session. The last few meetings had been uneventful with most of my time spent running around town to pick up supplies or make questionable deliveries. At any rate, working for the club had been the easiest job I could ask for, and the payments were enough to keep me from complaining.

However, every time I sat down in that meeting room, I couldn't help but worry that something crazy or dangerous might happen at any moment.

"I would like to start today's meeting with an announcement," said Miss Flamingo. She wasn't sitting down like everybody else in the room. "Roadrunner, would you come up here please?"

Wondering what Miss Flamingo was about to have me do, I stood up and walked over to her side of the table.

"Roadrunner, you have been with us for more than a month now," she said. "You have performed your duties well, and I believe you are a great asset for our club. That's why I have decided to give you a promotion."

"Oh," I replied, trying to find the right words. "Thank you, Miss Flamingo."

Everyone in the room gave a small round of applause. I had never been promoted before, so this was almost like a major achievement for me. Did this mean that I was going to get some sort of bonus or raise? My wallet was already feeling tickled.

"To honor this occasion, you will receive a bonus payment," said Miss Flamingo, handing me an envelope she had in her coat.

Hell yes! I thought as I grabbed the thick envelope and wedged it into my pocket.

"Your new position will be Raven's personal assistant," she said.

I suddenly didn't feel so jubilant. I looked over at Raven who seemed to be giving me an expressionless scowl, but I honestly couldn't tell what kind of expression it really was.

When I thought about it, she pretty much looked at everything that way.

"Personal assistant?" I asked Miss Flamingo. "What do you mean?"

"You'll be accompanying Raven on all of her duties," she said. "Many of her assignments are difficult for one person to do alone, and I believe you will be very helpful. You'll be expected to do whatever she asks of you, so long as her demands are practical."

I looked at Raven again. Her expression now looked a little menacing, much like a kid with spitballs in class waiting for the teacher to turn around.

"If you'll have a seat now, Roadrunner," said Miss Flamingo, "I would like to continue with the meeting."

When I took my seat, I tried to avoid eye contact with Raven. Being promoted suddenly wasn't as wondrous as I had made it out to be. There was no telling what assignments I would be carrying out with Raven, or what absurd demands she would have me do.

As usual, Miss Flamingo discussed club activities and figures that made little or no sense to me. I was starting to learn that it probably wasn't my place to really care about more than half of the topics covered during these meetings, but I did my best to follow along and tried to pick up on bits and pieces of everything being discussed.

When the discussions and announcements were over, everyone returned to what they typically did around the cabin: Oriole was behind the computer, Skylark was reading some book (it was a different one every meeting), Kookaburra was raiding the booze, Cormorant was tinkering with something mechanical, Raven was just sitting around, and Miss Flamingo was drinking something hot out of a mug with a pile of documents in front of her. At the very least, it looked as if *something* constructive was probably happening, but I could never really be sure.

After a few minutes of pretty much nothing, Oriole printed something out and showed it to Miss Flamingo. I didn't have much interest in what it was until Miss Flamingo spoke up.

"Raven," she said. "I have a job for you."

Raven walked over to Miss Flamingo and looked over the paper. Figuring that I was going to have to tag along, I stood up and went over to look it over myself. The paper mentioned something about retrieving something from Elm Valley College, but it was difficult to understand and oddly ambiguous.

"I'll do my best," said Raven dutifully. "Let's go, Roadrunner."

"What do we have to do?" I asked, following her out of the meeting room.

"We're going to the college," she said. "They're having night classes now, so it should be open."

"What's at the college?" I asked.

"Our target," she said.

"Okay," I said, getting impatient, "what's our target?"

"Think of our target as a hair stuck to a Band-Aid after you rip it off," she told me while we were heading down the stairs.

"That really doesn't tell me what it is," I said.

"Relax," she said, "you're just my personal assistant. You don't need to understand it completely."

"I think it'd be better if I *did* understand exactly what it is I'm helping you with," I said. "Wouldn't you think?"

"Nope. Wait here."

Raven hurried out to her car and returned to the cabin's living room with the bass guitar she had used at the show. When she sat down with it on the couch and started tuning it, I really had to know what she was doing.

"Why do you have that?" I asked her. "Aren't we supposed to leave now?"

"I need to play my lucky three hundred and sixty-six-note song," she replied shortly. "I do this before all of my assignments."

"Are you serious?" I said.

173

"Of course I'm serious," she said. "Three hundred and sixty-six is my lucky number, and I've never once failed an assignment for Miss Flamingo."

"Your lucky number?"

"I bought my bass on leap day," she said. "It's like the three hundred and sixty-sixth day of the year."

"Wouldn't that be the last day of December during a leap year?" I asked.

"Not without leap day!"

As soon as Raven started playing the riff, I remembered how much of a talented bassist she was. Fortunately, the notes were quick and the song didn't last too long at all. She sprung to her feet when she was finished, seemingly much more energetic than she was a few minutes ago.

"Alright, let's dominate!" she declared.

So that was that. There I was, sitting in Raven's little battery-powered car on my way to the college to get...our target. Her car smelled like linens and French fries, even though the air freshener dangling from her mirror was clearly in the shape of a raspberry. We didn't speak a word until we arrived at the college. Raven pulled up and parked as close as possible to the main office building.

"Now what?" I asked.

"Follow me," she said.

We walked casually into the main office building. Almost nobody else was around, making me feel slightly awkward to be one of the only people there. Raven glanced around, then headed down one of the hallways. She made it no more than ten feet before she stopped, glanced around again, and turned around to head in the opposite direction.

"Do you know where you're going?" I asked.

"I like to think I do," she replied.

I didn't want to ask too many questions if I never received a decent answer. Heaving a sigh, I just closed my mouth and followed Raven. Anything bad that happened was going to be her fault, not mine. I was just the assistant, after all.

She stopped in front of an unmarked door near the main office and took out the piece of paper Oriole had printed out.

After a quick examination, she folded the paper back up, put it in her pocket, then turned to me with an enthusiastic smirk.

"This is it," she said, grabbing the doorknob. "Huh, it's locked."

"So how do you think you'll get inside?" I asked.

"We're just going to have to break the door down," Raven concluded.

"We're not breaking the door down," I replied curtly. "That's just stupid."

"Do I need to remind you of your contract?" she asked deviously. "I have a job to do and you're my assistant."

"Yes, I know all about the stupid contract!" I grunted. "I'm just saying I think we should try something a little less forceful."

"Like what?" she asked irritably. "If you have an idea, then you should tell me."

"I don't know," I shrugged. "That's why we need to think this through more."

Raven let out a distraught sigh and crossed her arms.

"Look, Raven," I said, "do you actually think the two of us can break through this door on our own? And if we can *somehow* manage to do that, how are we gonna do it without anyone noticing? Smashing through doors isn't a sneaky tactic."

After giving me a mildly agitated look, Raven pressed her hand on the door and rubbed it gently.

"Well, it *does* seem extremely sturdy," she said.

You figured that out just by rubbing it? I thought.

Raven folded her arms again, running her eyes up and down the entire door to examine every millimeter. The hamster wheel in her head was definitely spinning to come up with a plan to overcome her seven-foot wooden foe.

"I would say we could take out the hinges," she said while in deep thought, "but they're on the other side...."

"What's the reason for trying to get into this room?" I asked her. "You're putting a lot of effort into figuring this out."

"Because this is where all the juicy stuff is!" she replied optimistically.

175

I'm not even gonna ask. Forget it. Whatever happens, happens.

"Okay, new plan," said Raven. "We'll wait for our opportunity, sitting right here."

The entire campus was littered with computers for student use, and it just so happened that two computers were stationed near the door we had to get through. Raven took a seat at one of them, so I just sat down next to her. I wasn't sure what we were waiting for, but figured I would just go along with Raven's plan for now.

Nearly an hour passed without this so-called opportunity arising. I did my best to kill boredom by playing solitaire and surfing the web, but my patience was beginning to dwindle. If I had known I would be camping out at the school, I would've packed something to eat.

My pocket was still bulging with the bonus Miss Flamingo had given me for my promotion. Curious, I took out the envelope and checked the money inside. When I counted out two thousand dollars, I had an overwhelming urge to break out with a hyperactive dance, but I merely put the money back in the envelope and wedged it back into my pocket.

"Psst! Hey, look!" Raven whispered. "Somebody just came out of that room!"

I was too engrossed in my wad of cash to notice what Raven was talking about at first. Mr. Gast, the physical education instructor, had walked out of the room, holding a clipboard and a large cup of what appeared to be coffee. As soon as he left the hallway and entered the main office, Raven scurried over to the unmarked door and attempted to get inside, only to find the door was locked again.

"Alright, listen closely," she told me. "We'll have to take the keys from that guy."

"Uh, okay," I said. "Are you going to ask him to just hand the keys over?"

"No," said Raven. "That most likely won't work. We'll have to use a little more force, probably against his will."

"That's the gym instructor!" I said. "There's no way we're gonna wrestle the keys from him. He's twice my size!"

Raven reached inside her jacket pocket and handed me a corked test tube filled with a clear liquid.

"Wait, what is this?" I asked skeptically, looking at the suspicious liquid.

"Put it in his drink when he's not looking," said Raven quietly. "We'll have to wait for the right time, but I'll make sure to distract him long enough for you to use that."

"So, you plan to poison him?" I shook my head. "You're insane, Raven. I think I prefer breaking down the door."

"It's not poison, jackass," said Raven, stroking the silver ornament hanging from her neck. "It's a phial of sleeping potion that Skylark made. It's completely non-lethal and highly effective."

I gave Raven a look of uncertainty. The situation had just grown from aggravating to ridiculous, and all I wanted to do was walk away and call it a night. Skylark was one of the club members whom I trusted more, and Raven told me that the sleep potion was safe to use. This was an uncomfortable dilemma, but I finally came to my decision.

"Gah, whatever," I muttered, putting the test tube in my other pocket, hearing it clink against my sapphire amulet. "Let's do it."

"Take your position in there," she said, pointing to the building's main seating area for students. "Act like you're doing something."

"With what?" I asked. "I don't have any of my school stuff."

"Improvise," she said. "Go!"

Making no argument, I headed over to the seating area and sat down at one of the tables. Taking deep breaths, I prepared myself for the criminal action I was about to take. A couple of minutes later, I could hear Raven talking to somebody down the hall, and I immediately whipped out my cell phone and pretended to be doing something on it. Soon after, Raven rounded the corner with the instructor following her. I didn't know what she had told him, but she looked pretty distressed.

"It was right out there!" said Raven, pointing out the window.

"Stay here," said Mr. Gast. "I'll go check it out."

He set his cup down on one of the tables and hurried out the nearest door. Noticing my cue, I rushed over to the cup, removed the lid, poured in the entire test tube of sleeping potion, and put the lid back on.

That really wasn't that hard, I thought.

"Good work," said Raven.

"What'd you tell him?" I asked.

"I said I saw someone in a black hoodie lurking around outside," she said. "Now take your seat before he comes back."

"Why do you want him to think we're not together?" I asked. "It really doesn't matter."

"Fine," she said, "I guess so."

Raven and I waited until Mr. Gast came back inside. He looked sweaty, as if he had been running around.

"Well, I couldn't find anyone," he told Raven.

"Oh, okay," said Raven. "Thanks anyway."

"I could keep you company if you feel insecure," said the instructor.

"No, that's okay," she said. "I have my friend to keep me safe."

"Alright, you stay alert," he said. "Contact anyone who works here if you run into trouble."

He picked up his cup and took a big swig, making me feel a little anxious as he gulped it down. I thought he might notice the sleeping potion; I poured in quite a bit. As he walked away without showing any sign of suspicion, I figured it was safe to assume we had gotten away with drugging the physical education instructor.

"How long does it take to kick in?" I whispered to Raven.

"A few minutes," she said.

"What do we do now?"

"We need to keep him occupied," she said. "If he passes out in the office surrounded by secretaries and instructors, our plan will be ruined."

"That means you have a plan to keep him occupied, I hope," I said.

"Not really," she replied. "We have to act quickly."

"Great, Raven!" I groaned. "You should've thought this through! C'mon, let's go!"

I immediately took off to catch up with Mr. Gast. He was about to enter the main office again when I called to him.

"Hey! Excuse me!" I called.

"What is it?" he asked, stopping in front of the office door.

"My friend changed her mind," I told him, making everything up as I went along. "She would feel much more secure if you could follow us out to the car."

"Oh, okay," he said. "I don't want any students to feel threatened or in danger."

"Thank you," I said.

Raven walked up to us, looking somewhat timid and embarrassed. Seeing her like that was pretty strange, even if it was just an act.

"I'm sorry to trouble you," she said modestly.

"No, I'll be more than happy to do this for you," he said. "There are a lot of dirt bags out there."

Raven and I looked at each other, both knowing what we had to do next. We started walking slowly, waiting for the potion to kick in. The last thing I wanted at this point was to get to the car and have to keep Mr. Gast around with meaningless conversations until he fell asleep.

When we walked out through the front exit, Raven started to head in the direction of the other parking lot. My initial reaction was to say something, but I quickly assumed that she was trying to buy us more time by "accidentally" forgetting where she parked.

"It's getting pretty cold now," I said, trying to ease the anticipation.

"Winter's getting closer," said Mr. Gast. "I really don't feel very cold right now, though. Maybe I'm just used to it."

I looked at Raven, who gave me a small smirk. Feeling warm apparently was one of the side effects of the sleeping potion, so that probably meant that it was kicking in. However,

179

the instructor still seemed very much awake when we made it to the parking lot.

"Oh, wait a minute," said Raven. "I feel so dumb! This isn't where I parked. I parked in the other parking lot."

The instructor appeared slightly agitated, but didn't say anything as we led him back across the campus. I swallowed hard, wishing that the potion would work a little faster. My hopes were raised as we reached the halfway point between the two parking lots when Mr. Gast stopped for a second.

"Oh man," he yawned. "I feel a little lightheaded."

"Are you okay?" I asked, trying to sound convincingly concerned.

"Yeah, I probably haven't been getting enough sleep lately," he said, taking a big swig of coffee and, consequently, more sleeping potion. "Let's keep going."

"It's really nice to know that Elm Valley has such a caring staff," said Raven.

"No problem," he said, sounding a little woozy. "We're responsible for the safety and well-being of our students."

I found it difficult not to feel a little guilty for putting the guy through this, but I didn't think I had much choice. When I finally heard the sound of a collapsing body behind me, I felt more relieved than I was willing to admit.

"Hey, wake up!" said Raven, waving her hands in front of the passed-out instructor. "Are you alright?"

After a few seconds of us pretending to be shocked, Mr. Gast signified his state of deep sleep with some genuine snoring. Raven quickly snatched the keys out of his pocket, looking around to see if anyone was watching.

"Quick, let's put him on that bench over there," she said, picking up his feet.

As we carried Mr. Gast to the nearest bench, I was shocked at how heavy he was. We both grunted under pressure as we attempted to keep him from dragging on the ground. He was snoring loudly the entire time, even as he slipped out of my grasp and bounced his head off the grass. Once we made it to the bench, we swung him onto it on the count of three. He landed haphazardly on the bench, then he quickly adjusted himself and immediately started snoring again.

"Follow me," said Raven without wasting any time.

The two of us swiftly entered the main office building again and headed straight to the locked door. Raven glanced around to make sure it was clear, then started trying each key to find the one that worked.

"Keep a lookout," she told me.

I watched up and down the hall, not believing what I was doing. We'd probably get arrested if we got caught and couldn't successfully play it off. Whatever we were trying to do, it had to have been really worth it.

"Hurry up," I hissed, keeping an eye on both ends of the hall. "I'm getting anxious."

"There are lots of keys," she said. "I'm going as fast as — got it!"

Hearing the door unlock was music to my ears. Without even thinking, Raven pushed the door open and pulled me inside, then quietly shut the door behind us. The lights were off, so the room was pitch black. I groped the wall for a switch and turned on the lights, finding myself in a room filled with filing cabinets and shelves stacked with paperwork.

Raven whipped out the paper that contained our objective and read it over quickly, then proceeded to dig through just about anything she could find. I couldn't stand watching her use her random-search method, so I thought I'd step in.

"What are you looking for?" I asked. "Maybe I can help."

"The student profile for Wyatt Halabi," she said.

There really wasn't an excuse to bring up any legal issues at this point, so I looked around for any indication of where the student profiles would be. I was pretty positive that student profiles are supposed to be confidential to the public, but we were already screwed if anyone happened to walk in on us, therefore my top priority was finding what we needed and getting out. When I found a section of filing cabinets labeled *Student Profiles: Elm Valley College*, I felt as if I had struck gold.

"Hey, I think I found the profiles," I said, opening one of the drawers to reveal a staggering number of folders. "Oh crap, I hope they're in alphabetical order."

"Good work," said Raven, opening another filing cabinet to dig through.

"What was the dude's name again?" I asked.

"Wyatt Halabi," said Raven.

"Never heard of him," I said, checking the names on the folder tabs. I appeared to be in the "R" section.

"Me neither," said Raven.

"Doesn't it bother you?" I asked, opening another drawer. "We don't even know this guy, and we're stealing his private information."

"Not at all," she replied. "A target's a target."

"What does Miss Flamingo want with his profile?" I asked.

"I don't know," Raven mumbled, checking another drawer. "Wait a minute…I think it might be here…aha!"

She pulled out a folder and showed it to me briefly, giving me just enough time to confirm the name on the tab. Closing the drawers quickly and quietly, Raven concealed the entire folder under her jacket and headed for the door.

"Hey, wait!" I said. "We're taking the whole folder? All of it?"

"Well, yeah," she said, giving me a dirty look. "What'd you expect?"

I noticed a copy machine and attempted to use a little rationalization.

"Why don't we make copies of the documents using that?" I asked, pointing at the copier.

"That'll take too much time and make too much noise," said Raven.

"But what if somebody notices the folder's missing?" I argued. "I don't really know how often they check student profiles, but I'm pretty sure they'll find out it's gone sooner or later."

"We'll return it before they do," said Raven impatiently.

"What? You mean we're coming back?"

182

I remembered everything we had to go through just to break into the room once, and I couldn't imagine trying to do it again.

"It might not be us," she told me. "Then again, it might be. Don't worry about it yet."

I wanted to protest, but all I could do was stand there and make ugly faces. Besides getting busted, having to repeat the situation was the only way it could get worse.

"We're leaving right now!" said Raven sternly. "Hurry up, unless you want me to tell Miss Flamingo that you were being insubordinate. I don't think she'd like to hear that. She might even demote you back to your starting position."

The facts were harsh, but in truth I was bound by contract to do everything Raven told me on the job. I bit my lip, gritted my teeth, and hurried out of the room with Raven, making sure the door was locked on the way out.

We returned to where Mr. Gast was to find him still fast asleep on the bench in the middle of the school grounds. Raven slipped the keys back into his pocket, along with fifty dollars she had.

"Why are you paying him?" I asked.

"We just knocked him out," she said. "This is my apology."

"So you give him fifty bucks? What do you think he'd possibly use it for?"

"Buy himself a thirty-pack and some pizza bagels," she said. "If this happened to me, I know I would."

Raven took off at a brisk pace back to the car with me following right behind her.

"How long will he stay asleep?" I asked.

"The potion usually wears off after a couple hours," she said.

"We're gonna leave him out there for that long?" I asked. "Shouldn't we tell somebody about him? We can say that he was escorting us because you saw a shady person lurking around, then he started feeling lightheaded and passed out."

"I don't wanna get involved," she said.

"We're already involved!" I said. "The last thing he'll remember when he wakes up is us! If he has any questions to ask, I'm pretty sure we'll be brought up!"

"And we'll deal with it *then*!" said Raven. "We need to complete our task, and I'd like to see you keep levelheaded while you talk to a staff member with stolen property in our possession."

"Whatever," I muttered.

On the drive back to the cabin, I had plenty of time to think about the assignment. What would've happened if there was someone else already in the room when we went in? I heaved a grateful sigh of relief knowing that didn't happen.

"Hey, Raven," I said.

"What?"

"Are all of your assignments as risky as this one?" I asked. "I mean, we just dodged some pretty nasty bullets back there. Do you know how much trouble we'd be in if we got caught?"

"Almost all of my assignments have some risk involved," she said. "Why, are you scared now? Don't tell me this is too hard for you."

"I didn't say that!" I said. "I just want to know what I'm getting into with this promotion. I would like to know what kind of stuff I'm gonna have to follow you into."

"That was one of the more risky assignments," she said. "However, our lives weren't on the line, so I can't give it more than a six out of ten on the risk meter."

"How would you rate your riskiest assignment?" I asked.

"Hmm...maybe a seven," she said. "I could've died, but I lived. If you want to see a nine or ten, ask Skylark or Kookaburra if you can go with them on one of their hunts. I doubt they'd agree. You might die. Or suffer eternally."

"Uh, I'll pass," I said, "but do those two really get into that much danger? It just doesn't seem real."

"They're demon hunters," said Raven. "Does that sound safe to you? I don't think so."

A few months ago, I never would have believed anything that Raven was telling me. It's crazy how much you can believe after one day. Meeting Sapphira was the pivotal point of my life, and now I was listening to Raven and actually feeling that her words carried legitimacy.

"You did good, Roadrunner," said Raven. "You could stand to follow directions a little better, but don't let that get you down. I'm grateful to have you as my partner."

That was sudden, I thought. *Never in a thousand years would I expect her to give so much praise all at once.*

"Glad I could help," I muttered.

Raven and I returned to the cabin to report back to Miss Flamingo. Everyone in the meeting room appeared to be doing the same exact thing as when we had left, and it was like they had no clue what we had just gotten away with. However, I was sure that nobody would be surprised if I explained how much trouble we went through to find the files, so I acted as if it was no big deal as Raven casually handed the folder to Miss Flamingo.

"We completed the assignment," said Raven. "Here is what you requested."

"Good job," said Miss Flamingo, taking the folder containing Wyatt Halabi's student profile. "Here are your payments."

"Miss Flamingo, can I ask you something?" I asked.

"Yes?" she said, flipping through the files.

"Who's that Wyatt guy?" I asked. "I've never heard of him before. Is he important?"

"You'll find out if the time comes," she replied blankly.

I took that as meaning "none of your business," so I just let it go without further questions.

~Opus 14~

"Wake up, Michael," I heard Sapphira say one morning.

If I ignore it, maybe it'll go away, I thought groggily.

"Wake up, Michael."

I don't wanna get up yet….

"Wake up, Michael."

"Hmmm…what?"

"Your phone is ringing. Should I answer it for you?"

I opened my eyes to find Sapphira standing next to my bed, holding my cell phone.

"I have the ringer off so it wouldn't wake me up," I said tiredly. "I don't care if someone's calling me."

"Very well," said Sapphira. She placed my phone on my nightstand and vanished.

I looked at the clock. Eleven thirty. Had I really slept in that late? Good thing it was Saturday.

The entire week had passed without any mention of the break-in I had done with Raven. I was paranoid every minute I spent in class, expecting the dean to parade up to me with a small army of cops and start asking questions about Mr. Gast or the stolen student profile. Nothing had happened so far, so I assumed I was in the clear. More accurately, I *hoped* I was in the clear.

Sitting up in bed, I rubbed my eyes and yawned loudly, then reached for my phone to see who called. Hayley's name showed up as a missed call, making it one of the few times I didn't mind having my phone wake me up. Not wasting another second, I immediately called her back.

"Hey, I saw you called me," I said when Hayley answered.

"Yeah," she said. "Did I wake you up? Sorry if I did."

"No, it's fine," I said.

I don't mind it when you wake me up, I wanted to say. *In fact, you could wake me up every morning.*

"I just got your voicemail from last night," said Hayley. "My phone was dead and I didn't find out until this morning. Anyway, I'd love to do something today. I'm free all day."

186

I had called Hayley last night to ask her out on another date, but I was immediately redirected to her voicemail. Hearing her positive response first thing in the morning was a thousand times better than any cup of bitter coffee.

"Great!" I said. "What time is best for you?"

"Um, one o'clock works for me," she said.

"Alright. Do you want to meet somewhere? I was thinking I could pick you up if you want."

"You mean pick me up from home?" she asked.

"Yeah, if that's fine with you," I said.

"Well…you could. You don't have to if you don't want."

I want to.

"It's up to you," I said. "I don't really mind."

There was a short pause. Oh, the anticipation of the short pause….

"Yeah, alright," she said. "I can give you the address."

I quickly found a pencil and piece of paper (which turned out to be the back of my psychology homework) and scribbled down Hayley's address.

"Okay, I'll be there at one to pick you up," I said. "We can think about what we want to do then."

"Alright, see you when you get here," she said.

I hung up and jumped into action, getting ready for my second date with Hayley, which was awesome. She allowed me to see where she lived, which was double awesome.

Hayley's home was about five miles west of town. While driving to pick her up, I had to follow the directions closely since I had never traveled west out of Elm Valley before. Regardless, the surrounding area looked the same no matter what road you took out of town.

Just as the clock in my car's radio changed to one o'clock, I noticed Hayley's address on one of the mailboxes. My timing couldn't have been any more perfect. There was a young woman outside the house as I pulled into the driveway, but I quickly realized that she wasn't Hayley. She walked up to my car, so I rolled down the window to talk to her. My guess was she was a little older than me. Not quite by ten years, maybe?

"Hello," she said. "You're Mike, right?"

"Yeah," I said. "Is Hayley here?"

"She should be out in a second," she said. "I'll go see if she's ready."

The young woman walked up to the door just as Hayley was coming out, and they nearly ran into each other. Hayley hurried over to my car and got into the passenger seat.

"Hi!" she said.

"Hey," I said. "How have you been?"

"I've been good," she replied.

"Who was that other girl?" I asked. "Your roommate?"

"My sister," said Hayley. "I moved in with her so I could be closer to the college. Her name's Jeanette."

"You really don't look alike," I said.

"Well, she's actually my stepsister," said Hayley, "but, yeah…. So, where are we going today?"

"It doesn't matter to me," I said. "Did you think of something you want to do?"

"Let's go to the office supply store!" she said enthusiastically.

"Do you need to buy something there?" I asked.

"Not really," she said. "I just wanna see what kinds of chairs they have. I like to sit in the office chairs and stuff."

"Uh, okay," I said, backing out of the driveway. "Are you looking for a new chair?"

"No, I just think it's fun," she said.

Minutes later, we arrived at the office supply store in downtown Elm Valley. I looked up at the store's sign as we were turning into the parking lot, thinking that it was the last place I expected to end up on a date. Once inside, I followed Hayley straight to the section for office chairs and desks. She took a seat in a big leather chair with huge armrests, wearing a soothed look on her face. Going along with what she was doing, I sat down in the hard, slightly uncomfortable chair next to her.

"This one's pretty nice," she said, patting the armrests of the leather chair. "It's like something a CEO would sit in and stare out a big window down at the city he wants to take over."

Just as I was finding the humor in what Hayley had said, the hairs on the back of my neck stood up. A chill rushed down my spine, and I knew it wasn't because of the air conditioning.

What the heck was that? I asked myself. *It reminds me of the time I was in that ghost car when that dead girl tried attacking me.*

I glanced nervously around, trying not to look too weird in front of Hayley. The thought of some ghastly being lurking in the aisles made my skin crawl. With a small sense of desperation, I reached into my pocket and clutched my sapphire amulet.

"Whoa, what's that?" said Hayley suddenly.

I whirled around to see what she was talking about, ready to grab her and run for the exit.

"Huh? What?" I said quickly.

"There's some kind of big sale over there," she replied, pointing to a big sign on the other side of the store. "Let's check it out!"

"Oh, yeah. We can do that," I said, feeling relieved.

Hayley looked at me and smiled.

"What's wrong? Did I scare you?" she asked.

"Scare me?" I said, playing it off. "How could you scare me?"

"I don't know," she said playfully. "You looked a little jumpy."

"That's my cat-like reflexes."

"Uh-huh...more like scaredy-cat reflexes."

As Hayley and I walked over to see what the big sale was, the ominous feeling drifted away. Whatever had caused that feeling must have just been passing through. My only hope was that it didn't notice me, since I was apparently a magnet for supernatural things now.

The big sale turned out to be for stuff used for mailing, such as envelopes and boxes of all sizes. From what I could gather, it appeared to be a really good deal. However, neither of us needed to mail anything, so it didn't do us any good.

"Is this all it is?" said Hayley flatly.

"What, are you disappointed?" I asked.

189

"I was hoping it'd be something more interesting," she said.

"How interesting did you think it'd be?" I asked. "It's an office supply store."

"Hey, don't be so mean," she said.

"I'm not being mean," I replied, "just honest."

Hayley gave me one of those fake pouting faces, making me chuckle a little out loud. Then she crossed her arms and let out a little sigh. Flirting, anyone? I do think so.

"Yeah, I guess," she said. "Let's go somewhere else!"

"Okay, where to?"

"Ice cream!" she replied with a twinkle in her eye. "Isn't there a place around here that has ice cream?"

"Uh, I think so," I said.

"Don't tell me you don't want ice cream because it's chilly outside," she said. "People don't follow that logic."

"I didn't say that," I said. "C'mon, let's get some ice cream."

On our way to the store's exit, Hayley's shoulder brushed against mine. Butterflies flew up in my stomach, but they were quickly frozen in ice as the ominous feeling crept back into me. Have you ever had butterfly ice cubes floating around in your stomach? It's strange, take it from me.

Whatever you are, go away! I thought. *Can't you see I'm working here?*

As if it could hear my thoughts, the thing seemed to get closer as the eerie feeling grew stronger. That feeling followed me as Hayley and I got into my car. Looking at her, I could tell that she wasn't able to sense it at all.

Another feeling suddenly surged inside me, completely different from the dark one that continued to linger. This new feeling was anything from strange, though. In fact, it was a very primitive feeling that guys often have when they look at a pretty girl. The only thing that disturbed me was how powerful and sudden it was. I mean, Hayley was a good-looking girl, but there was something a little off about how aggressive my desires had just become.

"Is something wrong?" Hayley asked me.

I realized that I had been staring and practically drooling at her. With a quick slap of reality, I immediately accommodated for my absentminded action.

"No, not at all," I said smoothly. "I was noticing how good you look today."

Hayley smiled and turned a little red.

"Thanks!" she said. "You look nice, too. I like that shirt."

"Oh, this?" I said. "It's nothing special, really."

"I like it," she said.

As we held eye contact, my desire began to surge to abnormal heights again. I had to painfully break our gaze to prevent myself from reaching animalistic levels of lust. My heart and breathing rate began to rise as I backed out of the parking space. Maybe if I could focus on driving, I'd come back to my senses.

By the time we reached the ice cream parlor, my primitive urges had dropped a little. Still, I had to grit my teeth to ignore the smell of Hayley's perfume wafting past me when we entered the restaurant. Even as we approached the counter, I had to take deep breaths to calm myself down. I knew it had been a while since I last had a girlfriend, but there was no way I could have been *that* deprived.

While waiting for our order, my phone went off in my pocket. I took it out to see who was calling, but there was nothing on the caller ID. Usually, a phone number comes up if I don't have that number in my contact list, but there was nothing. Hayley glanced at me, and I didn't want to appear awkward, so I hesitantly answered it.

"Hello?" I said.

"You need to be careful," said a woman's voice.

"Who is this?" I asked.

"This is Sapphira."

"Huh?" Now I was confused. "Where are you calling from?"

"You need to be careful," she repeated.

"Yeah, you said that already."

"There is a powerful demon who is aware of your presence," she warned.

191

My mouth got a little dry all of a sudden.

"Well, what should I do?" I asked, keeping a strong composure.

"Remain vigilant," she told me. "His name is Asmodeus. He manipulates humans through sexual desires. As long as you do not give in, he cannot control you."

"Oh," I said, "that actually explains quite a bit."

"You need not worry too much," said Sapphira. "Asmodeus is not particularly dangerous. However, he is powerful, so your amulet has a limited effect against him."

"Why don't you do something about him?" I asked angrily. "I'm in the middle of something."

"I concluded that Asmodeus is not enough of a threat for me to intervene," she said. "Would you like me to attempt to ward him off?"

"Yes, please," I grunted.

"Very well," said Sapphira.

The call suddenly ended. I looked back at Hayley, who was handing me my caramel sundae.

"Here you go," she said.

"Oh, thanks," I said, trying to appear chipper. "Let's take a seat somewhere."

The cool, creamy texture of my sundae did little to keep my mind off things. Just knowing that unseen entities were confronting each other somewhere nearby was unsettling. I couldn't help but imagine some beastly creature popping up in the middle of the restaurant, carrying Sapphira's severed head as a way of telling me that my days were done. Hopefully, she wouldn't get hurt while warding off that Asmodeus demon.

"Have you ever heard of a bacon sundae?" Hayley asked me out of the blue.

"That sounds a little weird to me," I replied.

"Believe it or not, bacon and ice cream go really good together," she said. "You should try it."

"Yeah, maybe someday," I said.

I couldn't sense the ominous feeling anymore, which made me feel a lot better. I also no longer had the urge to leap over the table and pounce on Hayley like a rabbit. These seemed like pretty good indicators that Sapphira was successfully keeping Asmodeus at bay.

I rubbed the bulge in my pocket where the amulet was, thinking about the limited protection it provided. How many things was it actually protecting me from? Maybe there was some way to increase its effectiveness.

I hadn't considered how long our date was going to be, even as we spent the entire day going to random places and doing random things. We drove around town, stopping to check out anything that looked interesting. Normally, I liked to have some sort of plan laid out, but I really didn't mind this time.

"Pencils are better for me," I said during one of our conversations in the car. "I like having an eraser because I make lots of mistakes when I write."

"It doesn't make much difference for me," said Hayley. "Do you think it's bad luck for a pencil to break on your first day of school? Someone told me that."

I remembered the first day of the school year when my pencil broke during my psychology class.

"Uh, I don't know," I said, hoping she wasn't right.

"It's just one of those weird superstitions I have," said Hayley. "You hear these things as a little kid, and sometimes it's hard to just dismiss them, even though you know it's just a bunch of hocus pocus."

"I hope that's all it is," I said, thinking about all of the things happening lately that were definitely more than superstition.

"Why do you say that?" she asked curiously. "Do you have any superstitions?"

"Not particularly," I replied. "I'm just a little more of a believer these days."

"Believer of supernatural things?" she asked.

"Yeah," I said, not wanting to go into detail.

We arrived at Hayley's house a little after ten. For the most part, our date had gone without a hitch, and I was a little disappointed that the day was about to be over.

"I had a great time," said Hayley sincerely.

193

"Good," I said, "so did I."

"We should do this more often," she told me.

"For sure," I said.

She looked at me, and we held each other's gaze for a few seconds.

"You're a lot of fun to be with," she said softly.

"You think so?" I said.

"Of course," she told me. "You get me out of the house. Because of you, I'm not always cooped up with my sister. Not like I don't like being with my sister...it's just that...I don't know. It's hard to explain, really."

"No, I know what you mean," I said. "I feel the same way about you. I'm not bored when I'm with you, and I enjoy it."

I don't remember exactly when I realized it, but we had slowly been inching closer to each other while we continued to talk in my car. How long were we sitting in her driveway like that? Did I keep the car running the entire time? Those questions hardly needed to be answered at the moment.

Our first kiss happened so suddenly that I was glad I was prepared for it. Hayley's lips were softer and warmer than I had imagined, and that might have messed with my head a little bit.

"Are you sure about this?" I asked. "You don't think we're taking this too fast?"

Hold on, what did I just say?

"Uh, well," she said softly. "Do *you* think we're going too fast?"

"No," I replied quickly, "not at all."

I leaned in for the second kiss. Unlike the first one, this kiss sealed the deal. Nobody had to tell me that it did, because I just knew. I don't want to say that a make-out session immediately followed, but that was exactly what happened. Hoist the anchor, matey! This ship was setting sail.

How great it would have been if this was the end of my tale. Had the lights dimmed and the curtains closed at that point, my happily-ever-after would have been just that. Alas, the stage was still set, and the play director had only just returned from his lunch break.

"Welcome home, Michael," said Sapphira when I returned to my apartment.

"Hey," I replied dreamily, my mind on other things.

"I have succeeded in keeping Asmodeus at bay for now," she told me.

"What? Oh, yeah," I said, regaining my train of thought. "Good."

"You appear to be in high spirits," said Sapphira.

"Yeah, you could say that," I replied.

"Would you like me to do anything for you?" she asked.

"Not right now, thanks," I said. "Maybe when I finish my homework."

"Very well."

My homework was finished before I knew it, despite the fact that I couldn't stop thinking about Hayley. Sapphira offered to make dinner, but I wasn't very hungry. In fact, I was pretty sleepy from running around with Hayley all day. After putting my school materials in my backpack, I went straight to bed.

That night, I had a dream. I dreamt that I was in a classroom with Hayley, and we were studying or something. Suddenly, Miyuki walked over to us.

"I didn't think *you* would be here," Miyuki told Hayley rudely.

"I'm not doing anything wrong," said Hayley defensively.

"Whatever," Miyuki muttered. "Can you just leave? I need some time here."

Without a word, Hayley quickly packed her things and stormed out of the room.

"That was a little mean," I told Miyuki.

"Oh well." She shrugged. "We're alone now, aren't we?"

"I guess," I said.

"That's good," said Miyuki.

She walked over to me and grabbed my shoulders, giving me a sultry look.

"I don't know," I said hesitantly, "this doesn't seem right."

"But it *is* right," she said, sitting on my lap.

As she started kissing me, I found it very difficult to stop. There was something entrancing about Miyuki's embrace. *This is a dream,* I thought. *I'm dreaming right now!*

"Do you realize that this is a dream?" Miyuki asked me, holding me tightly in her arms.

"Yeah," I replied.

"That means you can do whatever you want," she said, running her fingers through my hair. "What do you want to do with me?"

Before I could tell her any of my crazy desires, somebody flew from somewhere and tackled Miyuki right off my lap. As they hit the ground, I realized that Sapphira had just intervened with my dream.

"Sapphira!" I said angrily. "What are you doing?"

"Asmodeus is manipulating your mind," she told me while Miyuki squirmed underneath her like a rabid animal.

"Damn it," I grunted. "I'm just gonna wake up!"

The transition from dream world to the real world was fairly quick. However, I was horrified to see that Sapphira was in my room, and she was actually pinning down something on the floor next to my bed. I turned on my bedside lamp to get a better look, but I soon wished I had not seen what I did. The thing Sapphira was holding down looked shadowy and frightening. Sharp teeth gnawed in all directions while claws lashed out violently. In short, I nearly peed myself.

Over the creature's shrieks and growls, I could hear Sapphira saying something in some strange language. A magic circle appeared around her, illuminating the room with an eerie glow. I began to feel a deep vibration emanating from the circle. There was a bright flash that hurt my eyes...then it was over. The creature was gone.

"Allow me to explain the situation," said Sapphira like a news reporter.

"Oh, please do!" I said shakily.

"That was Asmodeus you just saw," she said. "He advanced on you while you were vulnerable in a dream state."

"That thing was a demon?" I asked in bewilderment.

"That is correct," said Sapphira. "That was Asmodeus. Humans are vulnerable while dreaming due to a lowered sense of awareness and heightened subconscious brain activity."

"Um, okay," I said, trying to absorb that explanation.

"Asmodeus attacks humans with sexual manipulation," Sapphira continued. "That is why you experienced the dream you had."

"Wait, you saw what I was dreaming?" I felt so embarrassed now.

"Yes," she said. "I apologize for entering your mind without permission, but I believed it was for your own good."

"I thought you said Asmodeus wasn't that dangerous," I muttered.

"He was attempting to lead you down a path of immorality," she explained. "You asked me to fend him off, so that is what I did. Otherwise, I would not have interfered because he poses no real threat."

"Down a path of immorality?" I said contemplatively. Thinking about what my dream was about, I easily understood what Sapphira meant.

"Is there anything else you would like me to do?" she asked.

"No," I replied. "You did good, though. Thanks."

"You are most welcome," she said. "Does this mean I am dismissed?"

"Yeah, you're dismissed," I said.

Sapphira vanished, leaving me to further contemplate the entire situation.

Asmodeus had tried to replace my feelings for Hayley with feelings for Miyuki instead, I thought. *It was a nice try on his part, but he was stupid for thinking I'd let go of the amazing relationship I have with Hayley.*

However, it made me aware of just how cunning demons could actually be.

~Opus 15~

The next day was intended to be one of those lazy days where you just stay home and do nothing. My encounter with Asmodeus made me want to lay low for a while and save my energy. A lot of things were going on in my life at the time, and my mind was running on low battery as it fought to keep up.

I had no homework left to do, so I was free from the lingering thought of responsibility. Miss Flamingo's generous paychecks eliminated any monetary concerns, and now Hayley was a part of the picture. Everything was just peachy as long as I didn't let the mysterious supernatural world intimidate me.

Then Sapphira showed up.

"Michael," she said, "there is someone here to see you."

I was sitting comfortably on the couch, contemplating my day of laziness. Noon hadn't even rolled around yet, and somebody was already wondering what I was up to. Something deep down inside was giving me a feeling that it wasn't anyone "normal" who had come to visit.

"Alright," I said, "who is it?"

"I do not know," said Sapphira.

"You didn't let them see you, did you?" I said, feeling a little worried. I quickly stood up and walked over to the door.

"It is no concern for this visitor to know of my existence," said Sapphira.

"What's that supposed to mean?" I asked, peering through the peephole into the hallway. "I don't see anyone."

"He is already aware that I am here with you," said Sapphira.

"Uh, okay," I said, confused.

"Would you care to meet him?" she asked.

I hesitated for a moment.

"Sure," I said.

Immediately, a little man appeared in my living room. More accurately, he was tiny, probably about five inches tall. Other than his size, I could immediately tell that he wasn't human from his slightly disfigured (and slightly ugly) face. Strangely enough, he was dressed in a tiny green pea coat with striped pants and bright orange shoes. Adding to the strangeness, he had little bug-like wings that allowed him to hover in the air. As he floated over to me, I didn't know if I wanted to laugh or run away.

"Hello there!" he said in a friendly, squeaky voice. "You must be Michael, right?"

"Yeah," I replied. I looked at Sapphira for reassurance, but there was nothing reassuring about her robotic gaze.

"Forgive me for not introducing myself," the tiny man said. "You can call me Toony."

"Toony?" I scratched my head. "Nice, uh, to meet you."

"You seem a little surprised, sonny boy," he told me with a gnarled, toothy grin. "The look on your face tells me you've never seen a hobgoblin before!"

"No...can't say I have," I said slowly. "What's a hobgoblin?"

"Oh, that really depends on who you ask!" he told me. "Just the same as my name!"

Now I'm really confused, I thought.

"Is there something I can do for you?" I asked. "You wanted to see me?"

"Ah, indeed," said Toony, swooping around my head like a giant gnat. "A favor is what I came to ask of you. You see, I'm looking for something, and rumor has it that you can help me."

"There are rumors about me?" I asked.

"Indeed there are!" said Toony. "Rumors in the other realm spread differently than you may be familiar with, so familiarity is not the key here. Lad, do you understand where I'm coming from?"

"No, I don't," I said impatiently. "What are you looking for? No guarantees I can help you out, though."

"It's a book," he said, swooping around the room again. "Are you aware of any?"

My mind immediately went to the weird grimoire, but for some reason, I tried to dodge the subject.

"I have lots of books," I told him. "Most are for school."

"I'm not talking about schoolbooks or romance novels or whatever it is your kind enjoy," said Toony. "A *grimoire* is what I'm looking for!"

So much for dodging the subject.

I wasn't sure if I really wanted to tell this Toony fellow about that grimoire. Who knew what he really was or what he would do with that book. The whole situation was too shady.

"Hold on," I said, taking authority. "I don't know who you are or what you're planning on doing, so I can't just go along with this without, like, knowing more stuff."

"My boy, what do you mean?" Toony asked, sounding suspiciously reassuring. "You actually know what book I'm talking about, judging by your defensive reaction."

"I might," I began, "but like I said, no guarantees."

"Ho ho! Stubborn, aren't you?" said Toony playfully.

He continued to swoop around the room, and I kept resisting the urge to bat him out of the air with my bare hand.

"Sapphira, is this guy legit?" I asked.

"You need to be more specific," she replied.

"Can we trust him?" I said impatiently.

"I do not know," she replied.

"Oh my, that's harsh!" said Toony.

"What are you planning to do with the book?" I asked.

"The book is out of place," he told me. "I want to keep it out of harm's way. More importantly, I just need to borrow it."

"That really doesn't answer my question," I grunted.

"I will give it back to you when I'm finished!" he said. "That is, if I think it will be safe with you."

"I don't even have it," I said.

"But you *want* it, am I right?" he said.

"Not necessarily," I replied. "Look, dude, you're a suspicious little bastard, and I'm not playing along with this game. I don't know what you're trying to pull, but I smell something fishy. I'm not helping you."

"Suit yourself." Toony shrugged. "Don't come crying to me when things get out of hand."

"When *what* gets out of hand?" I asked.

"You'll see," said Toony with his gnarled grin.

"Alright, now you're confusing me again," I muttered.

"A time will soon come when you'll want that book," he told me. "I just want something from it first. This is intended to be a mutual benefit."

"So what, you're some kind of prophet?" I said, unconvinced. "You just happen to know what I'll want someday?"

"Oh my, you're rather cocky for someone who doesn't know much about the other realm," said Toony. "Play it your way, I suppose."

"Sapphira, get this guy out of here," I said.

"No need," said Toony. "I can help myself out of here." Just like that, he vanished.

"What was *that* about?" I asked, feeling relieved that he was gone.

"He is a hobgoblin," said Sapphira. "They usually mean no harm, but their full intentions can be difficult to determine. As he was not repelled by your amulet, and I doubt he is powerful enough to counteract it, he is likely not evil."

"Hmph." I walked back to the couch, but didn't feel like sitting back down. "That little guy creeped me out a little. Now I'm feeling kind of antsy."

"Would you like me to conjure up some relaxation tonic for you?" Sapphira offered.

"I don't like that idea," I said. "I'll pass."

"There's no need to worry," said Sapphira. "It is safe and will help you relax."

"I said I'll pass," I repeated. "Maybe I'll see what Aaron's doing today. I was gonna stay home, but now I really don't feel like being here."

Sapphira lifted her hand, and my cell phone drifted out of my bedroom and floated over to me.

"Hey, thanks," I said, catching the phone out of the air.

"You are welcome," she said.

She's starting to learn how things work around here, I thought.

201

I called Aaron, and we made plans to meet at a bakery downtown. Why a bakery, Aaron didn't say. He insisted on it, so I agreed.

"I'm leaving now," I told Sapphira after I got ready. "Stay here in case that Toony dude comes back."

"What should I do if he returns?" she asked.

"If he needs to talk to me, have him leave a message," I said. "I don't want him showing up when I'm around other people, so tell him not to come looking for me. And make sure he doesn't break or steal anything."

"Understood."

I was beginning to feel as if I had a watchdog that could speak. Sapphira had proven herself to be a good protector, and that made me feel a little safer. The only thing was if it weren't for Sapphira in the first place, I wouldn't need all the extra protection.

"See ya," I said as I walked out the door.

"Have a good day," I heard Sapphira say behind me.

The bakery where Aaron wanted to meet was in a part of town I didn't know very well. He gave me general directions when we discussed our plans over the phone, but Aaron wasn't the best at giving directions. I ended up driving down every street, keeping an eye out for the benchmarks he gave me: an old gas station, a giant plywood gorilla, a purple fire hydrant, a tree with a fat bird living in it, etc. Although I found most of them, I still couldn't make any sense of where I was supposed to go.

After driving around like a lost tourist, I finally found the bakery. More precisely, I found Aaron's truck first. The bright yellow paint was like a beacon amidst the mostly gray, white, and black cars that seemed to fill every street. I parallel parked behind Aaron's truck and walked inside the bakery.

"There you are!" Aaron announced before I could even get a whiff of the baked aroma.

"Yeah, sorry it took so long," I said. "I got a little lost."

"How do you get lost in Elm Valley?" said Aaron flatly. "It ain't the city."

"Why are we at a bakery?" I asked, looking around. "Did you want a cake or something?"

"Doughnuts, man," said Aaron with a grin. "I wanted some doughnuts, but I didn't have any at home. The struggle was real."

"I was just curious," I shrugged. "It's just a random place to meet, don't you think?"

"It's not that random," said Aaron. "Now let's see. What kind of doughnuts do they have?"

The two of us peered through the glass display at all of the freshly made doughnuts. Just looking at them all made me crave some, and it was beginning to look like doughnuts were for lunch. After Aaron bought his share, I found myself taking out my wallet and purchasing my own bevy of doughnuts as well. We walked out of the bakery with our own bags and took a seat on a nearby bench.

"Oh yeah," said Aaron through a mouthful, "this is what I've been waiting for!"

"How long have you had doughnuts on the brain?" I asked, looking through my selection to see which one to eat first.

"Since last night," he told me. "I even had a dream about doughnuts."

"Hmm, you don't say," I said, taking a bite of my raspberry jelly doughnut.

"So, what's new in your world, Mike?" Aaron asked through another mouthful of the same doughnut.

Without needing to think about it, I immediately jumped to the important news.

"I have a girlfriend now," I boasted.

Aaron actually stopped chewing for a moment as he stared at me.

"Mike, you dog!" he said cheerfully. "You big player, you! Who is she?"

"Her name's Hayley," I said, not being able to hold back the bragging tone in my voice.

"Cool," he said. "Is she cute?"

"Aw, yeah," I said with a huge smile.

203

"Cheers to that!" said Aaron, holding up another doughnut. "So, that Japanese girl you were talking about. There's nothing stopping me from going after her now, right?"

"Uh, I wouldn't recommend it," I said, remembering that Miyuki had a boyfriend.

"C'mon, why not?" said Aaron. "You have a girlfriend now. That means all of your fantasies are null, void, and up for grabs."

"What fantasies?" I said. "It's not like that."

"Of course not," said Aaron, "not anymore. You've got your own woman to go home to now."

For a second, I thought he was referring to Sapphira. I quickly realized he was talking about Hayley, and there was no way Aaron would know that I've been shacking up with a woman this whole time, albeit a demon woman.

"Did you kiss her already?" he asked.

"Duh," I replied. "We're official."

"Did you, um, do anything else?" he said, elbowing me while moving his eyebrows up and down.

"Uh, not yet," I said quietly.

"Not yet, huh?" he said with a grin. "That's a pretty confident thing to say!"

"What'd you want me to say?" I asked.

"Nothing particular," he said. "All you have to do is take her back to your place, get her in the mood, maybe cook up a romantic meal or whatever, then strike while the iron's hot! Pow!"

"I don't need your advice," I said, reaching into my bag for another doughnut.

"Alright, do what works for you," said Aaron, stuffing another doughnut into his mouth.

Thanks to Aaron, I started thinking about what a romantic evening with Hayley would be like at my apartment. All I would have to do is tell Sapphira to disappear for a while, and everything would be peachy. That is, as long as things like Toony didn't make any more sudden appearances. With that thought, something else came to mind, and I couldn't help but ask Aaron.

"Hey, what do you know about hobgoblins?" I asked.

"Hmm?" Aaron finished his doughnut. "Isn't that the stuff in red blood cells that carries oxygen?"

"No, that's hemoglobin," I said. "I'm talking about a *hobgoblin*."

"Hobgoblin," said Aaron, taking a second to think. "Isn't that some kind of term for something? I don't really remember."

"I'm talking about the mythical creature," I said. "You've never heard of it?"

"Man, I'm not into that crap," said Aaron. "Why do you want to know?"

"Oh, just curious," I said.

"These doughnuts did the trick," said Aaron, crumpling up his bag and tossing it into a nearby trashcan.

Out of nowhere, I heard the sound of a machine gun being fired. For a second, it seemed as if somebody was shooting at us, then I realized the gunshots were coming from Aaron's pants. He reached into his pocket and took out his cell phone.

"Hello?" he answered. "I'm just hanging out with a buddy.... No, nothing important.... Alright, bye."

"Why would you have a ringtone like that turned up so loud?" I asked.

"So I can hear it," he said, standing up. "That was my uncle. He needs me for something, so I gotta go."

"Oh," I replied, "okay."

"I'll see ya later," said Aaron.

"Later," I said.

I remained seated on the bench for a moment, pondering my next course of action. Despite my original plan of staying at home and doing nothing, I didn't feel quite ready to go home. Hayley was probably bored at her house, so I decided to give her a call. When I attempted to use my phone, however, I couldn't get a signal.

"This piece of junk," I muttered. "I have decent service here. Why won't it work?"

Disgruntled, I shoved my phone back into my pocket, stood up, threw away my trash, and walked over to my car. With nothing else for me to do, I would just go back home and be lazy for the day. Sitting in my car, I put the key in the ignition. However, the car wouldn't start.

"You have to be kidding me," I said in frustration after several failed attempts to start the car.

My best option at this point was to call somebody for help. Cormorant was the only person I knew who could probably help me out, but I didn't have his phone number. The only way I could contact him was through Raven, and I really didn't want to call her. Regardless, it was probably the best thing to do, so I took out my phone again and selected Raven's number from my list of contacts.

A few minutes passed and none of my calls were still going through. Feeling quite pissed off at this point, I got out of my car and started walking, thinking that a change of location would help my phone. When I made it to the first crosswalk, I tried calling Raven again, but it was no use.

I strutted down the street to the next crosswalk and tried making another call, but there was nothing. Mental images of me smashing my phone against a wall flickered in my head, but I kept my cool.

I'll just ask someone if I can use their phone, I thought. *Someone is bound to let me do that.*

As I looked around for someone I could ask, a heart-lifting sight presented itself to me right on cue. A soldier dressed in full camouflage fatigues was walking up to me, and I immediately recognized who he was.

"Hey, Eli!" I called out. "Do you remember me?"

"You're Michael," he said with a solid demeanor.

"Yeah, that's right," I said.

"Do you need help with something?" he asked.

I was a little surprised that he figured it out so quickly.

"Uh, I do, actually," I said. "My car won't start, and my phone isn't letting me get through to anyone. Do you have a phone I could borrow for a minute?"

"No," he replied, "I don't have a phone."

"Aw," I groaned. "Why don't they have any payphones anywhere? It's times like this when payphones aren't obsolete."

"Where's your car?" Eli asked.

"It's a few blocks down," I said. "I can take you to it."

Eli followed me down the street to my car. For some reason, just having him nearby made me feel a little better.

"So, how have you been?" I asked him.

"I've been good," he replied. "What about you?"

"Except for just now, pretty good," I said. "What are you doing in town today?"

"Seeing the town," he said.

"You don't come here often?" I asked.

"Not very often," he said. "How are your friends?"

"They're doing alright, I think," I said. "I was just with one of them not too long ago. I met him to get doughnuts."

"What's his name?" Eli asked.

"Aaron," I said. "He's a little odd, but cool."

"I see," said Eli. "Have you seen your family recently?"

"Uh, no," I said. "It's been a while, actually. You know, it's kinda funny how I was also having car trouble the first time we met. Isn't that weird?"

"Why is that weird?" he asked.

"Well, it's just ironic," I said.

"Right, it is," he said with a smirk.

I wasn't sure if it was the fatigues or what, but Eli seemed like a natural protector. Having him around, I felt confident that he could do something to help me out with my car.

"This is my car," I told him when we made it back.

He placed his hand on my shoulder with a firm grip.

"Let's see what I can do, then," he said.

"I'll open the hood for you," I said.

"Try starting it first," he said.

I got inside my car and put the key in the ignition. When I tried starting it, I was surprised when it started right up. I felt a little stupid for dragging Eli along for nothing, but I was more relieved about my car working.

"Well, I guess it's working now," I told Eli with a grin. "Sorry for bringing you all this way for nothing."

"No worries," said Eli. "Will you be on your way?"

"Uh, yeah," I replied. "Thanks anyway."

"You're welcome," he said. "Take care."

Heading home, I once again felt the need to sit around and do nothing for the rest of the day. TV sounded like a good plan, maybe some video games. If only I had a more constructive hobby, then I would probably work on that all day. I used to put together model ships when I was a kid, but never picked the hobby back up after junior high school.

A muddy feeling gradually filled my head while I was driving, then slowly spread down through my body. I dismissed it as just tiredness at first, until it started getting worse. My initial concern was falling asleep at the wheel, but it didn't seem like my mind was impaired at all. There seemed to be a sludge-like aura surrounding me, and I was beginning to get concerned. Was there something wrong with me, or was it something else?

I made it back to the apartments, feeling no better. While I walked to the building entrance, I tried rubbing my eyes and taking deep breaths, but nothing eased the weird feeling. My balance, eyesight, and everything else seemed okay, though.

Right when I walked into my apartment, I was quickly confronted by Sapphira.

"Stop right there," she told me, holding her hand out.

Somewhat surprised, I immediately froze in place before I could close the door.

"What is it?" I asked. "Sapphira, it's me."

"I know it's you," she said, still holding her hand out like a traffic cop. "Welcome home, Michael."

"Why are you acting like that?" I asked. "Do you, um, notice something wrong?"

"Something is peculiar about you," she told me. "Also, you have a visitor."

"One thing at a time!" I said, closing the door to the apartment behind me. "Can I move from this spot?"

"I don't think that will be a problem," said Sapphira, putting her hand down. "Your visitor is asking to speak with you."

"Who is it?" I muttered, knowing the answer already.

"Toony," she inevitably replied.

"Tell him I'm dying," I said flatly, rubbing my head as I walked over to the couch.

"He says you'll regret not having an audience with him," she said.

"Are you actually talking to him right now?" I said, looking around.

"Yes, without words," she answered.

"Oh, alright," I sighed. "Come in, Toony."

I plopped down on the couch as the tiny hobgoblin appeared in midair. Without delay, he fluttered over to me with his little wings.

"Oh my, oh dear, oh my," he said as he approached me. "This certainly is unusual. No doubt you feel what I'm talking about, sonny."

"You mean this weird, heavy feeling I have?" I said. "Yeah, it's pretty hard for me to ignore."

"Any idea what this is?" Toony asked Sapphira.

"I am not familiar with this sort of energy," she replied, "but it appears to be malicious."

"Malicious." I chuckled, although I didn't feel amused in the slightest way.

"Now, I could be mistaken," said Toony, eyeing me, "but a curse is what this reminds me of."

"Curse?" I said meekly. "A real curse?"

"Is there anything you can do for the boy?" Toony asked Sapphira.

"I will do my best," she replied. "Stand up, Michael."

I got off the comfortable couch and stood in the middle of the living room. Sapphira stood directly in front of me and took both of my hands in hers. Her skin felt soft and smooth, but cold and strangely lifeless.

She began reciting something in a different language, but it didn't sound like Latin to me. Whatever she was saying, it created a magical circle of light that drew itself across the carpet. Elaborate symbols and markings began to fill the circle and surround me. Her sharp, yellow eyes peered into mine as her hands grew colder, eventually becoming like ice. When I moved a little out of discomfort, I noticed how rock hard her hold was on me. The unmovable strength behind her grasp was a little frightening and unlike anyone else's.

Suddenly, she stopped the incantation. The magic circle quickly vanished, but the muddy feeling did not. Taking a step back, I looked at Toony, who merely shrugged.

"I apologize," said Sapphira. "I am unable to have any effect on it."

"This sucks!" I croaked. "When the hell did I get cursed?"

"That's hard to say," said Toony. "It depends on the type of curse and what caused it, both of which I can't be certain. You might have had it placed on you a while ago, and it took some time to work. Or you might have already been cursed, but something had to activate its effects."

"But if I was already cursed," I said, "Sapphira would probably have known by now."

"This is the first I've noticed it," said Sapphira. "However, all I know is that this energy is far beyond my own power. It may have gone undetected because of that. Currently, I have no way of knowing what its effects will be."

"I have one thing to say, though," said Toony with a gnarled grin. "Such a curse as this is truly remarkable to behold! I believe only a very powerful entity is capable of something like this."

"How do you know that?" I asked.

"Just from experience," he replied. "Remember this, boy, I could be wrong. I'm no expert on the subject."

"So, how powerful was the thing that did this?" I asked, getting more anxious.

"Guessing far more powerful than your gal over there," said Toony, pointing to Sapphira. "That's rather surprising, since she's no weakling compared to most dwellers of the other realm. You snagged yourself a trophy demon slave, hee hee!"

I collapsed on the couch in a heap of hopelessness, wishing I could just pass out and sleep it off.

"I'm doomed," I groaned. "Doomed, man! Totally done for! I don't need this, damn it!"

"There, there," said Toony. "Not all hope is lost! There's bound to be something in that grimoire I mentioned earlier. We need to find it, is all."

"Oh, is that so?" I mumbled. "How do I know *you* weren't the one who did this to me?"

Toony burst out in laughter. With his squeaky voice, it was easily one of the most annoying things I'd ever heard.

"You're saying I possess more power than your demon slave?" he squawked.

"Then how'd you know I was gonna need that book so soon?" I asked angrily, sitting upright on the couch. "I knew you were a shady little bug!"

"Hey, no need for insults," said Toony. "I have that ability. It's a little similar to short-term memory, except in the future and not the past. Do you understand, lad?"

"I don't really care, lad!" I grunted. "Where's Chad? I'm getting that book right now!"

I took my cell phone out of my pocket and called Chad. Luckily, the phone seemed to work fine. While listening to the ringing on the other end of the line, I took some deep breaths in an attempt to lower my blood pressure.

"Hello?" Chad answered.

Yes! The call went through! I thought happily.

"Hey, what's up?" I said casually.

"Mike, how's it going?" said Chad.

"I have a favor to ask," I said. "There's an acquaintance of mine who was interested in taking a look at that grimoire you have. I was wondering if I could borrow it for a while."

"Oh, sure thing!" Chad agreed. "I don't have any uses for it, really. That won't be a problem."

"Great, thanks," I said. "When do you think I can get it?"

"Hmm, whenever is fine with me," said Chad. "Do you need it soon?"

211

"The sooner, the better," I told him. "I can even pick it up from your house."

"That works for me," said Chad. "I'll give you my address and directions to write down."

I scrambled to find a piece of paper and a pen, then jotted down the directions to Chad's house. Just by listening to him explain how to get there, I could tell he was much better at giving directions than Aaron.

"Alright, I'll head over there now," I told him.

"Yup, see ya when ya get here," he said before hanging up.

As soon as the call ended, Toony hovered over to me.

"So you *did* know the book's location," he said. "Ho ho, you're a sly one!"

"I'm going to get it now," I said, ignoring Toony. "Stay here, Sapphira."

"Understood."

"I better go with you," said Toony. "Monitoring your condition is a good idea."

"Fine," I muttered. "Just stay out of sight."

Toony vanished into thin air, and it made me a little uneasy knowing he could still keep track of me even though he was "gone." However, I had bigger problems to think about at the moment, so I was just going to deal with it.

The heavy, muddy feeling was still growing stronger, but the rate of increase seemed to be slowing down. As I hurried down the stairs, it was nice knowing that my mind and body still weren't impaired, even though I felt like I had just woken up from an anesthesia-induced nap.

Chad's directions took me right to his house with no problems. After making sure the address matched up, I walked up to the door and rang the doorbell. Within seconds, Chad greeted me.

"Mike, good to see ya!" he said, handing me the book. "Here's that for you."

"Thanks, man," I said. "I appreciate it."

"Are you busy right now?" he asked. "I'm free to hang out if you're down with that."

"Sorry, I can't," I said. "I need to get going. There's stuff to do."

"Right, I gotcha," he said. "In that case, take it easy, dawg."

"You too," I replied. "See you in history tomorrow."

"Hold on," said Chad.

"What's up?" I asked, getting impatient.

"I heard you have a girl," he said with a smile.

"Um, yup," I said. "Her name's Hayley. How'd you find out?"

"Aaron told me," he said. "He said you told him today."

"He already told you that so soon?" I asked.

Chad gave me a playful punch on the shoulder.

"Good work, man," he said. "Take good care of her."

"Yeah, I will," I said. "See ya."

"Later, Mike."

I would have loved to stay a while and talk about Hayley with Chad, but that wasn't happening today. As soon as I got back in my car, Toony appeared in the passenger seat.

"Hey, you got it!" he squeaked excitedly. "Let's take a look, shall we?"

"Whoa, not here!" I told him. "We should wait until we get back to the apartment where it's more private."

"Suit yourself, boy," he said before vanishing again.

Wasting no time, I drove back to my apartment. In my rush, I had almost forgotten about the car trouble I had earlier that day. There didn't appear to be any problems at this point. The last thing I wanted was to have my car break down. For all I knew, the curse on me would probably make that happen.

Surprisingly, my car held in there until I made it back. I burst into my apartment, clutching the grimoire to my chest as if it would float away if I were to let it go. Toony and Sapphira appeared almost simultaneously as I closed the door and locked it.

"Welcome home, Michael," said Sapphira.

"Golly," said Toony, "I can feel the energy from the curse is growing darn thick!"

213

"I concur," Sapphira added. "Michael's soul is likely condemned at this point."

"W-what?" I croaked. "What's that mean?"

"Look at it this way," Toony told me. "Pretend your soul is a lizard. Right now, that lizard just had one of its legs cut off. It's locked in a disease-filled cage guarded by a ferocious lizard-eating beast."

"That's terrible!" I replied with a shudder. "Of all the ways to explain it, why like that? Let's hurry up and do something!"

"Place the book on the floor," Toony instructed.

I did as Toony said, and he began flipping through it one page at a time. With each passing second, my anxiety meter went up another notch. Hopefully, it wasn't too late to reverse the damage, if the curse could be fixed at all. I didn't want my soul to be trapped like an injured lizard!

"Allow me," said Sapphira, kneeling down in front of the grimoire. With a single flip, she turned to a page near the back of the book.

"Look at you!" said Toony, sounding impressed.

"Is that the right spell thingy?" I asked.

Sapphira nodded.

"Wow, that's incredible," I said in awe. "You knew right where it was!"

"I know this book very well," she replied. "I was trapped by it for over two hundred years. However, I did not memorize the exact details of any spells that I had deemed unnecessary at the time, such as this one."

"Good news, lad," said Toony, "we might be able to set you right!"

"Oh, thank God," I breathed.

"This is one of two spells I assume will work," said Sapphira. "If this spell is not correct, it will have consequences."

I gulped hard.

"What consequences?" I said wearily.

"Your hair will turn gray and grow twice as fast," she explained.

"Uh, and what if the *other* spell is incorrect?" I asked.

"Your body will begin to rot and you will die within seven to fifteen weeks, depending on your metabolism."

"Then we'd better try this one first," I said, feeling a little sick.

"Stand up straight," Sapphira told me.

She took my hands like she did earlier and recited the incantation. Another magic circle formed on the carpet around me, and I noticed it was a little smaller this time. The symbols and markings inside it were also notably different. This process was a lot quicker than the previous one, and it was over in less than twenty seconds.

"How do you feel?" she asked when the magic circle disappeared.

I looked around. The muddy feeling had disappeared, and I found myself literally leaping for joy. For the record, I don't often leap for joy, so that should tell you just how good I felt.

"This is amazing!" I declared loudly. "That cursed feeling is gone! I think it worked!"

"Yes, I don't sense it as well," said Toony. "I believe it was a success!"

"So it seems," said Sapphira.

"Yeah! Alright!" I yelled, marching around the living room.

"You might want to keep it down, my boy," said Toony. "You have neighbors living below you."

"Oh, that's right," I said, stopping in my tracks. "I forgot."

"Well, if everything is settled here," said Toony, "I'll be borrowing this book now."

"You'll bring it back, right?" I asked. "It's not mine, and I don't want Chad to get mad if something happens to it."

"I'll return it to him," said Toony, lifting the book like an ant lifting a crumb. "Farewell, lad and lass! Ho ho!"

Before I could tell Toony that it would be better if I returned it to Chad myself, he vanished with the book.

"What if Chad sees Toony in his house?" I asked Sapphira. "I don't know what he would do."

"It should be nothing to worry about," said Sapphira. "Toony is more clever than that."

"You don't say," I muttered. "Honestly, I couldn't care less right now. I'm cured! I only wish I knew what cursed me to begin with. Whatever it was, I'd like to have an idea so I know what to look out for in the future."

"It's difficult to say," said Sapphira. "I assume it was another demon."

"Another one?" I rubbed the sapphire amulet in my pocket. "I don't like the thought of that."

"I do not detect any other spiritual entities nearby," said Sapphira. "It is safe here for now."

"It might be safe for the moment," I said, "but now I'm really starting to get concerned. Even with my amulet, a demon was able to place a curse on me."

"That curse could have been placed on you long before you received the amulet," she explained. "Additionally, the amulet will only have a minimal effect against very powerful entities."

"Can't I get it upgraded or something?" I asked. "Is there a spell for that?"

"It would require a virgin sacrifice," said Sapphira.

"Then couldn't you make another amulet?" I asked. "One that's more effective?"

"Yours is the most powerful amulet that does not require a virgin sacrifice," she said.

"I'm not sacrificing any virgins!" I told her. "What if you made another one just like this one? Would it increase the effect if I had two?"

"It doesn't work that way," she said.

"Ah, so this is basically the best I can get," I muttered, pulling out my amulet to look at it.

"I will protect you with all my strength," said Sapphira. "You should not worry."

"Hmm, thanks," I muttered. "Let me know if any threatening stuff pops up."

"Yes, I will."

"In that case," I said, falling back on the couch, "I'm staying right here all day. I really don't want to deal with anything else today."

Just as originally planned, I spent the rest of my lazy Sunday doing absolutely nothing constructive.

~Opus 16~

The following day, I entered the club conference room feeling sleepy for no apparent reason. In an attempt to get my juices flowing, I helped myself to some hot tea, although I never really liked tea very much. Something about sipping quietly on a hot mug in a room occupied by a secret organization made me feel strangely sophisticated.

Miss Flamingo entered the room with a stately stride and quickly took her seat at the end of the table. Everyone sat down with anticipation for today's meeting, though I couldn't say I was really looking forward to it.

"Raven," said Miss Flamingo only seconds after sitting down.

"Yes?" Raven asked.

"I've fully examined the documents you and Roadrunner retrieved for me last week," said Miss Flamingo. "Your next assignment is based off the information gained from those documents. Oriole, will you print out Raven's briefing report?"

"Yes, ma'am," Oriole replied as she immediately headed over to the laptop desk.

"Miss Flamingo?" I asked.

"What is it, Roadrunner?"

"Does this mean that me and Raven are going out on another assignment tonight?"

"That's right," said Miss Flamingo. "That's not a problem, is it?"

"Er, no," I said, choosing my words carefully. "It just seemed kind of soon. We just went on a risky one last time. Uh, not that I'm complaining, really."

"Consider it this way," said Miss Flamingo. "You and Raven are very important to the club right now. If I didn't need you to do something for me, then I wouldn't send you."

I guess that seems fair, I thought.

"Kookaburra. Skylark," said Miss Flamingo. "You two will also be given an assignment for tonight."

"Right," said Kookaburra.

"Okay," said Skylark.

I looked at Kookaburra and Skylark, who both appeared a little grim. They were about to be given a new assignment, meaning a malicious entity had probably emerged and was roaming around nearby. Any complaints I had about being given a new assignment so soon had gone completely out the window. At least my work involved dealing with regular humans.

As soon as the briefing report was printed, Oriole walked over and handed it to Raven. Without letting me look at it, Raven stood up with a dutiful twinkle in her eye.

"I'll get on it right away," she announced. "Roadrunner, c'mon."

I followed Raven out of the room and down the stairs, catching up to her before she could leave the cabin.

"Hey, Raven!" I said. "Let me see the report."

"Why do you want to see it?" she asked.

"We went over this last time," I said irritably. "The more I know about the assignment, the more I can help you."

"I'm glad you're so eager," she said, handing me the paper. "If you think it'll help, then take a look at it while I get my bass."

I had forgotten about Raven's lucky song that she insisted on playing before a mission. Making myself comfortable on the couch in the cabin living room, I looked over the briefing report to get an idea of what possible crimes I'd be committing this time.

As far as I could tell, our mission had to do with the person whose documents we had to take from the college: Wyatt Halabi. My first thought was that we were going back to the college to return the stolen documents, but as I read further, that didn't appear to be the case. Instead, it looked as if we were going to confront Wyatt himself and ask him a few questions. Just like last time, the report was confusing and ambiguous, so I wasn't able to understand much more of it.

Raven's lucky, plucky bass riff felt somewhat like a battle theme as I folded up the report and stuck it in my pocket. After the previous week's assignment, I was willing to let

219

anything help us complete our task, so I patiently waited for Raven to finish her song without any argument.

"You ready to go?" she asked as soon as the last note was plucked.

"Yeah," I replied.

The two of us squeezed into the little electric car and headed straight for downtown Elm Valley. For whatever reason, I was feeling strangely optimistic this time. With everything that had been going on, I wouldn't have been surprised if Raven's song really did have some kind of magical effect on our success. Either that, or I was just getting tired of being worried.

We pulled into a busy fast food restaurant in the heart of town called Sizzlin' Quickie. I had never heard of the place, but it looked popular since I could see the inside was packed with people. The long line for the drive-thru stretched all the way around the building as we took our place at the end of it.

"What are we doing here?" I asked Raven. "Are we getting something to eat?"

"*I* am," she said. "I don't know about you, but I'm a little hungry. Plus, it'll look less suspicious if we're actually eating."

"Suspicious? What do you mean?"

"This is where Wyatt Halabi works," she explained. "He should be off in about half an hour. Didn't you read the report? It said all of this in it."

"Um, I tried to."

"Oriole writes her reports really weird," said Raven, moving up in the drive-thru line. "Miss Flamingo demands they be written in a way so that non-club members have a hard time understanding them."

"So...what's the secret to decoding them?" I asked, unfolding the report and looking over it again.

"I don't know," she said. "You just learn, I guess. It's kind of like learning a new language."

No, it's not.

We had to wait a couple of minutes before we could place our orders. When we approached the speaker box, I figured it wouldn't hurt to grab something to eat for myself, so

I ordered two hotdogs and some mozzarella sticks. The wait to get the food was another handful of minutes, but the smell that flooded the car when we were handed the bags told me that it was worth it. Raven backed into a parking space facing the entrance so we could keep an eye out for Wyatt. She took out her cell phone, brought up a picture on it, and handed it to me.

"That's a picture of our target," she said. "Poofy dark hair, slightly dark complexion, five-foot eleven. He appears to be of Middle Eastern descent."

"Alright," I said, handing the phone back.

"Did you memorize his face?" she asked firmly, not taking her phone. "You need to make sure you know what he looks like."

"I got it," I muttered. "Take your phone."

Raven snatched her phone out of my hand and quickly grabbed a black case from the backseat. As small as her car was, I was surprised it even had a backseat.

"Open this," she said, thrusting the case into my lap. "We'll need what's in it."

I unlatched the lid of the case and looked inside. The only thing I found was a small phial containing a clear liquid.

"Oh no," I groaned. "Not again."

"What are you groaning about?" Raven asked, taking the phial out of the case. "It's just the sleeping potion."

"Yeah, I know," I said, "Do we really have to use it?"

"It's the best way to complete our mission," she said bluntly, putting the phial in her jacket pocket.

Before we started eating, Raven reached into her glove compartment and took out a plastic bottle with a nozzle, just like the kind you see with ketchup and mustard on condiment stands. She used it to squirt something onto her fries, drenching them until they became somewhat soggy.

"What's that?" I asked, knowing the answer could be anything from vitamin water to contact lens saline.

"Malt vinegar," she said. "I absolutely adore vinegar fries. You want some?"

"No," I replied with a grimace. "I hate vinegar."

The hotdogs I ordered were great, and I had to remember to check this restaurant out again. I was just about to start eating my second hotdog when someone walked out of the restaurant. A quick look was all I needed to see that it was Wyatt Halabi. He wasn't supposed to be off work for another fifteen minutes or so, but there was no mistaking his face.

"Hey, that's him," said Raven quietly. "Go get him."

"Why don't *you* go get him?" I asked.

"I'm still eating," she said, getting overly aggravated.

"I'm still eating, too," I replied stubbornly.

As Raven crudely sucked air in through her nose and loudly cleared her throat, I could tell right away that something bad was about to happen. She then spit a blob two feet through the air, which landed perfectly on my hotdog. Determined not to let her win, I casually took a bite, loogie and all, and swallowed it. With squinted eyes, Raven quickly grabbed her bottle of vinegar and sprayed it all over my food.

"Gah, what the hell, Raven?" I said angrily.

"Go!" she barked.

I had no idea what I was going to say to Wyatt as I walked over to his car. My only hope was that Raven would do something to help me out, but I wasn't betting on that.

"Excuse me," I said as I approached Wyatt before he got into his car. "Is your name Wyatt?"

"Yeah," he replied. "Do I know you?"

"My name's Mike," I said. "Um, I have a friend who wants to talk to you."

I wondered if I shouldn't have used my real name, but introducing myself as "Roadrunner" would seem a little strange.

"Er, okay." He looked a little skeptical. "Who's your friend?"

"She's in that car over there," I said, pointing at the electric car. "She goes to Elm Valley College with me."

"Oh yeah?" said Wyatt, scoping out the car to try to get a good look at Raven. He was obviously more interested now. "Why doesn't she ask me herself?"

222

"Well, that's the thing," I said. "She's a little shy. You should go over there and say something."

"I just got off work," he said, "so I was on my way home. My uniform smells like grease and chicken."

"That's alright," I said assuredly. "She likes the smell of food and honest work."

Wyatt chuckled and shook his head.

"Alright," he said. "Introduce me."

Wyatt followed me back to Raven's car. She was tilting the box of fries back to empty the crumbs into her mouth when I knocked on her window. With an expression that said, *What do you think you're doing?*, she rolled down her window.

"I brought someone with me," I told her with a grin. "Wyatt, this is Claire. Claire, Wyatt."

"Hello there," said Wyatt. "Your friend said you had something to tell me."

"That's right," said Raven nonchalantly.

"I told him that you've had your eye on him for a while," I said, trying to get Raven on the same page as me.

"Hey, I've seen you before," said Wyatt. "Weren't you in that band?"

Raven's eyes lit up so quickly that it actually surprised me.

"Were you at the Boney Feather?" she asked, suddenly sounding interested.

"Yeah, at the beginning of the school year," said Wyatt. "Your band played its last gig."

Raven got out of the car with an enthusiastic smile. She always seemed pretty passionate about her music, so this conversation was probably striking a chord with her, no pun intended.

"Our band was Triangular Lockjaw," she said. "I liked playing for them, but things happened. We all had to go our own ways, so we decided to pour our hearts into one last show."

"You guys rocked!" said Wyatt. "Do you have a CD out?"

223

Oh yeah, I forgot about asking for a CD, I thought. *I want one as well.*

"Not really," said Raven, "but I can burn one for you. The files are on the computer at our studio."

"That'd be great," said Wyatt. "I'd love to hear those songs again."

"Well, I could take you over there," said Raven. "It's not much, but you can check it out. It's not very far away."

"You'd do that?" Wyatt asked.

"Yeah, it's no problem," she said. "Then I can make that CD for you."

Wait a minute. Aren't we supposed to be on a mission? What are you doing, Raven?

"That'd be awesome!" said Wyatt eagerly. "I don't have anything else to do tonight. Should I just follow you there?"

"Yup." Raven spun her key ring around her finger and looked at me. "You ready to go, Ethan?"

"Ethan?" said Wyatt, sounding confused. "I thought you said your name was Mike."

"Uh, Ethan's my middle name," I lied. "Old friends and family call me Ethan."

"Oh," Wyatt chuckled. "I was a little confused for a second, but I gotcha. I'll meet you two at the studio then?"

"Yeah, just follow us," said Raven.

Raven and I got back into her car. I examined my vinegar-soaked hotdog, but the smell alone was enough to render it inedible for me. I tossed it into the bag with the rest of the trash and rolled it up tightly.

"Do you know what you're doing?" I asked Raven as we were exiting the parking lot. "We're on a mission. We can't mess around just because you want to make friends with a fan."

"I know that!" said Raven shortly. "Don't you trust me?"

"Well, I'm just making sure," I said. "I don't want to jeopardize the assignment."

"This is the perfect opportunity," she said. "My initial plan was to use the sleeping potion to kidnap him, but this

224

works out better. You said yourself that you're against the sleeping potion."

"What exactly are we doing with Wyatt?" I asked. "I still don't know."

"He's got some information," she explained. "It's our job to extract some things from him."

"When you say extract, I hope you mean only information," I said, concerned.

"Don't worry, he'll be fine," she said.

"Uh, whatever you say," I muttered. "So, does this studio even exist, or are we gonna take him back to the cabin and have Cormorant whack him upside the skull?"

"Yeah, the studio really does exist and we're going there," said Raven. "One other thing: never give your real name when on a mission. The club depends on secrecy. Hiding your true identity is important."

"But what if I bump into the guy in the future?" I asked. "I can't keep lying about my name to everyone we meet during an assignment."

"You didn't seem to have a problem when you introduced me as 'Claire,'" said Raven. "That was a good move, though, but what's the point of our club aliases if you don't even use them? That's why we have them."

"Well, I don't think it's that big of a deal," I said flatly. "As long as I don't mention the club itself, it should be fine to use our real names. And introducing myself as 'Roadrunner' might make things awkward."

Raven snickered quietly, and I could only wonder what was going through her head.

"You're an interesting person, Roadrunner," she said. "I don't know why, but you just are."

I'm not the interesting one here. You have it all backwards. Normal things just seem unusual to you.

Riding around while trapped in a tiny car with Raven is an experience that not too many people would enjoy. I can understand being in a car with a bickering spouse, whiney kids, or even obnoxious in-laws, but this girl was a league of her own when it came to a cruising companion. Whether it's good or bad is a total mystery to me, and I figure it just falls into one of those gray areas between "obviously crappy" and "illogically okay."

Less than twenty minutes away from Sizzlin' Quickie, just beyond the outskirts of town, was a piece of property occupied by nothing more than a small building. Raven pulled into the gravel driveway that was being overtaken by the grass. Sure enough, Wyatt pulled in right behind us. Deep down inside, I wanted to tell the poor guy to run and hide, but Miss Flamingo would have probably skinned me alive for compromising the mission. I had a mental image of her sitting in her cabin living room with my head mounted over the fireplace as she sipped her hot tea.

"This is the old recording studio!" said Raven as Wyatt looked around.

"It's out in the middle of nowhere," Wyatt commented. "You could jam to the max out here and nobody would notice."

"That's the idea," said Raven, looking through her keys. "Ethan, get my bass out of the car."

Reluctantly, I removed the bass guitar from the backseat and was surprised at how heavy it was. I had never held a bass before, but I assumed that the case was adding a lot of extra weight.

"Be careful with my baby," she said. "Any damage you do to it I'll do to you."

Wyatt laughed, but if only he knew that Raven was being dead serious.

Raven unlocked the door and switched on the lights. When I stepped inside, I was actually taken aback by how awesome it was. I had been expecting something a little more makeshift, but the studio appeared to be nearly professional. That really showed just how serious Triangular Lockjaw was with their music.

"Hey, this is really nice," said Wyatt.

"Damien, our lead singer, contributed the most to this studio," said Raven. "His dad used to be a producer, or something like that."

"No wonder you guys rocked so much!" said Wyatt. "You had all this awesome equipment."

226

"It's not the equipment that makes the band," said Raven pensively, "but it helped a bunch."

"Is it okay for us to be here?" I asked as I placed the bass guitar on the floor next to an amp. "That Damien guy won't get upset?"

"I doubt anyone else will show up," she said.

"So it's *not* okay," I said.

"It'll be fine," she said. "I'm here. If it was just you guys, then it'd be less than fine. Wait out here for a minute while I set up the chilleteria."

"The what?" I asked.

"The chill cafeteria," she said. "The chilleteria. That's what we called it."

I waited with Wyatt in the main entrance area, thinking about what Raven had in store next. I looked around at the equipment and wondered why the band would break up, but I figured it was for a pretty solid reason since they decided to abandon such a great setup in the studio.

"Alright, you can come in now," Raven called.

The chilleteria was nothing more than a break room at the back of the studio. Raven insisted that we all sit down for a minute and have something to drink. She made some instant lemonade with a powder mix that happened to be there and poured a glass for each of us.

"How long have you been in the band?" Wyatt asked as Raven handed him a glass.

"Oh, about two years," she replied. "I was the last person they recruited."

"It's too bad you had to split," said Wyatt, taking a sip. "Hey, this is pretty good."

"Drink all you want," said Raven.

Raven and Wyatt chatted for a few minutes about the band and other things. I didn't know what Raven had planned, but it sure didn't seem like she was getting on with it. Not wanting to cause any problems and having nothing to really say, I remained quiet and waited for some kind of cue.

"You're pretty quiet," Wyatt told me.

"I'm just tired," I said. "I'm normally not like this, but it's been a long day."

"Yeah, I see what you mean," he said, yawning deeply. "I'm pretty tired myself. Work was killer today, ya know?"

As he drank the last of his lemonade, I noticed that Raven was keeping a close eye on him. When he yawned again after the last gulp, I was certain I had figured out Raven's plan.

"Oh man," said Wyatt groggily, looking at the time on his cell phone. "I hate to cut this short, but I'm really sleepy. I think I'd best be leaving now."

"That's alright," said Raven. "I fully understand."

Wyatt stood up, swaying like he had one too many drinks.

"It was nice meeting...you...."

He could hardly finish his sentence before he started to collapse. Without a second thought, I jumped out of my chair and rushed over to catch him before he hit the floor.

"You used the potion, didn't you?" I asked Raven.

"I ran out of ideas, so I had to wing it." She shrugged. "It's not a big deal. We just ended up going back to plan A."

"I didn't realize we were even on plan B," I muttered, putting Wyatt back into his chair.

"Plan A was to use the potion to nab him while he was asleep," said Raven. "Plan B kinda happened on its own to avoid using the potion. I guess you can call this Plan AB, like the blood type, but without the weird medical science behind it."

"What are you talking about?" I was more annoyed about using the sleeping potion than caring about what she meant. "I don't like using that crap on people."

"Crap? You mean the sleeping potion?"

"Yes!"

"It's fine," she said, standing up and putting her hands on her hips. "I already told you it's non-lethal."

"I just don't think it's right," I argued. "Something about forcing someone to sleep for your advantage doesn't seem morally right."

228

"Morals don't run the world, Roadrunner," said Raven sternly, "and morals certainly don't run this club. Now take Wyatt into the recording room and bring the chair."

"What are we gonna do now?" I asked hesitantly.

"Just sit him up in the chair in the recording room," said Raven. "Move it!"

I let out a mild groan, hoisted the snoozing Wyatt onto my shoulder, and carried him into the recording room. After laying him down gently on the floor, I fetched the chair and seated him in it just as Raven had instructed. She walked into the room with a rope and tossed it to me.

"Tie him up nice and tight," she said. "Make sure he can't leave that chair."

Without a word, I got to work with the rope. I had no idea how to "officially" tie someone into a chair, but I did the best I could. While I was busy with the tying, Raven was setting up huge speakers in a circle around Wyatt so that they were all facing him. I really didn't want to hear her asinine explanation, so I simply let her do what she was doing.

"Hmm, looks good," she said when we were finished. "I already contacted Cormorant and he said to standby for further instructions."

"You mean we have to wait here?" I asked, feeling my eyelid twitch slightly.

"That's pretty much it," she said conclusively. "Make yourself at home, but don't touch anything that looks expensive."

"You do realize that Wyatt can easily report us, right?" I said, feeling inappropriately calm. "I'm pretty sure this counts as kidnapping or something like that."

"Don't worry," said Raven.

"You always say that," I mumbled. "What kind of information does this guy have that's so important?"

"Let me see that report," she said, holding her hand out.

I handed the briefing report to Raven and she scanned over it.

"It says that he's affiliated with the library that burned down," she said. "That means we need to ask him questions about that particular incident."

"What?" I couldn't believe my ears. "You mean he's the one who burned it down?"

"I said he's just affiliated with it," she said.

"I used to work there, so I'm affiliated with it, too!" I said. "That could mean anything!"

"Does he look familiar to you at all?" Raven asked, raising an eyebrow at me.

"No, not really," I replied, looking at Wyatt passed out in the chair. "He could've been a customer, but I'm pretty sure he didn't work there when I did."

"Check his car for clues," said Raven. "Look for anything that might be suspicious or possibly related to a fiery library."

I headed outside to Wyatt's car and opened the passenger door. The inside was messy, so I had to dig around. Most of what I found was trash, college papers, and things related to his job. After searching the car's interior and finding nothing, I checked the center console and found four lighters. I thought it seemed a little odd that he didn't have any cigarettes or ashtrays, so I snatched them up as evidence.

Before going back inside the studio, I opened the glove compartment and dug around to see what I could find. Looking through somebody else's stuff like that was something I never liked to do, but it made me feel a little better when I came across Wyatt's library card. Sure enough, it was issued by the library I used to work at. The report turned out to be correct when it mentioned that he was affiliated with the library, so I grabbed the library card as more evidence.

When I walked back inside the studio and presented the evidence to Raven, she took it all from me and examined everything with a thoughtful gleam in her eyes. She placed the four lighters and the library card on a table and crossed her arms.

"I thought the lighters were suspicious," I explained. "I couldn't find any signs of cigarettes or an ashtray in his car. The library was burned down, so I figured this could mean something."

"You make a good point," she said. "We'll definitely use this as evidence. The library card, too. Now we know for sure that he was associated with the library in some way."

Raven's phone starting ringing, and she quickly whipped it out of her pocket and answered it. I looked at Wyatt, unconscious and tied into his chair. Our payment for this assignment needed to be pretty hefty to make up for what we were doing. When Raven was done talking on the phone, I waited for her to tell me what to do next.

"Skylark and Kookaburra are here," she said, walking toward the door.

What are they doing here? I wondered. *Don't they normally hunt demons?*

Raven left the recording room and promptly returned with Kookaburra and Skylark. Skylark was carrying a large briefcase, which he placed on the table next to the evidence I found in Wyatt's car. Kookaburra looked at Wyatt tied up and grunted.

"What's going on, guys?" I asked.

"Miss Flamingo had us pick up ingredients for some potions," said Skylark as he opened his briefcase, "then we were told to come here."

I didn't really know what to say, so I just waited for Raven to say something instead. However, she apparently had nothing to talk about or ask, so I watched Skylark set up a chemistry set and prepare a bunch of phials full of who-knows-what. He started mixing various chemicals and ingredients together like a mad scientist. My concern only started to rise once I saw him fill a syringe with the concocted liquid.

"What's that for?" I asked, eyeing the needle in Skylark's hand.

"Oh, this?" he said. "My objective is to administer this into Wyatt Halabi's bloodstream. It cancels the effects of my sleeping potion."

"You mean it's a wakeup potion?" I asked.

"Yeah, pretty much," he said. "It's safe and non-lethal. Hey, Kookaburra, get the tourniquet."

Kookaburra grabbed a tourniquet out of Skylark's briefcase and walked over to Wyatt.

"How am I supposed to do this?" Kookaburra asked gruffly. "His arms are tied up."

"Just stab the needle into his jugular," said Raven.

"Whoa, is that even safe?" I said.

Skylark looked at me, then looked at Raven who shrugged.

"Well, I'll just look for a vein somewhere," said Skylark, examining Wyatt. "I can see one down by his right ankle."

"Alright, stab it," said Raven.

Deciding to keep all of my questions about sanitation and medical procedures to myself, I watched as Skylark injected the wakeup potion into Wyatt's ankle.

"That should do it," said Skylark, returning to his chemistry set.

"How long until it works?" Raven asked.

"A few minutes before he's fully awake again," said Skylark. "Here, this is for you."

He handed Raven another syringe full of who-knows-what, and I couldn't believe that he would just give her something like that. Being injected by Skylark seemed a lot safer than by Raven.

"Ooh, what's this for?" she asked, holding the syringe up to the light.

"It's my own amnesia potion," said Skylark. "I was told to make it for you."

"Awesome," said Raven, twirling the syringe in her hand like a baton.

"Yeah, just make sure to keep the cap on the needle until you use it," said Skylark warily as he packed everything up.

"Are we done here?" Kookaburra asked. "My meatball sub is gonna get cold."

"I believe our job tonight is finished," Skylark concluded. "I'll see you two later."

232

"See ya," I said unenthusiastically as Skylark and Kookaburra walked out the door.

"Now we wait for our sleeping beauty to wake up," said Raven, pulling up a chair and sitting down.

"Did Skylark and Kookaburra know what we were doing?" I asked.

"I don't know," said Raven. "I didn't tell them anything."

"Isn't it a little strange?" I asked. "They just showed up and gave us stuff that we needed."

"That's how it works in this club," Raven told me. "Maybe Cormorant filled them in after I talked to him on the phone just a little while ago."

"But Miss Flamingo said they had an assignment tonight before we even knew what we had to do," I said. "She acted as if she knew how this was all going to work out, so she put everything together before anyone left the cabin."

"How's that surprise you?" she asked. "First, Miss Flamingo is very good at arrangements and stuff. Second, she's psychic, or claims to be at least."

"Is she *really* psychic?" I asked quizzically.

Raven shot me an annoyed look.

"Just don't question it!" she said. "I don't know if she is or not, but it sure as hell seems like she is."

"In what ways?" I asked.

She rolled her eyes and sighed.

"Look, I'll let you in on something," she said. "Don't even try to figure Miss Flamingo out. I'm speaking from experience. You'll just wish you minded your own business. Is that good enough for you?"

"Uh, not really," I said flatly.

"You're thinking, though," said Raven. "That's good. You'd make a pretty good detective, Roadrunner. Have you ever thought of pursuing that kind of career?"

"I haven't really thought of any kind of career specifically," I said.

"A large root beer float," Wyatt mumbled, "...and a double...cheeseburger...coming up."

233

"Hey, he's waking up," said Raven. "Go away, pesky delta waves. Bring this person back to consciousness!"

Was he dreaming about his job or something? I thought.

"Hrrrm...uhh...what?"

Wyatt opened his eyes and groggily looked around. It didn't take very long for him to realize that he was tied down.

"What the...? Hey, what's this about? What's going on? What's with all these big-ass speakers around me?"

"There's no need to panic," said Raven, not sounding very convincing.

"I'm tied up!" Wyatt yelled, trying to break free. The chair scooted across the floor a few inches as he struggled with the ropes. "Let me go, damn it!"

"I will," said Raven, "but first I'll need some answers. If you just cooperate, everything will—"

"HELP!" Wyatt shouted. "Somebody help meeee!"

"Come on, man," said Raven, crossing her arms. "This'll be a million times easier for both of us if you just listen and play along. I'll let you go without any injuries. Physical injuries, at least. No guarantees about your mental health."

"What the hell do you want?" Wyatt spat.

"What do you know about the library in downtown?" Raven asked firmly.

"You mean the one that burned down?"

"That's the one," she said. "You wouldn't happen to know anything about that, would you?"

"Like what?" Wyatt asked angrily. "It burned down, like, a couple months ago, or something! I never really gave it much thought! Rrrr, let me go!"

"That's pretty interesting," said Raven like a professional interrogator. "People who don't give much thought to library fires typically don't carry library cards around with them."

She picked up Wyatt's library card off the table and showed it to him, causing his face to turn red.

"Where did you get that?" he snarled. "Were you going through my stuff?"

"No, Ethan did that," she said.

234

For a second, I had forgotten that my name was supposed to be Ethan. When Wyatt glared at me, I realized that Raven had just pinned that violation on me.

"What else can you tell me about the library?" Raven asked.

"What do you want me to say?" Wyatt spat. "I had nothing to do with it burning down! I'm telling the truth!"

"That's good enough for me," I told Raven impatiently. "You heard him."

"Shut it," she replied abruptly.

As Wyatt struggled some more to break free, Raven walked over to her bass and removed it from the case. She then grabbed a long cord and plugged one end into her instrument.

"Are you familiar with something called the brown note, Wyatt?" she asked.

"Not that I know of," he replied curtly.

Raven plugged the other end of the cord into one of the amps surrounding Wyatt. When they all made a quick popping sound, I noticed that all of the amps seemed to be hooked up together.

"The brown note is a theoretical low-frequency sound wave somewhere around five to nine hertz," Raven explained. "The human ear typically can't detect sound below twenty hertz."

"Yeah, and?" said Wyatt. "What are you getting at?"

"Prolonged exposure to the brown note is supposed to cause dizziness, nausea, and uncontrolled bowel movements," Raven continued as she adjusted the strings on her bass. "You wouldn't want to experience any of that, would you?"

"Will that really work?" I asked skeptically.

"It should," she said. "These subwoofers are customized to reach subsonic frequencies, and so is my bass guitar."

"That's not really what I meant," I said.

"Are you insane, woman?" Wyatt laughed. "You plan on torturing me with that? That's the stupidest thing I've ever heard."

"We'll see about that," said Raven, inserting earplugs. "Cover your ears, Ethan."

With a single strum of Raven's bass, I could instantly feel my entire body rumble as the subsonic sound waves emanated from the subwoofers. Although I couldn't hear anything, it was easy to tell that the speakers were turned up very loud. After a while, Raven stopped the note.

"How do you feel?" she asked Wyatt.

"Pretty fine, actually," he sneered.

"Oh yeah?" said Raven. "We'll just have to turn it up louder."

She cranked up the amp, then strummed again. This time, I felt as if my body was filled with jelly and like I was sitting on a washing machine doing its final spin. Raven kept the note going for a much longer time, and the look on Wyatt's face started to show signs of discomfort. When she stopped the note again, she immediately continued the interrogation.

"Do you remember anything about the library?" Raven asked.

"Ohh, I don't really know," Wyatt muttered.

"You have to be feeling something by now," said Raven with a grin.

"What makes you so sure?" said Wyatt stubbornly.

"Because *I* can start to feel it," she said. "What about you, Ethan?"

My head started to feel a little funny, to be honest. This brown note thing was probably more credible than I had thought.

"Kind of," I told her.

"If we're starting to feel a little funny," Raven told Wyatt, "then I can only imagine what *you* feel like, being in the middle of the sound. Let's turn it up a little louder."

I took a few steps back before Raven strummed again. The room itself started to look like it was vibrating, but I just assumed it was my eyes shaking in my skull. Before long, I started experiencing shortness of breath and discomfort. Wyatt, however, began to look pretty miserable. He started to scream something out, but his voice was drowned out by sound waves I couldn't even hear. When Raven finally stopped, Wyatt tilted his head back in relief.

236

"How do you feel now?" Raven asked him.

"A little strange, but I think I'll live," he replied.

"I don't know about this," I said. "This doesn't seem to be working."

Raven looked a little disappointed. She unplugged her bass, causing the speakers to make a loud, obnoxious sound that appeared to pierce Wyatt's head.

"Maybe I'll get the laptop," she said. "Do you know what a bass drop is, Wyatt?"

"Can't we do this in a more civilized way?" I asked. "Or at least in a way that actually works?"

"How about this?" said Raven, brandishing the syringe of amnesia potion in front of Wyatt.

I could see the fear immediately take form in his face as he looked at the syringe. Raven should have used this tactic from the start, as it was already being more effective than the brown note.

"W-what is that?" he croaked.

"Rattlesnake venom," she replied with a menacing grin. "I'm sure you don't need me to explain what'll happen if I pump this into you."

"You're lying!" said Wyatt with undertones of panic in his voice. "That's probably nothing at all!"

"No, it really is something," I added. "It's some pretty potent stuff."

"Do you want to call my bluff?" said Raven, pulling the cap off the needle. "It won't take very long to find out."

"Get that away from me!" Wyatt shrieked. "You're a witch! An evildoer!"

"When was the last time you visited the library?" Raven demanded loudly, inching closer to Wyatt.

"I d-don't know!" he sputtered. "A week before the fire!"

"What were you doing there?"

"Checking out some books!"

"What kind of books?" Raven asked, getting closer.

"Just some novels I wanted to read!" he croaked. "Honest, I swear! I never got to return them because the library burned down before I was done!"

"Where are these books?" Raven growled, pointing the syringe at Wyatt. "WHERE?"

"Ack! My house! Don't tell me you guys are here to collect them! If that's all you want, you can take them! Take every book I own if it makes up for it!"

Raven took one more advance toward Wyatt with the syringe, and he struggled so desperately to get away that the chair fell over. When he hit the ground, I winced at the sound it made. Raven stood directly over him as he sobbed in total fear, and I actually felt really bad for him. If only he knew that he wasn't in any real danger.

"That should be enough," said Raven. "Ethan, set him back upright."

"Sorry, dude," I said as I set the chair back on its legs.

"Shut up, you snotty-nosed prick!" he barked. "You went along with the whole thing. There I was, thinking you were going to set me up with a hot date, and this is what happens! If I make it out alive, I'll make sure you two go into the deep fryer for this!"

"Uh, are we done?" I muttered to Raven. "I think I'm ready to call it a day."

"Yeah, we're done," she replied. "I'm pretty sure he told us everything he knows. Hold onto him for me."

"Hold onto me, why?" Wyatt asked, his eyes bugging out.

"You'll wake up tomorrow, and this will all just be a dream," said Raven.

For somebody tied to a chair with another guy holding him down, Wyatt put up one hell of a thrashing fight as Raven injected him in the ankle with the amnesia potion. I just really hoped that it worked as well as the sleeping potion did, or I would be forever loathed by a man named Wyatt Halabi.

238

~Opus 17~

This was the plan as it stood: I had to give Wyatt a ride to his home with his car, using the address on his driver's license. Raven was to follow me in her car so I could get a ride back to the cabin after dropping off Wyatt. Normally, I wouldn't have had a problem with this plan, but the amnesia potion was making Wyatt a little loopy and partially brain dead.

"Flush the wig and whoopee cushion," he sputtered, rolling his head around in the passenger seat.

"I'll put it on my to-do list," I replied flatly, examining the name of the street I passed.

"Are you going the right way?" he asked me. Actually, I only assumed he was talking to me.

"I think so," I said. "Do you remember the way to your house?"

"Kentucky...not right," he groaned.

"We're not in Kentucky," I said.

"Take Kentucky Street!" he belched. "Left...turn left...."

I slammed on the brakes as I realized that I had just made it to the intersection of Kentucky Street. Luckily, Raven's car only weighed a little more than a cardboard box and had a short stopping distance, otherwise she would have rear-ended me.

"Good job, Spartan," Wyatt sputtered. "Cracker for yoooouuu...."

"Thanks, but I don't need a cracker," I said.

Wyatt slumped down in his seat, giggling. I noticed he was beginning to drool, and I hoped that his home was close by.

Your potions are really something else, Skylark, I thought. *I can't say I'm looking forward to ever taking one myself.*

The road Wyatt lived on was Nallard Street, and I was relieved when I saw that name on the next street sign. I tried looking for any address numbers to get a hint as to which way to turn, but I couldn't find any in the dark of night. Taking a guess, I turned right. A few houses down, I realized the address numbers were going the other way, so I pulled into a driveway and turned around.

"C'mon, can't you go the right way?" Raven hissed out her window while I was backing into the street.

Ignoring her, I continued down Nallard Street until I found a mailbox with the matching address. When I pulled into the driveway, Wyatt suddenly reacted.

"Home!" he shouted out of nowhere, making me jump.

"Yeah," I replied, not knowing what else to say.

Wyatt fiddled with the door handle for a few seconds before he was able to open it, then messed with the seatbelt buckle for a few more seconds before releasing it. I took the keys from his ignition and jingled them to get his attention.

"Do you have all your stuff?" I asked him.

"Ask my client," he muttered, taking his keys from me.

I exited Wyatt's car and walked over to Raven, who pulled in right behind me.

"Is he gonna be okay?" I asked her when I got in her car.

Both of us watched Wyatt stumble toward his front door. He tripped over his own feet and fell face down on the lawn.

"Eh, I'm sure he'll make it eventually," she said, shifting into reverse.

We backed out of the driveway with Wyatt still lying face down where he fell, and we headed in the direction of the cabin.

"So, that amnesia potion," I said, "it'll really work, right?"

"Did it seem like it was working?" Raven asked. "You were with him."

"He kinda remembered the way to his house," I said. "I'm not sure if he remembers us."

"Did you ask him if he knew who you were?" she asked. "Probably not."

"I didn't think of it," I replied irritably. "Sorry."

"Skylark knows what he's doing," said Raven. "You can't expect us to erase *all* of someone's memories. That'd be messed up."

"But how can he make something that only targets new memories?" I asked. "I don't see how that could work."

"Aren't you in psychology?" Raven pressed. "You should know how the brain works to some degree."

"Yeah, I suck at that class," I muttered.

"Ask Oriole to tutor you," she said. "She's smart. She can help. I'm sure she can provide satisfikation to your grade."

"Don't you mean 'satisfaction'?" I asked, raising an eyebrow.

"No," said Raven cockily. "It's my own word. It has a different meaning."

"I'm sure it does," I replied dismissively.

"Seriously, though, ask Oriole for help," said Raven. "I can help you, too. I'm not bad with psychology. We can come over to your place if it makes you comfortable. I already know where you live."

"That might be a little risky," I said.

"Why? What do you mean by that?"

"Well, I have a girlfriend," I explained. "If she found out I was at my apartment with some other girls, it'd be bad."

"Invite her, too!" she said. "You can't say you'd have a problem with being alone with a bunch of girls at your place."

"Four girls is a bit much," I said without thinking.

Oh crap! I thought. *Why did I let that slip?*

"Oh, four?" Raven had that devious smile. "Is there another girl? A mistress, perhaps?"

"No, it's not like that!" I replied defensively. "Just somebody I know. It's no big deal."

"We should totally have a mega study session at your place!" said Raven. "It'd be just like a harem story!"

"Quit using fake words," I said.

"I didn't use a fake word!"

"I'll talk to Oriole when we get back to the cabin," I said firmly. "We can discuss it there."

When we entered the meeting room back at the cabin, everyone else was already seated around the table. Miss Flamingo didn't appear to acknowledge us as we sat in the only empty seats remaining, but I knew she was aware of our arrival.

241

"Welcome back," she told us.

"We have completed our assignment," I said.

"Yes, Raven has already informed me over the phone," said Miss Flamingo. "You took longer to report back than expected."

"Sorry," I said.

"All of our work for this evening is complete," Miss Flamingo announced. "I would like to take this time to discuss something of an entirely different nature."

Oh no, I thought. *What's next?*

"As you all know," she said, "it's getting close to Halloween. How do you all feel about a Halloween party?"

That was unexpected. We were actually going to attempt something *fun*? Everyone else seemed to be thinking the same thing, as they blankly looked around at everyone else's blank faces.

"I think it's a great idea," said Cormorant.

"Anyone else?" Miss Flamingo asked.

There was a murmur of agreement as everyone gradually understood that this probably wasn't a joke.

"Would it be like a costume party?" Oriole asked.

"It can be," Miss Flamingo replied. "You can choose to dress up or not."

"Will there be food?" I asked.

"There can be," Miss Flamingo replied.

"I can bring sweet potato pie!" said Cormorant enthusiastically. "It's Mama's recipe."

"We can rent a venue for the party," said Miss Flamingo. "That way we won't expose the location of this cabin."

"What do you mean?" Skylark asked. "Expose the location of the cabin to who?"

Or what? I wondered.

"I'll allow you to invite guests," Miss Flamingo explained. "You'll tell them this is just a party with some college students and coworkers."

"Won't that be risky, though?" Oriole asked.

"It will be fine." Miss Flamingo took a sip from her mug. "Trust me."

To be honest, I was having some of the same doubts as Oriole. This seemed a little too risky to have outsiders involved. For some reason, I found it difficult not to trust Miss Flamingo. If she said it would be fine, then it would be.

"You should each try to bring at least one food item," said Miss Flamingo. "I'll also allow two guests per member."

"Does alcohol count as one food item?" Kookaburra asked.

"Alcohol hardly counts as food, Kookaburra," she replied.

"What if I bring a gallon?" he asked. "Or a two-liter?"

"*Food*, Kookaburra," she said. "Bring whatever you want, as long as one of those things is *food*."

"Then I'll bring a gallon of booze and chicken wings," Kookaburra grunted.

"Oriole, paper please," said Miss Flamingo.

Within seconds, Oriole provided our club leader with a pen and paper. Miss Flamingo scribbled down the list, reading out loud as she wrote.

"A gallon of booze and chicken wings from Kookaburra. Cormorant is bringing sweet potato pie."

"I'll get pizza and some kind of dessert," said Raven.

"Can I be in charge of salad?" Skylark asked. "And punch."

"Eggplant casserole," Oriole offered, "and cookies."

Miss Flamingo finished writing down the suggestions hurled at her. Inevitably, she asked me next.

"What are you bringing, Roadrunner?"

"Uh, what are *you* gonna bring?" I asked, not ready to answer her question.

"I asked you first," she told me.

I was never great at figuring out what to bring to parties. Pizza, baked sweets, punch, and alcohol were pretty much default items, but they were all taken. That's what I got for not speaking up sooner.

Hotdogs and hamburgers are pretty good, I thought, *but they're too simple. It should be something unique. Something shocking, yet hip and delectable.*

Why was I thinking about this so much?

I have limited cooking skills, so it needs to be something simple. I could just get something from the store. No, that would be lame. Why did I have to work in fast food? The only damn thing I can cook is hotdogs and hamburgers!

Miss Flamingo cleared her throat loudly.

"Roast beef," I said.

Roast beef? Is that the best I could do?

"Roast beef," Miss Flamingo repeated as she wrote it down.

Why did I say that? I've never roasted beef before in my life!

"And ganache-covered peanut butter fudge," I blurt out.

What the hell am I saying? I hardly know what ganache is. Isn't it chocolate?

"Hey, fancy stuff!" said Cormorant with a grin.

"Can you cook?" Oriole asked, giving me an interested look.

"It's never too late to learn, right?" I replied with a cheesy smile.

Oriole chuckled, but I still felt pretty stupid.

"If anyone dies from eating Roadrunner's food, we'll offer a proper burial," said Miss Flamingo, sounding scarily serious. "Does anyone have any requests for additional food items?"

Everyone shook their heads.

"This completes our meeting," she said, standing up. "Adjourned."

I walked down the stairs to the first floor, wondering how I was going to learn making roast beef and peanut butter fudge with ganache. Halloween was less than a month away, so there was still some time left for practice. The trick would be squeezing in cooking with studying and everything else.

Before I could make it out of the cabin, Oriole approached me.

"Hey, Roadrunner," she said.

"Yeah?" I replied.

"Raven mentioned that you could use some help in your psychology studies," she said. "I have no problem with lending a helping hand."

"That'd be nice," I said. "Are you sure you don't mind?"

"I'd love to help!" she said happily. "Tutoring is something I enjoy."

"Are you a student at Elm Valley College?" I asked.

"I graduated from there last year," she said. "I'm taking this year off, then I'll be going to a university next fall."

"Well, yeah, I'd appreciate you doing that for me," I told her. "I could really use the help."

"I told you she'd help," Raven chimed in out of the blue. "You'll pass your class with no problem. You might even be suspected of cheating. That's how good you'll do."

"Let's exchange phone numbers," Oriole told me. "Call me to set up a meeting."

"Alright," I said.

When I entered Oriole's phone number into my phone, it felt like I had just been given some kind of superpower. I drove home with a feeling of confidence. Psychology, prepare to be dominated!

Sapphira greeted me as I entered my apartment. I went straight to the kitchen and started looking around to see what I had, figuring I might as well get a head start on learning to cook.

"What are you doing?" Sapphira asked. "Are you looking for something to eat?"

"I need to learn to cook," I said, shuffling through the contents of my cabinets. "I'm supposed to bring some stuff for a Halloween party."

"I can help you," said Sapphira. "You'll learn to cook."

"Really? You know how to cook?"

"Cooking is not much different from magical brewing and chemical fabrication," she told me. "I possess a wide degree of skill and knowledge of both."

"Oh, sweet!" I said. "You just might save me a lot of trouble."

245

I had always thought Sapphira had the personality of a calculator, but she was proving not to be so bad.

"On the other hand," she said, "I could summon whatever food items you require. They will never expire."

"No, that's, um, not necessary," I said. "I kinda want to, like, put some of my own hard work and personal touch into this."

"As you wish," she said. "What do you need to cook?"

"Roast beef and peanut butter fudge covered in ganache," I said.

"Very well, I shall teach you."

Sapphira held out her hands and began reciting an incantation. A magic circle appeared underneath me, and I quickly realized that I had failed to explain the situation well. When I tried to exit the circle, my feet wouldn't move, as if I was standing in a puddle of superglue. The entire ritual was only about five seconds.

"What'd you do?" I said angrily.

"I transferred my knowledge of roast beef and peanut butter fudge covered with ganache over to you," she replied.

"I was hoping to do this without magic," I groaned. "This takes the fun out of it."

"I apologize," she said, bowing low.

I looked at the stove and tried thinking about roast beef. Suddenly, an explosion of knowledge about roast beef filled every corner of my mind. A huge list of recipes flooded my head and continued to grow as I calculated different ways to tweak the ingredients and processes. The wave of information hit me so hard and so quickly that I felt a little dizzy thinking about it all.

"Wow," I said quietly, leaning against the fridge. "I know a *lot* about roast beef."

"The transfer was successful," said Sapphira. "You should possess the same caliber of knowledge surrounding peanut butter fudge and ganache."

As soon as Sapphira said that, a very similar wave hit me just as forcefully with a plethora of information regarding peanut butter fudge and ganache. My mouth started to water a little bit, as if I already knew what all of those ideas would taste like.

"You did good, Sapphira," I said. "Next time, just wait for me to confirm something before you start slinging magic around like that."

"Affirmative," she replied.

Waking up the next morning, I was happy when I could still remember everything I had "learned" about the food I needed to make. Not only that, but it seemed as if my extensive knowledge of those two dishes had branched out into other cooking areas as well. If I could apply what I had gained from Sapphira to cooking other food, then I would be able to cook a hundred times better than I thought I ever would.

"I'm totally gonna blow the other club members away with my food," I snickered to myself as I got out of bed.

The cold air seeped through my jacket as I walked across the campus grounds. I shuddered a little, but I still wasn't ready to get out the winter coat. A part of me was clinging to the denial that summer was long gone.

Inside the building, an unforgettable sight caught my eye: a bold tattoo of a banana split. Trent was standing in front of a bulletin board, looking at what was posted. I still had plenty of time to kill before math, so I walked over to him.

"Hey, Trent," I said.

"What's up, Mike?" he said. "I'm just checking out the announcements."

"Anything interesting?" I asked, scanning the board.

"No, not really," he said. "What are you doing this Friday around five?"

"Um, nothing, as far as I know," I replied. "Why, is something going on?"

"You should come to my birthday party," said Trent. "I've invited a bunch of people. It'll be at my place."

"That's cool," I said. "I don't know for sure if I'll be able to make it, though."

"We'll have all kinds of food and stuff," he said. "B.Y.O.B. It's gonna be a good-sized bash."

Food, huh?

"If I make it out there, I'll probably bring some food for the party," I said boastfully. "I know how to cook a few things."

"Sure, that'd be great!" he said. "Bring whatever you want. I have to go meet someone now. Remember, Friday at five o'clock. I'll give you the directions to the place tomorrow in communications class."

"Gotcha," I said. "Hey, would it be okay if I brought my girlfriend?"

"The more, the merrier," Trent replied. "See you in communications tomorrow."

"See ya."

I figured it'd be good to bring Hayley with me. She could probably benefit from getting out and doing more, since she never seemed to have a very adventurous life. To be honest, I never had an adventurous life myself, so it could be a learning experience we could both undertake. This would be my first actual college party, and I was more stoked than I imagined I would be. October was turning out to be pretty exciting.

I placed my math homework on Mr. Pardee's desk shortly after entering the classroom, then took my usual seat in the back. While waiting for the bell to ring, I flipped open my textbook to see what would be covered in class that day. The material seemed self-explanatory to me, so I was expecting another smooth session.

Class started, and I noticed Miyuki hadn't shown up. That seemed a little strange, since she was always on time and never missed a class, at least to my knowledge. Maybe she already took a look at the day's lesson and figured it was something she could do without attending class. However, that really didn't seem like her.

About fifteen minutes into the period, I was already spacing out. The instructor was rambling on about stuff I had already figured out, so it was hard for me to pay attention. What actually caught my attention, though, was when the door opened and Miyuki walked in. Mr. Pardee smiled and nodded as she placed her homework on his desk, then he resumed his lesson.

So, she decided to come after all, I thought. *Nothing strange. People are late sometimes.*

As Miyuki walked over to the closest available seat, I noticed that something seemed wrong. There was no bounce in her step like usual, and she hung her head a little lower than I was used to seeing. It could have been my imagination, or maybe she could have been tired.

I finished the assignment right as class let out. On my way to drop it off at the desk, I stopped by Miyuki's seat as she was packing up.

"Running a little late today?" I said jokingly.

"Yeah," she replied in a dull tone.

"Is something the matter?" I asked. "You look a little down."

"Hmm, I don't wanna talk about it," she said.

"Alright, you don't have to," I told her. "I hope everything is going to be okay."

"I'm sure it will," she said with a weak smile.

She stood up and slung her book bag over her shoulder.

"Take it easy, Mike," she said.

"You too, Miyuki."

Man, I wonder what's up, I thought. *I hope it's nothing serious.*

English class was boring, to say the least. I kept thinking about the recipes I had obtained, and I figured I would stop at the grocery store and try some of them out. Dinner was definitely going to be roast beef that night, followed by some badass peanut butter fudge with ganache.

My biology lab didn't start until two and a half hours after English. During that time, I ventured to the library and texted Hayley to see if she wanted to spend some time together before our classes. She almost immediately agreed and showed up soon after I asked.

"Do you like roast beef?" I asked her while we were sitting at one of the tables.

"I love it!" she said.

"I'm going to try a new recipe I got," I told her. "I'm making it after I get out of biology."

"Aw, I wish I could try it," she said. "I have to watch Jeanette's son tonight."

"Your sister has a kid?" I asked.

"Yeah, he's almost two," said Hayley. "He's the cutest little thing!"

"Is Jeanette married?"

"No, it's her ex-boyfriend's son," she explained.

"Oh." I didn't want to press anymore, so I added, "Well, I'll make sure to save some leftovers for you."

"Yeah, awesome!" she said. "It'd better be good, or else!"

"I think it will be," I said, my mouth starting to water a little as I somehow anticipated the flavor.

The time I was spending with Hayley made my morning brighter. I inched my chair a little closer to her, getting ready to put my arm around her. That was when the eclipse moved in to cast its shadow over me. In other words, Raven had just shown up.

"Hey, I need to talk to you," she told me bluntly.

"Do you *need* to?" I replied stubbornly.

"Uh, yeah," she said, sounding irritated.

Hayley eyed Raven with a look of disgust, which Raven seemed to deflect right off herself. Didn't Raven realize she was being rude? Scratch that. What a dumb question. Of course not.

"I'll be right back, babe," I told Hayley.

I followed Raven, who led me out of the library.

"What are we doing?" I asked flatly.

"Don't act conspicuous," she said quietly. "Walk and talk, nice and casual."

"Okay," I said, "we're walking and talking...."

"I was just informed that the college staff found out that Wyatt Halabi's files went missing," she said.

A chill ran down my spine.

"How do you know?" I asked.

"I talked to Wyatt this morning," she said. "I came across him, so I stopped and asked if he remembered me. Luckily, he didn't."

"Then the amnesia potion worked," I said with relief.

250

"Anyway, we got into a small conversation," she continued, "and he happened to say he was on his way to the main office. He said he had to fill out his paperwork again because his files came up missing."

"Does that mean they don't know how it happened?" I asked.

A couple students were walking toward us, and Raven waited until they passed by before continuing the conversation.

"Not sure," she said, "but this is pretty lucky. All I wanted was to give him a copy of our CD, and I found this stuff out. He seemed a little confused since he didn't remember our first conversation, but he was happy all the same."

"Oh, you actually went through with the CD?" I smirked.

"He's a fan!" she said. "I'm not some coldhearted musician. When I tell a fan something, I mean what I say!"

"I didn't mean it like that," I said. "Calm down."

"Anyway, I wanted to make sure you knew that Wyatt forgot about everything that night," she said. "Also, it seems the stolen documents won't come back to haunt us."

"What about Mr. Gast?" I asked. "Remember the instructor we drugged? Is he fine?"

"Probably," said Raven. "We seem pretty clear."

"Cool," I said, stopping in the middle of the hallway. "Now can I go back to what I was doing?"

"Yeah, we're done here," she replied.

"If that was all you wanted, why didn't you just text me?" I asked.

"My phone's dead," she said hastily. "Later, Roadrunner."

I walked back to the library, feeling like a few pounds had been removed from my shoulders. Things seemed to be working out fine. When I made it back to the library, Hayley was still sitting in the same place, and I felt bad for just leaving her like that.

"I'm back," I said, taking my seat. "Sorry about that."

"Who was that?" she asked, sounding mildly annoyed.

"She works with me," I said. "She wanted to discuss some things about work."

"She couldn't do that here?"

"No, it was kinda classified," I explained. "She can be a little rude like that sometimes."

Hayley didn't say anything, but I could tell she was upset.

"She was the bassist for Triangular Lockjaw," I said, trying to ease the awkwardness. "They were the first band that played on the night you and I first met."

"Oh yeah," she said, "I thought she looked familiar."

"That was a good night," I said.

"It was."

You have crappy timing, Raven, I thought. *You should make sure to keep your phone charged in case important things like this come up.*

"I wanted to ask you something," I said. "I got invited to a birthday party this Friday at five. Would you like to come with?"

"Whose birthday?" she asked.

"This guy named Trent," I said. "He's in my communications class. He said I can bring you."

"That sounds interesting," she said. "I'm kinda shy, though."

"You'll be fine," I assured. "You'll be with me."

She flashed that cute little embarrassed smile that could turn steel into butter.

"I'll think about it."

Hayley's class started about an hour before biology. After she headed off, I decided to get something to eat at the commons to pass the time. I munched on some snacks and worked on my history assignment that wasn't due until the next day, trying to open up more time for cooking later on.

When I finally entered my biology class, Aaron and Lawrence were sitting in the usual spot, grinning at me from across the room. Wondering what could possibly be up, I walked over to them.

"Hey, lover boy," said Aaron teasingly.

Here we go.

"Hi," I replied flatly.

"You have a girlfriend, I hear," said Lawrence with a grin.

"Yup," I said. "Her name's Hayley."

"Cool," said Lawrence. "Good going, bro."

The three-hour biology lab session went by normally. We had been cultivating bacteria for a week, and my little single-celled organisms were living happily.

"Jorge wants to get together tonight," Aaron said near the end of class.

"What's going on?" Lawrence asked.

"I don't know," said Aaron. "Probably gonna hang out, play some games."

"Cool," said Lawrence.

"I won't be able to," I said.

"Uh oh, the ball and chain!" said Aaron obnoxiously, referring to Hayley.

"No, I have other things," I told him.

"Like what?" said Aaron in disbelief.

"Don't worry about it," I said.

"Hmm, gonna have a good night, eh?" Aaron elbowed me while moving his eyebrows up and down.

"What do you have to do?" Lawrence asked me.

"Cooking," I said.

Aaron started laughing like a baboon, which was far less annoying than how I thought he would respond to my answer.

"You mean cooking for real?" Lawrence sounded strangely astonished.

"Uh, yeah," I replied. "For real. I'm not just throwing something frozen in the microwave or oven. This is the real deal."

"What are you making, Chef Mike?" Aaron asked with a huge grin.

"Roast beef," I said proudly.

Aaron nodded, seemingly impressed.

"Well, best of luck," he told me. "Don't burn your place down. You share it with other people who might not appreciate that, since you live in an apartment and all."

"I'll do my best," I muttered.

Biology finally ended, and I wasted no time going straight to the store to pick up what I needed. The list of ingredients was already in my head, and I quickly checked out and headed straight home.

Carrying the bags full of groceries, I stopped at the apartment mailboxes to check my mail. I flipped through the usual junk mail and other things destined for the trash, but a particular envelope made me almost forget that I was in a hurry to get to my apartment. I read the return address twice to make sure I was seeing correctly.

My oldest brother, Sal, who I hadn't seen in years while he was in the military, had sent me a letter.

~Opus 18~

Dear Mikey,

I hope college life is treating you okay. There's no way I would ever spend all that money on school, but you were always smarter than me. Maybe you'll make something of yourself, so keep up the hard work, and don't let stupid things get you down!

I know I've been away for a long time now. I miss the snow because it never snows over here. We're lucky if it even rains. It must be getting colder where you are now. The desert here is harsh, so don't complain like you always do when you have to wear your heavy coat.

Anyway, the real reason I'm writing is to tell you a big surprise. I'm coming home for Christmas! I don't know the exact day I'm flying in, but I think it's early December. I'm looking forward to spending time with the family again.

Until then, take it easy and stay out of trouble.

Your brother,
Sal

P.S. Sorry for using snail mail. I would've emailed you but my laptop took a bullet. Don't ask why.

  I sat at the table in my apartment with Sal's letter in my hands. It had been two years since I last saw my oldest brother, and it had been a long time since I saw him before that. Now he was coming home for Christmas.

  "This is great!" I said out loud.

  "May I ask what is great?" Sapphira asked, standing across the table from me.

  "My brother is coming home for Christmas," I told her. "I don't get to see him very much anymore."

  "This is fortunate," said Sapphira.

I stood up and walked over to the window, gazing out for no reason at all.

"I bet there's gonna be a huge party at my parents' like last time Sal visited," I said pensively. "Man, I can't wait!"

"Do you love your family?" Sapphira asked me.

"Of course I do," I said. "Where'd that come from?"

"You are fortunate," she said.

"Yeah, hearing that from a demon is a little strange," I said. "I think I'm gonna get started on dinner. You're dismissed."

While I was busy cooking up one of the hundreds of recipes I possessed, I quickly learned that there was a difference between knowing how to do something and having the experience to do it. Although the roast beef was fairly simple, the ganache was really tricky. I wasn't very adept with a cooking knife, and trying to chop up all the dark chocolate was a rough endeavor. Perhaps I should've bought the chocolate chips instead of the big chocolate slab.

Despite my total lack of experience, I was surprised when everything turned out decently. Safe to say, it was a success. As I ate the roast beef, not only did I savor the flavor, but I thought of how it would amaze everyone at the club's Halloween party. If only I had a crock-pot, it would have been a little easier to make, although the roasting pan sufficed quite nicely.

When I finally tasted the peanut butter fudge and ganache, it almost put me on the floor. There was no way I had just made something so delicious, yet there I was eating it.

"Sapphira," I called out through a mouthful of fudge.

"Yes?" she said as soon as she appeared.

"You have to try this," I said, handing her a piece of fudge.

"I can not eat," she said. "I apologize."

"But can't you just taste it?" I insisted. "Chew it up and spit it out, or just lick it."

"The concept of taste is different for me than it is for you," she told me.

256

"Hmm, more for me then," I said, eating the piece I tried to offer to Sapphira. "I have to save some stuff for Hayley and the guys. They'll worship me."

"Do you wish to be idolized?" Sapphira asked.

"Uh, it was an expression," I said.

I put the beef and fudge in separate containers and stored them in the fridge. Although the beef would still be good later, it was a shame that nobody else got to taste it when it was freshly cooked. I would just have to make it again some other time. Trent's party was only a few days away, so I could unveil a new roast then.

With a full stomach and no homework, I was ready to relax for the rest of the evening. Hayley called me a little later just to chat, and I told her all about my cooking experience and how she would definitely love the fudge. I also told her about Sal coming home for Christmas, and that she would have to meet him.

"You can come to my family's Christmas party," I told her. "I'm sure they won't mind."

"Yeah," she said. "I'd like to if I have nothing going on."

This is going great! I thought. *Things are really looking up.*

For the rest of the evening, the aroma of my culinary successes lingered in my apartment. I ended up falling asleep on the couch, which I hated to do on a school night. My alarm was in my bedroom, and I didn't want to risk missing it and being late for class.

The next day, I was lucky enough to hear my alarm from the other room, so I made it to class on time. After a long and tedious psychology session, I met up with Trent in our communications class. He gave me a piece of paper with his address and a phone number if I needed to call about the party.

"Do you think you'll make it?" he asked.

"Yeah, I don't see why not," I told him. "I'm looking forward to it. My girlfriend seems pretty excited, too. She never really gets out a lot, so I'm trying to get her out and about."

Listen to me talking, I thought. *I used to be the same way.*

"Right on," said Trent. "I'd prefer if one of you could be a designated driver. If not, don't tell the cops where you really left from if you get pulled over."

"Don't worry," I said, "we're both underage and probably won't drink."

"Hey, just making sure," he chuckled, "but I won't argue against being responsible."

Mr. Holden spent most of the class going on about off-topic discussions. While I usually found his anecdotes to be entertaining, my mind was prancing through its own world. Before the end of the period, I scribbled down the day's assignment, then wandered off to history.

I passed by the bulletin board where I had seen the flyer for the event at the Boney Feather on the first day of class. Elm Valley College always had something going on, so I scanned over the announcements to see if anything interesting was coming up. The only interesting thing was a bake sale, which didn't intrigue me much anyway.

On my way to the other building where my history class was, I saw Chad walking ahead of me. He didn't seem to notice me, but I wasn't extremely eager to talk to him. I hardly spoke to Chad after borrowing the grimoire to rid myself of that freakish curse, and I was wondering if Toony had ever returned it. I didn't want to ask him if he got the book back, because if he didn't, then it would imply that I lost it or something. There was no point in trying to explain how a little bug-man borrowed it and kept it for himself. The whole situation made me feel awkward around Chad.

"Mike!" Chad called out. He must've noticed me while I was lost in thought.

"Hey," I replied.

"Ready for today's test?" he asked.

I suddenly felt as if there was a rock in my stomach.

"There's a test today?" I asked grimly. "I thought that was next week!"

"I'm just pullin' your leg!" he chuckled. "You should've seen the look on your face."

"Don't do that to me," I said, sighing in relief.

"I couldn't help myself," he said.

Figuring it was a good time to clear up some smoke, I brought up the grimoire, choosing my words carefully.

"Thanks again for letting me borrow that book," I said.

"Yeah, no problem," he said. "Just don't destroy it!"

So Toony hasn't returned it yet, I thought. *That idiot. I never should've trusted a hobgoblin!*

"Uh, don't worry about it," I said. "It's in good hands."

I was going to have to contact Toony as soon as I made it home, and hopefully Sapphira would help me with that.

The entirety of history class was spent with me wondering if I would be able to return Chad's book. Eventually, I began to question why Toony needed the book to begin with. My only hope was that he wasn't doing anything bad with it. That would be a responsibility I had no desire to uphold. Driving home, I felt a little paranoid.

I'm beginning to feel like an old man with everything on my mind, I thought.

When I entered my apartment, the first thing I did was ask Sapphira about Toony.

"I need a favor," I said.

"What is it, Michael?" she asked.

"Can you contact Toony for me? I want to talk to him."

"I will try."

Sapphira vanished into thin air. I placed my school supplies on the table and sat down on the couch to wait for her return. To my surprise, she reappeared only seconds later with good news.

"He should be here shortly," said Sapphira.

"Good," I replied. "Thank you."

"You are welcome."

Right on cue, Toony appeared in the middle of my living room, hovering in one spot with his tiny wings.

"How do you do, lad?" he greeted with a toothy grin. "Did you wish to speak with me?"

"Yeah, I do," I said, standing up.

"Let me guess," he said, "you want to ask about the grimoire. Am I correct to assume this?"

259

"Actually, yes," I said. "I need assurance that you aren't doing anything *undesirable* with it."

"No, no, not at all!" he said. Somehow, it was hard to fully believe him.

"If you're done with it, I'd like to have it back now," I said firmly.

There was a moment of silence as Toony seemed to be thinking of something, and I didn't like that at all.

"Oh, very well," he sighed.

That was easier than I thought.

He disappeared, then quickly returned with the grimoire. Seeing him carrying it was still entertaining, since it was bigger than him. Placing the book on the floor in front of me, he slowly backed away.

"I have nothing left I need to do with it," he said. "As promised, it has been returned to you in the very same condition it was in when you lent it to me."

I picked the book up and flipped through the pages. Everything seemed to be intact.

"Thank you," I told him. "This is all I needed."

"If that is all, then I'll be on my way," said Toony. "Until next time, ho ho!"

Hopefully there won't be a next time, I thought.

Toony vanished without a trace, leaving me to hope there wouldn't be any more encounters with him or any other hobgoblins.

"He is no longer in the vicinity," said Sapphira.

"That's nice to hear," I said. "I'll be right back. I want to return this now and just get it out of the way."

During the drive to Chad's house, I did my best to remember the route I had taken last time. Fortunately, it wasn't very complicated, and I arrived at his house with no problems. I rang the doorbell with the grimoire firmly in my grasp. The person who answered the door wasn't Chad, and I assumed it was his father.

"Hello," I said. "I'm Mike, one of Chad's friends. I wanted to return this book to him."

"Hey, I know that book!" the man said. "I work for the fire department, and we found that during the library fire."

This is Chad's dad after all, I thought.

"Chad was telling me about that," I said. "It's really weird how it was found completely unscathed by the fire."

"Yeah, yeah it is," he said. "I can give that to him for you."

I handed the book to Chad's dad, and a feeling of tranquility filled my bones. At last, the grimoire had been returned to a trustworthy keeper and out of hobgoblin hands.

"Thanks," I said. "Tell Chad I said hi."

"Will do!" he said, grinning the same grin that Chad always does.

With that done, I was finally able to breathe a little easier. The rest of the evening was peaceful as I worked on some homework and indulged in a marathon of video games. That peacefulness persisted into the next morning and throughout my math and English classes, continuing into the afternoon.

Then I had to attend the club meeting.

"Happy Thursday, Roadrunner!" Raven greeted as I entered the meeting room. She sounded as ambiguously sarcastic as ever as she wore a smile. It was the kind of smile that a ten-year-old wears when she gets praised for being good while she secretly has stolen candy stashed in her pockets.

"Hey," I replied. "How are you?"

"Better than a needle in a haystack, thanks for askin'," she said.

"I'll take it that means you're good," I said, taking my seat at the table.

"She's gonna ask you about her new hoodie," Cormorant told me.

Raven picked her new hoodie up off the chair and held it up for me to see. It was dark blue. That's really all there was to say about it.

"Uh, nice," I replied, not knowing what else to say.

"I know it's boring," she said, sniffing it. "I bought it because I thought it smelled like waffles. Now it doesn't anymore, but I still love it!"

261

She slipped it on, and it almost instantly seemed to connect with her. I'm nothing close to a fashion expert, but it matched her very well: dark and deceptively plain, yet mysterious and hinting toward a deeper meaning that nobody cared about. It's strange how clothes speak much louder as soon as somebody wears them.

Skylark and Kookaburra had yet to arrive. Oriole was busy typing away on the laptop. Raven was making a cup of what looked like hot chocolate. Cormorant was just standing by the door, texting on his phone. Miss Flamingo was sitting in her usual spot at the back of the table, sipping a hot mug and flipping through a stack of papers. Everything seemed normal so far.

"Now that Roadrunner is present, we can get this meeting underway shortly," said Miss Flamingo, setting her mug down.

Cormorant closed the door and took a seat, followed by Raven and Oriole. I looked at the two empty chairs usually occupied by Skylark and Kookaburra and had to ask about them.

"Miss Flamingo?" I said.

"Yes?"

"Are Skylark and Kookaburra coming tonight?" I asked.

"I had them meet here about an hour ago," said Miss Flamingo. "They are on a mission right now."

"Oh," I said quietly. "That's all I wanted to know."

The meeting started with Miss Flamingo going over the weekly financial figures, which still made little sense to me. From what I had gathered from past meetings, there seemed to be a significant money flow through the club. I also noticed a large number of associates who directly and indirectly affected the club's finances, but I was still clueless about the details. The entire time, I wondered how much of this the other members understood. Oriole probably knew a lot since she was in charge of information and documenting, and Cormorant likely knew because of his status as vice president. As long as this club wasn't part of a drug ring or something similar, I wasn't too concerned about it. However, I didn't think I could ever be at ease unless I fully understood exactly what this club was doing.

"That completes today's financial overview," Miss Flamingo announced. "Raven and Roadrunner, I have your next mission. Oriole, please bring me the document."

Oriole quickly printed off our mission and handed it to our club leader. After looking over it briefly, Miss Flamingo beckoned Raven over and handed the paper to her. Raven folded it up and tucked it into her hoodie pocket without taking a second to read it.

"We're heading out," Raven told me, walking briskly for the door.

"Can I read the mission overview?" I asked.

She slapped the folded paper into my hand, and I followed her out of the conference room. Once downstairs, I stretched out on one of the couches as Raven brought her bass in from her car. The document was still difficult for me to understand, and I had to wait for Raven to finish playing her lucky song so she could translate it for me.

"You need to let me know what this says," I said when she finished playing.

"When are you going to learn to decipher these?" she asked me sharply, putting her bass in its case.

"As soon as someone teaches me how to," I said curtly, handing her the document.

Apparently ignoring me, Raven looked over the document, then folded it back up and inserted it into her hoodie pocket. The crooked grin on her face slightly disturbed me.

"What's with that look?" I asked, not sure if I was prepared for the answer.

"This is going to be a fun one, my partner," she said in a bittersweet voice.

Ah hell, I thought.

"We're doing a stakeout," she said.

"A stakeout?" I stood up from the couch and gave Raven an inquisitive stare. "Like sitting out somewhere to keep an eye on somebody, right?"

"More or less," she said with her arms crossed, her grin still eating into my sense of security. "We're supposed to wait tonight and tomorrow evening."

That didn't seem too bad to me, since it sounded like all we had to do was sit around and keep an eye out for somebody. Despite the whole stalker thing going on, I always thought it'd be kind of fun to do a stakeout. However, the next evening was when Trent's birthday party was being held, and I really wanted to attend it.

"I was supposed to go to a birthday party tomorrow," I explained. "Will I be able to make it? It starts at five."

"We're supposed to be at our specified location at six tomorrow evening," Raven told me. "As long as you show up there at six, then I don't care what you do before then."

"Bah, never mind," I replied dully. "I don't wanna go there for a few minutes and leave. I was supposed to take my girlfriend there with me, but it wouldn't make sense if we're not staying long."

"Work sucks when it interferes with other plans, doesn't it?" said Raven.

"That's life," I shrugged.

My phone vibrated in my pocket, indicating that I had received a message. To my surprise, Raven's phone jingled at almost the exact same time as mine. I didn't recognize the phone number that sent it to me. The two of us checked our phones and found we had received the exact same message: information regarding a girl named Samantha Bridgman, including her picture.

"She's the target mentioned in our mission document," said Raven.

"We're stalking a girl?" I suddenly didn't feel very ready for our mission.

"You make it sound so terrible," Raven sneered. "What difference would it make if it was a male?"

"It just doesn't seem right," I explained. "It's easy to get guys in big trouble for stalking females."

"I promise I won't report you to the authorities," said Raven, holding up her right hand with her index, middle, and ring fingers up. "Scout's honor. I was actually a girl scout, so my honor carries meaning."

I didn't want to tell her that she was misunderstanding my point. Biting my tongue, I quietly accepted her assurance.

"Oh, I think I should tell you something," said Raven, tucking her phone away. "You received the same message on your phone as I did. That's a good thing. It means you're moving up in the world."

"Is that so?" I replied, not feeling so stoked. "Who sent it? Oriole?"

"Don't know, don't care, so don't ask," she replied swiftly.

The club seemed to adhere strictly to a policy that expects its members to simply shut up and don't ask questions. Such a way of running things prevented me from feeling completely at ease, as a lot of my questions remained shunned. Remembering the letter I had received from Sal, the same could be said for him while stationed overseas. Keeping your mouth shut and doing what you're told is the easiest way to stay out of trouble, but there was a sense of blind loyalty to that method. However, I figured it wasn't my place to understand everything the club did. There was bound to be a good reason to keep a lot of secrets, or so I reckoned.

Raven and I walked outside to her little electric car. Before I could squeeze into the tiny contraption, she tossed me a clipboard without warning, almost hitting me in the face.

"What's this for?" I asked.

"I'll need you to take an inventory of everything in the trunk," she told me sharply. "Just make a list on that paper. We're gonna need to make sure we have what we need for this assignment."

"I'm surprised this thing actually has a trunk," I replied.

She opened the back of the car, revealing the space right behind the seats. Looking at it from that angle showed that it had quite a bit more room than I had realized. Using the pen that was attached to the clipboard on a string, I began writing down everything I found:

One bass guitar, one pair of binoculars, two golf clubs (both putters), one stuffed teddy bear, one full roll of duct tape, one half bottle of fish oil supplements, one VCR, two lint rollers, one unopened can of aerosol spray, two bottles of moisturizing shampoo, one spool of fishing line, one power drill, zero drill bits, one pair of boots, one fingerless glove, eight sharpened number two pencils, one pair of shears, one nine-pound bowling ball, one unidentifiable piece of electronic scrap, one lug wrench, one spare tire (flat), one flashlight, and one cast iron skillet.

"How did you fit all this in here?" I asked, baffled.

"Organization is key," she said, taking the clipboard from me. "You didn't have to mention the bass."

"Well, I did," I shrugged.

"This looks good." She tossed the clipboard haphazardly into the trunk and closed it.

"Are we really gonna need all that stuff?" I asked.

"Maybe not *all* of it," she told me. "It's just good to have a wide inventory. Get in, we're going."

Once inside Raven's car, something suddenly came to mind and I had to inquire.

"That night when you climbed through my window," I said, "you had that tall ladder."

"Right," she said as she started the car.

"Where did you get that ladder? There's no way it could've fit in here."

"I found it," she said. "It was just lying around."

"You mean to tell me you found that big ol' ladder 'just lying around' somewhere nearby?" I chuckled. "You're a hoot."

"Does it matter?" she snapped. "Use what you can to do what you do! It's like a survival game, except nobody's dying."

"Right, right," I replied dismissively. "Anyway, what's the deal with this Samantha girl we're looking out for? I know we're doing a stakeout, but what *exactly* are we doing?"

"The document said to watch and report her actions," said Raven. "We only need to keep track of her at the specified location, so if she's not there, we're gonna be kinda bored."

"And what specified location is that?"

266

"Her house."

"Now I *really* feel like a stalker," I sighed. "If she's in her house, how are we supposed to keep an eye on her?"

"No clue," said Raven. "That's what makes it an adventure!"

We arrived at Samantha's house and parked across the street. Lights were on inside the house, indicating that someone was home. However, we were unable to see much from our position, and I was wondering how we would pull this assignment off.

Raven checked her phone, reading Samantha's information again.

"It says her room is on the second floor on the north side," she said.

"How do they know that?" I muttered.

"From where we are now, we can only see the east side of the house," she said. "We might need to move to a vantage point."

Before I could argue, Raven got out of the car and opened the trunk. Following suit, I got out of the car as well. Raven snatched the binoculars and handed me one of the putters.

"What's this for?" I asked, looking at the putter.

"In case something goes awry, we should be armed," she explained.

"You're really good at making me feel on edge," I told her, gripping the putter tightly.

Raven suddenly darted across the street, and I stuck close to her as we moved silently around to the north side of the house. Luckily, the darkness provided great cover, but I was still nervous about being spotted. While we were scanning the area, Raven tapped me on the shoulder.

"There's something in that tree over there," she whispered as she pointed.

I squinted to see through the darkness.

"It looks like a tree house," I whispered back.

"That's perfect!" she said. "We'll have a great view from up there!"

We hurried over to the tree, which had boards nailed to it for climbing up. Without a word, I tucked the golf club inside my jacket and followed Raven into the tree house. Once inside, I could see directly into the window of what was supposedly Samantha's room. Not only that, but we were well hidden among the branches and shadows.

"I can see right in there," said Raven, peering through the binoculars.

"This really doesn't feel right," I said, taking a seat on the wood floor.

"If it makes you feel better, I'll be the one who keeps an eye on her. You got Oriole's number the other day, so just text Oriole what's going on. Right now, Samantha's in there getting undressed."

"Huh?" I gazed over to get a look.

"Calm down, I'm kidding." Raven chortled. "You're such a typical man, Roadrunner."

"Very funny."

"There really is somebody in there, though," said Raven. "It looks like her. She matches the photo."

"What's she doing?" I asked.

"It's hard to say," said Raven, "but it certainly looks like something. It's like she's getting stuff together."

"What kind of stuff?" I asked, taking out my phone to text Oriole.

"Just stuff," she replied.

"That tells me nothing," I said flatly.

"Let Oriole know, anyway," she told me. "Try to word it well, okay? And make sure the light from the phone doesn't give us away."

Using my jacket to hide my phone's light, I started typing the message.

Target appears to be gathering materials in her room.

I sent the text message, feeling like a moron. Oriole would probably receive it and be just as confused as I was.

"Wait, they look like candles," said Raven, still peering through the binoculars. "She's lighting them. Yeah, definitely candles."

The materials include candles. Target is lighting them.

"Now she turned the lights off," said Raven.
I looked back at the window, and all I could see was the flickering candlelight.

Target has turned off bedroom lights.

About a minute or so passed, but nothing new appeared to be happening. I adjusted myself to get more comfortable on the wood floor as Raven continued to peer into the window.
"I can't see anything else," she said.
"What do we do?" I asked.
"Just keep watching," she told me. "We need to remain here until at least ten o'clock."
"That long?" I asked, scratching my head. "That's for more than another hour."
"Those are the orders," said Raven, pulling the binoculars away from her face.
We continued to wait, perched in the little tree house while the dim light flickered in the bedroom window. Being nestled there with nothing to do in the dark, I began to get a little sleepy. I did my best to keep from dozing off, but the boredom was killing me. Just as I was starting to nod off, my phone rang, tearing through the silence like a bullet. Startled, I fumbled for my phone.
"Turn that off!" Raven hissed. "It's making too much noise!"
Hayley was calling me, and I quickly answered it.
"Hey, babe," I answered.
"Hey," said Hayley sweetly. "What are you doing?"
"I'm at work," I replied, trying to keep my voice down.
"Oh, that's right," said Hayley. "Sorry, I forgot. You're not busy, are you?"

"Uh, yeah, at the moment," I told her. "Is there something you need to tell me?"

"No, not really," she said, sounding disappointed. "I just wanted to talk to you, that's all."

"I'll give you a call when I get done with work," I told her. "It should be, like, two hours or so."

"Alright," she said. "I love you."

"Love you too, babe," I said.

When I hung up, I could make out Raven's grin through the darkness.

"Aw, that's so sweet," she said.

I couldn't tell if she was mocking me or being sincere.

"Yeah, yeah," I replied.

"Hey, look!" Raven peered through the binoculars again. "There's somebody moving in there."

Looking into Samantha's window, I could see the silhouette of someone walking around. The room instantly turned pitch black, and I couldn't see a single thing anymore.

"The candles all went out," said Raven. "I can't see inside at all."

"How did the candles go out?" I asked, selecting Oriole's number in my phone's contact list.

"Not sure," she replied. "It's as if they all went out at once, though. That's peculiarly abnormal."

Noticed movement in room. Candles suddenly went out. Too dark to see inside.

"What now?" I asked Raven after sending the text. "We still have a half hour."

"We need to wait here until then," she told me.

The half hour came and went, but nothing else happened. The room remained pitch black, and it didn't seem like anything was going on. Raven and I climbed down from the tree house and headed back to the car, then we reported back at the cabin. The entire time, I wondered what was going on in that bedroom. Who was Samantha Bridgman, and why did we need to keep an eye on her? Whatever the case, I just

270

kept my mouth shut while my head buzzed with starving questions. Doing what I had to do without question was all I tried to be concerned about.

Once I made it home, I called Hayley back and explained how we would have to miss Trent's birthday party the next day. She didn't seem very disappointed as she assured me that it was okay with her, but I couldn't say I felt the same.

"I was looking forward to going," I told Hayley over the phone.

"I know, but your job is more important," she said. "We'll have more opportunities to, like, do fun things."

"Yeah," I replied.

~Opus 19~

The next day was Friday, meaning I had my three-hour chemistry lab in the afternoon. A long session like that typically didn't bother me much, but Jorge felt a little different. He often became increasingly bored and antsy throughout each session.

"I'm going to a birthday party tonight," he told me while sorting through test tubes. "You're invited. I was told to bring any friends."

"Birthday party?" I said, thinking about it. "Is it for someone named Trent?"

"Yeah, you know him!" said Jorge enthusiastically. "Are you coming? From what I hear, it's going to be a big bash."

"I was planning on it," I replied glumly, "but I have to do something for work. I won't make it."

"Bummer," he said. "Oh well, I'm sure there will be other parties and stuff."

"It's not a big deal," I said. "My job is more important."

I remembered the previous night when Raven and I observed Samantha in her room. Lighting candles and being in the dark for that amount of time was a little strange, but there wasn't anything too notable about that. However, the candles all blowing out at once made me curious, especially since the room remained pitch black after that. It was possible Samantha could have gone to sleep at that point, but I had a hunch that said otherwise.

Raven said we had to be at the specified location at six, which would give me a little more than two hours after chemistry. I planned on getting a good meal beforehand, owing to the possibility of this stakeout being much longer than the first one. My heart beat quicker in anticipation of the assignment, which I found a bit of excitement in. It was likely that I was getting used to my duties as a member of the club.

Chemistry wrapped up with a mini lecture about next week's session. Not wanting to appear overly anxious to get out of there, I consciously kept myself from packing up too quickly and springing out of the room.

"I'll catch you later, Jorge," I said on my way out.

"Alright, Mike," he replied. "Have a good one, man."

Before heading back home, I decided to swing through the drive-thru of a burger joint and fuel myself for the upcoming assignment. The restaurant had a few options I typically liked, and I settled with one of the larger combos they had to offer. Once the food was handed to me, the drive home in a burger-scented car made my stomach growl.

I entered my apartment, food in hand, and was greeted by Sapphira. Before I settled down to eat, I wanted to ask Sapphira about what I had witnessed at Samantha's house.

"What do you know about using candles for witchcraft rituals?" I asked her.

"Candles have been an important tool for centuries," she explained. "They are said to absorb a person's energy and release it into the air to produce an ideal atmosphere for magical practices. The color and type of wax are also crucial, depending on what the magic user is trying to achieve."

"Oh," I said.

Sapphira's response wasn't exactly what I was hoping for, but at least it provided a little insight for me. From what I could understand, candles were important for performing magic and weren't just clichéd decorations for establishing a mysterious environment.

"Do you wish to perform a magical ritual?" Sapphira asked.

"No," I said. "I was just curious, I guess."

"Keep this in mind, Michael," she told me, "improper use of magic can be harmful or dangerous. I advise that you consult me prior to performing any rituals of your own."

"I don't plan on performing that stuff," I replied, taking my food out of the paper bag.

"Is there anything else you wish of me?" she asked.

"Not now." I sat down at the table and unwrapped my burger. "You're dismissed."

"Very well."

When Sapphira vanished, I was left to contemplate my assignment a little more. Although there was little hard evidence of Samantha using witchcraft, my gut was telling me that something of that nature had happened last night. Why else would a club that dabbles in the supernatural be interested in her? There was more to this than merely a room full of candles.

A text message was sent to my phone at a quarter after five. In it were the details of the assignment, saying that we were to wait for Samantha at an arts and crafts store, follow her home, and report her actions until after midnight. A lump formed in my throat when I read the timeframe. Six hours was a long period of time to secretly keep an eye on someone. The big meal I had just eaten would probably hold me over that long, but I was now a little less excited about the mission.

Soon after receiving the text, Raven called me to confirm the objective.

"I'll pack something to eat so we don't starve," she told me. "Won't this be fun? I'm somewhat looking forward to this!"

"Uh, I guess," I replied.

"Gee, you sound bored already," she said. "What's wrong? You seemed so eager to do this before."

"No, it's nothing," I assured. "I'm ready for this."

"That's what I like to hear! I'll be at your place in a little bit. You're driving."

"Me? Why am I driving?"

"First, I *always* drive you around," she said sharply. "Second, my car was parked in front of the target's house last night. Using yours will reduce the chances of them noticing something suspicious. We're gonna be doing suspicious things tonight, but nobody needs to know that."

"You really have a way with explanations," I said.

"That's flattering!" she replied, probably being sarcastic. "I'll see you in a little. Be ready. Ciao."

In order to minimize criticism from Raven for being slow, I waited outside in the parking lot for her. As soon as she arrived, we immediately got into my car and were on our way. She was carrying a bag filled with everything we might need, which she placed in the backseat. The arts and crafts store we needed to go to was in a familiar place, so I drove us there with no problems. We arrived about ten minutes before six.

274

"We're making good time," Raven stated, grabbing her bag from the backseat. "Here, this is for you."

She handed me a juice box, which I looked at questioningly.

"Uh, thanks," I said.

"Make it last," she told me. "We only have one each."

"That's it?"

"That's it."

"Did you bring anything else?" I asked.

"What were you expecting? A three-course meal?"

"Well, I was expecting more."

Raven gave me a disgruntled look, which quickly turned into a smirk.

"I have some crackers for later," she said. "We're not gonna die from malnutrition. Six hours isn't terribly long."

"I'm not worried about malnutrition," I snapped. "I really don't care what you brought or how much you brought."

"You shouldn't let stupid things distract you from the task at hand," she said snobbishly. "Just focus, okay?"

Feeling irritated, I put the juice box in my cup holder and heaved a deep breath.

"I'm focused!" I told her. "I don't have any problems with this assignment."

"Then are you gonna let our target drive away?"

Raven pointed to a car across the parking lot, which was just backing out of the space. The car matched the description Raven had translated from Oriole's document the day before, and it was definitely Samantha's car. Not wanting to waste any time, I quickly pursued her.

"Why didn't you tell me she was out here already?" I grunted at Raven.

"That's a good question," she replied deviously.

Samantha pulled out of the parking lot and into the flow of traffic before I could catch up to her. I had to wait for a few cars to pass before I could turn onto the street.

"The target appears to be gaining distance," said Raven indifferently, toying with her silver ornament necklace. "Don't lose her."

275

"I'm not going to lose her," I said firmly.

"She's making a right up here," she said. "You need to be in the right lane."

"Can you just let me drive?" I muttered.

"Have you ever caused a car accident?" she asked. "I always had the feeling you were a safe driver."

"No accidents," I said, squeezing into an opening to get into the right lane. "I'd like to keep it that way."

"You'd better not get us into an accident," she said. "If you do, I'll have you bound and quartered using mopeds."

"OH MY GOD!"

As we were going around the corner, I yelled and slammed on the brakes for a split second, just to make the tires screech a little and cause the seat belts to lock. The sudden jolt made Raven cover her eyes and let out a squeal more high-pitched than the tires. As I laughed heartily at Raven's reaction, she gave me a scowl.

"Are you *crazy*?" she barked angrily. "What the hell was *that*?"

"Just a prank," I grinned.

"It wasn't funny," she sulked. "I almost had a heart attack. You'd have to drag a dead girl out of your car and explain to the authorities that your reckless driving took the life of an innocent victim."

I was enjoying the moment too much to reply, feeling that it was payback for all the crap I took from Raven. We had mostly caught up to Samantha at that point, and the trick was to stay far enough behind so that she wouldn't suspect we were following her. You could say that I was having a little too much fun with the assignment, but I made sure to keep myself from getting careless.

Shortly before arriving at Samantha's house, I circled the block to give her time to get inside her home. When we eventually parked across the street, it had become dark enough for me to feel comfortable about sneaking around. Raven and I took our position in the tree house one more time, ready for the second half of our assignment.

276

"Why did we have to follow her from the store?" I asked flatly when we were settled. "It seemed unnecessary."

"That's what our assignment said to do," Raven replied.

"Of course," I muttered.

"We'll do this just as before," said Raven, using the binoculars to peer through Samantha's window.

"Do you see anything?" I asked as I reached for my phone to send any informative text messages to Oriole.

"The lights are off," said Raven. "I don't think she's in there right now."

Target's bedroom is dark. Does not appear to be in room.

After I sent the text message, something came to mind.

"Hey, I just thought of something," I said.

"Yeah?"

"Should we be watching more than just her room?" I asked. "What if she's doing something important in another part of the house?"

Raven didn't answer right away, but seemed to think about what I had said.

"That's a good point," she said. "Go around the house and check inside the windows."

"Why don't *you* do that?" I asked. "I want to stay up here."

"You're my assistant," she told me sternly. "I have rank over you. You should know this by now."

"Won't you get lonely?" I replied sarcastically. "There'll be nobody here to keep you company but the squirrels."

"What do you mean?" she asked. "There are squirrels in here?"

"I don't know," I shrugged. "We're in a tree, after all. It's possible that squirrels, like, run through here all the time."

If I had realized the impact of my statement sooner, I would have said something else to terrorize Raven a little more.

"I hate squirrels!" she hissed. "They're like tree rats! Why did you have to say something so horrible? Stay here, I'll go around the other side of the house."

Raven thrust the binoculars into my chest, then headed down the ladder, moving a little quicker than usual. The darker side of me rejoiced a little, knowing that I was developing the necessary skills to annoy Raven. I would have to be careful, though. Who knew what crazy things she would do just to settle the score?

After about twenty minutes of nothing happening, Samantha's bedroom light finally turned on. I quickly took a look inside with the binoculars and watched Samantha walk across the window. I hastily texted Oriole, letting her know that the target was in her room.

This is crazy, I thought after my message sent. *I don't know what I'm going to do if she starts undressing. Watching it wouldn't be right, but it's my duty, I guess. Yeah, it's for the club, so there's nothing I can do about it.*

As it turned out, she never got undressed. In fact, she didn't do anything that needed to be reported. A lengthy amount of time passed with nothing notable happening. I inserted the straw into the juice box Raven gave me, then practically inhaled the entire thing. Those juice boxes were never big enough for me, even when I was a kid.

The sound of someone climbing up the ladder caught my attention. For a second, I thought I was screwed. Had someone noticed me? I reached for the putter by my side. When Raven crawled inside the tree house, I heaved a sigh of relief.

"I didn't see anything significant," she said.

"All that's happened was she came back to her room," I told her. "There's nothing else to report."

Raven took the binoculars and gazed into the room.

"That's her, alright," she said.

"You aren't afraid of the squirrels?" I teased. "I'm surprised you came back."

"I'm not afraid of them," she said. "I just don't like them. Hey, it looks like she's getting some more candles together."

"Are you sure that's what she's doing?" I asked.

"Positive."

I texted Oriole to let her know. After a couple minutes, the bedroom light went out again, and only the candles lit the room.

"It's just like last night!" said Raven.

"That's kinda strange, don't you think?" I said. "I wonder what she's doing in there."

"Hmm, I don't know," said Raven. "I still can't see anything from here."

"Maybe Samantha just likes candlelight," I said.

"Don't be dumb," she replied. "Maybe we could climb up the house and look directly in."

"Are you nuts?" I asked, knowing full well that she was.

"I know it's reckless," she told me. "How else do we find out what's really happening in there?"

"I don't think it's a necessary risk," I muttered.

The rest of the night was more or less an exact repeat of the previous night, including the part when the candles all seemed to go out simultaneously. Even with the room pitch black, the two of us remained in the tree house until midnight. When we reported back to the cabin's meeting room, Miss Flamingo was the only person there. Then again, she seemed to always be there.

"We completed our assignment," Raven told her dutifully.

"Well done," said Miss Flamingo. "Here are your payments."

She handed us our envelopes, and I tucked mine away into my pocket. My savings account was beginning to have a healthy balance in it because of these ludicrous tasks.

"There isn't much to report," I said.

"Oriole has all of your messages documented," said Miss Flamingo. "I'll review them soon. You two are dismissed."

That night, I lied in bed and wondered about Samantha. Something was giving me a strange vibe, but I was uncertain if it was because of my heightened spiritual connection or just my imagination. Regardless, something odd about Samantha was resting on my mind.

Things have a peculiar way of coming together. "Fate" and "coincidence" have been sworn enemies for much of mankind's history, and their feuds still continue to this day. I say this because of the string of events that practically fell into place the next day.

While I was enjoying my lazy Saturday afternoon, Aaron called me to hang out. He and Lawrence had met up somewhere, and they wanted to come to my place to get down on some games. Being the bored guy that I was, I agreed to their request. Not much time later, they showed up at my apartment and we fired up the video games.

Whether it was fate or coincidence, that was when Lawrence set the ball rolling.

"There's this girl I work with," he said while we were taking a frozen pizza break. "Her name's Samantha."

Neither of them noticed the fact that I had stopped in the middle of chewing at that point.

"Samantha?" said Aaron. "Is she hot?"

"She's cute, I'd say," Lawrence replied. "We've been talking a lot. I think I might ask her out soon."

"What's with everyone getting hitched lately?" said Aaron, sprinkling parmesan cheese on his pizza. "First Mike, now you. It's like the cupid is afraid of being laid off."

"You don't mean Samantha Bridgman, do you?" I asked Lawrence.

"Yeah, that's her," he said. "Do you know her?"

"Uh, not personally," I said.

"I know you don't like Harbert's, but you should come in to meet her sometime," said Lawrence. "I trust you, bro, and not only because you have a girlfriend."

"That's right," said Aaron cockily. "If I talk to her, she'd be swooning into my arms in no time!"

Lawrence gave Aaron an unsure look, and Aaron stared back at him and took a big bite of pizza.

"Yeah, I might do that," I said, taking a bold plunge into the situation. "Um, she seems like an interesting person. Do you know what her interests are?"

"She's kinda eccentric," said Lawrence.

"How so?"

"Just come in and talk to her," he said. "We both work tomorrow afternoon and evening, so come then."

"Heh heh, I'll be there, too," said Aaron.

A little extra information gathering wouldn't hurt, I thought. *This might be a good chance to learn what we missed from the last two nights.*

Sure enough, I found myself outside of Harbert's Groceries the next afternoon. The place I hated the most was turning into an inescapable part of my life. Gulping down my pride, I walked through the main entrance, all in the name of investigation. Scoping out the checkout lanes, I spotted Lawrence. Sure enough, Samantha was talking with him. Surprisingly, Aaron was nowhere to be found.

"Hey, it's Mike!" said Lawrence as I approached them.

"What's up?" I said casually.

"This is Mike, my other pal," said Lawrence to Samantha.

"Hi," she said, shaking my hand. "You can call me Sam."

"Nice to meet you," I said.

"We were just talking about peanut butter," said Lawrence. "Which do you like, smooth or crunchy?"

"Uh, smooth," I replied.

"You guys are boring," said Samantha. "Crunchy all the way!"

"I told you she was eccentric," Lawrence whispered audibly to me.

"It's not that weird," said Samantha. "At least I don't wear my socks in the shower like *some* people."

"I stopped doing that when I was eight!" said Lawrence.

"Hey, do I know you from somewhere?" Samantha asked me. "You go to college here, don't you?"

"Yeah," I replied. "It's my second year."

"Alright," she said. "I don't think you're in any of my classes, but I've seen you around."

"He's heard of your name before," said Lawrence. "He knew who you were when I told him about you."

281

"Really?" she said with an interested twinkle in her eye. "Where'd you hear about me? I didn't know I was that popular."

"Well, I can't really remember," I lied. "I just, like, heard about you from somewhere."

"I guess I took your job here when you left," she said, blowing off my answer. "If it wasn't for you, I'd probably be on the unemployment line right now."

"Funny how things work out, huh?" I said.

In the short time I had met Samantha, I could already see her quirkiness as described by Lawrence. Still, there was hardly anything that immediately warranted her as a user of magic. I would have to dig a little deeper to satisfy my curiosity at the very least. That was when the situation I had been dreading decided to present itself. Simply put, Bill Straussford had crawled out of his office dwelling. There was no mistaking the tall, lanky snake as he slithered across the store in our direction.

"Are we taking a break?" he said in his monotonous drone.

A hundred comments regarding my current thoughts and feelings swirled in my brain, but I remained silent and kept myself from pouring gas on the flames.

"No, just talking," said Lawrence.

"I need the workers to avoid distractions on the job," said Bill. "We don't want any more mishaps."

Before he walked away, his eyes met mine for a brief moment. While he slowly retreated to his office refuge, I knew this trip to the grocery store was over. Retreat was essential, otherwise I would probably romp down the aisles and knock things off the shelves with maniacal satisfaction.

"Mr. Straussford's a cool guy," said Samantha.

What did she just say?

"Yeah, he is," said Lawrence.

Lawrence! I should slap you for negligence! Why say such heinous things just to win the approval of one girl?

"Well, I gotta get going," I said. "It was nice meeting you, Sam."

282

"Likewise, Mike," she said. "Come visit us again."

"Later, bro," said Lawrence.

I walked out of the store feeling as if I had just wasted my time. Not only did I encounter my mortal enemy, but I was no closer to proving or disproving my suspicions of Samantha. Miss Flamingo was interested in her, so there was obviously something underneath the surface. I considered sending out Sapphira to spy on Samantha, but sending a demon to someone's house seemed worse than spying from a tree.

Later that evening, I was able to stop mulling over Samantha, or at least put my curiosity on the backburner of my mind. My time was instead occupied by studying for my history test, which was scheduled for the next class. With my nose buried in the textbook, my understanding of Chad's passion for history became a little clearer. Getting lost in the past was a way to escape from the present, if only for a little while.

During the Civil War, President Abraham Lincoln spent extensive amounts of time in a telegraph room, sending and receiving messages regarding multiple aspects of the war. Information is an invaluable tool in battle, and Lincoln pushed the limits of the new telegraph system to give the Union an upper hand. Without that network of information, the war's outcome probably would have been different.

"Knowledge is power," I said to myself while tapping my eraser on my notes.

The entire concept brought up thoughts of Miss Flamingo's club. She probably had an information network that extended well beyond the cabin's conference room, so I wondered if she had ways of compensating for any failures performed by the club members. If Raven and I hadn't gathered enough information on Samantha, would someone else finish the job for us? Someone who I've never met or even heard of?

I yawned loudly, staring at my open textbook with sleepy eyes. I felt that I had studied enough for the test, and I was satisfied with my notes. Putting everything away, I called it a night and headed to bed.

~Opus 20~

The remainder of October dragged by. Aside from the oddities of the club and being stuck with Sapphira, college life had mostly returned to normal. Psychology was still a pain in my butt, but Hayley was able to coach me through well enough to get passing grades. However, tutoring was far from the best reason why I was grateful to have Hayley. This may sound sappy, but I was madly in love with her.

Only one thing was left before bidding farewell to the month of October, and that was the Halloween party for the club. The night before the party, I did some grocery shopping for the roast beef and peanut butter fudge. Although the party's attendees were permitted to wear costumes, Hayley and I decided not to dress up. Not just because we thought it was stupid or embarrassing, but mainly because we were lazy.

On my way to the party, I picked Hayley up from her house. She told me the car smelled good from the roast beef, and I couldn't have agreed with her more. We showed up at the established venue at a quarter to eight. Despite Miss Flamingo's assurance, I was still a little uncomfortable about bringing someone to meet the rest of the club members. As we carried our food to the entrance, I wondered how I would introduce Hayley to everyone since we knew each other only by appointed nicknames. I swore Miss Flamingo only held this party to stress me out.

The banquet room was very nicely decorated for the occasion. Walking through the door, it was as if we stepped into a genuine horror movie (aside from the fluorescent lights and fresh smell). Even the carpet looked old and tattered.

"Wow, this looks really good!" said Hayley, glancing around at the ghoulish decorations.

"Somebody was pretty serious about Halloween this year," I said.

"You should know that I'm always serious," said a voice from next to me.

Miss Flamingo had practically appeared out of nowhere, wearing an elaborate masquerade costume. She had bright pink plumes feathering out from her head, and a black masquerade mask. Her crimson and black dress looked like something out of the Victorian Era. The entire getup somehow amplified her personality, and suited her very well.

"I'd like to introduce my girlfriend," I said once I got over the shock of Miss Flamingo's appearance. "This is Hayley."

"Hi," said Hayley shyly.

"This is my boss, Miss Flamingo." I just felt weird saying that.

"It's a pleasure," said Miss Flamingo, shaking Hayley's hand. "You two are the first ones here. The others should be arriving soon. Until then, you may put the food you brought on that long table over there."

Hayley and I took the roast beef and fudge to the other side of the room, placing it on the table like Miss Flamingo instructed. There were already some snacks laid out, such as cheese, crackers, and veggies. All child's play compared to what I had brought.

"I'm looking forward to tasting what you made, Roadrunner," said Miss Flamingo, who followed us to the food table.

"Roadrunner?" Hayley asked, looking at me with a questioning smile.

"Uh, it's an interesting story," I told her, not knowing how to explain.

"We have nicknames for everyone at work," said Miss Flamingo. "It's to promote a fun, friendly environment."

Fun and friendly. I had to bite my tongue not to laugh at that preposterous statement.

"Ah," said Hayley. "Does that mean 'Miss Flamingo' is a nickname, too?"

The icy stare that Hayley received sent a chill down my spine, even though the look wasn't directed at me. To my surprise, Miss Flamingo smiled.

"She's a cute one, Roadrunner," she told me. "Make yourselves comfortable. Who knows how long it'll take for the others to arrive."

The next person to show up was Skylark, dressed in a Star Trek outfit and carrying a covered bowl of orange punch. He was accompanied by a person completely hidden under a creepy monster costume, who was carrying a ton of salad in four large bowls stacked on top of one another. Miss Flamingo directed them over to the food table.

"The punch and salads have landed!" Skylark announced as he and his partner placed everything on the table.

"That's a lot of salad," I said, looking at the four large bowls of lettuce.

"It's easy to make," Skylark replied.

"What kind of punch is that?" Hayley asked.

"A combination of mango, orange, guava, and pitaya," said Skylark. "Pitaya is dragon fruit. This punch is the result of my own tropical blend."

"Ooh, that sounds good!" said Hayley.

"I don't believe we've met," said Skylark, shaking Hayley's hand. "You can call me Skylark."

"I'm Hayley."

"Nice to meet you, Hayley."

"Who's your buddy?" I asked, nodding toward the monster person.

"That's a secret," said Skylark with a smirk. "Let's go find a table, you hideous beast."

The hideous beast responded with a grunt as the two of them took a seat.

"You wanna take a seat somewhere?" I asked Hayley.

"Yeah," she replied.

We sat down at a nearby table, mainly so I could keep an eye on the food and hear people's reactions when they got seconds on what I brought.

The next person to walk into the banquet room was none other than Raven, carrying a stack of pizzas with cupcakes on top. I was surprised to see that she wasn't dressed up at all, because I took her for the type of person to go all out for something like this, especially Halloween. What didn't surprise me was that she showed up by herself, and it was the first time

I had ever really wondered about her social life outside of the club.

Raven set the pizzas and cupcakes on the table, and for whatever reason, walked right up to Hayley and I.

"Hey there, Roadrunner!" she said, sounding more cheerful than her stoic expression deemed appropriate.

"Hey," I replied.

Raven looked at Hayley, and they held eye contact for a very brief, yet very awkward moment.

"I've seen you before," said Raven. "You're that girl who was with my partner in the library."

Hayley's displeased smile made me swoop in to take control of this conversation as soon as I could.

"This is Hayley, my girlfriend," I explained. "This is Raven. We work together."

"Yeah, that's what you said before," said Hayley flatly.

"Hmm." Raven had a scheming look on her face, and it bothered me.

"What?" I asked.

"Does she know we call you 'Roadrunner' around here?"

"Miss Flamingo already explained the nickname thing to her," I said.

"I think it's pretty cool," said Raven. "Having nicknames makes things a little more interesting."

"Easy for you to say," I replied. "Your nickname is a real name."

"I wonder what your girlfriend's name would be if she worked with us?" said Raven.

It seemed like Raven was trying to strike up a friendly conversation with Hayley, but Hayley didn't seem interested at all.

"Swan, or something," I said.

Hayley gave me a confused look.

"Why would I be 'Swan'?" she asked.

"Um, it just kinda popped into my head," I replied.

Raven wasn't helping the situation by giving me the same purposeless look she always gave me. To make things worse, she then actually sat down at our table. I would have to keep things going well by having a casual conversation with Raven, which required some level of social skills I didn't think I had.

"What kind of pizza did you bring?" I asked Raven.

"All kinds," she said. "I don't really know. I didn't check."

"And I see you brought cupcakes, too," I said.

"Don't call it a cupcake. The politically correct term is 'budget cake.'"

"Is that so?" I asked, raising an eyebrow.

"They were made on a budget," said Raven, interlocking her fingers, "yet I don't think the correctness is literally political."

Hayley gave me another confused look, and I gave her a look that said I was just as confused as her but got used to it. I know it's a lot to say with a single look, but I think I pulled it off. Maybe I should have just shrugged.

"So, what did you bring?" Raven asked me intently. "I remember you saying something crazy."

"Roast beef," I said, "and peanut butter fudge covered with chocolate ganache. All homemade."

"Since when have you been so chef-like?" Raven asked.

"He's just naturally talented," Hayley told her dully.

Raven appeared mildly amused by that answer.

"I suppose," she said, toying with the silver trinket on her necklace. "He avariedly performs well at work, but I never took him for a good cook."

I could feel Hayley's annoyance levels rising by the second. Something would have to be done quickly before her levels reached critical. Fortunately, Oriole walked over to our table and saved the day.

"Hi!" Oriole greeted.

"Hello," I replied.

"Raven," said Oriole, "do you have a moment?"

"I have several," Raven answered.

"I need your help with something," said Oriole. "It's about my costume."

Raven stood up without a word, and the two of them walked out just like that. I felt overly relieved to have gotten out of that situation so easily.

Cormorant entered the banquet room shortly after Raven and Oriole walked out. He was wearing baggy track pants, a basketball jersey, and a big afro wig. Seeing him made me chuckle. He was with another black guy who was much shorter and dressed like a vampire. They were both carrying what I suspected to be the sweet potato pie Cormorant mentioned.

Moments after Cormorant's arrival, Kookaburra showed up with a girl. Neither of them were wearing a costume, but Kookaburra was most definitely carrying two half-gallons of something presumably alcoholic. The girl was carrying a tinfoil pan of chicken wings.

Raven and Oriole returned minutes later. Oriole was wearing some kind of fairy princess costume, complete with frilly, sparkling, poofy things, a magic wand, and wings. The crown on her head was covered with jewels, which suited her yellow dress.

I noticed somebody sitting alone at a table in the corner closest to the entrance. He was a young man, possibly around my age, and was wearing a black tuxedo with his hair slicked back. My initial thought was that he was dressed up as a business professional, but I couldn't tell for sure. Why would someone like that be at a Halloween party like this one? The outfit might have been a costume. Furthermore, who did he come with? All of the club members seemed to be sitting with their guests, and Miss Flamingo wouldn't just let someone join us...or would she?

The tuxedo dude wasn't interacting with anyone, nor did anyone else acknowledge him. He remained seated in the corner, staring off into space. Despite my slight curiosity, I was busy focusing on something more important.

"I'm starving," I said to Hayley, rubbing my hands together. "I can't wait to raid the grub."

"Yeah," she replied with a meager smile.

"Don't let Raven piss you off," I said. "She's just like that, but I don't think she means anything by it."

"It's fine," she replied, looking away.

I reached across the table and grabbed her hand. When she looked at me, I gave her a smile. She hesitated for a moment, then returned a smile more sincere than the words she had just uttered.

Miss Flamingo stood up in the back of the room, and everyone immediately gave her full attention. The masquerade costume she wore gave her an even more powerful presence, if that was even possible.

"Good evening, everyone," she announced. "I see that everyone has made it right on time. Let me take this moment to thank all those who have helped preparing for this event. There's a generous amount of food available, so I ask everyone to help themselves. Enjoy and have fun. That is all."

Like moths to a flame, we all headed straight for the food table. Since Hayley and I were right next to it, we were first in line. I heaped my plate with a little of everything that wasn't dessert, except for the roast beef I brought. I already knew what it tasted like, and I wanted there to be enough for everyone else.

Hayley's mood improved once we started eating. She seemed to have dismissed Raven's intrusion, or at least she was good at hiding her irritability.

That was when I realized that the young man in the tuxedo was still sitting in the same spot. He was the only person who didn't have a plate or something to drink. I would have just ignored him, but he suddenly looked over and noticed me eyeing him.

Have you ever made eye contact with a stranger and felt awkward about it? That sort of thing can make someone feel a little strange. This was *not* one of those cases. As soon as I made eye contact with this guy, an undeniably potent chill ran through my body. The force of this chill was so great that not only did it make me shiver, but it startled the crap out of me.

"What is it?" Hayley asked me when she noticed my reaction.

"Just a chill," I told her, trying not to look odd. "How's that sweet potato pie?"

"Scrumptious," she replied. "I've made it before, but this one puts mine to shame. Who made it? They really know what they're doing."

"Our vice president brought it," I told her.

"Which one is that?" she asked, looking around.

"The guy who looks like a basketball star at a disco club."

"Alright, I'll have to tell him how awesome it was!"

Using the very edges of my peripheral vision, I checked to see if the tuxedo dude was still looking at me. Oddly, he wasn't sitting at that corner table anymore. Looking around, I was unable to find him anywhere in the room, and that creeped me out a little more than having him stare at me. Something strange was happening, and I could feel it in my gut.

I took a sip of my punch, and the mysterious young man appeared out of thin air, standing next to our table. The sudden jolt of shock made me choke on my drink, spilling some of it on the table.

"Are you alright?" Hayley asked worriedly.

All I could reply with was coughing, but she quickly hurried to my side with a napkin to clean up the mess. I saw her go straight through the young man, and I quickly understood what was going on. He quietly watched as Hayley wiped off my face.

"Easy there!" said Cormorant on his way back to the food table. "Don't wanna perform the Heimlich!"

"Aw, your girlfriend's so cute," said Oriole in a somewhat dreamy voice. "She was right there to help you out."

Hayley turned red with embarrassment.

"Thanks, babe," I said, keeping a close eye on the tuxedo guy. "I just had some punch go down the wrong pipe."

"Be more careful, okay?" she said. "Although it was a little funny."

Hayley walked back through the young man before taking her seat, making me feel more uneasy.

"There's a draft in here," she said, rubbing her arms.

291

I almost didn't hear what she said, because this guy was just staring at me. Honestly, I had no idea what to do. How could I interact with him without Hayley noticing?

"Excuse me?"

The voice seemed to come out of nowhere, but I knew who said it. I looked up at the young man and could see there was desperation on his face.

"Excuse me?" he said again. His lips didn't move and his voice sounded distant.

The concept of spirits no longer surprised me the way it used to. Under normal circumstances, I would have wanted to talk to him. Looking around, all I could do was subtly shrug. I guess none of this supernatural stuff was a "normal circumstance" to begin with.

"Please," he said, "help me."

Something like this would happen, wouldn't it? I thought morbidly. *This is All Hallows' Eve, after all.*

"Please," he repeated.

The last thing I wanted was a begging ghost next to the table for the rest of the night. A begging dog is bad enough, but this was a whole new story. Heaving a huge sigh, I pushed back my chair and stood up.

"I'll be right back," I told Hayley.

"Okay," she said.

The young man became smoky in appearance as he drifted toward the door. My neck hairs stood up, and I rubbed the amulet in my pocket just to feel a little safer. On my way out of the banquet room, I glanced back and saw Miss Flamingo watching me, making my hairs stand up even straighter. A part of me wondered if she knew what was going on, but I exited without a second thought.

I left the building, finding myself alone in the parking lot. The sun had barely made it under the horizon, and darkness was quickly descending. Spirits seem to have a problem with daylight, which certainly doesn't make it easier for anyone who needs visible light on their retinas to see.

"Hello?" I called out in a voice slightly louder than a whisper. "Where'd you go?"

A smoky apparition slowly formed several feet in front of me, taking the shape of the young man in the tuxedo. Such an appearance was much nicer than suddenly popping out of nowhere.

"Will you help me?" he asked, still not moving his mouth.

"Uh…maybe," I replied. "I followed you out here, so I'll at least hear you out."

I patted the amulet in my pocket, wondering why it wasn't repelling the spirit. From what I had learned from Sapphira, it meant that this spirit was either super strong or not dangerous. I was hoping that it was the latter.

"My grave is nearby," he told me. "Something has been disturbing my rest."

"Okay," I said hesitantly. "Are you asking me to fix your grave or something?"

"Yes," he said. "You have an extraordinary level of sensitivity for the world beyond your own. I feel you are well suited for this favor."

I rustled my hair, not really wanting to oblige to his request. However, I couldn't just let it go.

"I'm in the middle of something right now," I explained. "I shouldn't just leave. They'll wonder where I went."

"My grave is right through those woods there," he said, pointing to the patch of woods behind the building. "It's only a short walk from here. Please."

I thought about it for a moment. This would've been the perfect time to just walk away, but of course I didn't.

"I'll try," I said finally.

"Thank you so much," he said, smiling.

"What do I have to do?" I asked.

The spirit disappeared without answering my question, leaving me alone again.

"Wait a second!" I called out. "What do I have to do? Hello? Hey!"

I glanced around, but there was no sign of anyone. With a distraught groan, my feet began moving in the direction of the woods. Whatever I had to do, I hoped it wasn't anything extreme.

Leaves crunched under every footstep as I trudged through the woods. The only source of light I had was from my phone's screen, which wasn't very much. Luckily, I had plenty of practice with walking through thick woods when I got lost with the guys on that camping trip.

Just as the spirit said, the walk through the woods wasn't very far at all. I emerged on the other side to find myself in a cemetery. Seeing the field of headstones stretching out before me in the night was a little discomforting. Furthermore, I had no idea where tuxedo dude's grave was. All I could do was stand there, scratch my head, and contemplate.

While I was trying to figure out what to do, I sensed something that can only be described as "movement" coming from my left. I strained my eyes as I carefully scanned the area where the sensation came from, but saw nothing. Treading cautiously, I followed my instincts and wandered into the cemetery.

The same feeling washed over me again, but it was much more distinct this time, and also much more unsettling. I hesitated, stopping abruptly. When the feeling quickly subsided, I continued onward, this time slower and more cautiously.

Not much time passed before I felt the sensation a third time, and it was even more potent, making me shiver as the uneasiness swept past me like a dirty wind. This time, I could see something moving in the darkness ahead of me. My heart started beating harder as I focused my eyes on the one spot where I saw the movement. Something deep inside was telling me this was the disturbance that the spirit was telling me about.

I practically dragged my feet, approaching like a tiger stalking a small, defenseless animal. Strangely, *I* felt like the small, defenseless animal this time — like a baby antelope with a death wish.

There was a good chance this thing had noticed me long before I noticed it, but it wasn't until I was about twenty feet away did it react. Taking a defensive stance, it suddenly became more visible, appearing as a four-legged animal the size of a large dog. A staring contest ensued as it let out a guttural, earthy growl. For a moment, I was paralyzed with fear. What if it charged at me? I'd be screwed, probably.

The life came back into my legs, and I slowly traversed to the left. Hidden in the shadows, I couldn't see the thing's face, but I knew it was following my every move. The thing moved with me, and I noticed it was staying between me and the headstone behind it, which was likely the grave of the spirit.

So...you're the perpetrator? I thought. *Does that mean I have to get rid of you? That blows.*

After rotating around the grave more than ninety degrees, the angle of light let me see the thing better. Standing roughly three feet tall, it resembled a dog with pitch black fur. Its eyes were still hidden, and I really wanted it to stay that way. The half tangible, half dreamlike appearance indicated that it wasn't a living creature.

Reaching into my pocket, I removed my amulet and held it out in front of me. Sweat began to form on my face and my legs trembled, but there was no turning back now. The confrontation had been established, so I was intent on following through until the end, sort of.

Swallowing hard, I began to advance on the creature, keeping the amulet ahead of me. The thing continued to stare at me and growl, and I wondered if I was making a mistake. I knew the amulet's abilities were limited, and I was taking my chance by betting that this creature was weaker than an average demon.

When I was less than ten feet away from the creature (yes, I got that close to it), it started to back away. Seeing it retreat gave me a boost of confidence, and I kept approaching. The amulet seemed to be effective in repelling it, as it kept backing away, farther from the grave. However, its constant coal-like growling was very intimidating. Despite what some would consider to be common sense, I kept my steady advance.

I have no idea how long this continued, and I wondered how far I would have to drive the creature back before it would just give up. The harrowing thought of staying by the grave just to keep this thing away crept into my mind, in which case the tuxedo dude would be out of luck.

Suddenly, the creature sank into the ground like a shadow. I wondered if it was gone, but a sharp growling sound behind me quickly answered that question. I whirled around and saw the creature had reappeared next to the grave, and anger immediately welled up inside me.

"Oh, come on," I muttered.

The creature continued to watch me closely. All of that effort proved ineffective in the end.

"Go away!" I shouted angrily, waving my fist. "Get the hell out of here!"

In response, the creature barked ferociously, making me stumble back. Apparently, screaming would get me nowhere, as the creature was obviously the louder one here. With nothing left in my repertoire of ideas, I decided to play my trump card.

"Sapphira!" I hissed.

To my relief, she immediately appeared before me.

"You called, Michael?" she asked.

"I need you to do something for me," I said, wiping the sweat off my forehead.

"Yes?" she replied.

I pointed at the creature.

"It's about that thing over there."

"That is a black dog," she explained. "They can be dangerous. However, this one seems to be displaying defensive behavior, which is very strange for a black dog."

"Awesome," I muttered. "Just get rid of it."

"How would you like me to go about this task?" Sapphira asked.

"I don't know!" I said shortly. "Use Night Slash, or something."

"I do not understand your request," she said.

"It was a bad joke," I said, chuckling in a way that implied my sanity was cracking. "That thing is disturbing the spirit of the person buried in that grave. I told the spirit I'd do something about it. Just do what you think will work."

"Very well."

Sapphira began to float, keeping her feet just inches off the ground, and circled the grave counterclockwise in a graceful manner. I couldn't see anything happening with my own eyes, but judging by the black dog's reaction, Sapphira's ritual was having some sort of effect. After a handful of revolutions, the black dog eventually fled the gravesite, vanishing amid the shadows. Sapphira ended the ritual and gently touched back on the ground.

"The entity has been expelled," she told me.

"Good job," I said. "That seemed pretty easy."

"It was a simple task," she said. "By occupying the area with my own possessive territory, I was able to cast out the black dog."

"What do you mean by 'possessive territory,' Sapphira?" I asked. "You mean you possessed the grave yourself?"

"Yes."

"That won't do any good," I groaned. "I'm pretty sure that spirit wants his grave to himself. Being in a demonic territory is probably more disturbing than that last thing!"

"Would you have me remove my territorial mark?" Sapphira asked.

"I think you should," I replied.

With a single wave of her hand, Sapphira removed her territorial mark. Within seconds, the black dog reappeared next to the headstone, and I scratched my head with frustration.

"There is another way for me to get rid of the entity," said Sapphira. "It will require more time and power, but it will leave this area free of any energies that may disturb the spirit of which you speak."

"Please do," I said flatly, looking at the time. "I really need to get back now. I'll leave it to you."

"Understood."

While Sapphira prepared to get rid of the black dog for good, I hurried back to the party. Hayley was probably wondering what happened to me, and I would have to think of some sort of excuse for being gone for so long. There's no way she would believe that I had been in the restroom for a half hour, so I'd need to formulate some other story.

I entered the banquet room casually. Hayley was still sitting in the same spot, chatting with Oriole, who had taken a seat at our table. When I approached, it appeared that they were having an enjoyable conversation.

"There you are, Mike!" said Hayley. "Did you take long enough?"

"I think I did," I said with a stupid grin.

"Where'd you go?" she inevitably asked.

"Restroom," I said, feeling like an idiot. "Then I had to make a phone call. I just lost track of time, I guess."

Luckily, the girls had been too engaged in a conversation to really pay attention to the authenticity of my story.

"We were talking about her costume," said Hayley, nodding at Oriole. "Isn't it beautiful?"

"Very pretty," I said indifferently, taking a seat.

"I worked hard to make it," said Oriole. "Raven had to help me with attaching the wings before I wore it here."

"You made that?" I suddenly felt a little more interested. "That's really amazing. I thought it was from a store."

"Nope," said Oriole. "By the way, that roast beef you made was really good. And that fudge stuff was out of this world!"

"Thanks," I said, beaming.

"There's Roadrunner!" I heard Kookaburra say from behind. "Good job on that food, man!"

Hearing such praise from Kookaburra indicated that he had been drinking, but it was good to hear nonetheless. Feeling a little worn out from the black dog situation, just about anything positive acted as a huge mood booster.

"I'm gonna get some more to eat," I told Hayley, standing back up.

"There's still a lot up there," she said.

The rest of the night went smoothly. Nobody else questioned my sudden, prolonged disappearance, including Miss Flamingo. She seemed occupied being in the company of

Cormorant and his guest. However, in the back of my mind, I couldn't shake the feeling that she somehow knew what I had just gotten myself involved in. That spirit had been in this room, so did she see him as well?

Before the party drew to a close, I noticed that Hayley appeared to be getting tired. She wasn't used to big social events, so it was no wonder that she was feeling a little drained. This worked out well, because I hadn't planned on staying too long myself.

"You awake?" I asked playfully.

"Yeah," she replied tiredly. "I'm just getting a little sleepy."

"Are you ready to go?" I rubbed her arm. "I'm ready to call it a night when you are."

"It doesn't matter," she said, yawning.

That was a clear enough answer for me. Hayley and I threw our trash away and made the round to say goodbye to everyone at the party. The last person to say bye to was Miss Flamingo.

"I'll see you later," she said. "Be careful out there. This is the night when many spirits are said to roam the earth."

I would've taken Miss Flamingo's last statement a little more lightly, except for the sharp stare she gave me while saying it. The hairs on my neck stood up again. Even with her mask on, I could feel Miss Flamingo's stare piercing my soul.

Hayley and I walked out to my car. I carried the leftovers while Hayley wrapped her arm around me. As we were getting into my car, I heard a distant voice call out to me from afar.

"Thank you."

Looking around, I saw nobody, but it was easy to tell who had said it. Not wanting to look like a weirdo in front of my girlfriend, I said nothing in reply.

~Opus 21~

Perhaps it's just me, but it seems like once Halloween is over, the rest of the following holidays quickly sneak up on you. It feels as if the year can't wait to end. That being said, Thanksgiving practically leapt out from around the corner and latched onto my face. Quite honestly, I hadn't given Thanksgiving much thought until I was attending a club meeting one evening.

Raven and I had just returned from a simple assignment of which we had to deliver biscuits and a box of rifle ammo to a person known simply as Tuba. We needed to drop the goods off behind a shed at some random house in the middle of nowhere. The job was actually very easy and fast, so I really didn't care less about this Tuba person and why they needed biscuits and bullets.

Before ending the meeting, Miss Flamingo stood up, signaling that she was preparing some kind of announcement.

"As you all may know," she stated, "this Thursday is Thanksgiving. We won't be having a meeting on that day, so this is the last club activity until next Monday. Thanksgiving is the day to give thanks to all of the people in our lives. As such, I would like to thank all of you for your hard work and dedication. I have prepared gifts for everyone here as your holiday bonuses."

If you want to pique the attention of your underlings, using the word "bonus" is a great way to do that. Miss Flamingo quickly went into the storage room and returned with a small box that had a hole cut in the top. She placed it on the table, and we all eyed it with anticipation.

"To be fair, you'll be drawing out of this box to see what prize you will receive," said Miss Flamingo.

The first person to approach the box was Cormorant. He stuck his hand through the opening and removed a piece of paper with something written on it. Everyone seemed to hold their breath as he looked at what it said.

"A home theater system," he said joyously. "Yeah, that's what I'm talkin' 'bout!"

After seeing the nice prize Cormorant got, everyone quickly took our turns to see what prizes we would receive. Kookaburra got a 32-inch television, Skylark got a mini refrigerator, Oriole got a really fancy camera, and Raven (to my horror) got a crossbow. The fiendish glow on her face made me shudder a little.

The prize I happened to receive was a tablet. I never had any interest in one, but there was probably some usefulness I could get out of it. My laptop worked just fine for me, so having a tablet seemed a little pointless. At the very least, I could sell it or give it away as a gift.

"All of your prizes are downstairs in the bedroom," said Miss Flamingo. "You can retrieve them there. That concludes this meeting. Have a happy Thanksgiving, everyone."

Everyone seemed pretty satisfied with their bonuses. I was somewhat satisfied, but the home theater or TV would have been nice. Kookaburra had a look of delight on his face as he wrapped his beefy arms around his TV and hauled it outside. As Raven examined her crossbow, a small grin spread across her face.

"Do you know the things I can do with this?" she said, clutching the weapon close to her chest.

"I'm afraid to know," I muttered, snatching up my tablet.

"Hey, that's a really nice tablet," Skylark told me. "It's supposed to be the best one you can get right now."

"I wouldn't know," I said, looking at the box. "Maybe it'll be handy for something."

Despite my enthusiasm to use the tablet for *something*, it remained in its box for a while.

I spent Thanksgiving alone at home. Hayley had plans with her family all day, but was going to spend the next day with me. The peace and quiet was nice, and I mainly relaxed and did nothing worth mentioning all day. My Thanksgiving dinner was a turkey sandwich with instant mashed potatoes, which was all I needed.

"I can prepare a feast for you," Sapphira offered as I mixed the powdered potatoes with water. "It is understood that

301

Thanksgiving is a special occasion for humans of your culture, and bountiful food is a longstanding tradition."

"No, I'm fine with this," I told her. "There's no reason to go all out. Even if I did, I could make something myself."

Later that evening, when I was talking to Hayley over the phone, we discussed our plans for the next day. She wanted to spend some quality time with me and agreed to come over to my place. We could watch some movies, make something to eat, and do other awesome things that couples do during quality time together.

Calm yourself, Michael, I thought. *Don't get overly excited about this. It's going to be just another day with Hayley, except you'll be spending it in the privacy of your home.*

"I can't wait for tomorrow," she said happily over the phone.

"You'll have fun," I said. "I'll do my best to make sure of that."

After hanging up, the weight of the situation came down on me. First, Hayley was coming to my apartment for the first time. Second, my apartment was a mess. I glanced around at the clutter and realized it wouldn't be good to have my girlfriend see the man cave in its current state. Random clothes and trash had been scattered around, untouched since before I could remember. Video game stuff littered the living room. Almost nothing was organized. Although it was within the boundaries of being a civilized home, it was far from presentable.

Into the wee hours of the night, I rushed around to clean the apartment. The task seemed simple at first, but became more daunting the more I worked. Organizing and putting things away was never my specialty, and I quickly found myself getting frustrated.

After putting most of my stuff away in a neat and orderly fashion, I decided to save the actual cleaning for the next day. Upon waking up the following morning, the first thought that crossed my mind was cleaning the bathroom, which included scrubbing the toilet. Not a pleasant thought to start the day with.

I blew the dust off of the bleach bottle and toilet scrubber, then went to work on places that most people prefer to forget about. While hunched over in the darkest corners of my bathroom with a sponge and disinfectant, the thought of asking Sapphira for help kept coming up. However, there was a sense of pride in doing the work myself, and I wasn't about to take the wimpy way out. This was all for my girlfriend, and I was going to do it with my own sweat, tears, and blood!

At long last, I reached the point that I thought would never come: the apartment was cleaned and organized. Not only did it look better, but the scent of a disinfected home put the cherry on top. I stood in my living room, feeling accomplished and proud.

"Hey, Sapphira!" I called.

"Yes?" she answered upon appearing.

"What do you think of the place?" I asked, beaming.

"Very nice," she said in her usual toneless tone.

"Alright, here's the plan," I explained. "My girlfriend is coming over today. You know what that means?"

"I will remain out of sight and undetected," she said. "Is that correct?"

"Right," I replied. "Uh, that's about it, I think."

"I understand," she said. "Anything else you need from me?"

"That's all," I said. "If I need anything, I'll let you know."

"Understood."

I called Hayley to let her know I was about to leave to pick her up. On my way to her house, I could barely hold in my excitement as I jammed to my victory music. This was going to be a great day, I just knew it.

As soon as she got in my car, I could tell that she was sharing the same level of excitement as me. The smile on her face said it all.

"Hi!" she greeted perkily.

"Hi, babe," I said. "You all ready?"

"Yup!"

After a quick kiss, I shifted into reverse and we were on our way.

"How was your Thanksgiving?" I asked on the way back to my place.

"Good," she said. "It's nice to see my family. How was yours? You weren't too lonely, I hope?"

"Nah, it was peaceful," I said. "I didn't feel lonely because I knew I'd be with you today."

She blushed a little. That cute look never got old.

"This is my first time at your place," she said.

"It's nothing special," I told her. "I hope you know that I slaved last night and this morning to clean it up for you."

We made it back to the apartment complex, and I showed her up to my place. After I opened the door and she walked inside, it was as if a slot machine was going off in my head. If there was an emotion called "flashing lights and ringing bells," then I was certainly feeling it at that point.

"Wow, this place is nice," she said.

"Don't think it's normally like this," I said, closing the door behind us.

"Well, if I'm going to come over again, then it better be normally like this," she said playfully.

"Yes, your highness," I replied. "Take your shoes off. Make yourself comfortable. *Mi casa es su casa.*"

"I see you have some movies," said Hayley, looking at the DVDs by the TV. "Can I look through these?"

"Go ahead," I told her. "Can I get you something to drink?"

"Just some water," she said, browsing my movie collection.

I brought her a glass of water as she picked out a selection. She wore a big smile as she showed it to me.

"You have *Marshall and Mud Flap* on DVD!" she beamed.

"The first four seasons," I said. "When season five comes out, I'll have it, too."

"I love this show!" she said excitedly. "Can we watch it?"

"Sure, sure," I said.

I popped the DVD into the player as Hayley made herself comfortable on the couch, then I cuddled up next to her. Wherever this day was going, I wanted to get there smoothly and naturally, and this seemed like a good way to start things off. Sitting next to her like that made me feel like I was flying, and right now we were sailing through the clouds.

They say the good die young, and I guess that also goes for good times. Being in such a perfect situation only seemed to attract the ugly hand that yanks people out of blissful situations. I should have expected the knock on my door at that moment, putting a black mark on the perfect picture Hayley and I were painting.

"Who's that?" I muttered, standing up.

When I peeked through the peephole, I almost jumped when I saw Miss Flamingo's rocky stare on the other side of the door. How did she get inside the building without a key? Wondering how this situation would possibly turn out, I took a deep breath and opened the door. Cormorant was standing there too, making me wonder just how serious this unexpected visit was.

"Hello," I said.

"Good afternoon, Roadrunner," said Miss Flamingo.

"Hey there," Cormorant greeted.

"I'm not interrupting anything, am I?" Miss Flamingo asked. "I have business to conduct here."

"Uh, well," I glanced back at Hayley sitting on the couch, "I'm not *particularly* busy at the moment."

"Good." Miss Flamingo stepped inside my apartment. "Should we remove our shoes?"

"That'd be nice," I replied. "I just cleaned the place. So, what brings you two here?"

Miss Flamingo took her shoes off and placed them by the door. She was wearing thick socks that I assumed were wool.

"An inspection," she told me, looking around the apartment. "All of my new recruits must undergo a mandatory home inspection. I would have done this sooner, but I had other things to take care of first."

"Oh. Okay."

I looked at Hayley again, who seemed a little intimidated by Cormorant.

"You two have met Hayley," I said, trying to make the situation a little more comfortable. "She was with me at the Halloween party."

"Hi," said Hayley shyly.

"Hello," said Miss Flamingo flatly, not even looking at Hayley.

"Hey there," said Cormorant, notably friendlier than Miss Flamingo.

Miss Flamingo strutted into the bedroom, and I immediately followed. Although she was doing an "inspection", I still didn't like the idea of having someone going through my place the way she was.

"Is there anything I need to do?" I asked her.

She gazed around the room for a few seconds.

"Not as of now," she replied. "I'll let you know if I need your assistance."

Miss Flamingo walked back into the living room and looked around some more, then went back into the bedroom, all while Cormorant stood by the door like a guard. Watching her made me nervous. I still had no idea if she was actually psychic, but I still wondered if she could sense Sapphira in any way. My only hope was that Sapphira understood what was going on and had left the area completely. I also didn't want to try communicating with Sapphira in any way, risking the chance that Miss Flamingo would notice something.

"Hmm," I heard Miss Flamingo say as she walked over to my bedside table.

"What is it?" I asked.

"This caught my eye," she said, pointing to my sapphire amulet.

Uh oh, I thought nervously. *Does she know what that is?*

"Yeah," I said, choosing my words carefully, "it has my birthstone in it."

"May I take a look at it?" she asked.

"Well, it's kinda valuable," I said. "I normally don't let other people handle it."

"Then I'll look at it without touching it," she told me.

Crap, I thought. *She's good.*

Kneeling down by the table, Miss Flamingo put her face inches away from the amulet. I could only imagine what she was thinking and what kinds of deductions were going through her head. After a short moment of silence, she stood up and started walking toward the bedroom door.

"So, what do you think?" I asked her before she left the room.

"I think I'll inspect the kitchen next," she said without hesitation.

That wasn't quite the answer I was looking for, but I decided to just go with it. I followed her into the kitchen where she stood and looked around some more. Hayley remained on the couch and gave me a questioning stare, and Cormorant was still standing by the entrance like he usually did. Was he thinking about stopping me if I decided to leave for some reason? Was he expecting someone (or some*thing*) to try to enter the apartment and interfere with the inspection? Perhaps he was ready to make a quick escape if something crazy happened.

"Hey, Cormorant," I called over, "you can come in and make yourself comfortable."

"He's to stand by the door until the inspection is complete," said Miss Flamingo, opening the fridge.

"It's my job." Cormorant shrugged with a smile.

Miss Flamingo reached into the fridge and took out the plate with the sandwich that Sapphira had summoned through a hell portal. I felt my heart skip as she held the plate up to examine it closely.

"What kind of a sandwich is this?" she asked me.

Keeping cool, I smirked and attempted to draw some humor from the situation.

"You're the psychic one. Can't you figure it out?"

I could practically feel her eyes drilling into my face as she gave me an incredibly rigid look, like her expression was carved into a boulder.

"Ham," I added quietly.

She briefly looked at the sandwich again, then placed it back in the fridge.

"Hmph, I see," she said. "Very well, this completes the inspection. Sorry to intrude, Roadrunner."

"Are we leaving, Miss Flamingo?" Cormorant asked.

"Yes," she replied, walking over to the door.

There was an awkward silence as Miss Flamingo put her shoes on. Hayley continued to sit in the same spot on the couch, looking as if she wasn't sure what to do. In a way, I didn't blame her.

"Have a good day, you two," said Miss Flamingo as she was leaving.

"Wait a minute," I said, following her and Cormorant into the hallway. I closed the door behind me and made sure nobody else was around.

"What is it?" she asked.

"There's just something on my mind," I said. "It's about the club. We're supposed to be about supernatural stuff from what I was told."

"I'm listening," said Miss Flamingo.

"Well, it's just that I haven't seen us do any kind of supernatural stuff," I explained.

"Do you have any beliefs about the supernatural?" she asked firmly.

"To an extent," I said with a forced grin.

"What are you getting at?" she asked. Even if she wasn't trying, she was being a little intimidating.

"I...uh...don't know."

"I'm sorry if you find the club boring," said Miss Flamingo, "but it's not about having fun or doing things that might be deemed as cool."

"I know that," I explained, trying to be respectful without sounding like a wuss. "I don't know what I'm trying to say."

"I think I have a general understanding," said Miss Flamingo. "I'll see you at the next meeting, Roadrunner."

She walked off, leaving me to think about what I had just tried to explain.

"Later," said Cormorant before following Miss Flamingo.

I walked back into the apartment and took my seat next to Hayley. That had happened and ended so quickly that it was almost as if it didn't happen at all.

"What was that about?" Hayley asked.

"I guess she needs to inspect the homes of everyone she hires," I said.

"Why's that?" Hayley asked with a puzzled look.

"No idea," I said.

"That's really weird," she said. "I've never heard of something like that."

"Me neither," I said.

There was an awkwardness that lingered for some time after that, but it wasn't until I made dinner did that feeling disappear. As we ate our spaghetti and garlic toast, we seemed to forget all about Miss Flamingo's strange visit. That was proof that true love prevails over weirdness!

After dinner, we watched a streamed movie off my game console. The movie was also Hayley's pick, and it was a little too girly for my taste. However, such a movie was practically tradition for the current situation, and I wasn't going to complain over something so insignificant. Additionally, we only made it about a quarter of the way through before Hayley wrapped her arm around me tightly, tighter than she ever had before.

"I'm having a really great time, Mike," she told me. "Thanks for letting me come over."

"Sure thing," I told her. "We can do this more often from now on."

"This is the best Thanksgiving I've ever had," she said, looking directly into my eyes.

"It's not Thanksgiving anymore, goofball."

"Whatever, dork."

309

After the initial kiss, I pushed Hayley back and pinned her against the couch. It truly was the best Thanksgiving I could remember, even though it wasn't Thanksgiving anymore.

~Opus 22~

"Joy to the wooooorld, it's Christmas break!" Aaron sang loudly as he, Lawrence, and I exited our biology class. It was the last class of the year until they started up again in early January.

"What are you guys doing for Christmas?" Lawrence asked us.

"No idea, really," said Aaron. "I think my family's doing something. We usually have a party. What are you doing?"

"I have a date with Sam on Christmas Eve," said Lawrence.

"Good for you, man," I told Lawrence. "What are you two gonna do?"

"See a movie," he replied. "We need to get there early because they won't be open as late. I already bought us tickets."

"Lawrence is getting in touch with his inner pimp for Christmas," said Aaron. "What about you, Mike?"

"I'm taking Hayley to meet my family," I said. "We're staying there for a few days."

"Where do your parents live?" Lawrence asked.

"Warren Woods," I replied. "It's a town north of Elm Valley. It's a little smaller, too."

"Taking the girl to meet the parents, huh?" Aaron elbowed me playfully. "It's getting serious between you two!"

All of Aaron's joking aside, spending Christmas with Hayley at my parents' house was a big step in our relationship. However, that wasn't the only thing I was looking forward to. Sal was going to be there, which was a huge plus. The Christmas bonus I had received from Miss Flamingo provided enough money to afford more than just cards for everyone, which was another plus. Furthermore, the club meetings before and after Christmas were cancelled, leaving plenty of time to have off. This Christmas was already looking great.

As soon as I made it back to my apartment, I went to work on wrapping everyone's gifts. I was terrible with wrapping paper, so the job took a little longer than anticipated. All of that cutting and taping reminded me of the little art

311

projects I had to do in elementary school, which I never enjoyed doing. When I finally finished wrapping the last present, I actually felt a little worn out.

"Glad that's done," I said to myself.

I stashed the presents in my closet until the trip. The plan was to go to my parents' house on Christmas Eve and have our party, dinner, and other stuff. Christmas day would be for being lazy and eating leftovers. The day after Christmas would be when Hayley and I leave back to Elm Valley. Pretty simple and straightforward, right?

On the morning of Christmas Eve, I sprang out of bed feeling pumped and ready to go. After a quick breakfast and a speedy shower, I called Hayley to let her know that I was about to head out. All of the presents were stuffed into a big sack, so I slung it over my back like Santa Claus and was on my way.

"Sapphira, I'm leaving now!" I called before walking out the door.

"Have a good time," she said. "I will be waiting for your return."

I almost wished her a merry Christmas, but that just didn't seem quite right. She was a demon and probably had no intentions of enjoying the season, and I was okay with that.

The first major snowfall was about a week before that day, followed by a couple more days of snow. Consequentially, there was a good accumulation of snow in time for Christmas. Many people who don't like snow say they can accept it for Christmas because it helped with the holiday spirit. I, on the other hand, couldn't care less what days had snow. The snow had forced me to finally start wearing my winter coat, and that was all that mattered. My thin jacket would be hanging in my closet until next spring.

When I picked Hayley up from her house, she was all bundled up in a scarf, knit cap, and furry boots. Just looking at her made me feel cold, and I had to bring it up as soon as she got in my car.

"You look like a stylish penguin," I told her.

"It's freezing outside!" she said, shivering. "Aren't you freezing?"

"I'm not *that* cold," I said. "I'll crank up the heat for you."

The drive from Elm Valley to my old home was about an hour-long trip. A good portion of the trip was easy because I could take the interstate, and the rest required going down all kinds of other streets and back roads. I had only made the trip a few times in my life, but it was still easy to remember where to go. Maybe it was an innate ability to be able to find your way back to your home and family, or maybe I was just a gifted navigator.

"Tell me a little about Warren Woods," said Hayley as we were traveling.

"It's the town I grew up in," I told her. "It's nothing special. Elm Valley is a little bigger."

"I've heard about that town before," said Hayley. "Isn't there a state park between Elm Valley and Warren Woods?"

"Um, I think there might be," I said. "I'm not sure."

"I'm a little nervous about meeting your family," she said shyly. "I've never been good with new people."

"It'll be okay, babe," I said, placing my hand on her knee. "They'll love you. All you have to do is keep being adorable."

Before long, I found myself in familiar territory as we entered the town where I grew up. Good old Warren Woods, still the same as it had been since my childhood. Feeling like a tour guide of sorts, I kept pointing things out to Hayley, such as where I used to go, and offered stories about certain places. I even took a slight detour to show her my elementary school, which was now closed for Christmas.

When I turned onto the street where I used to live, a wave of nostalgia rolled over me, and it felt like I had never even left. My old house was located outside of town, sitting on seven acres of land with woods to the east and neighboring farmland to the west. I had never considered myself a country boy, but the isolation from town offers a kind of tranquility that suburbia doesn't. That said, I don't think living in the country was quite my thing, and I was happy with my stuffy apartment in the midst of town. An occasional getaway to the countryside was good enough for me.

We made it at last to the house of my childhood. Everything was the exact same, from the big front porch to the stone chimney that gently puffed smoke up into the air. The sparkling snow made it look like a picturesque gingerbread house. I didn't mention to Hayley that our house was quite large, and the look of awe on her face was what I was aiming for. Although my family wasn't necessarily rich, a lot of time and hard work went into turning our house into the posh home that it became.

"Mike, you didn't tell me you had such a nice house!" said Hayley, wide-eyed as we drove up the driveway.

"Eh, it is what it is," I replied modestly.

Hayley and I weren't the first to arrive. I noticed the green SUV that belonged to my Uncle Bill and Aunt Katie, who lived only a couple towns over. They were usually the first ones to show up at family events, so seeing their vehicle was no surprise to me.

We hadn't even made it to the porch when the front door flew open. My mom came up to me with arms wide open and a smile on her face, hugging me before I could say anything.

"There's my baby boy!" she said happily. "I've missed you so much!"

"Merry Christmas, Mom," I said.

"Oh, and you must be Hayley," she said. "It's good to meet you!"

"Nice to meet you, too."

Mom hugged Hayley just as I heard the sound of scampering paws come running out of the house. Our half husky, half wolf leapt down the porch steps, practically bowling me over.

"Hey, Shadow!" I exclaimed, trying to pet the hyper dog while he jumped all over me. "How ya doin', boy?"

"Aw, he's cute," said Hayley. "Is he a husky?"

"Half husky and half wolf," said Mom. "He's a crazy one. Shadow, get inside! Go on!"

The dog ran back inside the house, eagerly waiting for us to follow. As soon as we walked through the door, he started jumping and licking again. My dad walked into the room at the sound of the commotion.

"Hey there, Mike," he greeted. "How've you been?"

"Good, Dad," I said, hugging him. "Merry Christmas. This is Hayley, my girlfriend."

"I've heard a lot about you in Mike's emails," he said, shaking her hand. "Nice meeting you."

"Nice meeting you, too."

"You know," Dad told her, "Mike says a lot about you. You should see the mushy things he says in those emails."

"Oh, stop it, Jeremy," Mom said. "You'll embarrass him."

Thank you, Mom, I thought.

I followed my parents into the living room where everyone else was. There was my younger sister, Elizabeth, who was a senior in high school. Uncle Bill and Aunt Katie were sitting next to each other. Before I knew what happened, Sal suddenly came out of nowhere and hugged me, lifting me off the floor. I even felt my back crack and ribs pop. He was much taller and bigger than me, so there was no escaping his grasp.

"Little Mikey!" he said loudly. "How's my baby brother?"

"Good," I managed to say.

"Set him down, Sal," said Mom. "He's turning red."

I could instantly feel my blood flowing again as soon as I was freed from my brother's death squeeze.

"It's great to see you again!" I told Sal. "How long have you been back?"

"Since last night," he said. "Originally, I was gonna be here sooner, but had delays and paperwork and stuff. You know how it is."

"Do you two want something to drink?" Mom offered Hayley and I. "We have stuff in the kitchen to drink and snack on if you want it."

"Could I use your bathroom?" Hayley asked timidly. "It was a long ride."

"No, you can't," said Sal.

When Hayley looked taken aback, everyone just laughed.

"Don't let him intimidate you," I told her. "He likes to mess with people."

"I'll show you where it is, dear," said Mom. "Follow me."

After Hayley left with Mom, Sal looked at me with a stern expression.

"How do *you* know I'm just playing?" he said fiercely.

Although I knew he was just messing around, there wasn't much I could do when he snatched me up and held me upside down. Dad and Uncle Bill just laughed as Sal carried me around like that.

"Let's say hi to our sister," he said, taking me over to Elizabeth.

"Hi, Lizzie," I said while upside down.

"Hi, Mike," she chuckled.

"I miss doing these things to you, little Mikey," said Sal, letting me down on the floor.

"Yeah, you never tortured Jake," I said, standing up slowly to equal out my blood distribution yet again. "Speaking of, where is the middle brother?"

"He should be here later today," said Dad. "He's bringing his fiancé."

"Jacob's engaged?" I was shocked. "When did this happen?"

"A couple months ago," said Dad. "I thought you knew."

"Nobody told me!" I replied.

"Geez, get with the program, Mike," Elizabeth teased.

"Even I knew," said Sal, "and I was halfway across the world!"

"I guess we forgot to tell you, Mike." Dad shrugged. "We had a lot of people to tell, so it's only natural that we'd forget one person."

"Wow, how thoughtful," I said flatly. "Who's he getting married to?"

"Her name's Yvonne," said Dad. "You'll meet her when they get here."

Mom and Hayley returned to the living room. I let Hayley take a seat in one of the recliners while I pulled up a wooden chair from the dining room. We spent the next couple hours having typical family time, chatting and catching up on everyone's lives. When we got onto the topic of jobs, I knew what was coming and braced myself for the inevitable.

"So, what's this job you have, Mike?" Mom asked. "I remember you saying something about it."

"Oh, it's a research team," I said.

"What kind of research do you do?" Mom asked.

"All kinds of stuff," I said. "Uh, it varies each time."

"Who's the research for?" Dad asked.

Oh boy, that's a tough one to get around, I thought.

"Um, different clients," I said. "If someone needs information, they contact us and we get it for them."

"Are your clients college students?" Uncle Bill asked.

"Eh, sometimes," I said.

"You don't sound too enthusiastic about it," said Dad.

"It's a decent job," I said. "It pays well."

"That's good," said Mom.

"It's probably better than my job," Elizabeth muttered.

"I told you horror stories about fast food jobs," I said, "but you didn't listen."

"I needed a job!" she said. "Nowhere else was hiring. Give me a break."

The interrogation over my secretive occupation finally shifted gears. Lying about my club duties was necessary, but I still didn't like doing it. I imagined that I had a chip planted in my brain that monitored everything I said, and that it would detonate if I mentioned too much about the club. The thought made me chuckle, although I wasn't fully amused.

Jacob showed up just in time for dinner. He was four years older than me, making him two years younger than Sal. I met Yvonne, his fiancé, and I was a little surprised. Jacob was always shallow about his type of women, so it was surprising to see that Yvonne was a little larger than his normal selections.

However, Yvonne turned out to be a sweet person, so it goes to show that beauty is only skin deep. People don't eat fruits for the skins and rinds.

"Mike, I've been meaning to ask you something," said Jacob as we took a seat in the living room. "What games do you play online?"

The question caught me off guard. Jacob hardly ever played video games, and I wondered for a second if this person was an imposter who looked like my brother.

"Since when do you play video games?" I asked.

"I just started getting into them earlier this year," he told me. "I only have a few people to play with online, so maybe you'd join me online sometime."

"Sure, let me get something to write with," I said. "I'll give you my online info."

I went to the kitchen and found a pen and paper, then I quickly wrote down my information and gave it to Jacob.

"Awesome," he said, pocketing the paper.

"You know what we used to do for fun when I was a kid?" Dad asked intrusively.

"Wrangle cattle and split wood?" said Jacob with a grin.

"Very funny, Jake," said Dad. "I'm just saying that we couldn't do this online stuff with each other. Being able to always keep in touch with everyone makes special gatherings like this a little less special, ya know?"

"Hmm." Uncle Bill seemed to be contemplating something as he sipped his beer. "You've always been the old school one, Jeremy."

"Heh, I just think it's unhealthy to spend so much time in front of computers and TVs," Dad explained, "but that's just my opinion."

"You're turning into an old man, Dad," said Elizabeth while texting on her phone much faster than I ever could.

Dad chuckled and crossed his arms.

Mom strutted into the living room, wearing her apron. That particular apron was older than Sal, and she'd been using it almost every day she's had it. There were two passions in my mother's life: cooking and the apron she wears for cooking. It's almost like her cape, except worn in front rather than behind.

"Dinner's almost ready!" she sang. "Katie, can you help me out?"

"Sure, Doris," said Aunt Katie, standing up.

"Ooh, I can't wait!" said Sal, rubbing his hands together. "Mom's Christmas dinners were always so damn good!"

"Are you ready for this?" I said to Hayley. "I guarantee you'll eat until you can't move."

"That sounds alright to me." She smiled.

"You two are cute together," Elizabeth told me.

"Of course we are!" I boasted, making Hayley blush.

"Did you meet each other in college?" Jacob asked.

"Yeah," I said. "It was at a talent show thing at the beginning of the semester."

"I met Yvonne through one of my friends," said Jacob. "He hooked us up, and it was love at first sight."

When Jacob and Yvonne kissed, Sal let out a snorted laugh.

"What's with all you guys getting hitched so soon?" he said. "I'm loving my freedom as my own man."

"Whatever, Salvador," Elizabeth sneered. "You were heartbroken when that one chick dumped you way back when."

Sal snorted again and stood up.

"I'm going into the kitchen," he said as he walked away. "I'm not waiting in line behind y'all."

The rest of us slowly congregated in the kitchen to check out the food situation. Mom eventually shooed us out into the dining room where we took our seats. My mouth watered in anticipation as the aromas teased my nose. When Mom and Aunt Katie brought the dishes out, I clutched my fork as I prepared for mass food intake. We said grace, then plowed into the feast. My first plate was heaped with the delicious goodness, and I knew it wasn't going to be my only helping.

"Doris, I can't explain how much I love your cooking," said Uncle Bill as he cut into the baked ham.

319

"We got the ham from a farmer Jeremy knows," said Mom, pouring herself a glass of red wine.

"It helps to know farmers," said Dad with a grin. "He's been a buddy for a long time. You just can't compete with fresh meat."

"How is it?" I asked Hayley.

Her mouth was stuffed, so all she could do was smile and nod. She took a drink of grapefruit juice, looking utterly satisfied.

"Really good!" she said.

"Save room for dessert," said Mom. "We have tiramisu and Sachertorte, along with other goodies."

The main course left me feeling like there was a yoga ball in my stomach. Somehow, I was still able to eat a piece of tiramisu and a piece of Sachertorte. In the end, I was painfully stuffed, and it felt great.

When everyone had finished eating, we eventually headed back to the living room for presents. The last time I opened presents on Christmas morning was years ago. At some point, we started doing it on Christmas Eve. Not that it really mattered to me, but I missed the excitement of waking up on Christmas morning, jumping out of bed, and bouncing down the stairs in a mad dash to the mound of presents under the tree.

I headed out to my car to retrieve my big bag of presents. Upon returning to the living room, everyone laughed at me as I carried the load to the Christmas tree.

"Check you out with your giant sack!" Jacob snickered.

"You're like Saint Nick," said Dad.

"I wanted to make sure I got something for everyone," I said. "I needed a big bag to carry it all."

"Where'd you put your reindeer?" Sal joked. "I didn't see them outside."

"Leave poor Mike alone," said Mom.

Mom to the rescue again. I looked over at Hayley, who was also chuckling at me. It could've been worse, though. At least they weren't throwing rotten produce at me.

Elizabeth passed out the presents, which is what she did every year. For some reason, she enjoyed it. I unwrapped my gifts one by one with the anticipation of getting something big or fancy. Clothes and gift cards seemed to be my mainstay this year, which I didn't have much problem with. A lot of my clothes were starting to get a little ragged, and gift cards were always enjoyable.

My excitement peaked when Elizabeth handed me a present that said *From Hayley* on it. I looked at my girlfriend, who gave me a warm smile.

"When did you sneak this under the tree?" I asked.

"I'm a ninja," she replied playfully.

"What did little bro get from his girly friend?" Sal teased.

I unwrapped the present, wondering what she could've gotten for me. A true loss for words overcame me when I found it was a cookbook. Initially, I was confused, but it suddenly made sense to me.

"I thought you'd like it," said Hayley bashfully. "You seemed to enjoy cooking."

"It's great," I said. "Thanks, babe."

When I hugged her, you could've sworn that everyone else was watching puppies make finger paintings. Was my relationship with Hayley really that adorable? I wasn't complaining, but it was a little odd how people viewed it that way.

"Looks like she's accepted you as the head cook," said Uncle Bill. "She's given you a responsibility!"

"You can cook?" Dad asked me. "When did this happen?"

"Uh, I just decided to pick it up one day," I said. "I'm living on my own, so it's nice to know the basics."

"He makes the best roast beef ever," said Hayley. I could sense a little bragging in her voice, and it made me feel empowered.

There was no way I could tell them that Sapphira had planted the knowledge into my mind with magic. Remembering that actually made me feel somewhat phony, but I figured not to sweat it. I was going to use Hayley's cookbook to learn more through my own effort.

"Oh, there's a present here for Hayley," said Elizabeth, handing the present to my girlfriend. "Guess who it's from?"

"Man, this is like watching a love comedy!" Sal blurted. "What did you get her, Mikey?"

Hayley unwrapped her present, revealing the digital camera I bought for her. When she gasped with excitement, I knew I had done well.

"A camera!" she exclaimed. "I needed a new one, but I never told anyone! How did you know?"

"I just know." I grinned, feeling lucky for picking the perfect gift when I honestly didn't know what to get her.

We finished off the night by playing some card games. As we enjoyed the quality time together, I could see that Hayley was beginning to loosen up and become more comfortable with my family. Similarly, everyone seemed to love Hayley, and even though they didn't say it, I could tell they were happy for our relationship.

Before winding down for the night, it seemed like a good idea to get the extra pillow and blanket out of my car before I got too tired and lazy to do so. Just as I was about to pop the trunk, I glanced around the yard. The snow reflected the light from the waning moon, illuminating everything nicely. A deep feeling of nostalgia flooded me again, to the point where I actually ventured into the backyard, as if something had led me back there. While I gazed across the moonlit snow, I could sense a warm and loving sensation descend upon me.

In fact, it was a *really* warm and loving feeling.

A glowing light seemed to radiate from around me, indicating that something strange was happening. However, the unexplainable sense of calmness and security was a dead giveaway as to what was going on. I was suddenly approached by a tall figure whose ethereal appearance outshone the silver moonlight and its snowy reflections.

"Merry Christmas, Michael," he said in a caressing voice.

"Merry Christmas, Lemuel," I replied.

Sapphira's parole angel smiled at me, chasing away the chill of the December air.

"How are you doing?" he asked.

"Good," I replied, not sure what to really say.

"That's good," he said. "Shall we take a little walk?"

Without hesitation, I walked with Lemuel through the yard. The powdery snow was lighter and softer than I had ever felt as I treaded through it.

"You appear to be doing quite well," said Lemuel.

"Yeah, I guess," I said.

"You have a family who cares for you very much," he said. "Consider yourself blessed."

"This is one of the few times a year I get to see them," I told him. "It's been a great time so far."

"That's good to hear," said Lemuel.

We continued walking in silence for a little. When we reached the halfway point between our house and the back boundary of the yard, I stopped and looked back at the house.

"So, why are you here?" I asked. "Is there something you need to tell me?"

"I'm just checking up on you," he replied. "I hope I'm not imposing."

"No, that's not a problem," I said. "I figured you can keep watch on me at all times, so there must be a good reason to come to me."

"It's nice to have personal encounters," said Lemuel. "Speaking like this is a better way to communicate."

That makes sense.

"How is your relationship with Hayley?" he asked me.

"Really good," I said. "She's a great person. I'm really happy just being with her."

"Very good," said Lemuel. "Just remember not to let love blind you. Love is a double-edged sword and must be wielded with caution and care."

"I know," I said.

"This really is my favorite time of year," said Lemuel. "Seeing people smile and hearing them laugh is beautiful. The compassion and kindness of the human heart burns as bright as the sun around this time. People may stress a lot during the holidays, but when you see the underlying love cut through those problems, you realize that it's all worth it."

I didn't know what to say and honestly didn't feel the need to open my mouth at all. Lemuel's words soaked into my soul, making it feel as if I were standing in the July sun.

"There is one thing I want to say," said Lemuel. "How are you doing with Sapphira?"

"Alright," I replied. "She's pretty helpful, even though she's super dense and takes things way too literally."

"I'm glad to see you are enjoying your pact with her," said Lemuel. "However, I must remind you that she is a demon."

"I know," I said. "I keep that in mind every time I see her."

"That's very important," he told me. "No matter how helpful or loyal she is, you need to remember that she does not feel any sense of compassion toward you. Sapphira hates humans, and you are no exception. In her eyes, you are lowly and deserve to be tormented. Her pact is the only reason why she can never act upon that."

A freight train of reality blasted through me.

"Sapphira hates me?" I said quietly. "I never thought of it that way."

"She is a demon," Lemuel repeated. "I don't think I need to explain it more than that."

While I stewed in my thoughts over the current conversation, Lemuel turned and looked at my house. I still don't know exactly why he chuckled softly right then, and I'm not sure if I ever will.

"Well, I think it's about time for me to go," he said. "I apologize for keeping you out for so long."

"It's okay," I replied. "It was good seeing you again."

"Take care of yourself," said Lemuel. "May the grace of God be with you."

He spread his white wings, which stretched farther than I had imagined they could. Taking flight like a bullet out of a gun, he disappeared into the night sky a hundred times faster than a rocket. Not a sound nor gust of wind accompanied his impressive exit. However, the cold air quickly returned, and the snow felt much heavier as I headed back to my car to retrieve the pillow and blanket I had almost forgotten about.

"There you are," said Mom as I entered the house. "Did you get lost?"

"I just thought I'd take a look at the yard," I said, stomping the snow off my feet.

Mom took the pillow and blanket from me as I took off my shoes.

"You feel really warm," she told me. "I can feel the heat coming off you. Are you feeling sick?"

"Huh? No, I'm fine," I said, wondering if Lemuel's warmth had somehow stuck to me.

"You look more vibrant," she said with a smile.

"I guess I'm just a dashing fellow," I joked.

I showed Hayley my old room, which had just a bed, dresser, and lamp these days. Everything else was now in my apartment. I spread the blanket I brought on the floor to serve as my sleeping spot.

"You can have the bed," I told her. "It's only big enough for one person."

"Okay," she said.

"Are you tired?" I asked. "You can go to sleep anytime you want."

"Yeah, I'm about to." She yawned.

Dad walked in and stood in the doorway.

"You getting settled in?" he asked. "When you get the time, Mike, come down."

"I'll be right there," I replied.

I showed Hayley where the upstairs bathroom was, then went downstairs to see what Dad wanted. I found him in the living room with Mom, Sal, Jacob, and Elizabeth. Mom beckoned me to take a seat. Dad was holding four presents, all the same size.

"This is the first time we've all been together like this in a while," said Dad. "I wanted to take this chance to give all of our kids their special presents at the same time."

He handed a present to me and each of my siblings. When I tore off the wrapping paper, it turned out to be a framed family portrait of us. However, it wasn't just one of our random family portraits, but it was the one we had taken while on vacation in Hawaii. I was ten years old at that time, and I remember it being the most awesome family trip we had taken.

"Aw, this was in Hawaii!" Elizabeth squealed. "I remember taking this picture!"

"We knew this picture was very special to us all as a family," said Mom, "so we decided to make high quality copies for all of you. We used mahogany picture frames for all of them."

"It's kinda big," said Sal. "It'll be hard taking it back with me."

"Well, it's for when you come back for good," said Dad. "You'll have it for your house."

"I know where I'm putting this when I get home," said Jacob. "Right above the fireplace, on the mantle! That's a great spot."

"What about you?" Dad asked me. "I know you don't have much space in your apartment, but you should be able to find a nice place for your picture."

"Uh, I'm sure I'll find one," I said, eyeing the picture. "Maybe I'll hang it on the wall."

"Can you put nails in apartment walls?" Elizabeth asked. "I thought there were rules like that."

"They have special hooks that stick to the wall," I told her. "I can buy some. They're probably pretty cheap."

"Alright, I'm going to bed now," said Mom. "It's been a long day. Merry Christmas, kids."

We had a good group hug, then everyone headed to the sack. I took the picture back to the bedroom to show Hayley, who was already lying in bed.

"Aw, that's nice," she said, looking at the picture. "You looked so cute!"

I placed the picture on the dresser. Looking at it, there was already a sense of homeliness to my old room again. It's amazing what a simple photograph can do to brighten up a room.

"Oh, your phone was going off," said Hayley. "I didn't see who it was."

I'm by my phone all day and nobody calls me. As soon as I'm away for not even ten minutes, it goes off.

When I checked my missed calls, the name that popped up was Raven's. The cheer of the holiday might have had something to do with it, but I actually didn't feel disappointed, annoyed, or any other negative emotion due to Raven's unexpected call.

"Who was it?" Hayley asked.

"Raven," I replied.

"Oh."

"What could she want?" I wondered. "I sort of don't wanna call her back."

"Then don't," said Hayley bluntly.

"I probably should," I sighed. "It might be about work."

I pressed the call back button and listened to the ringing on the other end of the line. Just before the voicemail kicked in, Raven picked up.

"Hey," she answered, "where are you?"

"At my parents' house," I said. "It's very far away from Elm Valley, just so you know."

"Crap sauce!" she grunted. "I went to your apartment, but that plan's shot down now."

"What do you mean?" I asked. "What were you doing there?"

"I wanted to give you your present," she said in a totally unsweetened voice.

"My present?"

"Is that so strange?" she asked. "It's Christmas."

"No, just...I didn't think you would —"

"Does this mean you didn't get a present for me?" she asked sternly.

I paused for a moment. Now she made me feel like the bad guy, and I didn't know what to say.

"Don't worry about it," she said. "I didn't expect you to."

"Sorry," I said. "I got caught up with a bunch of stuff."

"Don't sweat it, Roadrunner," she said. "I'll see you later. Have a very merry one."

"Yeah," I said. "You too."

I hung up feeling a little awkward.

"What was that about?" Hayley asked, staring intently at me.

"She went to my place to drop off a present," I said. "I wasn't there, so she called me."

"Did you get her a present, too?" Hayley looked a little upset.

"No," I said. "I didn't even think about it, really."

Hayley sat there quietly. I walked over and took a seat on the bed next to her.

"What's wrong?" I asked, rubbing her back. "You look a little upset about something."

"I don't like that girl," she told me. "There's just something about her."

"Don't even worry about her," I said. "She's a little weird, but she's my coworker."

"Is that all it is?" Hayley muttered dismally.

Oh no, here we go, I thought.

"There's no reason to feel jealous," I said. "I don't think of her as anything other than the person I work with."

"I'm not jealous!" said Hayley. "It's just, I don't know, I don't like her, that's all."

"I understand how you feel," I said. "Raven is, uh, an *odd* person. I just got used to it because I see her all the time."

Hayley seemed to sulk a little deeper this time, and I was seriously running out of things to say to her.

"I'm sorry," she said. "I don't know what I'm thinking."

I hugged her and stroked her hair.

"You're the only one I think about," I told her softly. "Trust me, okay?"

Hayley sighed, then cracked a small smile.

"Yeah," she replied.

328

She lay down and I pulled the blanket over her. When she was all tucked in, I kissed her on the forehead.

"Good night, babe," I said. "I love you."

"I love you, too."

After turning off the lights, I made myself comfortable on the floor. A few minutes later, I heard Hayley's breathing change as she drifted into sleep. The sound of my girlfriend gently snoring made me feel strangely fuzzy inside as I soon fell into a deep sleep.

~Opus 23~

Christmas day came and went so fast that I hardly had time to know what happened. The smell of leftovers constantly lingered throughout the house, acting like a lure to draw us into the kitchen all day. Along with doing nothing but watch movies from sunup to sundown, it was easily the laziest day I could remember in a long time. When it was finally time to go to bed, I did so while feeling completely unproductive and proud of it.

Alas, the following morning snuck up on me, and it was time to hit the road. Hayley was the smart one since she packed everything the night before. While she was taking her morning shower, I had to work on getting everything ready for the trip back home.

"You two don't have to go so soon," Mom told me as I was stuffing my suitcase. "You're more than welcome to stay here as long as you want."

"I know," I said, "but we really do have to get going. I told Hayley's sister that I'd have her home before one o'clock this afternoon. I think they have plans."

"Alright," said Mom. "The news said there's a winter storm coming through, and I'd feel better if you two just stayed here until it passed."

"It's gonna be fine," I said. "I've driven in snowstorms before, Mom. Don't worry about it."

I carried our suitcases downstairs. Shadow ran up to me and started wagging his tail excitedly. Setting the luggage by the door, I petted his head.

"He knows you're leaving," said Jacob, taking a bite of his breakfast pastry.

"I'll be back, boy," I told Shadow, scratching behind his ears. "You be good while I'm gone."

The second I opened the door to take the luggage to the car, snow blew into the house by a frigid gust. Deciding to tough it out without a coat, I ran to the car, a suitcase in each hand, and quickly opened the trunk. Freezing winds blew snow up my shirt, making my teeth chatter. Slamming the trunk shut, I ran back into the house and closed the door.

"You looked cold out there." Jacob laughed.

"A little bit," I replied, shaking the snow out of my hair.

I walked into the kitchen to get something to eat. Sal was standing by the microwave making popcorn, wearing his camo pajamas.

"Popcorn for breakfast?" I asked him.

"It's better than MREs," he said groggily.

Rummaging through the fridge, I grabbed a bunch of random leftovers and put them on a plate. When Sal's popcorn was done, I heated the plate up in the microwave, then helped myself to a breakfast hodgepodge. Washing it down with a tall glass of grapefruit juice, I was fueled for the trip back.

Hayley came downstairs, smelling sweet after her shower. She made herself a quick bowl of cereal and joined the rest of us in the dining room.

"Feel free to stop by anytime," Dad told me.

"This is still your home, you know," said Mom.

"I know," I said, trying to avoid the sappiness of the conversation. "Are Aunt and Uncle still asleep?"

"I heard snoring coming from the room they're in," said Elizabeth.

"I find it funny how they're always the first to arrive and the last to wake up," said Jacob.

"Hey, Lizzie," I said. "Are you still thinking about Elm Valley after graduating? You're almost done with high school."

"Uh, probably," she said. "I'd like to check the place out before I enroll, though."

"You can come out anytime," I told her. "I'll be in town if you ever visit."

"Okay, cool!" she said.

"Our last one is about to graduate," said Mom with a soft smile. "You're all growing up so fast."

"Good, now they can pay their own damn bills," Dad joked.

After breakfast, Hayley and I got all bundled up to face the arctic fury outside. We said our goodbyes and prepared to venture into the winter storm that seemed to be building its strength. In that short amount of time, my footprints from putting the luggage in the car had almost been covered. This snowstorm was looking like a formidable foe, and I was ready to take it on.

I started the car and let it warm up as I brushed off all the snow and ice from the windows. Winter was always a pain. Anyone who has *never* had to clean off their car in the freezing cold before driving on dangerous roads is a lucky individual.

When the car was cleaned off enough, I tossed the snowbrush in the backseat and got behind the wheel. Cranking on the defrosters, the windows slowly cleared until I was able to see comfortably through them. Shifting into drive, the wintry journey began.

Driving through town wasn't too bad. The roads appeared to have just been plowed, although they were starting to get covered again. I was used to driving in such kinds of conditions, so it was a breeze for me. However, I quickly realized it was going to take a lot longer to get back because I was driving slower. Although I had told Jeanette that I would have Hayley back by one o'clock, I was sure she'd understand that the storm made that timeframe impossible.

After leaving the city limits of Warren Woods, the storm started to really pick up. Wind blew increasingly harder, reducing visibility by quite a bit as it carried large quantities of snow with it. The roads were beginning to get drifted over as it was becoming harder to see where the sides of the pavement were.

"It's really nasty out," said Hayley worriedly.

"Yeah," I said. "It'll be fine, babe. I've driven through this kind of stuff before."

Before long, I had to use the mailboxes and street signs to mark both sides of the road. As long as I stayed between them, it would be fine. Hayley clutched the door handle tightly as the wind shook the car. Every time the level of traction underneath the tires shifted, the car would jerk a little bit, adding to her anxiety. I tried to assure her that we were fine, but it didn't seem to make her feel better.

"What's wrong?" I asked her. "Don't you trust my driving?"

"That's not it," she replied. "I've been in an accident before. It was because of icy roads. It wasn't even a blizzard that time."

"I'm going to get you home safely," I said. "I promise."

I put my hand on her leg, and she freaked out.

"Keep your hands on the wheel!" she barked.

"Okay, fine," I said. "I was just trying to calm you down."

"You can do that when we're still alive," she said crankily.

I breathed deeply, trying to keep my cool while behind the wheel in a snowstorm.

Geez, what's her problem? I thought.

My main concern was to make it off all of the back roads and to the interstate. I usually felt much safer on the highways because they're straighter and often the most cleared, but snowstorms can make things unpredictable. There was a chance that the interstate would be just as bad as the back roads, but it wouldn't stop me.

At some point before reaching the interstate, the visibility suddenly became atrocious, and I couldn't even see the front of the car. Everything was engulfed in white, and I had to slow down to a crawl. Hayley remained completely silent, but I could tell she was like a balloon that was filled to its limits. One more pump of air would cause her to pop, and that would be problematic for me.

I decided to pull over to the side of the road. Driving on slippery roads is one thing, but not being able to see is a completely different beast.

"We should've stayed at your parents'," Hayley muttered.

"Calm down," I said, starting to feel annoyed.

"What are we gonna do?" she asked. "Just sit here?"

"I can't see anything right now," I said. "Whiteouts don't last forever. We'll move when I can see and stop when I can't."

Hayley sighed and shook her head. I honestly didn't know what to tell her. Looking around, I could make out the faint outline of some kind of building ahead of us. Through the clear patches of wind, I saw that it was a convenience store.

"Look, there's a store up ahead," I said. "If it makes you feel better, we could stay there for a little. Maybe the wind will die down some."

"Whatever," she muttered.

I hit the gas, only to find that we weren't going anywhere. After giving it a little more gas, we still didn't move at all.

"Damn, we're stuck," I grunted. "How did we get stuck in such a small period of time?"

Hayley sighed again, and that only made me angrier.

"Stay here," I said, getting out of the car. "I'm gonna go check it out. I'll be right back."

The cold wind blew relentlessly as I hurried to the store. I entered through the front entrance and took a look around. The clerk noticed me, so I approached him.

"Hey," I said, "I'm with my girlfriend, and we're thinking about staying here for a little bit."

The clerk was a creepily skinny guy with pale skin, a bushy mustache, and huge gauges in his ears. He looked at me in a way that said my business was none of his concern.

"Uh, sure," he replied monotonously.

"Oh, and can I ask a favor? My car got stuck on the side of the road. It's really close to here. Is there any way I can get some assistance or something? Like some help to get it to the parking lot just so it's off the road."

"Uh, sure," he said again, as if someone had recorded his previous statement and replayed it.

He went to the back and returned moments later with a really burley guy with a thick beard and arms as big around as my legs. One of his eyes looked like it was blind, and his hands were scarred and leathery.

"You havin' car troubles?" he asked me.

"Yeah," I replied. "It's stuck, and I just want to get it off the road and into the parking lot here. My girlfriend and I are thinking about taking shelter here from the storm."

334

"What were ya doin' drivin' in this crap?" he grunted. "It's dangerous."

"Uh, I miscalculated," I replied.

"Alright, I'll be right back," the big guy said.

He walked to the back of the store and returned with a snow shovel and some mats.

"C'mon, let's go," he told me. "We'll be back, Lenny."

I showed the big guy where the car was, and the two of us started moving snow out from around it. We had to act quickly because more snow kept falling and blowing. As soon as most of the snow was cleared, we placed the mats under my front tires to provide extra traction. I hopped into the car and started it up, and the big guy pushed from behind as I hit the gas. To my relief, the car took off fairly easily, and I drove to the store and parked it.

"I'm going inside," said Hayley, heading in without any hesitation.

"Thanks a lot," I told the big guy.

"It's a good thing you were still on the road," he said. "If not, ya would've been buried for good."

When we went back inside, the skinny guy was still behind the counter.

"Did it work?" he asked.

"All good, Lenny," said the big guy.

A woman walked up to the counter, wearing the same uniform as the other two guys. Despite her hardened appearance, she gave me a warm smile.

"Are you the one who needed help with a stuck car?" she asked me.

"Yeah," I replied. "Thanks to this guy, we got out fine."

"That's good," she said. "Are you planning on staying here for a bit?"

"If that's alright," I said. "I have my girlfriend with me, and it'd make her feel better if we were out of the storm."

"Go right ahead," the woman told me. "I'm Jane, the manager here, so you have my permission to wait it out. I'd rather you do that than be out there."

"Thanks," I said. "I'm Mike."

"Daryl," the big guy said. "That's Lenny behind the counter."

Hayley walked up to me, and I put my arm around her.

"We can stay here as long as we have to," I told her.

"Good," she said. "Thanks for doing this for us, Jane."

"No problem," said Jane. "I'll show you the break room. You two can make yourselves comfortable there."

We followed Jane to the back of the store, past the "Employees Only" sign. She showed us the break room, which was just a little room with a small table, some chairs, an old TV, a microwave, and a coffee maker. Hayley and I took a seat. My chair creaked as I sat down on it.

"Would you like some day-old doughnuts?" Jane offered. "I can't offer you any fresh ones for free."

"I'll take one," I said. "A powdered one if you have any."

"Sure thing," said Jane. "Help yourselves to the coffee. We have cream and sugar over there. The remote for the TV is right here, so you can mess with it however much you want."

"Cool," I said. "Thanks."

She left the room, returning shortly after with a powdered doughnut on a napkin.

"We only have standard cable," said Jane, handing me the doughnut. "I'll be in the office right outside the door if you need anything."

As soon as Jane walked out, Hayley went straight to the coffee maker and poured a cup. She loaded it up with sugar and cream, sipping the steaming cup with a stern expression on her face. She had told me that she was sensitive to caffeine, but given the situation, I figured it would probably do her some good. When she sat down next to me, I hugged her closely.

"I told you it would be alright," I told her. "We'll just stay here until it clears up. At least until the wind dies down and stops blowing all that snow around."

"Hmm." Hayley took another sip of coffee. "Oh, I should call Jeanette and tell her that I'll be home late."

Fortunately, Hayley's phone had enough service to get through to her sister. She briefly explained the situation, and it sounded as if Jeanette understood just fine. When she hung up, Hayley looked a little more relaxed.

"She said it's fine," said Hayley. "She's glad we're safe and would rather us stay here until the weather lets up."

"That's good," I said, holding her tightly.

"How's the doughnut?" she asked me.

"Pretty good," I replied. "How's the coffee?"

"Alright," she said, resting her head on my chest.

"The caffeine won't make you wired?" I asked.

"I wouldn't worry about it," she told me. "Being wired right now might be a good thing."

I spent the next couple of hours flipping through the TV. Nothing particularly interesting was on, but it was enough to kill the time. Hayley had fallen asleep on my lap, and her gentle breathing helped soothe me to the point where I had forgotten about the storm outside. The occasional gust of wind shook the building, reminding me of the circumstances we had found ourselves in, but it really wasn't all that bad.

After a few hours, I walked out to the front of the store to check out the weather. When I peered out the window, I saw that it hadn't gotten any better. Although I had parked right in front of the window, the blowing snow still made it difficult to see my car at some points. Everything else was just a solid whiteness.

"It's still snowing," said Lenny, who was still standing in the same spot behind the counter.

"I noticed." I sighed.

"I'm supposed to be off my shift in an hour," he said, "but I don't feel safe driving in that."

"I don't blame you," I replied, still peering out the window at the whiteness.

Amid the swirling torrent of snow and icy cold, I noticed something approaching. Watching closely, I could see the faint silhouette of a car slowly making its way across the parking lot. It crept through the flurry before parking next to my car.

"Hey, there's someone there," I said.

A woman exited the car, bundled in a thick sheath of coats. She hurried to the passenger side of the car, where she opened the door. I watched as she helped a small child out of the car, and both of them quickly made their way into the store. When they passed through the doors, I could easily see that it was a mother with her daughter, as the child looked almost exactly like the woman.

"Hi," said the woman breathily to Lenny. "It's really bad out, so we had to stop somewhere."

"You're not the only ones," I told the woman. "I'm staying here with my girlfriend until it clears up."

"It won't be too much of a bother if we do the same, will it?" the woman asked Lenny. Her eyes were full of desperation, and her daughter looked tired and scared.

"Uh, sure," said Lenny. "Let me ask the manager."

Lenny walked off, looking as numb to the world as he did when I asked him the same question.

"It should be fine," I told the woman. "There's a break room we're staying in, and there's still plenty of room left. The manager seems really nice."

"Oh, that's good," she replied. "We were on our way back from my parents' house, but the storm was a little worse than I thought it would be. Before I knew it, we were caught up in it."

"Your story is the same as mine." I chuckled.

Jane showed up shortly later and greeted the woman the same way she greeted me. She agreed to let the woman and daughter stay in the break room until the conditions improved.

"Thank you so much," said the woman.

"It's no trouble," said Jane. "I'm Jane, by the way."

"Kathy," said the woman. "This is my daughter, Tiffany."

As Lenny once again returned to his post, I followed everyone else back to the break room. Hayley was pouring another cup of coffee when I walked in. She looked at Kathy and Tiffany questioningly.

"We found some more survivors!" I said.

"Did you get stuck in the storm, too?" Hayley asked them.

"Yeah." Kathy sighed, taking a seat.

"Me and my boyfriend have been here since this morning," said Hayley. "It's not clearing up any?"

"Doesn't look that way," I said.

"Check the weather on TV," said Jane.

I picked up the remote and flipped to the news. The weather radar showed a massive system sweeping across the country, and we were right in the middle of it.

"Wow, it's big," said Kathy.

"The whole thing stretches from Mexico to Canada," I said.

"Shh, they're talking about our area now," said Jane.

"The system is moving quickly through the indicated area," said the reporter. "It's expected to completely pass by within the next five or six hours."

"Five or six hours," Kathy muttered.

At that moment, Tiffany started to cry. She buried her face in her mother's shoulder. I looked at Hayley, who grimaced at the TV.

"I don't wanna die here!" the little girl sobbed.

"We're not going to die," said Kathy.

"What are we gonna do until then?" said Hayley, looking at me with a disgruntled face.

"I don't know." I shrugged. "Sit and wait, I guess."

Daryl barged into the room, covered in snow. He pulled off his knit hat and gloves then tossed them on the table.

"Took the trash out," he said gruffly. "And it looks like I'm stuck here. My ride don't wanna leave the house. Ain't blamin' nobody, though, not in this storm."

"You're not the only one," said Jane firmly. "Lenny's not leaving, and I'm certainly not driving in that."

"The weatherman said it should pass in five or six hours," I told him.

"Damn it!" Daryl grunted. "So, we're gonna sit here the whole time?"

"What else do you have planned?" Jane asked calmly.

"It's really not that bad," I said. "We'll be bored for a few hours, that's all."

"I know, I know," said Daryl, "but it still pisses me off. I'm gonna be stuck at work all day while the next shift crew gets the day off."

"Now would be a good time to close shop," said Jane, ignoring Daryl's ranting, "otherwise Lenny will stand behind that counter all day with no customers to take care of."

"Will he really?" Hayley asked.

"He's like a parrot," said Daryl. "Stands in the same spot and doesn't stop talkin'."

"He seemed quiet to me," I said.

Jane and Daryl both started laughing.

"Everyone says that," said Daryl. "You got no clue."

"If anyone wants to buy anything, such as food, I suggest doing it now," said Jane. "Once we shut the registers down, we won't be able to make any transactions."

"You can't let us have anything for free?" Kathy asked.

"I can only offer the day-old doughnuts and coffee," said Jane. "I'm running a business in a tough economy. Sorry."

As the store's workers started closing up, the rest of us browsed the aisles. The store wasn't big at all, but there was still plenty of food to choose from. I was trying to help Hayley decide what she wanted, but she didn't seem very cooperative.

"How about these?" I said, picking something off one of the shelves. "Peanut Butter Dunk Monkeys!"

"Nah," she said dismissively.

"You can't deny these," I said. "They're totally awesome. I thought you liked peanut butter."

"I do," she said.

"Then try these," I said. "If you don't like them, I'll get you something else. What looks good to you?"

"I don't know."

"Come on, you have to help me out here," I said. "They still have some doughnuts. We don't have to pay for those."

"Then get them. I don't care."

She walked over to the drink coolers, leaving me to decide what food to get. I rolled my eyes, thinking that she didn't have to be so uptight. We weren't in danger anymore.

Jeanette said it would be fine if we made it back late. What was her problem?

I snatched a bunch of random snacks, figuring that Hayley couldn't complain about what I got if she wouldn't tell me what she wanted. When I walked over to the counter, I dumped everything out for Lenny to ring up.

"Is this everything?" he asked, sounding like I was just another nameless customer.

"Yeah," I said.

When everything was checked out, he put them in a bag and handed them to me.

"Is your girlfriend mad or something?" he asked me.

"I don't know," I muttered. "She's just being moody."

"If you need any dating advice, I can oblige," he said.

"Uh, thanks," I said, "but that won't be necessary."

Hayley walked up to me carrying two bottles and showed me one.

"Would you drink this?" she asked, showing me the bottled green tea.

"Yeah, that's good," I said. "What about for you?"

"Chocolate milk," she said, holding it up. "Chocolate apparently makes you feel good because it's an aphrodisiac."

After she bought the drinks, Lenny immediately started closing down the register. Hayley and I went back to the break room where Kathy and Tiffany were heating up some canned soup in the microwave.

"I'll be right back," I said, placing the bag on the table.

"Where are you going?" Hayley asked.

"Restroom," I said, walking out.

The store didn't have a public restroom, so I had to ask Lenny where the employee restroom was. When I found it, I took a deep breath to contemplate the situation while I did my business.

What a story this'll make, I thought. *This is almost as crazy as the time we got lost in the woods.*

While I was washing my hands, I heard the restroom door open. The person who walked in was probably the last person I expected to see, and I had to blink a few times to make

341

sure I was seeing correctly. There was no mistaking the Army fatigues and unforgettable face.

"Eli?" I said, stunned.

"Michael," he said. "How are you?"

"Uh, good," I replied. "What are you doing here?"

"Just stopping by," he said.

"In this weather? Did you get lost in the storm?"

Before Eli could answer, the door swung open again and Daryl walked in.

"I thought I heard voices in here," he said, looking at Eli. "Haven't seen you before. You just get here?"

"Yes," Eli replied.

"Let me guess, lookin' for a place to wait out the storm?" said Daryl with a smirk. "We're pretty popular as a storm shelter."

"No, I was passing through," said Eli.

"Passing through?" said Daryl, raising his eyebrows. "You must be drivin' a tank to make it through that snow! Judging by your getup, you probably drive some kind of armored juggernaut!"

"I only have my motorcycle," said Eli.

That shocked me even more. He was out in that storm with a motorcycle, which was beyond dangerous. His fatigues could probably fare well against moderate cold, but that freezing wind could go straight through a person.

"A *motorcycle*?" Daryl bellowed. "Are ya outta yer gourd? What are ya doin' on a motorcycle in this weather? Craziest thing I ever did hear!"

"My Abigor Steed functions perfectly in most conditions," said Eli. "I have no problems with the current weather."

"But aren't you freezing out there?" I asked. "I couldn't imagine riding a bike while wearing just what you have on. You could get sick, or worse!"

"I'll be fine," he said. "How about you, Michael? Are you doing well these days?"

"Uh, yeah," I replied, feeling confused.

Jane appeared, looking shocked to see so many people standing around in the restroom.

"What is this, a potty party?" she asked. "Daryl, can you help me with something? Oh...hello."

"Hello," said Eli.

"Are you looking for a place to stay?" she asked.

"No, I'll be on my way," said Eli. "Take care of yourself, Michael. May we meet again."

Just like that, Eli turned and walked out. Daryl and Jane gave him strange looks, shrugged at each other, and walked out. I simply stood in place, wondering what Eli was doing. My imagination could have been playing tricks on me, but it seemed as if he knew where I was and had come to see me.

I went out to the main part of the store and watched out the window. Eli mounted his motorcycle, his clothes blowing in the powerful gusts of wind that blew snow all around him. The roar of his motorcycle echoed loudly through the building, and he drove off, disappearing into the whiteness.

"Who was that?" Lenny asked as he was mopping.

"A guy I know," I replied.

"He has to be cold," said Lenny.

"Yeah."

"It's really strange, though," said Lenny. "I didn't even know he was here."

"You didn't?" I asked. "Weren't you here the whole time?"

"I was, but I didn't see him come in," said Lenny. "I didn't hear the motorcycle or anything. He might've come in through the backdoor."

"Maybe."

I was utterly perplexed. Eli always seemed a little different, but now I felt really strange about him. There was a possibility of him being a spirit, but other people saw him and spoke with him. Powerful spirits might have that kind of ability, but it was hard to say. If he was a demon, then he wouldn't have been able to get so close to me. The amulet was still in my pocket. However, Sapphira mentioned that the amulet didn't protect against merely annoying entities, but Eli

343

wasn't particularly annoying or bothersome…just odd. He even helped me out before, so I doubted he was dangerous.

Is there something I'm missing here? I wondered. *Some kind of loophole? I don't know if this is even worth worrying over.*

There was no point in dwelling about it too much. The tiredness was beginning to set in and I couldn't afford to direct my energy toward Eli's mysteriousness. When I walked back into the break room, Hayley was munching away at the Peanut Butter Dunk Monkeys. With a grin on my face, I sat down next to her.

"How are they?" I asked.

"Awesome," she replied.

"I told you," I said.

She tried hiding her smile, but it didn't work.

Some time passed with meager attempts to entertain ourselves. Hayley and I chatted with Kathy while Tiffany watched cartoons. I explained how we were coming back from my parents' house just as they were, and the low visibility forced us to stop. Finally, Daryl and Lenny joined us in the break room, both taking seats around the limitedly small table.

"That soldier guy yer buddy?" Daryl asked me.

"More like an acquaintance," I said.

"He's nuts!" Daryl chuckled. "Let's hope he's not out there somewhere layin' frozen stiff in a snow drift."

"That's not very nice to say," said Kathy.

"It's true, though!" said Daryl. "Temperatures like that can kill a man, especially ridin' a motorcycle. If he don't wreck first, that is."

Jane entered the room and went straight for the coffee maker.

"He should've stayed here," she said. "The storm should be over in a few hours."

"Maybe he was in a hurry," said Lenny.

"What could be so important that you'd risk your life like that?" said Jane, taking a seat. "It's dangerous out there."

"Who are they talking about?" Hayley asked.

"A guy I know named Eli," I said. "He was just here not too long ago, but he decided to tough it out and not stay."

"Really?" said Hayley in disbelief. "And you said he was on a motorcycle?"

"He called it his Alamo Steed or somethin'," said Daryl. "Said it was good in the snow. Still crazy, if ya ask me."

"Well, it's out of our hands now," said Jane. "So, does anyone have any ideas to pass the time?"

"Snowball fight," said Lenny.

"Ha! No," said Daryl.

"We have several decks of cards," said Jane. "How's that sound?"

Everyone either shrugged or muttered in agreement, aside from Tiffany, who was still occupied with the TV. Jane reached into a cabinet and took out the cards. We settled with Texas hold 'em, then Jane shuffled and dealt.

Playing card games passed the time quickly, and I hardly noticed that the wind stopped shaking the building. After a few hours of getting my butt kicked at various games, I walked out of the break room to see what it was like outside. A giant wave of relief came over me when I saw that the snow had stopped blowing and that I could see the other side of the street easily. When I told everyone the good news, we all went outside to check it out.

"Hey, it looks like they plowed the road!" said Kathy.

"I'll have to call my ride and tell him to hurry," said Daryl. "I'm ready to go home!"

"It's about time," said Hayley, putting her arm around me.

"Yeah," I replied.

"You all make sure to drive carefully," said Jane. "Even though the storm has passed, the roads are more than likely still icy in most places."

"Thanks a million," I said, shaking Jane's hand. "Who knows where we would be right now if it weren't for you."

"Sure, glad I could help," she said happily.

I quickly hurried over to my car, which was almost completely buried in snow. Hayley used the brush to help clean the snow off, but I just used my sleeves since I couldn't wait to get back on the road again.

The moment of truth arrived when we pulled out of the parking lot and onto the plowed road. Hayley pulled her knit cap over her eyes and leaned the seat back.

"I'm going to sleep," she said. "Wake me up when we get back to Elm Valley."

"Alright," I said.

Even though Christmas had come and gone, it still lived on through that day, and I understood what Lemuel had said about the kindness in people's hearts. At that point, I made a mental note to always stop by that convenience store every time I made a trip to my parents' house.

~Intermezzo: Scherzo~
Presto

.:Aluminum Ordeal:.

~Opus 0.33~

I don't make New Year's resolutions. When I used to make them, I almost never followed through with what I said I would do. After a while, the very idea of making a resolution would slip my mind completely, and the first of January would be just another cold day in the middle of winter. The holiday rush would finally be doused, and the national stress level seemed to drop slightly.

However, if I would have made a New Year's resolution this time, it would probably have something to do with sticking to my college pathway. That seemed redundant, though, since that was a resolution I had made a long time ago. Despite some missteps, I still remained strong to that determination, which was the only relevant resolution I had going for me.

Now that we were in the earliest days of January, Christmas break was nearing its end. Aaron had come to my place the night before, and after a long night of gaming and nonconstructive time-killing, he decided to spend the night. He fell asleep on my couch, wrapped up in the same spare blanket I had taken to my parents' house.

I was sound asleep in my bed when something jolted me awake. Still in a sleepy daze from the weird dream I was having, the blurry outline of someone standing next to my bed forced me into a more awakened state. Blinking to focus my vision, I noticed that the person standing there was Sapphira.

"What are you doing?" I asked groggily. "There's somebody here. Don't let him see you."

"I must tell you something," she told me.

"Quiet!" I hissed. "Aaron can't know you're here."

"I apologize," she replied quietly, bowing to me.

I sat up in bed and rubbed my eyes.

"What is it?" I yawned.

"It appears a spell has been cast on me," she said.

I looked at her.

"What do you mean?" I asked.

348

"There is some sort of magical restrictor placed on me," she explained. "Because of this restrictor, I am unable to hide myself from your world."

A lump formed in my throat.

"Huh?" was all I could say.

"I cannot leave the physical world," she said, "thus I am unable to hide. My pact with you has brought me fully into the physical world, so I will be fully detectable by humans if I do not hide."

Without realizing it, I was already on my feet. Sneaking quietly and swiftly, I went into the living room to check on Aaron. His loud snoring was a sure sign that he was still out. When I turned around to go back into my room, Sapphira was standing behind me right in the open. If Aaron were to suddenly wake up, he'd see her for sure. Feeling slightly panicked, I pushed Sapphira back into my room and closed the door.

"What were you doing?" I hissed angrily. "If he was awake, you'd be spotted!"

"I apologize," she said, bowing again, "but another effect of the restriction spell is that I must remain close to you at all times."

"You gotta be kidding me," I groaned, hanging my head. "How far away can you get?"

Sapphira took a few steps back, leaving a total distance of about six feet between us. I moved back, and Sapphira moved with me in a perfectly synchronized fashion. Exiting my room, I closed the door behind me and attempted to walk away. As soon as I was about six feet from the door, I heard her bump into the other side. When I tried to walk farther away, it simply didn't happen. To describe it the best I can, it felt like going against the current of a rushing river. The harder I pressed against it, the harder it pressed against me, resulting in my inability to move in that direction at all.

I went back into my room, closed the door, sat on the floor, and buried my face into the carpet.

"Not good," I muttered. "This is so not cool. Not cool, man. Not cool, not good."

Sapphira stood there silently with no expression at all. She didn't care about the situation. If anyone found out she existed, it'd be my problem and not hers. Seeing her without any worry made me really angry, but I suppressed my annoyance and tried to act rationally.

"How did this happen?" I asked her.

"I am uncertain," she replied. "The spell is akin to the magical workings of a powerful demon, but my powers are now too limited for me to ascertain any details."

"A demon," I muttered. "Fantastic. You couldn't do anything to prevent this?"

"No," she said. "I was quickly overwhelmed. Whatever caused this is either very cunning or more powerful than me."

"What are we supposed to do, then?" I asked, scratching my head. "We can't let anyone know who you are. I'll probably have to, like, disguise you."

"Under normal circumstances, I could easily alter my appearance," she said. "However, my powers are too limited."

"That really blows," I muttered, burying my face back into the carpet.

"There is something we can do," she said. "All it requires of you is to find a very common ingredient."

"Really?" I said, perking up. "What ingredient?"

"Aluminum," she said.

"Eh?"

"Metals contain magical properties imbued in their essences," Sapphira explained. "Aluminum can be used for illusionary magic, and it should be able to amplify my powers enough so that I may alter my appearance."

I sprung up, feeling a second wind from Sapphira's proposal.

"I have some aluminum foil!" I said. "We'll have to be quiet."

The sound of Aaron's snoring indicated that he was still sleeping. Sapphira and I snuck past the living room to the kitchen. I opened the drawer as quietly as I could, grabbed the entire box of foil, then tiptoed back into my bedroom.

"Is this enough?" I asked, removing the roll of aluminum from the box.

"Possibly," she said. "Shall I commence the spell of appearance alteration?"

"Yes, yes," I said impatiently, handing her the roll of foil.

Sapphira placed the aluminum foil on the floor and held her hands over it. She began reciting some sort of incantation in a different language, possibly Hebrew or Sanskrit, but I really had no idea. Several minutes passed with no perceived effects, and I was beginning to wonder if it would work.

At some point, I noticed something happening with the aluminum. Some kind of visual distortion was taking place around the roll of foil, similar to heat waves but not quite the same. Staying transfixed on the aluminum for so long, I was in for a shock when I looked back at Sapphira and saw that her appearance was actually beginning to change. Her dark hair was losing some of its sheen, and her complexion was becoming gradually more wrinkled. Even her sharp, yellow eyes turned brown.

Sapphira ceased the incantation, and the distortion around the roll of aluminum foil immediately vanished. When all was said and done, Sapphira looked just like an ordinary, middle-aged person. Her odd outfit was still the same, but it looked more like it was made from normal fabric and not all fluttery and otherworldly. Awestruck, it was hard for me to look away.

"I-it worked!" I said happily. "You look like a regular woman now!"

"What should you have me do now?" she asked. Although her appearance had changed, her mannerisms were the same.

"Um, I guess that's it," I said. "Is the foil, like, okay to keep?"

"It should not be any different than before," she said.

I picked the roll of foil up, but immediately dropped it. At first, I thought it had burned me, but it was actually icy cold.

"Gah, it's cold," I said, putting it back in the box quickly.

"That's a mere side effect of draining its magical essence," said Sapphira. "It should replenish itself shortly, thereby warming it back to normal temperature."

"Hey, are you talking to yourself?"

Aaron's voice from the other side of the door startled me. Before I could respond, he barged right in, seeing Sapphira and the foil in my hand. I couldn't tell if he looked more confused or sleepy.

"This is my Aunt Grace," I quickly lied. "She's here to visit for a little while."

"Uh, alright," said Aaron. "What's with the foil?"

I tried to think of something quick, or I'd come across as suspicious.

"She found it and brought it in here," I said, "so I was taking it back. It's...uh, just something she does."

"Okay," Aaron replied, looking at me questioningly.

I walked up to him and whispered in his ear.

"She's a little special," I told him. "You know, not all there sometimes."

"Oh yeah, I got it," he said. "Nice to meet you, Grace."

"Same here, darlin'!"

My mouth fell wide open. It was good that she immediately conformed to a casual style of communication, but hearing her speak warmly with a Southern accent while wearing a smile was crazily weird.

Aaron went into the bathroom, and my fingers were starting to go numb from the freezing foil in my hand. I went into the kitchen (with Sapphira right behind me) and placed the foil back into its drawer. When Aaron came out of the bathroom, he went straight into the kitchen and opened the refrigerator, then removed the box of leftover fried chicken from the night before.

"Are you gonna want the rest of this?" he asked, showing me the chicken.

"You can have it," I told him.

"Righteous. I'll just take a breast and a thigh. It'll be a snack after I get home."

"I don't have any containers you can use," I said. "Just take the whole box."

"I don't want the whole box," he said. "Where's that foil?"

"In that drawer next to you."

I watched Aaron open the drawer and reach in. Surely he would notice how cold the metal was.

"Damn, this foil is cold!" he said. "Why's it like that?"

"Beats me." I shrugged.

Having Aaron and Sapphira standing in the same room was still unsettling for me, even though she was disguised and posing as a goofy aunt. When Aaron exited the apartment, I took a seat on the couch and rustled my hair.

"We can't keep this up," I told Sapphira. "Is there any way to lift this spell on you?"

"Perhaps there is something in the grimoire that can help," she said in her usual lackluster tone, "although I am not certain."

"I thought you knew that book inside and out," I said. "You said you learned about almost everything in it since you were trapped inside it for so long."

"This is another effect of the restricting spell placed on me," said Sapphira. "I am unable to recall many things, including most of the contents in that book."

"Well, it still might be worth it," I said conclusively. "I'll have to get it from Chad again. Maybe I really should just keep it. All this stupidity keeps surrounding me, so it'd make sense if it stayed here."

I lay down on the couch, which was still warm from Aaron sleeping there. Closing my eyes, I prepared to get a little more sleep before doing anything else that day. However, that didn't happen. There was a loud knocking on my door, so I shoved off the couch to see who it was. Peering out the peephole, Aaron's pudgy face took up the entire view.

"Did you forget something?" I asked when I opened the door.

"I can't leave," he told me, stepping into the apartment. "It looks like an ice storm hit last night. The roads are glazed over completely. I fell on my ass just walking out to my car, and once again on the way back in here."

"You're kidding," I said morbidly.

"Nope," he said. "I'm probably gonna be all bruised up."

"Not your ass," I said. "You mean the roads are completely iced over?"

"Check for yourself," he said. "Look outside."

I went over to the window and looked out. Just as Aaron had said, everything was covered in an ice coating. From my apartment, it was still easy to see that the road was solid ice. In those conditions, schools and businesses shut down because it's virtually impossible to drive anywhere. On top of that, it was snowing pretty heavily. Although the lack of wind didn't make it as bad as the storm Hayley and I got stuck in, it would be difficult for the plows to keep the roads cleared.

"Oh no," I groaned.

"What's wrong?" Aaron asked. "Did you have somewhere to go?"

"Um, kind of," I replied dismally. "It wasn't important."

Aaron placed his foil-wrapped chicken on the table.

"Looks like we're gonna have a repeat of yesterday!" he said. "Video games all day. It won't be so bad."

Now I can't go get that book from Chad, I thought. *Even if I did, how would we have some kind of magic ritual without Aaron knowing?*

"I'm going to do the laundry," I told Aaron. "You can stay here and get a head start on some games."

"Alright," he said, sitting on the couch.

"Let's go, Aunt Grace," I told Sapphira. "I'll show you how a washing machine works."

"That's so sweet of you!" she replied in her Aunt Grace persona.

I tossed all of my dirty clothes in my laundry basket, thinking about how screwed this situation was. While I was concerned about removing the spell from Sapphira, what really bothered me was who or what caused it. My understanding was that demons were left alone by other supernatural entities, and it seemed as if it would make more sense for me to be the target instead. Whatever did this to Sapphira must've had some understanding of my relationship with her and how she was like my protector. This worried me, meaning that this person or thing was more intelligent than Asmodeus.

With my basket full of laundry, Sapphira and I headed down to the apartment building's laundry room. There was nobody else there, which made me feel a little more at ease and gave me the opportunity to further discuss the problem with Sapphira.

"Looks like we're stuck here," I said as I loaded the washing machine. "Hopefully, they'll have the roads cleared by tonight."

"There may be something we can do," said Sapphira. "All we need is a very common ingredient to act as a magical amplifier for me."

"I'm glad you still remember *some* things," I said. "What do we need this time?"

"Aluminum," she said.

"Again?" I couldn't help but laugh out loud. "Are we going to change *my* appearance, too?"

"That is unnecessary," said Sapphira. "As well as illusion magic, the magical properties of aluminum can aid in travel."

"You don't say," I said. "That's, er, really random."

"Do you have any more aluminum we can use?" she asked.

"Can't we use the same foil?" I asked.

"We will need to wait for it to regenerate its magical essence," she told me. "That may take up to several hours."

I tossed the last bit of laundry into the washer and poured in the detergent, trying to think of a plan.

"I don't have any more aluminum cans," I said, "and I'm not digging through the dumpster out back to get them. Other than the foil, I can't think of anything I have with that much aluminum in it. Maybe I can find a folding chair? I wonder if my car has any built into it. It's a pretty ubiquitous material...."

I closed the top of the washer and hopped up to sit on it. There was a sign saying not to sit on the washers and dryers, but I really didn't care at that point.

"So, what were you going to do with the aluminum?" I asked. "Will you make it safer to drive on the roads?"

"I cannot remember how to perform any rituals that ensure safe travels that way," said Sapphira. "The method I want to propose will be far more efficient, yet tricky and dangerous. In fact, I'm not sure if I will have enough power to successfully perform the ritual."

"Okay," I said dully, "what's your plan?"

"Teleportation," she said.

The washer suddenly kicked into its first cycle, but that didn't jar me as much as what I had just been told.

~Opus 0.67~

"Wait a minute," I said abruptly. "Run that by me again."

"The magical essence of aluminum, when combined with my own power, might allow you to instantly travel from here to your friend's house," Sapphira explained. "In other words, you could bypass the dangers of the road by teleporting there."

I was lost for words. That definitely intrigued me. Who hasn't wished they could teleport at some point in their lives? Still, that was far too drastic for me to quickly consider.

"That's crazy," I said, shaking my head. "I'm not very sure about that idea."

"It's not as far-fetched as you may think," she said. "It'll take some effort, but there may be a way for your physical body to travel along the astral plane. You can think of it as wrapping yourself in a cloak of subspace, similar to the human concept of wormholes proposed in—"

"Whoa, whoa, stop right there," I interrupted. "I don't need to know how it works."

"This choice is entirely yours," she told me. "You can choose to wait for the roads to be favorable and drive to your friend's house and retrieve the grimoire."

"But you said we'd have to wait for the aluminum to recharge its essence, or something like that," I said. "Either way, we're gonna have to wait."

"That's correct," said Sapphira.

"How much longer for the aluminum to be ready?" I asked. "You said several hours, right?"

"It is hard to say," she said. "My restricted powers interfere with my ability to calculate the metal's rate of replenishment, but it typically takes only a few hours. I don't believe that I drained all of its essence, so it may be ready sooner."

I scratched my chin, weighing my options. Teleporting seemed really cool, though. As I slid down off the washer, my decision was made as soon as my feet touched the floor.

"Teleporting it is," I said firmly. "There's a good chance that the aluminum will be ready before the roads are safe, especially with all the ice and how it's snowing so hard."

"Very well," she said. "I'll do my best."

"The only problem is finding a place to do this," I said. "Aaron's gonna be at my place, and I don't want to perform anything crazy while he's there."

"We could produce doppelgängers of ourselves with the aluminum," said Sapphira. "They could distract Aaron while we perform the teleporting ritual."

"Yeah, but wouldn't that drain the aluminum's essence?" I said. "Then we'd have to wait for it to recharge again."

"That's true," said Sapphira. "Also, the doppelgängers would not be able to speak because the spell would be purely a visual illusion. Additional magic would be needed to alter the appearance of my doppelgänger because I am already using illusionary magic on myself."

"We'll need a different plan," I told her. "I would say we could use this laundry room, but I don't want to risk someone else walking in since it's for everyone in the building."

"I could perform a barrier spell around the room to prevent entry from the outside," she said. "In my weakened state, it would require candles and another metal such as lead or iron."

"Or I could just lock the door," I said. "Alright, we'll do that."

I carried the laundry basket and detergent back up to my apartment. Aaron was playing a game, looking focused and unaware of what was going on.

"Dude, I tried eating that chicken I wrapped up," he said. "It was completely frozen!"

"Uh, maybe all the ice outside had something to do with it," I said, feeling stupid.

"Maybe," he said, too immersed in the game to care.

When I checked the aluminum foil in the drawer, it was still cold to the touch. I considered warming it up in the oven, but I figured its coldness had nothing to do with thermal energy. If that was the case, it would've been room temperature by now, but it was still cold enough to freeze Aaron's chicken.

I sat down next to Aaron and beckoned to Sapphira to sit next to me. While I watched him blow things up in the virtual world, Sapphira sat there like a mannequin. The stress and uncertainty of the situation was giving me the jitters, and I had to stop my legs from bouncing anxiously.

"You wanna play?" Aaron asked, handing me the controller.

"Nah, I'm not feelin' it right now," I replied.

"Alright, I'll keep going," he said.

There was still some time before the laundry would need to be put in the dryer. To keep my mind off things, I had to do something constructive. I was a little burnt out from video games from the previous day, so I would have to find something else to do.

"Is anyone hungry?" I asked. "I'll make something."

"Like what?" Aaron asked.

"I have a new cookbook I got from Hayley," I said. "Maybe I'll find something in it."

"Alright," said Aaron.

When I walked into my room to get the book, I thought of how awkward it must have looked to have my "aunt" follow me everywhere I went. The cookbook was on my dresser, and I grabbed it and went into the kitchen.

"Do you want to watch me cook?" I asked Sapphira, trying to make her look a little less awkward in front of Aaron.

"Sure thing, darlin'!" she replied.

I wanted to find something fairly simple to cook. Flipping through the pages, the recipe that stood out was one for tacos. I happened to have all of the necessary ingredients, including tortillas. All that was missing was tomatoes, but I didn't need them. There was already some hamburger meat thawed out in the fridge, so I was good to go.

While I prepared everything, Sapphira checked the aluminum. After chopping up the lettuce, I looked at the clock and saw that it was time to take the laundry out of the washer.

"You need my help with this?" Aaron asked me, coming into the kitchen.

"If you can," I said.

"I can cook," he said. "I'm not stupid."

"I'm making tacos," I told him. "It should be pretty easy."

"Cool," he replied. "What do you need me to do?"

"I'm gonna check the laundry," I said. "You can start cooking the meat for me. Like, season it and stuff, too. I have the instructions right here in this book."

"Will do," he said. "If I burn the place down, it's not my fault."

Sapphira and I headed back to the laundry room. The washer had already finished, so I threw everything into one of the dryers, then quickly went back to the apartment. Aaron said he could cook, but I really didn't have that much faith in him. Call me terrible, I know. However, I'd heard stories about Aaron and stovetops.

"The aluminum appeared to be nearly ready," Sapphira told me. "Its restoration is happening faster than I anticipated."

"Awesome!" I said. "I'm looking forward to this. I can't believe I'm actually going to teleport! This is unbelievable!"

"There's no guarantee that it will work," said Sapphira.

"Don't ruin the mood," I said flatly. "I have the chance to be the next big thing in the history of human transportation! Although, nobody will know about it."

When I entered my apartment, the absence of smoke and fire alarms was a good sign. Aaron was in the kitchen, stirring up the ground beef in the skillet. He actually handled it quite nicely, though I gave him an incredibly simple task.

"How's it coming?" I asked.

"Looking good," he replied, giving a thumbs-up.

The tacos turned out to be really good. My first time trying the cookbook from Hayley was a great success, and Aaron and I chowed down. Sapphira couldn't eat any, and I had to explain that she was on a strict diet. As much as I wanted to stuff myself with the delicious tacos, the anticipation of teleporting curbed my appetite.

While cleaning up the kitchen a bit, I checked the aluminum again and it seemed to be at room temperature. Just to make sure, I waited until Aaron was out of earshot before asking Sapphira.

"Is it ready?" I whispered.

She placed her hand on it. After a few seconds, she nodded. Excitement built up inside me, but I had to keep my game face on. I checked the time and saw that the laundry was ready to be taken out of the dryer. My next concern was taking the aluminum foil with me without arousing Aaron's suspicion, but he was too engrossed in the game he was playing to notice much when I left the apartment.

Sapphira and I entered the laundry room and I quickly locked the door behind me. I assumed the entire process of teleportation wouldn't take more than several minutes. While Sapphira began the ritual with the aluminum, I folded my laundry as fast as I could, my hands shaking from excitement.

"The preparations are complete," said Sapphira as I folded the last bit of laundry. "We are ready to teleport."

"Sweet," I said. "What do I have to do?"

"Hold my hand," she said. "Make sure to grasp tightly."

"Okay," I said, grabbing her hand. "Now what?"

"Visualize where you want to go," she said. "Since this is your first time, it will be easiest to go to places you have been before. If you are unable to create a clear image in your mind's eye, it may interfere with the jump."

I tried to remember Chad's house in as much detail as possible. Luckily, I had been there a few times before. Things such as colors and surroundings were probably important, and I closed my eyes to help myself remember the best I could.

"Once you have a clear image in your mind," said Sapphira, "imagine yourself being there. Imagine not having to walk or drive there. Know that you can arrive by transcending the usual laws of physical travel. Allow the astral plane to be your medium. Believe that your destination is already beneath your feet. Feel it in your heart."

Attempting to abandon all logical knowledge of the physical world wasn't easy. I slowed my breathing, focusing on

Chad's house. The room was starting to feel like it was slowly spinning, but I did my best to keep my concentration. A dreamlike feeling washed over me, followed by a vibrating feeling that emanated from my chest. I began to feel weightless. Throughout, I kept my thoughts on Chad's house, telling myself that I could arrive instantly.

Suddenly, I felt as if I had been sucked through a vacuum tube. The unexpected sensation startled me and I opened my eyes without thinking, making me immediately feel heavy. I staggered to the ground, quickly realizing that I was no longer in the laundry room, but also not at Chad's house. Before I could determine where I had ended up, a swirling sensation in my head ran straight down my spine, causing my stomach to lurch uncontrollably. Seconds later, I was looking at my tacos in a chunky puddle down at my feet.

"Urrgghhh," I groaned. "Where...are we?"

I looked around, seeing that we ended up in an alley between two buildings. There was still snow on the ground, so I figured we couldn't have gone too far. Had it been warm and sunny, I would have been quite concerned.

"We are still in Elm Valley," said Sapphira. "However, you broke your concentration during travel, resulting in a premature exit from the jump. Shall we try again?"

"Hold on a sec," I said, clutching my gut. "Let me...catch my breath."

"Teleporting can put a strain on your physical body," said Sapphira. "With practice, it will become easier as you learn to channel the energy more effectively."

"Cool," I muttered, "but I don't think I'll be doing this too often."

A cold breeze blew past me, making me shiver. I hadn't even thought about dressing warm for the occasion. One moment I was in a warm building, and now I was out in the cold. Still, the fact that I had actually teleported was boggling, even though it didn't work quite right. As another breeze swept up my shirt, I decided to hurry up and get this over with.

"Let's finish this," I said, trying to ignore the cold.

I grabbed Sapphira's hand again and tried to visualize Chad's house. The freezing air made it more difficult to focus this time, but the process only took about half the time as before. When the sudden jolt of teleporting happened again, I was ready for it. With my eyes still closed, I felt my feet quickly touch the ground. Stumbling over, Sapphira kept me from falling into the snow. However, I still threw up.

"Ooohhhh," I moaned, rubbing my aching stomach.

We turned up in somebody's yard between the house and fence. The area definitely looked like Chad's neighborhood, but it was hard to say for sure. Weak and shivering, I made my way to the street. To my surprise, we were on the street Chad lived on, and I could see his house several houses down. While the teleportation wasn't spot on, it was close enough for me.

I hurried over to Chad's house, trying not to slip on the ice that covered everything. Chad answered the door, looking confused when he saw me standing there without a coat.

"Mike?" he said. "What are you doin', man? Ain't you freezing?"

"Eh, I'm just d-doing my t-toughness workout," I said through chattering teeth.

"Did you walk here?" he asked, realizing my car wasn't in the driveway.

"All p-part of the workout!" I said, trying to appear enthusiastic. "It builds c-character! M-my aunt says so."

Chad looked at Sapphira and chuckled.

"Man, you're nuts!" he said.

"I have a f-favor to ask," I told him. "C-can you lend m-me the b-book again?"

"I'll let you have it under one condition," he said. "If you take it, you're gonna keep it!"

"Works for m-me," I said.

"Dude, come inside for a little," he said. "You look like you might die."

"No, I shouldn't," I said. "The sh-shock from the t-temperature change is n-not healthy."

"If you insist." He shrugged.

363

Chad quickly returned with the book and handed it to me. I pressed it against my chest, feeling how warm it was compared to the freezing air.

"Th-thanks," I said.

"Yeah," he said. "We should hang out sometime. If you don't die from hypothermia, that is."

We both laughed, and even that took some effort from my end. After he closed the door, I scurried around the neighborhood in search of a place to teleport without anyone seeing. The cold air was beginning to get a little more bearable, but I think it was because I was going numb.

There was a small section of woods with no houses around, and I figured it was a good place to perform the teleportation. Sapphira and I trudged into the woods. Snow piled into my shoes, stinging my ankles, but it didn't slow me down. When I felt we were nice and secluded, we began the process.

This time was going to be the trickiest. I was able to get to Chad's house even though the teleportation wasn't very accurate. However, the laundry room was locked, so I would have to jump inside the room. Focusing on the laundry room, we suddenly made the jump through time and space.

Appearing in front of the apartment building, I held my wrenched stomach and was able to keep myself from vomiting. Without my keys, I wouldn't be able to get inside the building. We snuck around to the side where we had the least chance of being spotted. Swallowing hard and trying to calm my angry gut, I shakily clutched Sapphira's hand again.

"Michael," she said before getting started.

"Huh?" I grunted.

"This is the last jump we'll be able to make," she said. "After this, we will have depleted all of the aluminum's power."

"Great," I muttered. "Let's g-get this right, then."

To my despair, I found myself staring at the laundry room door from the hallway. Although I was grateful that we didn't appear in someone's apartment, I was still locked out of the laundry room. My only hope was to go to the main office and ask them to unlock it for me.

I made my way up to my apartment, feeling worn out from all of the teleporting. My stomach was cramped, my vision was blurred, but I had the grimoire. When I entered my apartment, Aaron was still playing games.

"I'll be right back," I said, grabbing my keys and coat. "I gotta visit the main office."

I placed the grimoire on my dresser and walked slowly back into the living room.

"Are you okay?" Aaron asked me. "You look terrible."

"I'm fine," I assured.

"But you're all pale and stuff," he said.

"It's nothing," I replied, walking out.

Sapphira and I walked over to the main office, located in another building. The sidewalks had been salted, so I didn't worry about slipping. Once at the office, I notified the clerk of my situation. She followed me back to the laundry room and unlocked it for me.

"Thank you," I said. "It's been a long morning."

"Yup," she said unenthusiastically.

I returned to my apartment with my laundry and foil. Aaron stayed over for a few more hours until the roads were slightly less hazardous. As soon as he was gone, Sapphira and I looked through the grimoire to find a spell that would negate the one placed on Sapphira. We needed a spell that Sapphira could perform in her weakened state, and we were in luck. The ritual took roughly an hour, but proved successful in the end.

The next day, I still didn't feel quite right from all of the teleporting. Although it was an awesome experience, I really didn't want to do it again unless I absolutely had to. Until then, I vowed to stick to walking and driving whenever I had somewhere to be, since those methods didn't wreak havoc on my body and mind.

~3rd Movement: Rhapsody~

<u>Con Spirito</u>

.:Sapphire Fulfillment:.

~Opus 24~

The end of the semester was fast approaching, which meant that finals were lurking around the corner. Another stressful part of a new semester was signing up for upcoming classes. Class signups could be finished months in advance, but I considered it the one thing I would always put off. This year, I managed to sign up for my classes a few weeks beforehand, so you could say I did it last hour rather than last minute. A small triumph for me while the other students ran themselves ragged to sign up at the last possible second.

"As you all know, finals are almost here," said Mrs. Flynn near the end of psychology class one day. "I'm going to hand out your study guides, which will help you with everything covered in this class' final exam. Completing the study guide isn't mandatory, but I will grade it if you turn it in, strictly for the sake of knowing what areas you need help with. Please hand it in by this Friday so I'll have time to grade it before the exam."

When I received my copy of the study guide, I was disheartened by how many pages it was. Flipping through it, it served as a grave reminder of everything I dealt with to keep my grade afloat in psychology. As much as it pained me, I knew I would have to complete it and turn it in, since I couldn't afford to fail the exam.

I took my usual seat in communications next to Trent. Funny how college doesn't have assigned seating arrangements, yet most people still sit in the same seats each class. Perhaps we were just too lazy to break the mold that we were raised into. Personally, I had no emotional attachments to my particular seat, so it had to be some kind of conditioning. Oddly enough, psychology class had conditioned me to notice conditioning. Very strange, if I do say so myself.

Trent was notably lacking in energy that day. I assumed he was probably hungover, since the stories he had told me about his birthday party implied that he was quite the party animal. Feeling like I could relate, my own energy levels had dipped pretty low, which was typical of this time of year. Cold weather, no more major holidays, classes starting back up—it was a recipe for gloominess.

"Looking kinda tired today, Trent," I said.

"Yup," he replied groggily. "Long night, man."

"I figured." I chuckled.

And that was the extent of the conversation.

Fortunately for me, there was something in my near future that I was looking forward to. Hayley's birthday was coming up, and I had plans to take her out somewhere. Nothing grandiose, but simple and heartfelt. I had already bought her a personalized teddy bear and some chocolate, so all I had to do was top it off with a date night. She mentioned something about ice skating at one point, so that was definitely a possibility, even though I vowed never to ice skate again since I had busted my face when I was a kid.

Just as Mr. Holden was starting class, a large, portly man stepped into the room. I had seen him once before, and it took me a moment to recognize him. He was none other than Mr. Landon, the dean of Elm Valley College. The sturdy look on his face showed that he was going about serious business, and he stopped a few steps after walking through the door.

"Excuse the interruption," he said to Mr. Holden.

Mr. Holden stopped writing on the dry erase board.

"Is there something I can help you with, Mr. Landon?" Mr. Holden asked from the front of the classroom.

Another man walked into the room, who I immediately recognized as Mr. Gast, the physical education instructor. When Mr. Gast pointed at me and whispered to Mr. Landon, a bad feeling bubbled up inside me.

"You there," Mr. Landon told me. "Can I see you for a second?"

This can't be good, I thought as I stood up. *Don't tell me this is about when me and Raven drugged Mr. Gast and stole those files. That was back in October, so it seems odd that it would take that long to come back and bite me.*

Everyone in the classroom had their eyes on me as I walked over to the dean.

"How long is this going to take?" I asked Mr. Landon.

"Hmm, that depends," said Mr. Landon sternly.

"We won't be covering any new material today," Mr. Holden told me. "We're just going to have a review session, so you won't be missing out on too much."

"You should gather your belongings," Mr. Landon told me.

As I packed everything into my bag, Trent gave me a perplexed look. I attempted to look like everything was fine, but a harrowing feeling prevented me from showing any outward confidence.

"What's your name?" the dean asked me.

"Michael," I replied.

"Come with me, Michael."

I followed Mr. Landon and Mr. Gast out of the room, unable to shake the feeling that I was headed to the gallows. Mr. Landon's heels clicked loudly down the empty hallways with each step, adding to the tension like a clock counting down my final seconds.

Just remain calm, I thought. *There's no guarantee this is about that night. Maybe Mr. Gast thinks I'm gonna be the next big thing in cross country, so he notified the dean.*

"Do you know why we called you out here?" Mr. Landon asked me while we were walking.

"No," I replied.

"There was an incident in October," he said firmly. "We think you might be able to provide some information for us."

I'm doomed.

"Oh," I said.

"We'll talk about it when we get to my office," said Mr. Landon.

We exited the building and headed across the snowy campus. I glanced at the bench where Raven and I had placed Mr. Gast when he passed out from the sleeping potion, and I wondered how he must've felt when he woke up. Although I got paid well for doing that assignment, it wouldn't be worth it if I got kicked out of college. I rubbed the amulet in my pocket, hoping it would provide the slightest form of help, but I knew it didn't work like that.

369

Upon entering the main building, the events of that night played through my head when I looked around. There was the seating area where I had put sleeping potion in Mr. Gast's drink. There were the computers Raven and I were using while waiting for our opportunity. There was the door to the file room where we stole the documents concerning Wyatt Halabi. There I was, about to eat dirt for everything I did that night.

I followed Mr. Landon and Mr. Gast into the dean's office, and I was a little surprised to see Raven sitting there. It looked like they were planning a double execution on that fine day. As soon as Raven saw me, a devious smile spread across her face. My only assumption was that she had something up her sleeve in case the situation got hairy, and that somehow made me feel a little better. Only a little, though.

Closing the door, the dean and physical education instructor took their seats on the other side of the desk, and I took my seat next to Raven. The chair felt hard and uncomfortable, not like the ones in the classrooms. Mr. Landon cleared his throat before beginning the interrogation.

"There was an incident in October," he began. "Do either of you know a student here named Wyatt Halabi?"

"Sort of," I said.

"No," said Raven.

I looked at her, but she avoided eye contact.

"Well, all of his student documents came up missing one night," said Mr. Landon. "Mr. Gast was the last person in the file room before we noticed the documents had been tampered with. Somehow, the documents were later returned. None of our staff admits to have been involved. This was after we had Wyatt fill out all of his paperwork again, so that was a major inconvenience to him."

Now that Mr. Landon mentioned it, I never actually knew what happened to Wyatt's documents after the fact. There was probably no telling how those documents were returned, and I decided it would be easier to not think about it at all, although Miss Flamingo was probably responsible in some way.

Mr. Landon paused to take a sip of water, most likely doing it on purpose just to make Raven and I stew in guilt longer.

"Mr. Gast has a long history of good health, being the physical education instructor and head of the health department here at Elm Valley College," said Mr. Landon. "However, on the night before the documents were identified as missing, Mr. Gast had a peculiar…how would you put it, Mr. Gast?"

"I blacked out," said Mr. Gast, "and for no apparent reason."

"Strange, wouldn't you say?" Mr. Landon asked.

I nodded, but Raven didn't respond at all. Was she trying to get us killed?

"He says the last thing he remembers is being with two students," the dean continued. "You two, particularly. He didn't know your names, so it took a while to identify you. What were you two doing that night?"

"There was a shady person lurking around," said Raven. "I was scared, so we asked Mr. Gast to escort us back to our car."

"Then what?" the dean asked.

"Mr. Gast got sick or something," said Raven. "He collapsed, so we placed him on a bench."

"Then what?"

"We left the campus," said Raven.

"You didn't think to notify any staff members of Mr. Gast's condition?"

"We were terrified," said Raven, starting to get somewhat emotional, which I could tell was a full-blown act. "There was a weird stalker person, and a teacher suddenly collapsed. It was fight or flight, so we flew."

"Hmm, I see," said Mr. Landon. "What are your thoughts, Mr. Gast?"

"It's as they said," said Mr. Gast. "I was escorting them because the girl said she saw somebody suspicious. Suddenly, I became woozy and blacked out, then woke up on a bench nearly two hours or so later."

371

He's not gonna mention the fifty dollars Raven left him? I thought. *I guess I'd keep it a secret, too, if I were him.*

"What did this suspicious person look like?" Mr. Landon asked.

"He was wearing a black hoodie with the hood over his head," said Raven. "That's all I remember. It was so creepy!"

"What was he doing?"

"Snooping around, it looked like," said Raven. "Like a burglar or a ninja...sticking to the shadows. He was outside, probably trying to see if anyone was around."

"Did you talk to him, or interact in any way?"

"It was like we noticed each other at the same time," she continued. "As soon as he realized he'd been spotted, he took off. That was when I ran to Mr. Gast for help."

"What were you doing during this?" the dean asked me.

"Uh, I was keeping her company," I said.

As lame as my answer was, the dean seemed to buy it. Even more surprising, the improvised story of a shady person to distract Mr. Gast provided us with a red herring. At least for now, it looked like the school officials were going to be on the hunt for a person in a black hoodie.

Mr. Landon and Mr. Gast exchanged looks. Raising his eyebrows, Mr. Landon took a gulp of water.

"Is there anything else you can tell us that you think might help?" he asked.

"Nope," I replied.

"Not really," said Raven.

"Alright then," said Mr. Landon, pushing his chair back. "Thanks for your cooperation. I apologize for taking up your time. You two were a big help."

"Glad we could help," said Raven.

"Uh, yeah," I said.

"You're free to go," said Mr. Landon. "Good luck on the upcoming finals."

It felt as if the noose had been cut from around my neck as Raven and I exited the dean's office. While we were walking down the hall, Raven glanced behind her, then started laughing villainously.

"That was *intense!*" she said.

"That was horrifying," I said flatly. "I thought we were done for."

"You did?" said Raven. "C'mon, Roadrunner! You gotta have more faith in us than that! We work for Miss Flamingo, and she'd never steer us astray."

"That was as far astray as I ever want to be," I muttered.

"You were sweating bullets in there," she teased. "I could tell."

"You can't tell me that when those two showed up to drag you out of class that it didn't make you feel intimidated," I said.

"The only thing we have to fear is fear itself!" she said boldly.

"Yeah, whatever." I sighed. "Anyway, now they suspect it was that guy in the black hoodie you said you saw. Who knows how long it'll take them to find out the truth?"

"You two know about the guy in the black hoodie?"

A girl with freckles in the seating area had overheard our conversation. She was sitting with a group of girls, and one of them happened to be Samantha. When Samantha noticed me, she smiled and waved.

"Wait," I said to the freckled girl. "You mean *you* know about the guy in the black hoodie?"

"There was a rumor going around," the girl told us. "Apparently, a student overheard a teacher talking about it."

"Mike, you know about the rumor?" Samantha asked, walking up to Raven and I.

"Yeah," I said, feeling a little uncomfortable.

"This girl said she actually saw him," said the girl with freckles, pointing at Raven. "Isn't that right?"

"That's right," said Raven nonchalantly. "I was the one who reported him."

All of the girls looked as if they had just met a celebrity as they gasped, all wide-eyed.

"How many people know about this?" I asked.

"I don't know," Samantha shrugged. "Maybe a hundred, I'd say."

"A *hundred*?"

I looked at Raven, but her expression offered nothing.

"Is it true?" Samantha asked. "A guy in a black hoodie really was creeping around?"

"Yup," said Raven, just digging the hole deeper. "I saw him right outside those windows over there."

The girls gasped as they looked over at the windows where the alleged creep was spotted. I wanted to just walk away, but part of me was darkly entertained by the girls' ignorance.

"Some people are saying he's a rapist," one of the girls whispered to us. "Others think he was an alien."

"That's quite a difference in theories," I said.

"He's known as the Campus Creeper," said another girl.

"Hey, I'm gonna get going," said Samantha. "Uh, Mike?"

"Yeah?"

"I want to ask you something. You aren't busy, are you?" She looked at Raven. "You too. I don't think we've met."

"Call me Raven."

"Ooh, I like that name."

"Sure, I have a moment," I said. "What is it?"

"This way," said Samantha. "Bye, girls."

Samantha waved to her friends before we followed her out of the building. I wondered what she wanted to talk about, and why she didn't want to discuss it in front of her friends. Since there were still classes going on, hardly anyone was out wandering around, giving her a chance to talk to us personally.

"Do you two believe in witchcraft?" she asked us.

The sudden question wasn't all that surprising. However, I was now excited because I still hadn't let go of my suspicions of her affiliations with the supernatural.

"Yeah," I said. "We do."

"I figured as much," said Samantha. "You two give off good vibes, and I assumed it was because I could trust you with this kind of talk. I rarely feel that way about anyone, but when I do, I'm always right."

"Supernatural stuff is part of our belief system!" said Raven.

"That's good," said Samantha. "Ever since I heard about the Campus Creeper, I thought there was something unusual surrounding it. That's why I've made it a little hobby to find out more about it. Some people are saying he's connected to the missing student files, and a powerful feeling is telling me that it may be true."

"You heard about the missing files?" I asked.

"Rumors spread like wildfire here," said Samantha. "Well, what do you say? Will you help me out with my investigation? It involves using magic and divination techniques, just so you know."

Samantha had practically pushed us into a corner, more so than the dean had. I really had no idea how I should have responded, but luckily Raven was right on it.

"It's hard to say," said Raven. "If anything comes up, we'll see what we can do, but no promises."

The smile on Samantha's face showed that she was still satisfied, even with that answer.

"Alright," she said. "Thanks for listening. I'm sure we'll meet again someday. See you later."

Samantha headed off in a different direction as Raven and I continued walking. An interesting new development had leapt onto the scene out of nowhere, and it was up to us to determine how to handle it.

"I'll have to contact Miss Flamingo about this," said Raven.

"So, there really was something going on with Samantha after all," I said. "It's crazy how we still managed to get the scoop on her even though our assignment turned up nothing."

"That's how the club works," said Raven arrogantly. "Don't you know this by now? And you've been working with us for how long?"

"Well, excuse me!" I grunted. "I'm sorry if all of the club's oddness is still odd to me."

Raven quickly strutted off without a word. One thing that I did know about the club after all this time was that my partner still pushed my buttons.

My annoyance was easily overshadowed by what we had just learned about Samantha, and I could only imagine what this would lead to. I was really skeptical about helping her get to the bottom of the Campus Creeper rumor, since that was the free ticket out of a heap of trouble concerning the theft of Wyatt's student documents.

I returned to my communications class. Mr. Holden was discussing something we had covered earlier in the semester, just as he said he would. He acknowledged my return with a nod, and I took my seat next to Trent.

"What was that about?" Trent asked quietly.

I wasn't one for spreading rumors, but it was presumably too late to make a difference.

"Have you heard about the Campus Creeper?" I whispered.

"Some weird guy in a hoodie who sneaks around," he said. "Who doesn't know?"

"They just wanted to see if I knew anything about it," I said.

"Well, did you?" he asked.

"Not really," I lied. "Nothing that isn't already known about it."

For the rest of class, my mind wandered aimlessly around the topics regarding everything that had happened so far that day. I glanced at the clock, realizing that it was still morning and that the day was far from over. The concept of going through the rest of the day placed bricks on my motivation, and I foresaw a nap as soon as I was to make it home.

I headed straight for my history class as soon as communications let out, feeling determined to get Monday's last class over and done with. While waiting for class to begin, I paid little attention to the rest of the students who slowly filled the empty seats. In my daze, I didn't even notice Chad walking in until he sat down next to me.

"Wassup, Mike?" he said cheerfully.

"Yo," I said.

"Did you talk to the other guys?" he asked. "We're probably gonna get together tonight. Maybe grab a bite somewhere. You down?"

"Maybe," I replied dully.

"You feeling alright?" he asked. "You look a little bummed."

"No, I'm fine," I said. "Just have a lot on my mind."

"Everything going good with your woman?"

"Yeah," I said. "This time of year always gets to me, ya know?"

"Yup, I know how it is," said Chad, opening his folder. "You finish that homework?"

"Oh yeah, I almost forgot."

Chad and I placed our assignment on Mr. Weechik's desk. Feeling a little blah was nothing new to me, but forgetting to hand in my homework wasn't like me at all. I found it hard to believe that I was actually getting worn out from the mental overload surrounding everything in my life, since I was usually good at handling that sort of thing. However, I had to admit that my life over the last semester was unlike how it had ever been. The library fire seemed to be a major turning point for me, and I was still feeling the ripples caused by it. How different would my life be at this point if I still had my job at the library?

Get ahold of yourself, I thought. *Since when have you been so philosophical? This is no time to get melancholic about stupid, petty things you have no control over.*

I thought about asking Chad if he knew of the Campus Creeper, but decided against it. The last thing I wanted was to give everyone the impression that I was obsessed with it, especially since I was partly responsible for its origin. That thought tickled me a little, since it was quite ironic how something like that became such a rumor. Perhaps it would become one of those legendary stories that some colleges and schools have.

Class dragged by slower than a thirsty person eats toast, and I was almost too lethargic to leave the room when dismissed. I told Chad to inform me of the details later of whatever was going on that night, then headed home. During the drive to my apartment, my attempt to get energized with music barely got my blood flowing.

Sapphira greeted me as usual when I opened my door. Placing my bag on the table, I went straight into my room and crawled into bed. There was math homework due the next day, but that was going to wait.

Awaking a couple hours later, my energy levels had increased significantly. However, something still felt off. There was some kind of murky feeling lingering over my head, and I wasn't quite sure what it was.

Doing my homework, I saw that my productivity wasn't suffering at all. However, there was something missing from my usual flow. Exactly what that was proved hard to pinpoint, but I didn't let it get to me since it wasn't getting in my way.

Hayley called me later that afternoon to chat. Talking to her made me feel better, and I figured I was just missing my girl. I told her that I was planning to meet with the guys that night and invited her along. She said she was willing to join us, and I told her I'd let her know the details when I found out more.

I kept myself entertained by cooking some simple appetizers out of my cookbook. They weren't anything special, but the constructiveness provided a satisfactory way to pass the time while I awaited hearing from the guys. The intrinsic rewards of making food were starting to present themselves to me, and I found myself increasingly pulled away from the exploding zombie heads in the virtual world, opting out for the stovetop and cutting board instead.

While I was indulging in my homemade cheese ball with multigrain crackers, my phone went off. Chad's name showed up on the caller ID and I answered it as quickly as possible. He gave me the details of where and when we'd be meeting. I told him Hayley would be coming with me, and he said that Lawrence was bringing Samantha. When I heard her name, I couldn't tell if I was glad or disappointed, but I for sure wasn't indifferent. Hopefully, she would have something interesting to tell me, but wouldn't arouse the suspicions of everyone else.

I informed Hayley of the plan and picked her up shortly after. She had met my friends during brief run-ins at the college, but this was her first time actually hanging out with them. I assured her that she had nothing to be worried about, but Hayley was Hayley, so naturally she was a little nervous.

Our meeting point was Zoe Café, where we had met once before. The difference was that this time I could afford to pay for myself and Hayley, plus our share of the tip. In fact, I could afford to pick up everyone's tab, but they weren't going to know that.

Aaron's yellow truck was already in the parking lot, and it looked like everyone was already inside. Hayley and I entered the restaurant, and I heard someone calling us over. Aaron, Chad, and Jorge were seated at the biggest table in the corner of the restaurant.

"Hey, guys," I greeted as we walked over to them. "Where's Lawrence and Sam?"

"They're on their way," said Jorge.

"Don't think they dipped out on us," said Aaron. "This is a mandatory crew gathering. I'd give Lawrence forty lashes if he missed this."

"Then I'm glad I could make it," I said, taking my seat.

"I knew you would," said Aaron, pointing his fork at me. "It's Lawrence I'm worried about."

I handed Hayley a menu, then flipped open my own. This was the second time I had eaten at Zoe Café, and just like the first time, I was able to choose whatever I wanted without having to look at the price.

"Order whatever you want, babe," I told Hayley. "It's on me."

"You won't complain if I order the most expensive thing they have?" she asked playfully.

"Only if you don't eat it," I told her.

"Mr. Moneybags over here!" said Jorge. "That research job or whatever it is must pay well."

"It's mostly about how I handle my finances," I said modestly.

"I remember when you were a broke bloke," said Aaron. "One of your awesome friends had to pay for your meal so you could eat that day, isn't that right?"

"You may have saved my life that day." I chuckled.

Lawrence and Samantha showed up a few minutes later. There was something about sitting at a table with a large group that gave me a feeling of power. Strength in numbers or something along those lines. On top of that, being in good company always made things better.

"I had frog legs for the first time last week," said Jorge as we waited for our food.

"Frog legs are delicious," said Samantha. "They kinda taste like chicken."

"If only people were willing to accept that, they wouldn't be missing out," said Jorge with a mild smirk.

"You wanna try some frog legs sometime?" I asked Hayley.

"Ew, no!" she said, scrunching her face.

"How about chocolate-covered ants?" said Samantha. "Those are good, too."

"You wanna try some chocolate-covered ants?" I asked Hayley teasingly.

"Actually, I have," she said. "I like them."

"Huh? Really?" I asked, bewildered.

Aaron started laughing like a baboon.

"She got you with that one!" he told me.

"And toasted crickets with hot sauce," said Hayley. "That's my favorite bug snack."

"I heard crickets are pretty good," said Jorge.

"You all are insane," said Lawrence with an eyebrow raised.

"What's wrong, Lawrence?" said Aaron. "You don't like the idea of exotic cuisine?"

"Not exactly," Lawrence replied.

"Where's the sense of adventure?" Aaron sneered. "If it looks good, eat it."

"I think less intelligent life forms have perished that way," said Lawrence flatly.

"See what your boyfriend has to deal with when he's with us?" said Aaron to Hayley.

Hayley giggled and shook her head.

"Your friends are crazy," she told me. "But a good kind of crazy."

"Yup," I replied.

Our meal was one of the more enjoyable ones I had in a while. They say that food is better when eaten with others, and that was very hard to argue against. To make things better, I could tell that Hayley was having a good time as well. Watching her gradually come out of her shell was one of the more rewarding aspects of my relationship with her.

We stayed for quite a bit of time after we finished eating. The random and motley conversations were flowing like wine, and it wasn't until we were drunk on good times did we finally call it a night. I paid for my part of the tab, shelling out an amount of money that would've made me cringe not too long ago. However, that was then and this was now.

Hayley had to use the restroom, so I waited for her by the entrance. Lawrence was warming up the car when Samantha walked up to me.

"About what I said to you earlier," she said. "I don't want you to feel obligated or anything."

I patted the amulet in my pocket.

"Don't worry about it," I began, "but it's like Raven said. We don't know if we'll be able to help you, but if there's something we can do, you can count on us."

Samantha smiled, and I wondered why I would say that. Now I really was obligated.

"Thanks," she said sincerely. "I'll see ya around, Mike."

"See ya."

When Hayley came out of the restroom, I wrapped my arm around her as we went out to my car. When I dropped her off at her house, I walked her to the door.

"Did you have fun?" I asked.

She looked down at the ground for a moment, then looked up at me.

"Yeah," she said, sounding a little tired.

"Good," I said. "Have a good night."

"You too."

I kissed her goodnight, then got into my car and drove off. As I was heading back to my apartment, the strange feeling of emptiness crept back into my mind. Was it just me, or was I already missing everyone?

My nap earlier that afternoon had offset my sleeping pattern slightly. As I wound down with some late night TV, I couldn't help but shake this strange fog lingering over me. Oddly, it worsened the more I thought about Aaron and my other friends.

My friends, I thought. *These people are the closest to me, but who are they exactly? What do they think of me? Just what is this feeling of importance I have when I think of them? I know what Hayley means to me, but what about the others?*

It was slightly disturbing how these thoughts suddenly began to present themselves. What was more disturbing was the fact that the voice in my head speaking these thoughts didn't seem like my own.

~Opus 25~

Aaron and I were hanging out for lunch at a sports bar. I wasn't much into sports, nor was I old enough to drink, but the place was renowned for its fantastic burgers and steak fries. The reputation proved true, because my mushroom and Swiss cheeseburger on a toasted bun was so good it was diabolical.

"The game is called *Bereft of Freewill 2: Breeding Violence.*"

Aaron was trying to describe an upcoming video game to me, but it was hard for me to get interested. I wasn't into those hack-and-slash games like he was, since they were too fast-paced and in-your-face for me. However, they seemed to cater to Aaron's innate aggression quite nicely.

"Are you going to get it?" I asked, already knowing the answer.

"Duh!" he replied. "They're having a midnight launch at my favorite game store. Everyone there gets a free poster, and anyone who preordered the game will get the soundtrack for free! The first game had a brutally epic soundtrack, and I expect nothing less from this one! I would have to be dead in order for me to miss that!"

"That sounds kinda cool," I said, now feeling partially intrigued.

"You can come with," he told me. "Those crowds are always the most interesting. You're bound to witness something memorable."

"Isn't that game store you like out of town?" I asked. "I don't really feel like going that far."

"Dude, I've got this," Aaron assured. "My buddy is going to give me a ride. His name's Rudy, and I doubt he would mind you tagging along."

"I have classes in the morning," I said. "I can't be out all night. My math class is at eight, then I have English right after."

"What are you doing in those classes tomorrow?" Aaron asked. "Taking any tests? Doing any projects?"

"Study sessions for exams," I said.

"Is that all?" Aaron stirred his drink with his straw. "How are your grades in those classes?"

383

"I'm getting an A in both."

"Then what the hell?" said Aaron. "You don't need to study for those classes. Both study sessions are, like, gonna be a waste of time unless you're going for perfect attendance, which you already screwed up last year."

"I didn't screw up," I said, irritated. "I had the flu."

"It'll be fun, dude," he told me. "One time at a midnight launch we got free food. These guys who worked at a sandwich shop showed up and started whipping sandwiches into the crowd. People went crazy, grabbing sandwiches and stuff. It was awesome!"

Aaron had a point. I really didn't need to attend those study sessions at all. Any reviewing for my math and English exams could be done at home, and they'd be brief since I already knew most of the material. On top of that, a good chunk of my psychology study guide was completed, so I didn't need to worry too much about that.

"Alright," I said, "I gotta see this for myself if it's really as exciting as you say it is."

"It depends," said Aaron. "Some times are more fun than others, but you don't know until you get there. I'm gonna call Rudy and let him know that you're coming."

While Aaron called his buddy, I looked up at one of the TVs. There was a boxing match going on, and one of the guys totally got laid out with a jab to the face. Thinking about the Roman Empire, the guy who lost probably would've been fed to the lions. That extra incentive of life and death might have provided a different outcome in a match, since people tend to fight differently when their lives are on the line. I took another bite of my burger and thought how much it would suck to be a Roman who didn't have a good social standing.

"Rudy says it's fine," said Aaron, putting his phone into his pocket. "I gotta warn you, he's quite the character."

"What do you mean?" I asked.

"He's quite the character," Aaron repeated. "Some of the things he tells me!"

"Like what?"

384

"Well, he was doing dishes one time," said Aaron. "He was washing a cheese grater. He told me he didn't realize he was grating through the sponge until his fingers started to bleed."

"And we're gonna trust this guy to drive us somewhere?" I was starting to feel unsure about Aaron's buddy.

"It's fine," said Aaron. "He's cool."

After lunch, I followed Aaron back to his place. We were going to hang out there until that evening, then Rudy was going to pick us up and take us to the game store. I had no homework due the next day, so I didn't have to worry about getting home to finish any.

"Dad, I brought Mike over," said Aaron once we were in the house.

Aaron's dad was sitting at the computer in his underwear. He looked a lot like Aaron, but with full facial hair. He looked at me and smiled.

"Hey there, Mike!" he said. "It's been awhile. How've you been?"

"Pretty good," I replied.

"We're going to that midnight launch tonight," said Aaron. "He's gonna hang out here until Rudy gets us."

"Alright," said his dad. "Your mom's working a double today, so she won't be home until about one in the morning."

I followed Aaron up to his room where we played video games and watched weird movies. His room was exactly as I remembered it from the last time I was over, except his collection of games, CDs, and movies had grown.

Around nine o'clock, Aaron got a phone call from Rudy. He was on his way to pick us up, which I thought was pretty early for a midnight release.

"See ya soon," said Aaron, hanging up.

"Already?" I asked. "Do you usually go this early?"

"We gotta reserve a good place in line," he said. "The sooner we get there, the sooner we can leave. Plus, the more stuff we get to witness."

"Have you ever been the first in line?" I asked.

Aaron laughed.

"If you want to be the first in line for a midnight launch, then you gotta pitch a tent," he said.

"Yeah, right," I replied in disbelief.

"Dead serious," he said. "Those guys are hardcore about their dedication. There's typically at least one at every launch. When a new system comes out, it's ten times worse."

I couldn't imagine camping out in front of a store just to be the first one to get my hands on a video game. Then again, I wasn't exactly a diehard gamer, so that just wasn't my thing. Who am I to tell someone that their lifestyle is extreme or absurd?

Aaron and I got ready to wait for Rudy at the end of the driveway. A significant amount of snow had fallen while we were in the house all day, but the roads were mostly cleared. I just hoped the weather wasn't going to get nasty while we were waiting outside the store.

I heard the distant sound of an engine gradually getting louder. Expecting to see a big truck or something come around the corner, it turned out to be an old car, and not exactly a muscle car at that.

"There's Rudy," said Aaron, watching the vehicle approach.

When the car pulled up in front of us, I couldn't help but wonder what was keeping it in one piece (aside from the clearly visible duct tape that appeared to be holding the front end together). Thick smog belched from the exhaust as the car clunked to a halt. Aaron opened the front passenger door, which creaked and popped like a cable suspension bridge in an earthquake.

"Hey, Rudy! What's up," Aaron greeted.

"Same old, same old," said Rudy.

Rudy was a scruffy guy with a messy haircut and patchy facial hair. My guess was he was probably in his mid-thirties, maybe a little older.

"This is my buddy Mike," said Aaron.

"What's up?" Rudy said to me.

"Not much," I replied. "Nice to meet you."

"You can get shotgun, Mike," said Aaron. "I'll stretch out in the backseat."

I sat in the front passenger seat and had to make room for my feet in all of the trash on the floor. Empty cans and bags littered practically every inch of the car's interior, and it smelled like an exhaust leak inside a dumpster. That's not an exaggeration.

"Thanks for the ride, dude," said Aaron when he was in the car.

"You got that gas money?" Rudy asked him.

Aaron handed him some cash, which he stuffed into his coat pocket. After shifting into gear, the car lurched forward and we were on our way.

"So, how long you known each other?" Rudy asked as we were heading down the road.

"Since last school year," I said.

"Oh yeah," said Rudy, scratching his patchy beard, "you guys are in college."

"Did you go to Elm Valley?" I asked.

Rudy barked a wheezy laugh.

"Hell no!" he replied. "Ain't no way I'm going to college. Waste of time, what it is. And a waste of money, too."

"Rudy's an idiot, Mike," said Aaron. "He's proud of it, too."

"Hey, I see it like this," said Rudy raucously. "If I can go to work, pay my bills, and eat, then I'm as smart as I need to be. I don't need no degree or whatever."

"I think working for a degree makes me feel good," I said. "It sucks and it's expensive, but if I play my cards right, it'll be worth it."

Rudy gave another wheezy laugh.

"Where'd you find this guy, Aaron?" he guffawed.

"College," Aaron replied flatly. "We said that."

"Yeah, one of *them* folks," said Rudy. "What's your name again? Mike?"

"Uh, yeah," I said.

"Well hey, to each their own," said Rudy. "You look like you've never served a single day behind bars, am I right?"

"That's right," I replied.

"Damn, ain't that something?" said Rudy, shaking his head. "I forget that people like you exist."

What kind of people do you normally associate with? I wondered.

"Look at you, all clean and everything," Rudy told me. "You got the whitest teeth I think I've ever seen. What's the worst dental procedure you've had done?"

"Um, I had some cavities filled."

"That ain't nothing, give me a break. You don't know what it's like to have a root canal when the only painkiller available is rubbing alcohol, and that stuff doesn't taste the greatest. I know from experience."

"Did that really happen to you?" I asked.

"I've been places, done things. I've moved all over the country my entire life, and I never really stayed in one area long enough to grow attached to it before I moved out here. Take my word for it, drinking rubbing alcohol with a throbbing toothache wasn't my only crazy experience."

"You mean you *drank* the rubbing alcohol?" I asked in awe.

"How else was I gonna get drunk enough to have a root canal?" he replied gravelly.

Several miles were traveled with Rudy spilling his wild anecdotes. As my ears were filled with some of the most bizarre, amusing, and often unsettling tales I've ever heard, I started looking forward to the moment when I could get out of that car. Not saying Rudy was a bad guy, but I wouldn't necessarily coin him as a good guy either.

While I was listening to how Rudy once mounted a customized, fully automatic BB gun to his customized, motorized skateboard, the rearview mirrors suddenly lit up with the unmistakable blue and red lights of a police car. Honestly, I wasn't very surprised that we were getting pulled over. Rudy was doing fifty-five in a forty-five speed zone for the past few miles, after all.

"Damn it all!" said Rudy frantically, pulling over. "Hide the stuff! Hide the stuff!"

"W-what stuff?" I asked nervously, looking around.

Rudy busted out with some of the wheeziest, hoarsest laughing I thought was humanly possible.

"I'm screwing with ya, kid!" he guffawed. "I've been clean for months! Ain't nothing in this car to be worried about."

"Oh," I said, forcing my blood pressure down, "that's a frickin' relief."

"What'd you do this time, Rudy?" Aaron asked nonchalantly.

"Hmm, guess I was speeding," said Rudy. "I always forget that it's only forty-five through here. Ever since they lowered the speed limit from fifty-five back in 2005 or something, I've been messing it up."

"Um, I think it was actually *thirty*-five miles an hour through here before," said Aaron.

"Oh yeah," Rudy replied, as though he just had a major epiphany. "Guess I've always sped through here, then."

I could tell I was in for a spectacle before the officer even made it to Rudy's window.

"Good evening," said the cop to Rudy.

"Good evening, Officer Carson," Rudy replied.

Do these two know each other? I thought.

"Do you know why I pulled you over?" Officer Carson asked.

"Speeding, right?" said Rudy with a two-faced grin.

"You were going fifty-five miles an hour in a forty-five," said Officer Carson. "Do you have your license, registration, and proof of insurance this time, Rudy?"

Yup, they know each other, I thought.

Rudy reached over and opened the glove compartment in front of me. For whatever reason, I was half expecting a rat to fly out at me when he opened it to retrieve his paperwork. He handed everything to Officer Carson, who walked back to his police cruiser.

"How did he know your name?" Aaron asked Rudy.

"I've, um, been involved with him before," he replied.

"Oh yeah?" Aaron raised his eyebrows.

I don't claim to be a master of being pulled over, but it seemed like Officer Carson was in his car for a long time. Rudy was going on about his previous offenses, and I was beginning to wonder how this was going to end. After a while, Officer Carson walked back to Rudy's door.

"I need you to step out of the car," he said firmly. "Everyone else stay seated and keep your hands up."

Should've seen this coming, I thought, holding my hands out in front of my face.

"What's going on?" Rudy asked. "What'd I do?"

"Step out of the car," the officer repeated. "Don't make me tell you again."

Rudy opened the door and exited the vehicle. Almost immediately, he was put in handcuffs.

"The hell is this?" Rudy demanded. "On what grounds do you have the right to handcuff me?"

"You have a warrant out for your arrest," I heard Officer Carson explain.

"That thing in Delaware last month?" Rudy spat. "I had that sorted out!"

"Not according to the information I have on you," the officer said. "You're charged with failure to appear in court."

"This is outrageous!" said Rudy. "I'm not going through with this!"

There was something darkly entertaining about watching a handcuffed man take off running, only to be tackled mere seconds later. Since Rudy's hands were cuffed behind his back, he couldn't prevent himself from falling flat on his face.

"Oh my God," said Aaron as Rudy was taken to the cop car.

"How long have you known this guy?" I asked.

"A couple years," Aaron told me. "He's a crazy dude."

"I see that."

I wanted to turn around and see what was going on outside, but part of me thought it would be best to just mind my own business. Not much later, Officer Carson appeared on my side of the car and told Aaron and me to get out.

"Keep your hands where I can see them," he said as we opened our doors.

Aaron and I stepped out of the car.

"I'll need to see some identification," he told us.

"What's gonna happen to him?" Aaron asked as we took out our licenses.

"He'll be escorted to jail," said Officer Carson, taking our licenses. "Hang tight here."

Within the next minute, another police car showed up. I shivered in the freezing cold as snow started to gently fall. Officer Carson told the other officers what was going on before conducting a search of Rudy's car. Feeling lost for words, I heaved an audible sigh.

"Sorry I got you into this," said Aaron. "I really didn't expect this to happen."

"You didn't?" I said, chuckling ironically. "I was almost waiting for it to happen."

"Rudy's a good guy," Aaron insisted. "He's got some screws loose, maybe a few missing, but he's a good guy."

I felt that strange, empty feeling creep back into my mind, and it seemed to make me even more agitated.

"What are we going to do now?" I asked, irritated. "Will the cops take us to where we're going?"

"I don't think they work that way," said Aaron. "They might take us back to the station if we can't find a ride for ourselves. Don't worry, Mike. I've got us covered."

"Oh, how assuring," I muttered angrily. "Kinda like how you had us covered with Rudy?"

"Dude, chill the hell out," said Aaron firmly. "I know where we are. There's a place just down the road no more than a mile or so. We can walk there and have someone pick us up."

"Alright, whatever," I muttered.

"The car's clean," said one of the other officers who was going through the car.

What a poor choice of words, I thought as I remembered all the trash in the car.

"Here you go, fellas," said Officer Carson, handing back our licenses to us. "You two are good to go, but I can't say the same for your friend."

I looked at the back of the police cruiser where Rudy was, but I couldn't see inside.

"Thank you, sir," said Aaron, sounding more polite than I was used to. "We can have someone pick us up."

"Where are you being picked up?" Officer Carson asked.

"We'll wait at a gas station or something down the road," said Aaron. "A couple strapping young lads like us won't have any problem walking that short distance."

"Well, alright," said Officer Carson. "You two watch yourselves out there. Stay out of trouble, okay?"

"Yes, sir," we said in unison.

We headed off down the road, and just as we were out of earshot, I had to set something straight.

"Why did you tell him we could walk?" I groaned. "He might've offered us a ride."

"And have us eating out of his hands?" Aaron replied. "No thanks."

"What do you mean?" I asked angrily. "Is this some kind of tough guy act?"

"Make it sound so bad, why don't ya?" said Aaron.

"Man, I hate snow," I muttered, trudging forward.

"It builds character." Aaron chuckled.

"Now you sound like my dad."

The walk to the gas station was bearable, but I cursed under my breath almost every step of the way. For some reason, I was feeling especially irritated, and the weird feeling over my head wasn't helping any. If Aaron had more trustworthy acquaintances, we wouldn't have been in such an aggravating situation.

Calm down, I told myself. *I shouldn't be so angry over something like this. As annoying as it is, I don't understand why I'm so bent out of shape. Maybe I'm turning into an old man already.*

When we entered the warm building, my feet and legs were covered in snow. I stomped it off on the mat in front of the

392

entrance as Aaron made his phone call. My temper started to drop, and I figured it was the warm air soothing me or something.

"Hey, what's up?" said Aaron on the phone. "I have a favor to ask. Can you give me and Mike a ride? I'll give you gas money."

While Aaron was setting up a possible ride for us, I ventured through the convenience store and found the hotdogs. Even though I was a little hungry, my main motive for standing by the hotdogs was to get the heat from the cooker. Just as the feeling was starting to come back into my toes, Aaron showed up by my side.

"Those dogs look tasty," he commented.

"Did you find a ride?" I asked bluntly.

"Yeah," said Aaron. "Jorge should be here in about ten or fifteen minutes."

"That's good," I said.

"In the meantime," said Aaron, reaching for the hotdog buns, "I'm getting something to eat."

"Yeah, I might as well do the same," I said.

Both of us made up our own hotdogs. I loaded mine up with chili and cheese, which seemed like the perfect thing after walking through the snow. Normally, I would've gotten a slushie, but the last thing I wanted at the moment was ice inside me.

"Don't you want any ketchup or mustard on that?" Aaron asked as he loaded up the condiments.

"I already have chili and cheese," I said. "I don't need anything else."

"What's an American meal without ketchup?" he said, putting an obscene amount of ketchup on his hotdog. "It's like the national gravy!"

Jorge showed up just as Aaron had said. Both of us climbed into his SUV, which was a vast improvement over the jalopy that Rudy had.

"Tell me again. What happened?" said Jorge with an amused grin.

"The guy giving us a ride got arrested before we got there," I said.

"I thought he was supposed to be your buddy, Aaron." Jorge chuckled.

"He is," Aaron replied, licking the ketchup off his wrists. "He shouldn't have been speeding."

"What did he do in Delaware?" I asked. "Isn't that what caused all that?"

"Uh, I'm not sure," said Aaron. "It's Rudy we're talking about, so it could be anything."

Anything? I thought. *Including murder or assault with a weapon?*

Jorge chuckled again and shook his head, apparently thinking the same thing I was.

"So, what's the game you're getting?" he asked.

"Bereft of Freewill 2: Breeding Violence," Aaron answered proudly.

"Sounds kinda wicked," said Jorge.

"Only the most wicked," said Aaron. "They considered giving it an 'Adults Only' rating because the violence is so graphic and detailed! But the gameplay is what it's all about."

"That's what I look for in a game," I said. "As long as the game is fun and plays well, I don't care if flowers burst out of the things you defeat."

"Um, that's kinda weird, Mike," said Aaron. "Flowers?"

"What are you gonna do, Jorge?" I asked. "We're gonna be there until midnight."

"I'll just hang out with you guys," he said. "I don't have morning classes tomorrow, so it's no big deal."

"Thanks again, dude," said Aaron. "Mucho appreciation."

When we arrived at the game store, there was already a small congregation outside. The three of us quickly took our place in line as more people showed up behind us. Within the course of a half hour, the line had more than doubled. I was amazed that so many people were waiting for a game that I had never heard of.

The conversations we had with other people were mainly about video games. It was a good chance for everyone to brag about their virtual achievements, and the crowd gradually became more rowdy over time. A group of people behind us was the loudest of all, and it was easy to see that they were drunk. The bottles of juice they were chugging were probably more than just juice, as they grew rowdier as the bottles became emptier.

One of the store employees walked out and addressed the crowd. She caught everyone's attention with more than just her words and gestures, though. I won't lie, she was very attractive.

"Listen up, everybody!" she called out. "We're going to hand out our free posters for the game! Anyone who wants one can take one and *only one!*"

"Woooo! Yeeeaahhh!"

The drunkards in line were having trouble suppressing their libidos as the attractive girl tried to talk. There was no way she couldn't hear their annoying remarks, but she was doing a good job of ignoring them. She and another employee (a dude, mind you) handed out posters to the people in line. Aaron quickly snatched one, and I figured I'd take one as well. Jorge passed, saying the poster was too brutal for his liking. He offered to put the posters in his SUV so we wouldn't have to hold them.

At one point, somebody pulled their car up and turned up the stereo. The way the bass thumped, it was obvious they had subwoofers. The drunk people started dancing like morons, doing pathetic and hilarious breakdancing on the icy, slushy ground.

Around eleven-thirty, the attractive employee came back out to make another announcement. As the rowdy drunks made another uproar at her appearance, I wondered why the store didn't have a less attractive employee come out instead.

"Anyone with a preorder will get a free soundtrack with the game!" she announced. "We're going to have those of you with preorders come to the front of the line."

"Yeah, baby!"

"Woooo! She said 'preorder'! Haaawww!"

"Take it off! Yeeaahhh!"

"Will you jackasses shut the hell up?"

"What'd you say, punk?"

"Keep your hands off me!"

Just when I was able to see it coming, it already started happening. Fists started flying as the wrong people got too personal with each other. Half the crowd scrambled to flee while the other half rushed into the brawl. Of course, Aaron, Jorge, and I were caught in the middle.

"Holy crap!" Aaron shouted, pushing through the crowd to get away from the hotspot. "Metal concert skills, activate!"

While struggling to make sense of where to go in the flurry of people, I slid on a patch of ice and fell into another guy. We didn't fall over, but the strong smell of booze on his breath was combined with the furious look on his face, and that told me that I was in trouble. He swung at me with a wide haymaker, which I somehow blocked with my arm. When he swung with his other arm, somebody else happened to stumble between us and take the hit for me. This other guy was much bigger and unfazed, and he knocked the drunk guy out with a single punch.

When I managed to escape from the madness, I looked at my arm that blocked the drunk guy's punch. There was a bruise forming, and I was glad that it wasn't on my face. Somehow, the fight quickly resolved itself. Everyone who deserved to be knocked out was lying on the ground.

"Mike!"

Aaron hurried over to me, looking completely unscathed. Jorge's nose was bleeding a little bit, but it didn't look too serious.

"Are you okay?" I asked Jorge. "Who hit you?"

"The ground did," he said, wiping his face. "I slipped when trying to get away."

"What about you?" Aaron asked me.

I showed him my arm.

"He was aiming for my face, but I blocked it," I said. "Then he accidentally hit another guy who took him out."

The cops showed up minutes later to take care of the rest. As they were handcuffing people, I recognized Officer Carson. He stopped when he noticed us.

"You guys again?" he said.

"Small world, huh?" I said, forcing myself to laugh.

"You didn't get hurt, did you?" he asked.

"I did," said Jorge, sniffing through his clogged nose. "My nose stopped bleeding, so I'm fine."

"How did you kids manage to find so many crazy people tonight?" Officer Carson asked. "Be careful, okay?"

"Yes, sir," we said in unison.

Officer Carson went back to speak with the other cops. Aaron took his place at the beginning of the line with everyone else with a preorder who didn't get arrested. When he walked out of the store, he was carrying a bag and wearing a huge grin.

"Awesome night, huh?" he said, elbowing me. "I told you it'd be worth it. Oh yeah, sorry Jorge. You really got the wrong end of this deal."

"It's straight," Jorge replied, gently touching his nose.

"Are you sure you don't want a poster?" Aaron asked. "It'd serve as a souvenir for this eventful night!"

"That's alright," said Jorge. "I don't think I'll forget this very easily anyway."

While riding back to Aaron's house, there was no denying what he had said to me earlier that day. The entire experience was quite memorable, and I was somehow glad I went along with it. When I got home, I looked for the tape, then hung my poster up in my room. The brutal depiction of the game on my wall fit the memory of the midnight launch party to a T.

~Opus 26~

I called Hayley on the morning of her birthday to sing her an off-key birthday song. For the record, it's the only song I ever sing to anyone. You'd be hard-pressed to find me stretching my vocal cords for any other reason. If I ever had another need to serenade Hayley, I'd be more likely to stand outside her window with my radio and have a recorded artist do the singing for me.

"Aw, thanks babe!" she cooed over the phone. "But your singing is terrible."

"All just for you," I replied softly. "Are you ready for tonight? It's gonna be fun."

"I can't wait," she said. "You'll come get me, right?"

"Of course," I said. "Four o'clock. Make sure you're ready when I get there."

"Okay!"

Today was going to be the perfect day. I would take her out to dinner somewhere nice, but nothing over the top. I also decided to go with the ice skating idea, thinking it'd be a lot of fun. Lastly, I would bring her back to my place to wind down the evening.

"Ooh, this is going to be awesome!" I declared excitedly after hanging up.

My phone rang again in my hand, and I wondered if Hayley had forgotten to tell me something. A heavy frown dragged my face toward the floor when I saw Raven's name on the caller ID.

"Yeah?" I answered morosely.

"We've been assigned a task today," she told me.

"What do you mean?" I asked. "I have plans today."

"I informed Miss Flamingo about Samantha," said Raven. "We need to head to the cabin right now."

"For what?" I asked grumpily. "How long are we gonna be there?"

"I don't know!" she snapped back. "I don't have all the answers! Why are you suddenly asking so many questions?"

398

"It's Hayley's birthday," I told her. "We already made plans for today. I'm picking her up at four."

"No excuses!" said Raven. "If you don't show up for this assignment, you're going into the furnace! Got it?"

"Rrrrgh!" I moaned. "I'll get ready to head out."

"Good, I'll see you soon!" she replied, suddenly sounding insincerely chipper.

I quickly got ready to go, wanting to get this done before I had to get Hayley. It was almost eleven, giving me about five hours to do whatever I was going to have to do. On the way to the cabin, I hoped and prayed that it would be something simple and quick.

When I reached the end of the long dirt driveway, I was flustered to see the little windup toy Raven drove wasn't there yet. After all that crap she gave me over the phone, she was going to make *me* wait. The world's goofy sense of humor was probably making someone chuckle, but it certainly wasn't me.

There was, however, another car parked there that I didn't recognize. I wondered if it was Miss Flamingo's new car, but the thought suddenly occurred that I had never actually seen Miss Flamingo's car. Maybe she happened to have it parked out front that day, owing to the fact that she even had a car to begin with. She seemed like the type of person who could just show up wherever, or perhaps she had a healthy supply of aluminum in stock.

The door to the meeting room was closed, so I knocked. Immediately, I got a reply from inside the room.

"Yes?" I heard Miss Flamingo say.

"It's Roadrunner," I replied.

"Wait until Raven is with you," she said.

I sighed, then headed back downstairs. Taking a seat in front of the crackling fireplace, I gazed up at the big moose head on the wall. I had never seen a moose in real life, but judging by the size of the head alone, they must be pretty massive.

"Hurry up, Raven," I muttered, looking at the time on my phone. "I've been here fifteen minutes already."

After a few more painful minutes of waiting, the cabin door swung open. Raven stepped inside, appearing disgruntled and disheveled. She closed the door and stomped the snow off her boots, then leaned her bass upright against the wall.

"You're here early," she said.

"And you're here finally," I said. "I couldn't get into the meeting room unless you were with me."

"In case you haven't noticed," she said snootily, "there's snow out there. I hate driving in snow. It stresses me out, and stress is bad for my skin."

"Yeah," I sneered, "if you wrecked that little car going twenty miles an hour, you'd be done for."

"What grudges have you against my diminuate car?" she asked, cocking her head to the side.

"What's wrong with you today?" I asked, changing the subject. "You look like you just rolled out of bed."

"Maybe I did just roll out of bed," she replied.

"Are we having a problem here?"

Miss Flamingo had somehow made it down the stairs without us noticing. She was standing there with her arms crossed, looking a little displeased that two of her subordinates were arguing. Raven and I didn't say anything, both acting like dogs that had just been yelled at. Miss Flamingo silently walked back up the stairs, and the two of us followed without a word.

Upon entering the meeting room, there was another person who I didn't recognize. Seated in a chair close to Miss Flamingo's spot, he was a tall Native American who looked to be in his thirties or possibly forties. His long, dark, flowing hair was almost too beautiful to be a man's, and his clothes, although modern and casual, had a hint of tribal flair that matched his ethnicity.

"This is Mr. 29," said Miss Flamingo, closing the door behind her. "He is your client for this assignment."

"Hello," he greeted with a smile.

Mr. 29? I thought. *What's that about? I know Native Americans traditionally had unique names, but this is a new one.*

Raven and I took our seats at the other end of the table. This was quickly looking like another interrogation similar to when Mr. Landon and Mr. Gast had called us to the dean's office.

400

"Mr. 29, you may begin," said Miss Flamingo.

"Thank you," he said, looking at Raven and I. "You two attend Elm Valley College. Are you familiar with a rumor regarding the Campus Creeper?"

"Yeah," I replied. "They say a suspicious person in a black hoodie was seen on campus."

Miss Flamingo looked at me with a solid stare.

"I understand that you two are responsible for this rumor," she said firmly.

"Uh, that's right," I said. "We used that story for—"

"I know," said Miss Flamingo abruptly. "Mr. 29?"

"You two are familiar with another student who attends the same college," said Mr. 29. "A girl named Samantha Bridgman, correct?"

"Yes," I said.

"Samantha has been trying to uncover the mystery of the Campus Creeper," he continued. "I would like to know more about this situation."

"Should we tell her the truth about the rumor?" I asked. "Otherwise, she'll just be on a wild goose chase for some story we made up."

"No," said Miss Flamingo. "To uphold the club's secrecy, it is very important that you never disclose the truth to her. We are not worried about her finding out on her own."

"Does that mean that she *won't* find out on her own?" I asked.

"That's none of your concern," she replied.

"Due to recent information given by you two," said Mr. 29, "I now believe that Ms. Bridgman is a Wiccan."

"A Wiccan?" I asked. "You mean like a witch?"

"In some regards, yes," said Miss Flamingo. "Take care not to use the two terms interchangeably, though."

"I need to know what kind of magic she is using and how she's using it," said Mr. 29. "That is all. I'm not interested in the girl or anything else she does, or even what purposes her magic is for."

"Go to her house," said Miss Flamingo. "Look around and take note of anything magical or anything that could be

401

used for magic. This includes candles, sculptures, mysterious tools, and especially grimoires."

That last word made my ears twitch, as if someone had come up from behind me with a feather duster and tickled the back of my neck.

"You want us to go inside her house?" I asked, dumbfounded.

Mr. 29 reached into his pocket and removed a key, which he slid across the table to us. I was going to catch it, but Raven snatched it up before I could.

"That's a duplicate of her house key," said Mr. 29. "It should get you inside."

"Nobody should be at her home until four o'clock," said Miss Flamingo. "I take it that this timeframe works well for everyone?"

I looked at Miss Flamingo, who was looking at me as if that last statement was aimed at me solely.

"I don't think I can do this," I said. "We're breaking into someone's house."

"We're not breaking in," said Raven. "We have a key, so it's legit."

"That's not my point," I protested.

"I understand your unwillingness to perform this assignment," said Miss Flamingo. "However, it will be made worth your while."

Undoubtedly, she was referring to the hefty paycheck I was bound to have waiting for me upon returning. Miss Flamingo and Mr. 29 were looking at us as if they were finished speaking, so we simply stood up and walked out of the room. Raven used an app on her phone to tune her bass and perform her lucky song, then we were on our way back to Samantha's house yet again. I had to drive, of course.

There weren't any cars in the driveway at Samantha's house, but I was still nervous about being caught. I insisted on making absolutely sure that nobody was home, but Raven went right ahead and unlocked the door with the duplicate key. Gulping hard, I followed her into the house.

"Alright," said Raven when we were in, "we need to find magical objects. Candles, sculptures, mysterious tools, and *especially* grimoires! Do you know what a grimoire is?"

"Sure do," I said. "Where do we start?"

"Tell me what a grimoire is, Roadrunner," said Raven sharply. "This is important information that you must make yourself familiar with."

"A book containing magic and conjuration spells," I said impatiently. "I understand fully. Trust me."

"Well, aren't you confident!" said Raven deviously. "You sound like you know all about books containing magical spells."

A snide remark like that from Raven would usually be answered with a quick comeback or sarcastic retort. However, I somewhat stumbled over my own thoughts, because not only was she right, but she was acting as if she were on to me. At any rate, I couldn't let her know the truth.

"I'll check down here," I said. "You check upstairs."

"Who died and made you boss?" Raven sneered. "Last I checked, I'm still alive. But sure, I'll go along with your plan."

As Raven headed up the stairs, I was relieved that she agreed to my plan. I knew that Samantha's bedroom was upstairs, and I really didn't feel comfortable about going through a girl's room at all. That was also where the most magical items would be, and I was sure that Raven would be able to identify them better than me.

Stupid Raven, I thought to myself as I searched the living room. *She's always acting like she's better than me and like she knows more than me. If it weren't for me helping her, she'd be totally out of luck. I can't stand the way she acts. It pisses me off. If I could, I'd knock her teeth out and string them together to make a necklace, then strangle her with it.*

I stopped what I was doing. As true as it was that Raven irritated me, I was feeling much more vicious toward her than usual. That empty feeling of loneliness and dissatisfaction began to radiate down my spine, and I shook my head to try and get a grip on myself. It was the same feeling I had felt several times recently before, and it was kind of disturbing.

However, there was also something invigorating and exciting about it, as if it were compelling me to harbor those thoughts.

Feeling a little nervous and uneasy, I stroked the sapphire amulet in my pocket, telling myself to just get over it. This time of year always did funny things to my mind, so it must have been stress and lack of sunlight. While I continued to search through the house, the disturbing feeling gradually subsided.

I searched the entire downstairs, even looking out for secret hiding places, but found nothing of the magical variety. I took extra caution to make sure everything was put back in its place and didn't appear as if it had been tampered with. Deciding to see how Raven was coming along, I headed up the stairs. I heard her voice coming from one of the bedrooms, and I peeked inside to see who she was talking to. She was on the phone, and I quickly recognized the room as Samantha's. There was a dresser drawer open in front of Raven filled with candles, dreamcatchers, scribbles of magical symbols on papers, and other odds and ends that oozed of witchcraft.

"I understand," said Raven on the phone. "Very well. Bye."

She hung up and looked at me with a tilted smirk.

"Look at this goldmine!" she said. "This is strong evidence that Samantha is into magic. Wouldn't you say so?"

"It seems like it," I said, gazing into the drawer. "Who were you talking to?"

"Miss Flamingo," she said. "She wants us to get a sample of something."

Raven reached into her pocket and removed an empty phial.

"Do you always carry empty phials with you?" I asked.

"No," she said. "Just a coincidence. I forgot I had this."

She removed a little jar filled with a blue fluid out of the drawer, which looked almost like antifreeze. Very carefully, she poured some of the blue fluid into her phial, filling it up about halfway, then sealed it with a rubber stopper.

"Alright," she said, putting everything back into the drawer and closing it, "let's move out!"

404

We quickly left the house, locked the door, and hurried back to the cabin. For the first time since arriving at Samantha's house that day, my heart rate finally began to slow down to normal. I was glad that we didn't get caught, but as I learned with Wyatt's files, it can sometimes take a while for things to come around and bite you. Hopefully, nobody would notice that we were in the house.

"What are we gonna do now?" I asked Raven on our way back.

"We need to give this phial to Miss Flamingo," she said. "Then I don't know."

I looked at the time, which was now one-thirty. As long as everything went smoothly, there was a possibility that I'd be back in time to pick Hayley up at four. With such a stressful morning, I was really ready to spend time with my girlfriend and relax.

Back at the cabin, I saw that Mr. 29's car was still parked out front, but Skylark's car was also there now. I assumed he had been summoned by Miss Flamingo and that the blue liquid we had procured was part of it.

"Looks like Skylark's here," said Raven as we walked to the cabin's entrance. "Get ready for some weird science!"

"Yay," I muttered.

Sure enough, Skylark was in the meeting room along with Mr. 29 and Miss Flamingo. We presented the phial of blue liquid to Miss Flamingo, who took it from us and showed it to Mr. 29.

"Looks like antifreeze," said Mr. 29.

That's what I thought, too, I thought.

"Skylark," said Miss Flamingo, "I need you to perform the Gumball Procedure on the contents of this phial. After performing the procedure, the liquid should bubble up and turn pink. If not, then it's not what we're looking for."

"Okay," said Skylark.

He took the phial from Mr. 29 and looked at Raven and me.

"Would you two give me hand?" he asked. "This is a three-person thing I gotta do."

"Uh, sure," I replied. "What's the Gumball Procedure?"

"It's the codename for the experiment we'll use to identify this liquid," said Skylark. "Do either of you have experience in chemistry?"

Raven shook her head.

"I do," I said. "I'm taking chemistry classes right now."

"Good, good," said Skylark, looking pleased. "Let's go to the kitchen."

Raven, Skylark, and I headed to the kitchen. Skylark quickly began setting up an elaborate chemistry set, and it was easy to see that he had done something like this many times before. He knew where everything was and prepared everything as if it were second nature.

"The result we're looking for is a bubbling, pink substance," said Skylark, hooking up various tubes and chambers.

"Alright," I said.

Looking at the setup, I could tell this was going to be far more advanced and complicated than what we were doing in my chemistry lab sessions. When Skylark placed a worn out notebook on the table and opened it to a page filled with magical symbols, I knew for certain that this was unlike anything we'd done in school.

"What is this, alchemy?" Raven asked, peering at the magical symbols in the book. "Looks fun."

"Eh, somewhat," said Skylark. "Alchemy is sort of like outdated chemistry, though, so this is a little different."

When the setup was complete, Skylark left the room and returned with his briefcase shortly later. He opened it, revealing a wide selection of all kinds of tools and various things that I could only describe as "things." There was a box of rubber gloves, which Skylark removed first, telling us that protecting our hands was important.

"Okay, looks good," said Skylark. "Let's begin."

During the Gumball Procedure, I understood the parts about mixing chemicals and heating them. However, everything that required magical invocations and drawing symbols was up to Skylark. The procedure was more difficult than what I was used to, and I made sure to follow Skylark's instructions as closely as possible. Luckily, Skylark proved to be a very good lab partner. Strangely enough, even Raven was doing her part well, although she was clearly more flustered than us.

"We're doing good, guys," said Skylark in the middle of the experiment. "Keep it up. I'm adding the liquid you brought now."

I wasn't sure how long the procedure was taking since we were constantly mixing, stirring, extracting, heating, cooling, drawing, reciting, and repeating. What I did know was that it was a really *long* procedure. For all it was worth, there had better been a bubbling, pink substance at the end of that road.

When everything was finally boiled down to a single flask, Skylark paused for a moment and took a deep breath.

"Alright, moment of truth," he said, looking at the funky gunk inside the flask. "All we have to do is add this last chemical to it."

"I'll do it," said Raven, grabbing the phial of "last chemical" to add to the concoction.

She was obviously getting impatient at this point, as we were all ready for this experiment to be over. Before Skylark could say anything else, she started pouring the chemical into the flask.

"Wait, don't do it so fast!" Skylark told her.

It was too late. Raven practically dumped the chemical in, causing a violent reaction. The gunk in the flask instantly turned bright pink and fizzed up like a geyser, spraying Raven's hand. She screamed, dropping the phial she was holding, which hit the floor and shattered. In under a second, the pink foam had eaten through Raven's glove and came into contact with her skin.

"Ow, ow, ow!" she shouted frantically.

Without another thought, I immediately turned on the sink for her to wash off the pink foam before it ate her hand off. Raven hurried over to the sink, but Skylark grabbed her and pulled her back.

407

"Don't!" he said. "It'll explode in that much water!"

He quickly grabbed the roll of paper towels and started cleaning her hand. I could just imagine seeing nothing but a skeletal hand under that foam, so I looked away in disgust.

"It's alright," said Skylark. "The substance eats through latex much, much, much faster than skin. You should have nothing more than a mild chemical burn."

I heaved a huge sigh of relief when I saw that Raven's hand was still intact, albeit red from irritation. As Skylark applied an ointment to her skin, Miss Flamingo walked into the kitchen.

"What's going on in here?" she asked sternly. "Is everyone alright?"

"Just a minor accident," said Skylark. "Raven suffered a mild chemical burn, but she'll be fine."

Miss Flamingo looked at me with sharp eyes, as if to say it was my turn to share my part of the story.

"Um...it turned pink and bubbly," I told her, not knowing what else to say.

"I see," said Miss Flamingo, looking at the pink foam covering the table and floor.

Skylark began wrapping Raven's hand in bandages as Miss Flamingo walked over to her.

"Are you going to be alright?" she asked Raven.

"I believe so," said Raven with a pained grin.

"All this noise and screaming made me think someone was getting killed," said Miss Flamingo.

"It was scary!" said Raven, looking more excited than afraid.

"I can attest to that," I chimed in.

"When you're finished, clean this up and report back upstairs," said Miss Flamingo before turning and walking out.

That was the first time I had seen Miss Flamingo show any sort of concern for another living person. I found it somewhat strange at first, but was relieved that she seemed to care even the slightest for her subordinates.

While we cleaned up the mess and put everything away, nobody said much at all. Raven didn't show the slightest hint of weakness after her frightening experience, and I honestly admired that. She always talked big and tough, but now she was showing that she was more than just talk. In the end, my respect meter for Raven had moved up a few notches.

As cleanup was about finished, I was suddenly struck with a realization just as terrifying as Raven's accident. I checked my phone and was horrified to see that it was a quarter after four. Time had completely flown out the window while I was busy helping Skylark.

"Oh crap!" I shouted. "I gotta go!"

"What's up?" Skylark asked.

"I was supposed to pick my girlfriend up for her birthday at four!" I said, starting to sweat. "She's gonna kill me!"

Without wasting another second, I quickly called Hayley. She didn't try leaving me any messages, but she was probably feeling really disappointed.

"Hey," she said flatly when she picked up.

"Hi, babe," I said. "I'm really, really sorry, but I'm running kinda late. I'll be over there to get you as soon as I can."

"Alright," she said. "Bye."

"Bye."

I hung up, probably looking pretty grim.

"What'd she say?" Skylark asked.

"She sounded upset," I said dully. "I didn't realize how long this Operation Bubblegum was going to be!"

"It's the Gumball Procedure," Skylark corrected. "Don't worry about it, we'll handle it from here."

I looked at Raven, who just rolled her eyes.

"Go on," she said. "You'd better hurry."

Running up the stairs, I barged into the meeting room. Miss Flamingo and Mr. 29 looked like they were having a casual conversation with coffee.

"We've completed the assignment," I said quickly, "and I just realized I'm late for something important."

Not saying anything, Miss Flamingo walked over and handed me my envelope.

"Drive safely," was all she said.

"Thank you! Mr. 29, it was nice meeting you."

I bolted out of the cabin to my car and sped down the driveway. The drive into town had never felt so long, even though I was speeding a little. When I was almost to Hayley's house, I suddenly remembered that I had Hayley's presents back in my apartment. Cursing loudly, I was about to pull a U-turn when I got an idea.

"Sapphira!" I called out.

Sapphira appeared in the passenger seat almost immediately.

"What is it, Michael?"

"Can you bring me Hayley's presents?" I asked. "The box of chocolates and the teddy bear."

Holding out her hands, Sapphira created a magic circle on my dashboard. In a matter of seconds, the box of chocolates popped out of it, which Sapphira caught. Shortly after, the teddy bear popped out.

"Are these the requested items?" she asked.

"Yes!" I said. "Thank you. You're dismissed."

"Understood."

I hated using magic like that, but this was an emergency. Despite my unwillingness to ask Sapphira for help, Hayley didn't need to wait any longer than what she already had. Once I made it to her house, I could tell just by the way she walked to the car that she was upset.

"Happy birthday, Hayley," I said when she got in. "I'm really sorry I'm late. I got called into work."

"You had to work?" she asked.

"Yeah," I said. "There was an accident and Raven got hurt, but she's fine."

Hayley was quiet for a moment.

"You were with Raven today?"

"There was work we had to do," I said. "It was crazy."

I handed Hayley the chocolates and teddy bear.

"Here, I got these for you. I know you like these kinds of chocolates, and that teddy bear is customized."

"Thanks," she said.

To say the least, the rest of the evening was awkward. During dinner, Hayley didn't seem to want to talk much. Even when I took her ice-skating, she appeared to have fun, but there was still some sort of undermining moodiness beneath her. I could understand her for being upset, but cut me some slack here.

At last, the time came when I was planning to take her back to my place. We were walking back to my car from the skating rink, my arm around her.

"You wanna go back to my place?" I asked her. "We can just lounge around and be lazy. I can even make some appetizers out of that cookbook you got me."

Hayley didn't answer me right away. She looked away for a moment, and I could tell something was going on in that head of hers.

"I don't know," she said finally. "I think I want to relax at home tonight."

"Are you sure?" I said. "We can do whatever you want. I made this awesome schnitzel thing the other day, and I think you'd really like it."

"Not tonight," she sighed. "There's this show I want to watch."

"You can watch it at my place," I said.

"No, that's alright."

We stopped at my car. I had to unlock it for Hayley to get in.

"What show is it?" I asked.

"A detective show," she replied. "It's pretty good."

"I didn't know you liked detective shows," I said.

"It's interesting," she said, still avoiding eye contact. "It taught me a few things. Pretty much every lie can be exposed with a little investigative work. It's just that most lies probably aren't worth the effort."

I looked at her, not believing what I was hearing. Was this her way of calling me a liar?

"What's the matter?" I finally asked.

"Unlock the door, Mike."

"Tell me what's wrong. I can tell you're still mad."

411

Another moment of silence. It was the kind of silence that begged for sound, even nails on a chalkboard. When the sound did return, it happened to be the sound of Hayley repeatedly pulling on the locked car door handle. I would have gladly traded nails on a chalkboard over that.

"I'll take you home," I said quietly, unlocking the car.

Not a single word was spoken on the way back to her house. While I was feeling bad for making her mad, she was still being unreasonable, so I wasn't able to pin all the guilt on myself. When I pulled up to her house, she continued to stare out the window in silence. Even after putting the car into park, I noticed she didn't seem to be in a hurry to get out.

"I need to talk to you about something," she said finally.

"Alright, sure," I said eagerly.

Finally, I thought. *Let's just discuss this like we should.*

I turned the car off, realizing this was probably going to be a long talk.

Hayley sighed.

"I don't think this is going to work out," she told me. "This thing between you and me."

The rest of the conversation doesn't need to be explained in detail, as I'm sure you can fill in the blanks with your imagination. On top of that, I really can't remember the details very well myself, and I honestly don't want to remember. What Hayley said at the end of the conversation was where the important part picks up again.

"I feel like I'm not good enough for you, and I don't think you're good enough for me."

Rather than to self-mutilate my dignity by holding up an argument against the steel wall of Hayley's complicated emotional hurricane, I settled to end it quickly and painlessly.

"If that's what you want," I said.

"It is what I want," she replied stubbornly.

She got out of the car, hesitated briefly, and then grabbed the chocolates and teddy bear.

"Thanks for the presents," she told me.

As soon as she closed the car door, I started the car, slammed it into reverse, and got the hell out of there. Just like that, and it was all over. The drive back to my place was a long one, and all of my anger slowly grew to a boil until I threw open the door to my apartment and stomped inside. When I was safe inside my own abode, the volcano suddenly erupted.

"That bitch!" I bellowed, slamming the door behind me. "Stupid, ungrateful bitch!"

Sapphira had appeared, but I was too mad to pay her any mind.

"Is something wrong, Michael?" she asked.

"Hayley dumped me!" I growled, pacing back and forth in the living room. "For no good reason! I *know* it was because she thought I was going to cheat on her, which I would *never* do! It never even crossed my mind! But did she listen? No! Did she think everything I did for her was a joke? She must have, because she didn't even show the slightest damn bit of gratitude! Stupid, insecure woman! Thinking all of my love and affection was an act just to keep her close to me! 'Thanks for the presents,' she says. Well, you're welcome, Hayley! *You're welcome!* What a crock of…arrrggghhhhhhh!"

"Shall I bring upon her the pain and anguish of a thousand deaths?" Sapphira asked.

"No, no, forget it." I breathed, calming myself down. "I just had a moment, but damn it, Hayley."

I collapsed onto the couch and slumped into the cushions.

"Is there anything you would have me do for you?" Sapphira offered.

What is there that you can do, Sapphira? I thought. *There should be something. It's not like you really give a crap about me anyway, so what should I care what I make you do for me from now on?*

"Just leave me alone," I muttered. "I'll call you if I need something."

"Understood."

The rest of the night, I brainlessly watched some TV as I tried to forget about Hayley. Getting over her would take some time, but it reminded me of what was truly important. My dedication to my studies had swayed because of my

413

relationship with a girl, and now it was time to get back on track. However, all of that enthusiasm I had toward my college degree had gone away, and it was going to take more than TV and magic to get it back.

~Opus 27~

There are advantages to being single. You're free to do as you please without being held back or tied down. However, when you've been dumped, it's usually the list of negative things that you mull over first. Rather than going on and on about how much I was missing Hayley only two days after the breakup, I'm going to cut to the chase. Hayley was the reason why I was possessed to sign up for Psychology II. We were going to be in the same class, and her help was the main thing that got me through the first semester of that class.

Now, it was totally possible for me to go to the office and schedule another class to replace Psychology II. However, I wasn't a quitter, and I really had to prove to myself that I didn't need Hayley for anything. Besides, Oriole had said she could tutor me, so screw you, Hayley!

Something about a broken man is more pitiful than any other broken thing. More pitiful than a broken vinyl record on the floor by a band nobody cared about, but they had that one song that everyone can hum but can't tell you the lyrics, song name, or band name…to amble down the corridors of oblivion for eons and ages.

I had temporarily become a shut-in and a hermit to the world. Even though I thirsted to experiment in the kitchen, it was hard for me to look at the cookbook I got from Hayley. Still, I had every intention of holding onto it because the awesomeness contained within its pages could not go to waste. Even so, I had succumbed back to the ways of frozen pizzas, fast food, and instant ramen, sometimes all in one sitting. Imagine me shoveling down the grotesque excuses for American cuisine while sitting in my boxers as the stubbly hairs on my face grew coarser with each passing moment.

Mind you, this was *two days* after Hayley had dumped me, and I was already reduced to a mere sack of indignant pudding while my questionable journey of recovery left me crawling facedown across an endless desert.

Regardless of the circumstances, final exams were still right around the corner. Getting lost in my studying was the best way for me to get my mind off things, as I could slowly feel myself getting used to life as the way it used to be. While locked inside my apartment with little to no contact with the outside world, I powered through my study guide for psychology and turned it in to Mrs. Flynn. The following Monday, I got it back and studied extra hard to correct everything I had gotten wrong.

On the day of the exam, it was like a gunslinger duel as I stared at the beast in front of me. Feeling confident, I picked up my pencil and stormed through the exam. There was no way I could lose to it now. My grade and my career were on the line! Furthermore, I still needed to prove to myself that I didn't need Hayley's help to succeed. I was my own man again, and I was gonna stomp on this exam with my own two feet.

I could practically smell gunpowder smoking out of my pencil as I set it down on the table. Taking a look at my finished exam, a smile spread from ear to ear. Not wanting to risk any chance of failure, I carefully looked over the entire exam, checking my answers and making sure that I didn't forget anything or leave any obvious mistakes. When I was certain of my victory, I placed the exam on Mrs. Flynn's desk, packed up my stuff, and strolled out of the room.

Now that I got the worst exam out of the way, the rest of exam week is gonna be a breeze, I thought.

And it was. One by one, I knocked out each exam. When I sat down to take my math exam, the anticipation of completely dominating it made my hands tremble. Miyuki walked into the room, giving me a confident smile when she saw me, and I couldn't help but smile confidently back.

Shortly after Hayley had broken up with me, I had had a conversation with Miyuki. She had broken up with her boyfriend a few months before, and she was able to relate to my situation. Having someone to simply talk with can really help, especially if they can relate.

"Are you as ready as I am to take this exam?" she asked me when she took her seat.

"For sure," I told her. "I'm going to ace it, just watch me."

"Did you hear what happened to the testing center?" she asked. "I thought there was a place used specifically for taking exams."

"Now that you mention it," I said, thinking it over, "we've been taking the exams in the classrooms. What's going on with the testing center?"

"I wondered if you knew," Miyuki replied. "It's just conjecture."

Anything could have happened to prevent the testing center from being used, such as new policies or renovations. Although I was curious, there was just no more room inside my head to think about it.

"This is the first I've thought of it," I said. "I'm just here to take my exam, ya know?"

Miyuki seemed satisfied with my answer.

"Well, good luck," she said.

Math was my strongest subject, and I blew through the exam like it was nothing. I took the time to check over all of my work when I finished the last problem, and I still finished before just about everyone else. Placing my exam on Mr. Pardee's desk, he gave me a courteous nod before I strutted out of the room. Miyuki was still working diligently as she was hunched over the exam, and I silently wished her luck.

The last exam I had was for chemistry. As usual for that class, it was a group project, so I teamed up with Jorge and Paxton just like always. When we received our exam instructions, I quickly looked over them and chuckled. Compared to the Gumball Procedure I had to help Skylark with, this exam was going to be cake.

The Gumball Procedure. I had to help out right before meeting Hayley for her birthday. Part of me wondered if she wouldn't have broken up with me if it wasn't for that crazy experiment. That was the main reason why I was late to pick her up. Thinking about it that way, it was hard for me not to feel angry toward Skylark for failing to mention how long the procedure would be.

Forget about it, I thought. *Hayley was still upset about Raven being my partner for work. If she didn't break up with me when she did, she probably would've done so eventually.*

"Are there any last questions before you begin?" Mr. Youngren asked the class.

Time to focus, I thought. *Clear my mind of meaningless pondering, at least for now. It's game time.*

"You may begin," said Mr. Youngren, taking a seat at his desk.

Jorge, Paxton, and I immediately got started setting up everything. When the chemical reactions were underway, I was able to concentrate on the task at hand. As I had expected, this procedure was much less difficult than the Gumball Procedure. Nonetheless, every reaction and result we had to record was interesting, even borderline bizarre. The most mind-blowing part was the final step; we ended up with the exact same substance as when we started, down to the thousandth of a decimal when measuring the weight, volume, and density.

"Uh, were we supposed to end up with what we started with?" Jorge asked, scratching his head as he looked at the final measurements.

Mr. Youngren walked over to examine our finished result.

"Very good," he said. "Are you ready to hand in your papers now?"

"I think so," I said, briefly looking over my worksheet.

Taking our papers, Mr. Youngren smiled.

"Looks like you're the first group done," he said. "Nice work."

When Mr. Youngren walked away, the three of us smiled and rejoiced quietly. Everyone else in the room glanced over at us, probably feeling jealous that they were still stuck in class. We closed down our lab station and left the room, feeling accomplished that we had done so well.

"That was a breeze," said Paxton. "I thought it'd be harder than that."

418

"Yeah, me too," said Jorge. "You really seemed like you knew what you were doing, Mike. It's like you took control and just went with it."

"Meh," I said modestly, shrugging.

Did you underestimate me that much? I thought, feeling somewhat annoyed. *Looks like I showed everyone.*

We split up to go our separate ways, saying bye to each other. I was feeling like a conquering hero as I strutted down the hallway with springs beneath my feet. Exams were done and I felt really confident about each of them. My college career wouldn't falter, no matter what. Nothing could stop me now...not even seeing Hayley walking toward me at that very moment.

We made eye contact for a second, and the springs beneath my feet quickly turned into cement shoes. She quickly diverted her gaze, moving to the far side of the hallway as she picked up her pace. The breeze we created when we passed each other was like a freezing chill that made my neck hairs stand up. I heaved a sigh and kept walking, because that's all I could do.

That evening, I was hanging out with Aaron, Chad, Jorge, and Lawrence at my apartment. We were celebrating the end of exams with pizza and video games, even though what we were doing was akin to a typical night of hanging out anyway. The end of exams was just an excuse to do it again, I suppose.

"You're lookin' kinda scruffy, Mike," Chad told me. "When's the last time you shaved?"

"A while ago," I said, rubbing the stubble on my chin.

"I was getting a little worried, bro," said Lawrence. "You've been acting really down since you broke up with Hayley."

"I didn't break up with her," I replied. "She did the breaking."

"She was an insecure chick," Aaron told me, pouring a glass of root beer from the two-liter bottle. "Just be glad she didn't take any of your stuff. All of my girlfriends ended up with at least one of my things when we broke up. Clothes, movies, CDs, you name it."

"Whatever," I said dully. "I'm trying not to think about it. Let's eat pizza, play games, and be merry."

"Be merry!" said Jorge, holding up his glass. "To Mike, for being one of the guys again!"

We clinked our glasses together like a bunch of pirates. At that moment, I realized that my friends were what really mattered. They'd be with me through thick and thin. However, that was exactly when that weird feeling crept up inside me again. Taking a look at all my friends, I started to second-guess myself. I started to wonder if my friends really *were* that important to me, or if they were actually holding me back.

"Wait a minute," said Lawrence. "If Mike's one of the guys because he's single, what's that make me? I'm dating Samantha."

"You're still a guy," said Aaron. "Just not entirely."

"What's that mean?" Lawrence asked.

"Shut up!" I said loudly. "Enough talk about relationships and our statuses as 'guys.' We're here to have fun."

"Yeah, what Mike said," said Jorge.

"Isn't your brother online now?" Chad asked me. "It's after eight."

"Oh yeah," I said, looking at the time. "Jake should be already playing. I'll get the game set up."

Ever since I started playing games online with Jacob, I had a reason to use my headset that allowed players to talk to one another. Having my brother on my team made the gameplay experience that much better, and it was almost like the old days when we would sit in the living room as kids and play together. The only major difference was that Sal couldn't unplug the game console, or Elizabeth couldn't accidentally trip over the controller cords. Jacob probably stopped playing video games because of our siblings ruining the experience. In that sense, it was better this way.

While I was playing the game, my character kept dying because my online teammates were being negligent. Usually, I didn't get very upset because it was just a game. For some reason, a higher level of aggression was showing through, and it was hard for me to contain it.

"Ah, you bastards!" I shouted into my headset mic when a player on the other team got me from behind. "You're supposed to cover me! How many of you people actually play this game?"

"A little hostile today, aren't we, bro?" said Lawrence.

"Who asked you?" I grunted.

Jacob was talking to me through my headset, trying to tell me where the opposing team members were.

"There's a sniper in that second story window," he told me. "Don't run out into the open."

"I'll get him," I said. "I'll just use my rocket launcher and blow him away."

Right when I said that, the sniper picked me off with a single shot. That final kill gave the opposing team enough points to win the match.

"That was a good shot," said Jorge. "I'm surprised he got you from that far away."

"I'm taking a break," I muttered, passing the controller to Chad. "You want the headset, too?"

"Yeah, I'll take that," he said, putting on the headset. "Yo, what's up, Mike's brother?"

I went to the kitchen for a breadstick. Dipping it in marinara sauce, I could feel the anger coursing through me. Something about it was very unusual, yet it felt so good, as if it had an insatiable appetite that was slowly being fulfilled.

Get a grip, Mike, I told myself. *This isn't like you. Nothing good can come from being so mad about stupid things. But...it just feels so good. It feels so right.*

"Are there anymore breadsticks left?" Aaron asked me, coming into the kitchen. "You better not have eaten the last one."

There was an urge to tell Aaron to go screw himself, but I was able to suppress it.

"There's one more," I said. "Cool your jets, man."

"Good," he said, grabbing the last breadstick. "Let me see that marinara sauce."

"It's all gone," I said, showing him the empty container.

"Damn it, Mike," he groaned. "Oh well."

You got a problem with me, Aaron?

"Ahhh." I rubbed my head, trying to relieve my unreasonable anger.

"You okay?" Aaron asked. "Headache?"

"Uh, y-yeah," I said. "All of that studying for the exams must have, like, overloaded my brain."

"That's probably just your brain relaxing," he said through a mouthful of breadstick. "You know how, like, you're the most sore right when you stretch out to relax. Your brain's probably doing the same thing."

"Maybe."

My raging thoughts eased up throughout the rest of the night, and I was able to enjoy the company of my friends again. After a tiresome night of intense online gaming, the apartment seemed eerily quiet after everyone went home. I stacked the pizza boxes up by the trash and proceeded to do the dishes, ready to wind down before going to bed.

"Michael," said Sapphira as she appeared while I was finishing the dishes.

"Huh?" I responded.

"There is something I must tell you."

"What?" I asked, drying off my hands.

"I have confirmed the presence of a demon nearby," she told me.

My stomach felt like it had been tied into a pretzel. Anytime Sapphira said she had something to tell me, it usually wasn't good. However, this was a little more than what I had prepared for.

"Another demon?" I asked, glancing around. "It's not Asmodeus, is it?"

"No," she said. "The spiritual energy signature of this demon closely resembles the one of a demon named Valefar."

"Uh, alright," I said slowly. "Is there something special that this one does?"

"Valefar is renowned for his mischievous behavior," said Sapphira. "He has been known to move and steal objects."

"So, he's a thief," I grunted. "Has he stolen anything from me?"

"Since his relation with you is still partially underdeveloped, he can only steal small things," she told me. "He has already stolen a cracker from your pantry, but I have returned it."

"A cracker?"

"If he continues to steal anything else from you, I will do my best to return it all," she said.

"Oh man." I groaned. "This is just not what I need."

"However, Valefar's true power isn't thievery," said Sapphira. "He can also destroy relationships between people."

"Destroy relationships?" I asked. "What exactly do you mean by that?"

"He can turn friends against one another," she said. "He does this by putting angry thoughts and feelings in people's minds and hearts, causing them to lash out at each other with false hatred."

My jaw dropped as I realized what Sapphira had just said.

"I've noticed that!" I said. "All of those crazy thoughts I've been having whenever I think about my friends! That was Valefar doing that?"

"Yes," said Sapphira, "more than likely. There is also a good chance that some of your friends have begun to feel that same resentment toward you, just as Valefar intends."

"That's why Hayley broke up with me!" I growled. "I don't believe it!"

"That is not true," said Sapphira. "Hayley's relationship with you was more intimate than friendship. That sort of relationship is Asmodeus' territory, and I have not detected him since he was cast out. Hayley likely broke up with you of her own free will."

"Oh," I said quietly. "Well then, how long has Valefar been doing this?"

"I first detected his presence fifteen days ago," said Sapphira.

"That long ago?" I said. "You didn't tell me!"

"I apologize," she said, bowing. "I wanted to be sure of Valefar's presence before telling you, to prevent making you feel stressed. After tonight, I am now certain that it is Valefar."

"You still should've told me," I said, irritated. "Demons can be so frickin' unreliable!"

I walked into the living room, trying to contemplate a solution to Valefar's troublemaking.

"Can't you just get rid of him the way you got rid of Asmodeus?" I asked, sinking into my beanbag.

"Unfortunately, I cannot," said Sapphira. "He is a unique demon, therefore he requires special magic to effectively cast him out."

"Is there anything in the grimoire?" I asked dully.

"No," said Sapphira. "I am certain of this."

Using her finger, she started drawing something made from light in midair. When she was done, there was a magical emblem floating in the air in front of me.

"Magic spells effective against Valefar bear this emblem," she said. "It is used to designate the specific type of magic used to cast out demons in his category. Unfortunately, I have never dealt with such magic and cannot perform it without instructions."

"Hold on for a second," I said.

Grabbing a pencil and paper, I quickly sketched the emblem to the best of my ability.

"I'll need to know what it looks like if I happen to come across it," I said, looking at the picture I drew. "Yeah, that looks pretty accurate."

"It is a rare type of magic," said Sapphira. "You may have difficulty finding anything of its nature."

"Don't get me so down," I muttered. "It's already hard enough dealing with all of this."

"I apologize."

"In the meantime, isn't there *anything* you can do to help against Valefar?"

"Your amulet is all I can provide," she told me. "If it wasn't for that, Valefar would have completely invaded your mind by now, preventing you from suppressing the angry thoughts at all. You would also be missing many things."

"So, the amulet is only partially effective." I rustled my hair. "That means he's a powerful demon."

"Moderately powerful," said Sapphira. "As long as you have the amulet, his influence should not escalate much higher than it is now."

I sat on the couch, pondering what I could do. The first thing that came to mind was to bring this to the attention of the club. However, I still wasn't comfortable with sharing my supernatural secrets with them, especially Miss Flamingo. There was no telling how she would react and how that would affect my status within the club. She would probably promote me to a demon hunter, which I seriously wouldn't want. Either that, or she would use my close connection with the supernatural to put a shorter leash on me, which I also seriously didn't want.

"I want you to keep me updated on Valefar," I told Sapphira. "Any actions he takes, let me know."

"Understood," she said.

"One more thing," I added. "I've been wondering about something. How is it that you're not repelled by my amulet? Does it have to do with our pact?"

"Simply put, the amulet is a symbol of our pact," she told me. "For that reason, it has no effect on me. Also, my name and your birthstone in the amulet are beyond coincidental. Would you like to hear a detailed explanation?"

"No," I said. "Dismissed."

"Very well."

When Sapphira disappeared, I took my amulet out of my pocket and held it out in front of me. The light refracted through the sapphire in an almost hypnotic way. It was hard to imagine that such a simple trinket had helped me so much and had kept me out of danger. There was no telling what I would've gotten into if I hadn't been protected by it.

425

Before turning in for the night, I flipped through the grimoire, examining random information. There were all sorts of texts that I couldn't understand because they were in other languages, and the ones in English were sometimes hard to read and understand. However, a bunch of pictures and drawings filled just about every page, and most of them were somewhat interesting.

Ever since Hayley had dumped me, going through the grimoire had become an everyday thing. Just by looking around in it, I had already become familiar with some things, such as the symbols and characteristics of the classical elements like water, wind, earth, fire, etc. There probably wasn't any use to that knowledge, but I was still drawn to the book, since it was what had gotten me into my weird situation to begin with.

I stopped when I came across the page containing the spell used to summon Sapphira. That was where it all started, with that stupid idea we had out in the woods. The thought occurred to me that Sapphira could've just as easily been assigned to Aaron, Chad, Lawrence, or Jorge, and it would've been them dealing with Sapphira and everything that it entitled.

Closing the book, I took a deep breath and exhaled slowly. There was no point in thinking about the things that could've been, since I was knee deep in the things that were reality. According to theorists, every decision creates another alternate world for every possible result for that decision. I really didn't know or care, but it was boggling to assume that somewhere out there, each of my friends were in the same situation I found myself in.

"Blah," I muttered, standing up. "What am I thinking? I should just go to bed and try to forget about it."

And that's exactly what I did.

~Opus 28~

I was sitting in the living room of the cabin, waiting for the meeting to begin. Kookaburra and Raven were in a heated chess battle, and Kookaburra was doing surprisingly well. Not that I would call him a muscular meathead, but that was certainly my initial assumption before watching this match. Secretly, I was hoping for Raven to suffer agonizing defeat.

"Check," said Kookaburra, sliding his bishop into position.

Raven studied the board closely. She moved her king out of danger, but Kookaburra immediately moved his other bishop into place.

"Check," he said again.

Raven's poker face was immaculate, but I could tell what she was feeling. The way she toyed with the silver ornament on her necklace indicated her frustration. She moved her knight in front of the king, only to have it taken out by Kookaburra's queen.

"Check."

"Uh, Kookaburra," said Oriole, "that's checkmate."

"Oh, is that what that is?" he grunted, looking at the board. "Checkmate then."

There was a small round of applause, as if everyone was like, "Holy crap, Kookaburra won."

"Good game, rookie," said Raven, shaking Kookaburra's hand.

"Who're ya callin' a rookie?" he said. "I've played this game before."

"Who's next?" said Raven. "Step up!"

"Shouldn't Kookaburra challenge someone next?" Skylark asked. "He won."

"Uh, I'm done," said Kookaburra, standing up. "I just used up my brainpower for the day."

Way to shoot down my newfound respect for your unexpected intelligence, I thought.

"Challenge Roadrunner, Raven," said Cormorant. "If I was a bettin' man, I'd say he seems like a good chess player."

"Um, not particularly," I said.

"Bring it on, Roadster!" said Raven, grinning menacingly.

"Did you just give me a nickname for my nickname?" I muttered.

"Come on!" she egged on. "I'll set it up."

"I'm not really feeling the chess vibe right now," I said.

"Aw, lame," she said, flicking her dead king over on its side.

"Chess is a classic game of wits," said Skylark. "It's said that it was used for peaceful negotiations between conflicting countries. There's a story of a peasant who once challenged a king to chess to prevent his home from being used as royal farmland...."

"Here we go," Kookaburra mumbled, rolling his eyes.

"At one point in the game, the peasant made a move that he wanted to correct. However, he had already taken his hand off the piece. He reached for the piece to move it back, and the king pulled out a dagger and chopped the guy's hand off."

"That's...lovely," said Oriole with a grimace.

Miss Flamingo walked into the living room, blowing on a steaming mug of something that smelled strange, presumably tea.

"The meeting will begin shortly," she said.

Within minutes, everyone had gathered like usual in the meeting room. Miss Flamingo began the session by stating there were no significant financial reports that needed to be addressed, as if hearing about all of this mysterious money flow ever did me any good to begin with.

"We're reaching a crucial point regarding the club's activities," she announced.

Does it really make a difference if it's crucial or not? I thought.

"You'll all be assigned a task today," she said firmly. "Oriole, the documents."

Oriole printed out three documents. She handed one to Kookaburra and Skylark, one to Raven and I, and one she shared with Cormorant. I was a little surprised to see Oriole and

Cormorant given an assignment, since they typically stayed back at the cabin.

While we were overlooking our assignments, Miss Flamingo took out a cell phone. I watched her texting and thought it seemed a little unprofessional to be sending messages while conducting a meeting. Moments later, I felt my phone vibrate. The sender's number wasn't in my list of contacts, but I had a feeling that I knew who it was from before I read it.

> This is Miss Flamingo. I need you to bring me Exhibit C-12. You'll understand what I mean. Keep this a secret between us.

I looked up at Miss Flamingo, who was sipping from her mug as if nothing had happened. An uncomfortable feeling churned inside me as I wondered what she meant and why I had to keep it a secret from Raven.

"A simple mission, this will be!" Raven told me after reading the document. "Don't screw this up, okay?"

"As long as you don't screw it up first," I said.

"Good answer," she said. "Cormorant, I need something from the supply room."

"Okay," said Cormorant.

"You need permission to go into the supply room?" I asked.

"Of course you do," said Raven. "You can't just waltz in there on a whim and take something."

She opened the door to the small room next to the meeting room and rummaged around. When she came out, she was holding a little notebook with a weird pencil. Not wanting to ask, I just quietly followed as she briskly walked out of the meeting room.

When we were in her little electric car, Raven filled me in on the situation. We were supposed to go to the Elm Valley Museum and perform some kind of basic rite. I had never been to the Elm Valley Museum, but I heard it wasn't anything grandiose like one you would find in a big city. Chad was the one who told me about the museum since he was a big history buff.

"What's this rite we're supposed to perform?" I asked. "We're not conjuring spirits, I hope."

"No, nothing that fun," said Raven, sounding a little disappointed. "We're going to use those supplies I brought with us. That notebook had its pages replaced with paper made from papyrus granted with some kind of mystical powers by an African shaman. The pencil is charcoal, and something was done to it to make it special in a magical sort of way. I don't remember what. Don't touch the charcoal, though. It'll smudge on your hands and clothes."

"And what are we doing with these magical art supplies?" I asked.

"You'll see when we get there," she said.

The museum wasn't located in a busy part of town, but was closer to the outskirts. When we pulled up, I noticed how small the building was for a museum. The apartment building I lived in was larger. I suppose every museum isn't home to a tyrannosaurus skeleton.

Raven and I were the only visitors when we walked in. An elderly woman sitting at the counter greeted us and asked us to sign the visitor's log. When I jotted my (made up) name, I noticed Chad's name appearing three times on that one page, making me chuckle. The boy loved history.

We walked around for a little bit, posing as normal visitors (as I was still unsure as to what I was really doing there). After a few minutes, Raven said that she forgot something in the car, then hurried out. Looking around at the artifacts from Elm Valley's past, I thought about Miss Flamingo's text. She told me to bring her Exhibit C-12. Looking at the exhibit title cards, I realized each one was assigned a code, probably to help the people working at the museum keep organized.

I'm supposed to steal something from here? I thought. *That's madness!*

I glanced at the old woman seated at the door, thinking that it'd be challenging to sneak something big out of the museum. The museum was a single room, so I was virtually in her line of sight at all times. There didn't appear to be any cameras anywhere, but I wasn't certain. Why didn't Miss Flamingo give me something that could help me out? Surely she must've known this wouldn't be an easy task, and I was honestly wishing for some sleeping potion to knock the elderly woman out.

Going to each exhibit, I checked the title cards for the one labeled C-12. For the most part, the codes were in alphabetical and numerical order, so I was able to locate my target fairly easily. Exhibit C-12 happened to be a small piece of paper, which was a relief. However, it was locked inside a display case. I would have to find a way to get inside the display case without alerting the old woman. On top of that, I also had to make sure Raven didn't notice. This assignment was pretty much set up to fail.

The piece of paper had some writings on it, which I immediately recognized as magical. The description even said it was believed to have been used many years ago for occult purposes. Upon further inspection, I noticed one of the emblems on the paper. My heart about skipped a beat.

"No way," I said to myself.

I took out my wallet and removed the paper with my drawing of the emblem Sapphira had shown me. Just as I had thought, the drawing I had made perfectly matched the one on the piece of paper I had to steal.

"It's gotta be a coincidence," I said to myself. "It *has* to be. There's no way Miss Flamingo would know."

Raven came back in, and I quickly put my drawing back into my wallet before she could see. When she approached me, she removed some of the papyrus pages from her coat, along with the charcoal pencil.

"Time to take some 'notes' for that history report!" she said loudly.

"What took you so long?" I asked quietly. "You were gone too long just to get those out of the car."

"I had to take care of some things," she whispered, giving a thumbs-up. "Don't be surprised when something happens."

"What do you mean?"

"Don't worry," she said. "Just let me do this."

As Raven went to do her thing, I was left to figure out how I would do *my* thing. Before I could think of anything at all, a sudden power outage interrupted me, and I became aware of what Raven was talking about.

"Oh dear," said the old woman. "The power went out."

"Aw, and I was supposed to get work done for my history report," said Raven, pretending to be disappointed.

"Let me go check the fuses," said the old woman, getting up from her desk.

I watched her slowly walk toward a door in the back of the museum. A sudden plan struck me, and I walked over to her desk. When the old woman walked into the other room, I looked at Raven to make sure she wasn't paying attention to me. Raven seemed busy scribbling on the papyrus pages, which she tucked away in certain places around the museum.

Looking around the old lady's desk, I found a key ring. Not wasting a moment, I snatched the keys and hurried to the display case holding Exhibit C-12. Praying that one of the keys would unlock it, a wave of excitement went through me when one of the keys turned the lock and made a clicking noise. I quickly lifted the glass, snatched the paper, locked the case, and returned the keys to where I found them, all while making sure Raven and the old woman didn't see.

Wiping the nervous sweat from my forehead, I tried not to laugh out loud at the fact that I had just pulled it off. Valefar's thieving prowess may have aided me somehow. With Exhibit C-12 safely in my pocket, I decided to see what exactly Raven was doing before the old woman returned. I walked over to her as she was about to scribble on another piece of papyrus.

"Do you mind?" she asked as I was looking over her shoulder.

"I'm just seeing what you're doing," I said.

"Magical inscriptions," she told me. "What were you doing just now? You looked like you were rushing around."

"Just keeping an eye out," I lied. "Making sure the coast was clear and stuff."

Raven started drawing on the piece of papyrus, and it didn't take long for me to recognize what it was. I had seen it in the grimoire countless times: the symbol that represented fire.

"What is that for?" I asked aggressively. "That's a magical symbol for fire!"

"What are you talking about?" she asked. "How do you know?"

"I just do!" I told her. "Were you drawing that on all of the papers you stashed around here?"

"Be quiet!" Raven hissed, looking around. "Yes, it's the same symbol on all of the pages! What's your deal?"

The flickering memory of the library popped into my mind. I recalled the blazing inferno that night, as ashes and embers licked the night sky. Chad's dad had said that particular fire seemed exceptionally voracious, not stopping until every last part of the building had been completely burned away. Everything except for the grimoire, a magical book.

"Why are you placing those all over the museum?" I demanded. "Do you even know what you're doing?"

"Does it really matter?" she said angrily. "I'm just doing what Miss Flamingo wants. I don't really care if I don't know the details. It's how all the members do their assignments!"

I looked at Raven through squinted eyes. Whether she was playing dumb or was just ignorant didn't matter.

"You're going to burn this place down," I said sternly. "Isn't that right?"

Raven looked taken aback.

"What the hell are you saying?" she said.

"You were there on the night of the library fire, weren't you?" I said, getting right up in her face. "You're a little arsonist, aren't you?"

Rather than firing back at me like I expected, she looked away for a second, as if to think about what she had to say.

"No," she said quietly, "I didn't have anything to do with the library fire."

"That's crap," I said.

"I don't care if you don't believe me," she said, finishing the drawing of the fire symbol. "It won't change the fact that I had nothing to do with it."

"Sure, whatever."

"Did you forget why we interrogated Wyatt? To get answers about the library and the fire. Why would we dig for answers we already have?"

"It's probably part of Miss Flamingo's elaborate schemes!" I said. "She could have us running around in circles just to keep us in the dark and off her trail. We always get left in the dark anyway!"

The lights came back on, and I was able to clearly see the look on Raven's face. As always, it was difficult to tell what she was thinking judging by her expression, but I could tell that she was definitely thinking something. Guilt, was it? Maybe her feelings were just hurt because of my accusations.

"We're running off the generator now, kids," said the old lady as she walked back to her desk. "Something happened with the main power line."

Raven swiftly tucked the final piece of paper away, turned around, and headed straight for the exit without a word. Making sure nobody was looking, I removed the last piece of paper Raven had hidden, crumpled it up, and stuffed it into my coat pocket before walking out.

The drive back to the cabin was unusually quiet. Although I was able to successfully steal Exhibit C-12, there was still a bad taste in my mouth. My suspicions for the club were soaring, and I didn't know what to think. It was hard to determine how much of my yelling at Raven was Valefar's doing…perhaps it was *all* his doing. However, it was something that I had to get off my chest.

"We need to stop somewhere," I told Raven out of the blue.

"Stop where?" she asked flatly.

"Somewhere with a restroom," I said.

"Can't you wait until we get back?" she asked.

"No!" I said. "It's sort of an emergency."

Without an argument, Raven pulled into the next restaurant's parking lot. She seemed to be extra submissive all of a sudden, probably because I let her have it back at the museum.

Once in the restroom, I flushed the piece of papyrus down the toilet. Removing Exhibit C-12 from my pocket, I snapped a picture of it with my phone. After a few attempts, I managed to get a good picture that showed all of the text. By showing Sapphira the picture, she would be able to perform the spell against Valefar after I gave the paper to Miss Flamingo.

When Raven and I returned to the cabin, I headed straight up to the meeting room. Skylark and Kookaburra had already returned, so I couldn't give Miss Flamingo the stolen exhibit yet.

"We finished our assignment," I told her dully.

"Excellent," she said, handing me my payment.

Raven walked in shortly after and received her payment as well. She looked at me and smirked, and that just got my blood pressure rising.

"Wait here until Cormorant and Oriole return," said Miss Flamingo. "It shouldn't be much longer."

Kookaburra was helping himself to some gin. After my assignment, I was inclined to have some as well, despite not being the legal age.

"Roadrunner," said Skylark. "Want to play a game?"

"Not really," I said.

"I'll play a drinking game with you, Skylark," said Kookaburra.

"No thanks," said Skylark. "I remember last time. I was so drunk that I couldn't move."

There was the sound of hearty laughter coming from the hallway. Cormorant opened the door, carrying a wooden crate filled with who-knows-what. Oriole was right behind him with a pair of deer antlers mounted on a plaque.

"I remember that story," said Cormorant, setting the crate on the table. "I had to hold Skylark's head as he threw up into the toilet!"

"We've completed our assignment," said Oriole, holding up the antlers.

"Very good," said Miss Flamingo, sipping from her mug. "Set those next to the crate, Oriole."

"You're mounting more antlers on the wall?" Kookaburra asked.

"Of course," said Miss Flamingo. "I use antlers in all of my decorating."

Cormorant and Oriole took their envelopes from Miss Flamingo before the meeting was brought to an end, then everyone headed out. When I was the last one in the room, I handed Miss Flamingo the stolen exhibit. Without saying anything, she handed me another envelope containing the payment for my extra assignment.

As I followed everyone else outside, I clenched my fists. There was no way I could let this slide anymore. Once all of the club members were outside together, I swallowed hard before saying what I needed to say. Although I had attempted to have this discussion with the club members once before, it felt necessary to bring up again with no holds barred.

"Hey, guys!" I said. "I've got something to say."

Everyone stopped and looked at me. Raven seemed to know what was coming, as she remained off to the side.

"Doesn't anyone ever wonder about what we're doing?" I asked. "I mean, I've been with you guys for a while now, and there's still so much I don't understand about this club."

"Like what?" Cormorant asked.

"Well, a few things," I replied. "Like all of the money Miss Flamingo talks about. She makes it sound like a business more than a club. It's just all too weird for me!"

"A lot of what we do is kept secret," said Skylark, "even from each other. It's just how things go around here."

"That's what I keep hearing, and it's starting to get really annoying!" I said. "How can you keep doing this stuff without really understanding what it's all about? Can anyone here honestly tell me just *who exactly* is Miss Flamingo? Does anyone know what her purpose for this club even is? Anyone? *Anyone?*"

"Just hold on a second," Kookaburra warned.

"No, I'm not finished yet," I said sharply. "I was with Raven tonight, and I noticed she was writing some kind of fire charms or some crap on some paper, then hid them around the museum we went to."

"Uh, we're not supposed to discuss our assignments with other members," said Oriole nervously, glancing around.

"I recognized the emblems as being related to fire," I continued, ignoring Oriole. "That's what made me think of the library fire."

Everyone looked at each other, and I could see that the library was a sensitive topic by their reactions.

"A friend of mine has a fireman for a dad," I explained. "I heard from him that the fire at the library was very unique. First of all, it didn't seem affected by the fire department's attempts to put it out. Not affected in the slightest way! Absolutely everything was burned down—"

I stopped myself, not wanting to accidentally mention the grimoire.

"Absolutely everything was burned down before the fire put itself out. That's why I think the club had something to do with it."

"You figured out that the library fire was magic-related, huh?" said Kookaburra gruffly. "You're smarter than I thought."

"Kookaburra, don't," said Oriole.

"Then it really was the club that did it," I sneered. "And Raven insisted that she wasn't there on the night of the fire!"

"That's because Raven wasn't there," said Cormorant.

"You mean it was one of you?" I asked, looking everyone in the eye.

"Phoenix was there," said Skylark glumly. "His last assignment before his stroke required him to go to the library."

"Phoenix?" I said. "You mean the guy I replaced?"

"Well, he was here before you," said Cormorant. "Calling you his replacement is unfair to you and him. He was hospitalized for a week, but health complications led to his death."

437

"How do you know he was there?" I asked. "You guys just said our missions are kept secret from one another."

"Does it really matter?" Kookaburra grunted.

I looked at Raven, who was still standing off to the side. She was giving me a firm glare, but there was something softer beneath it. All of a sudden, I felt really bad.

"We don't know for sure if Phoenix was the one who *caused* the fire," said Oriole. "However, if what you say is true, it does sound as if the fire was magic-related."

"So, you're all just fine with that?" I asked. "You have no idea if we're going around burning places down? You're perfectly okay with not knowing what we're doing?"

"Alright, I've had enough of listening to you!" said Kookaburra, walking toward me. "Do you really want to know what it's all about? Do you *really* want to know?"

The intimidating air that Kookaburra gave off would have normally made me step back, but there was something giving me the courage to stand my ground as he stood over me. Perhaps Valefar was fueling my aggression, or possibly I was just too fed up with it all.

"I *do* want to know," I said bluntly.

"Well, too bad," he said, "because nobody knows. We've all been here longer than you, but none of us know much more about this so-called 'club' than you do! But I'll tell you one thing. The reason why we all just shut up and do our jobs. You can't tell me that all of the crap you've been put through during your club services hasn't been because of the *money*."

In fact, Kookaburra had hit the nail on the head. If it wasn't for the generous pay from Miss Flamingo, I wouldn't have even joined. Kookaburra's answer was the same answer that had ended this conversation the first time. Money was truly a powerful thing.

"Each one of us here is in it for the money," he continued. "I won't tell you any different. *They* wouldn't tell you any different. *You* wouldn't tell us any different. Am I right?"

I looked away, not wanting to openly admit that he was completely correct.

"So, just keep your mouth shut and do your duties," Kookaburra growled. "It's dangerous to talk about the stuff you're saying. To be honest, I'm too scared to tell you what'll happen if you keep flappin' your trap. It ain't pretty, I'll say that. Just accept it as is. You've given a bunch of reasons for us to like and respect you, so don't blow it. Got it?"

I was speechless. Optimistically, I managed to get a lot off my chest and cleared things up with my fellow club members. On the flip side, it still pissed me off knowing that it didn't change anything in the big picture.

"It's good, though," said Raven, walking closer to the rest of us. "Roadrunner has always shown that he likes to think for himself. He's not just some lapdog who follows orders."

"I understand how that's honorable," said Cormorant, "but it's dangerous in this club. I'm just concerned for the kid's safety, is all."

Raven looked at me with her typical stoic expression.

"It's fine to think what you want," she told me. "Just don't be too open about it. Miss Flamingo is very secretive and mysterious, and she can acquire information like you wouldn't believe. No doubt she knows about everything you just mentioned."

"Whatever," I muttered. "I'll see you all later."

As I headed home, I couldn't help but feel relieved and angry at the same time. Knowing that the rest of the club members were on the same page as me was good. However, it was still hard for me to accept things as the way they were. It was true that I had considered leaving the club to do honest work, but the pay was almost intoxicating. I had a very healthy amount of money sitting in my savings account now all thanks to the club, and it was hard to just give it up.

Additionally, I had learned that the library fire was most likely part of the club's activities, but I still couldn't understand why Miss Flamingo would want to burn the library down.

Is she after the grimoire? I wondered. *That would make sense, since it contains a lot of information regarding magic and the supernatural. At the same time, would she really need the book? There's just no telling! Maybe Kookaburra and the others are right, and I should just ignore everything that I don't understand. That just doesn't seem right, though.*

I made it home, feeling worn out. Valefar's presence in my mind was setting in heavily, and I knew that I had to fight back as quickly as possible. However, something was different. Nobody was there to greet me as I came home.

"Sapphira?" I called out into the quiet apartment. "Where are you?"

A few seconds later, she appeared in the living room.

"I apologize," she said. "Valefar appears to be making an advance, so I was attempting to ward him off."

Taking out my phone, I brought up the picture of the spell that was written on the stolen exhibit.

"Here," I said, handing her the phone. "Is this what we need?"

"I believe so," said Sapphira as she examined the photo. "It bears the correct emblem that indicates what kind of magic this is. Although it is not the most effective spell for this matter, I believe it will be sufficient. Shall I get to work now?"

"Do you need to ask?" I said impatiently. "Yes, do it. Hurry up, I can feel Valefar's influence getting stronger."

"Understood," she said, handing my phone back.

I tucked my phone back in my pocket. Out of nowhere, Sapphira grasped the top of my head with both hands, her sudden action startling me. She began reciting something, and I could feel myself getting dizzy. I didn't know if the room was starting to spin or if it was just me, but I closed my eyes to keep myself from getting sick.

An empty feeling in my head began to radiate as I heard weird humming sounds around me. Not daring to open my eyes, I tried to keep my balance. My body started to feel like it was floating, and I couldn't tell if my feet were still on the floor. The entire experience was quite frightening, and I wondered if I should've used the bathroom before going through with it. That's how scared I was.

Sapphira's voice grew louder and louder as the strange sensations became more intense. Out of nowhere, my eyes popped open, and I shoved Sapphira back for apparently no reason. Numerous magical circles were floating around me, glowing like neon signs. I found myself taking some steps back, looking at Sapphira with nothing but hatred in my heart, although I couldn't find any reason to justify those feelings.

"Get away from me, you worthless skank!" I bellowed.

"Michael, you must fight Valefar's influence," she told me in her usual calm voice. "The ritual is not complete yet."

"I don't care!" I growled angrily. "There's no reason to do this!"

"You mustn't let Valefar gain influence over you," she said. "You are still in control. If you allow him to possess you, it will be out of my ability to exorcise him."

It felt as if two minds were clashing inside my head. Half of me wanted to finish the ritual, and the other was just blindly raging. I grabbed my head and groaned, trying to gain control of myself.

"Grraaahhhh! Sapphira, finish it!"

She quickly clutched my head and began reciting the incantation again. I felt myself struggling against her, but her grasp on me was rock solid. Fighting for control of my own body, I closed my eyes as tightly as I could. I felt my fists hitting Sapphira with all my strength, but it was like punching a metal post. To keep myself from breaking my hands, I grabbed onto my shirt and clenched with all my might.

Slowly, I could feel myself regaining control of my body and mind. A calmness began to drift through me, and my breathing began to slow down to normal. I hadn't realized how tensed every muscle in my body was until they began to relax. After a while, Sapphira stopped the incantation and released my head. I collapsed to the floor, trembling.

"It was successful," said Sapphira. "I no longer sense Valefar's presence."

I got back up to my feet, wiping off the sweat dripping down my face. I felt like I had just climbed a mountain.

"Good," I said weakly. "Very good."

I put on my coat. As I was about to leave the apartment, Sapphira stopped me.

"Where are you going?" she asked me.

441

"I'm going to the store," I said tiredly. "I really want some chocolate ice cream right now. I really, really do."

~Opus 29~

The months of February and March were mostly uneventful. To say the least, my life as a college student was finally beginning to return to the equilibrium that I so desperately sought out to achieve. I managed to pass my psychology exam with a score of eighty-two percent, which was more than good enough for me. My degree was so close now that I could almost taste it, and I had to remain steadfast in my determination for just a little longer.

This semester only had me take three classes to obtain the required number of credits for my degree. My classes were trigonometry, which wasn't too difficult for me, German, which was a little tricky but didn't give me much problem, and the next level of psychology, which was a pain in the neck. Having only three classes gave me plenty more free time, making it the most breezy college semester thus far.

I continued to work for Miss Flamingo, deciding to do my best to ignore everything shady or hard to understand. Just as everyone else in the club had always said, the money was an overwhelming incentive to keep quiet and do what I had to do. Nobody brought up the discussion I had about blindly following orders without understanding the club's true motives, and everyone moved on as if nothing had ever happened.

Oriole had been tutoring me in psychology, which was proving to be much more difficult this semester, and I was still having significant problems understanding the material. To make it worse, Hayley was in the same class as me, and the underlying awkwardness of seeing her in class made it even harder for me to concentrate on what I could hardly concentrate on to begin with. She would always look at me like she had something to say, but didn't have the guts to say it. That was fine with me, because I had nothing to say to her.

While I found myself in the rut of college life yet again, time inevitably began to blow past without me noticing. Before long, spring break had come. The snow was finally gone, and while there was still the chill of late March in the air, I was able to put away my winter coat in exchange for my lighter jacket on the days when the sun was warmest.

A surprise arrived one day during the transitioning seasons. Elizabeth had paid me a visit during a trip to Elm Valley College. A school program she was in offered her the chance to talk to a college guidance counselor, and she took the opportunity since she was interested in attending next fall.

"Hi, Mike!" said my sister when I opened the door.

"Lizzie?" I said, confused. "What are you doing here?"

"Visiting the college," she said. "You said I could stop by to see you whenever."

"Well, I guess I did say that," I replied. "Come in."

"Don't worry," she said, stepping into my apartment, "I'll be staying with a friend today, so you won't be stuck babysitting me."

"If I had to babysit you," I said, "then I'd leave you to your own devices. You're almost a big college student now."

"I thought you'd say that," she said, looking around. "This is your place, huh? Not bad."

"It's not much, but it's home," I said humbly.

"Don't trash the place," she said. "I might be living here when I attend college."

"What?" I asked. "Why do you say that?"

"That's what Mom and Dad told me," she said.

"But I might still be living here!" I replied. "Does that mean we'll have to shack up together?"

"Oh, don't make it into such a big deal," she said as she grinned. "It's not that weird for siblings to be roommates, is it? If it's college life, then we just have to accept whatever living situations we can get."

"Mom and Dad really told you that?" I asked flatly. "That sounds a lot like Dad, for sure."

"It'll reduce the rent you have to pay," said Elizabeth. "Then you'll have more money for whatever it is you do."

"But this is only a one-bedroom apartment!" I told her.

"We can share the same room," she said, "or you can sleep on the couch."

Just as I was about to object, Elizabeth busted out with laughter.

"I'm just pulling your leg." She chortled. "I'll most likely be living with my friend."

Don't get me wrong, I love my little sister. However, I already had to live with her for my entire life, and I don't think I could handle living with her in an apartment, especially one with only one bedroom. She had actually made me paranoid there for a minute.

Elizabeth's visit was fairly brief. She explained her meeting with the college's guidance counselor and what she was going to do. After taking a quick look around the apartment, she received a call from her friend and had to go. When I closed the door behind her, I breathed a sigh of relief knowing that my apartment was still going to be my own. Having to share living space with my sister had been an underlying terror that had haunted me for a while, and now I was certain that I had sidestepped that train.

On another note, Aaron had been talking about going on another trip for spring break. He assured us that it was only half the drive, and it could only be for one day if we left early enough. Rather than going camping in some desolate place in the woods, he was thinking about a simple fishing trip.

Aaron, Chad, Lawrence, Jorge, and I had met for lunch at a simple burger joint to discuss our plans for spring break. That was when Aaron brought up the idea for fishing.

"Fishing?" Lawrence asked. "I've never been fishing."

"Never?" said Aaron in disbelief.

"It's been a few years since I've gone fishing," I said. "I have my fishing pole in my closet."

"I don't have a fishing pole," said Lawrence.

"I can bring an extra one," said Aaron. "What do y'all say?"

With a little pushing and prodding, Aaron was able to convince everyone to take a day to go fishing. He really seemed like he wanted to go, and I didn't think it was a bad idea myself.

"It won't be overnight," said Aaron. "We all remember what happened last time we spent the night in the woods."

445

"Yeah, let's not repeat that," said Jorge. "I still feel like an idiot for not knowing about the panic button thing. But I'll drive again. Gas isn't a problem for me."

"What about fishing licenses?" Lawrence asked. "Don't we have to pay for them?"

"They're easy to get as long as it's in-state," I said. "We're not leaving the state, are we?"

"Nope," said Aaron, squirting more ketchup on his burger.

"That should reduce the price a lot, too," I said. "If anyone needs help buying one, I'll pitch in some cash."

"Then it's settled!" said Aaron. "Fishing it is!"

The morning of the fishing trip was reminiscent of the morning of the camping trip. All of us met at the college and piled into Jorge's SUV. There was much less stuff to carry this time, so packing was a breeze.

"It's too bad we can't just fly to where we want to go," I said during the drive. "Think of how much easier it would be if everyone had an airplane."

"Or jet packs," Lawrence chimed in.

"I don't really like flying," said Chad. "It makes me all anxious, especially during turbulence."

"Flying is fun!" said Aaron. "Every time the airplane lands on the runway, I put my hands up and say, 'Touchdown!' You know, like in football."

As Aaron had said, the drive wasn't nearly as long as the drive for the camping trip. When we arrived at the lake, my legs didn't feel so cramped as I got out of the SUV. Everyone retrieved their fishing poles and tackle, and I felt like I was in a fishing league or something as we walked up to the bait shop.

"I don't really know much about bait," said Jorge, "like what fish take what."

"I'll cover it," said Aaron. "If I get some wax worms and night crawlers, we'll be straight."

We walked into the bait shop, and the familiar smell of fishing filled my nostrils. That smell took me back to the days when I would go fishing with my dad and brothers. As Aaron talked to the guy working at the counter, I looked around at all of the things for sale. Since I was still an amateur fisherman, most of the equipment in the shop was overkill for what we were doing, and it was surprising that some people actually use all of that advanced stuff.

"Alright, ladies," said Aaron after purchasing the bait. "Let's do some fish hunting! Remember not to catch anything illegal."

"Huh?" Lawrence asked concernedly. "Like what?"

"We only have basic licenses," said Jorge. "Some fish require an advanced license to catch, or have regulations."

"Like trout or shellfish," said Aaron.

Lawrence suddenly looked quite worried, so I tried to console him.

"Don't worry about it, man," I said. "Chances are you won't catch anything like that in this lake. Well, maybe some trout...."

Since we didn't have a boat, we had to walk to the end of the dock. There still weren't too many people out, so I didn't worry about snagging someone who was out on the water. While I was setting up my rod, Aaron had to show Lawrence what to do.

"Honestly, dude," said Aaron as he attached Lawrence's bobber, "you need to get out more."

"I am out more!" said Lawrence, annoyed. "That's why I'm here."

I cast my line out, and the waiting game began. Fishing is like ten percent reeling in fish, ninety percent reeling in nothing. That makes it a great opportunity to just relax and enjoy the great outdoors.

Aaron cast his line out like a professional, going much farther than mine. He was more of an outdoorsman than me, so he was more accustomed to fishing than the rest of us. You wouldn't think that by how much he plays video games day in and day out.

A couple hours went by with moderate success. We had a large cooler for storing the fish we had caught, and it was looking like we would have plenty for a decent fish fry. The sun had been out all day, which helped chase away some of the chill lingering since that morning. All in all, we were enjoying ourselves. Even Lawrence found humor in being slapped in the face by the fish he was trying to get off his hook.

"If we catch enough fish, we'd be able to have ourselves a little party!" said Chad. "A fish fry, ya know what I'm sayin'?"

"It'd be crazy if we became known around Elm Valley as the fried fish kings," I said. "We could have a huge college party and serve fish to everyone."

"We'd have to have some other stuff to go with it," said Chad, "like cornbread and greens and such. You can cook, Mike. Side dishes can be up to you."

"Think about how famous we'd get," said Lawrence. "People from all over would come to our party."

"That'd be awesome!" said Aaron. "It'd be like taking a shower in chocolate milk! No, that'd be disgusting, actually. I take it back."

"And we could invite all the girls," said Jorge suavely. "That'd be the best part."

"Eh, I think I'm done with girls," I muttered, staring at my motionless bobber floating on the water. "At least for now."

"Oh, don't be like that, dude," Aaron smirked. "What about that one chick you're always around?"

"Huh?" I asked. "Who?"

"You know," said Aaron. "That girl with the emo-looking hair that covers half her face."

"Yeah, she seems to hang around you a lot," said Jorge. "I think she's in some kind of band, or she used to be."

"Ha! Don't make me laugh," I snorted. "I just work with her. There's no way!"

"Why not?" Aaron asked. "She's kinda cute."

"She's all yours, man," I said dismissively. "Proceed with caution. Handle with care. Keep your arms and legs inside the vehicle at all costs."

"It sounds like you're overreacting, dawg," said Chad. "She probably ain't that bad."

"Hey, I caught another fish!" said Lawrence excitedly.

"Well, don't just scream at it," said Aaron. "Reel it in!"

"It's a big one!" Lawrence grunted as he wrestled with the line. "Oops...aw, it got away. It ate my bait, too."

"Damn it, Lawrence!" Aaron muttered. "That one counts as your share."

"One of us will probably catch it," I said, casting my line out again.

"How about it, Mike?" Jorge asked after a brief silence. "What's your relationship with that girl?"

"I work with her," I replied. "Every time you guys see me with her, we're discussing our job."

"And?" said Chad with a huge grin.

"That's it," I said.

"Have you thought about asking her out?" Aaron pried.

"Oh my God," I muttered. "Drop it, guys. I don't think of Raven that way at all. She's too much of an oddball. She might even be on drugs, I can't tell."

"So, her name's Raven, huh?" said Aaron pensively.

"Well, it's her nickname," I said, wondering if I wasn't supposed to disclose that information.

"I believe you," Lawrence told me. "If you say there's nothing between you two, then I believe it."

"Thank you, Lawrence," I said with a smile.

"You mean to tell me there's nobody you have in mind?" Aaron asked me.

"I'm focused on finishing my degree right now," I said firmly. "What about you, Aaron? You always interrogate me about women, so where do you stand?"

"I wouldn't mind getting to know that Raven chick," he replied smugly. "And it might be kinda taboo, but I think your ex is hot, too."

"You have the worst taste in women," I laughed.

"Dude, you don't date your friend's exes," said Jorge. "That's just common bro morality."

"I'm just being honest." Aaron shrugged.

"Ah, this takes me back to the years of high school drama," said Chad.

"There are plenty more fish in the sea," said Lawrence. "Don't worry about it, Mike."

449

"Just focus on catching *your* fish," Aaron told Lawrence.

"I already did." Lawrence smirked. "Samantha is my trophy catch."

"Aw, good one!" said Chad, giving Lawrence a high-five.

"Hey, Chad," said Jorge, casting his line back out. "Did you hear anything else about that museum fire?"

I cringed at the question. The day after Raven and I had visited the Elm Valley Museum, a mysterious fire happened to break out inside the building. Firefighters were able to put the fire out before it spread too far, but a handful of the exhibits were destroyed, mainly in the section where the stolen exhibit was displayed. That being the case, nobody would ever know that I had stolen Exhibit C-12 because it was assumed to have been destroyed.

Word of the fire had spread quickly through town, and there were all kinds of speculations about there being a connection with the library fire. I actually hadn't heard about it until a little while after, but I just wanted to forget all about it. The very thought of it made my blood pressure rise. Why couldn't people stop talking about it?

"They don't know much," said Chad. "They don't think it was an electrical fire, so they really don't know how it started."

"At least the place didn't get completely destroyed," said Jorge.

Remembering my visit to the museum, I thought about the pieces of paper Raven had placed and how I had destroyed one of them without her knowing. Something was telling me that was the reason why the building was spared.

"Do you think it's connected to the library incident, Chad?" Lawrence asked.

I hung my head slightly. If only they knew.

"Maybe," said Chad. "It's hard to say. There ain't any evidence connecting the two."

"People like to make connections between things," said Lawrence. "It makes things interesting, I think."

"I say it's arsonists!" Aaron blurted.

I coughed, feeling a lump in my throat.

"What was that about weird papers being discovered inside the museum?" Lawrence asked.

Come on, guys, I thought. *Just let it be.*

"Yeah, there were," Chad told him. "My dad said they were hidden in tight places. There were some weird symbols drawn on them, but it was hard to make out because the papers were decaying real fast. Before they could analyze for fingerprints and stuff, the papers had completely rotted away. They could actually see the decomposition happening right in front of their eyes!"

"That's scary," said Lawrence.

"Yeah, that's really strange," said Jorge. "Almost sounds like cult magic."

"Blah, blah, blah, magic," Aaron muttered. "It was arsonists, I say."

Actually, it was magic AND arson, I thought.

"Mike, what are your thoughts?" Chad asked me.

"It was aliens," I replied sarcastically.

"Oh yeah, I didn't consider that possibility!" Jorge chortled.

"You act like you have a dirty little secret," said Aaron, nudging my arm.

Although Aaron was just playing, it was a good thing I wasn't hooked up to a polygraph machine, otherwise the brief nervous burst in my chest would've set something off.

"Maybe I do," I said nonchalantly.

"Could you imagine if it really was Mike?" said Jorge jokingly. "One of the last guys we'd expect would be the one burning places down!"

"Those are the ones you gotta look out for!" said Chad.

"So, that makes you pretty suspicious, Mike," Lawrence chimed in.

"Watch what you say," I said with a smirk. "I know where y'all live."

At the end of the day, we had caught a moderate amount of fish, and it was enough for a small fish fry among the five of us. We bought some extra ice for the cooler to keep the fish fresh during the drive back. When everything was packed into the SUV, we began the trip back to Elm Valley.

Not long after hitting the road, I reached behind the back seat and took my tablet out of my bag. Since receiving it, I practically had to force myself to use it so I wouldn't feel as if it was going to waste. For some reason, there was something keeping me from getting rid of it.

"Is that your new tablet?" Chad asked me as I turned it on.

"Yeah," I replied. "I'm trying to use it more often."

"Don't you have a laptop?" Aaron asked. "What's the point of having a tablet?"

"It was a gift," I said. "I guess it makes me feel more up to date with modern technology."

"Do you have Internet out here?" Chad asked.

"Jorge has Wi-Fi in his car," I said, accessing the Internet.

"Ooh, fancy-pants," said Aaron. "You guys have all the cool stuff."

I kept myself busy with some simple online games. However, I soon became bored and put the tablet back into my bag and engaged in random conversations with the guys for the rest of the trip.

That weekend, the five of us gathered at Aaron's place for the fish fry. Since the weather was nice, we held it outside and used a portable deep fryer. Aaron's dad had an awesome recipe for fried fish that blew my mind when I tried it. Although it wasn't the grandiose party that we had joked about, it still met my standards for a great time with great company.

~Opus 30~

My German class was first thing in the morning, starting at eight o'clock. I entered the classroom about fifteen minutes early, which was quite early for me. Jorge and Samantha were my classmates, and it was nice to have familiar faces in the same class. When I walked into the room, there were only a couple other people in there, including Samantha. She smiled as I took my seat next to her.

"Good morning," she said.

"Good morning," I said tiredly.

She rolled her pencil back and forth on the table.

"I've been thinking," she said. "You remember how I asked for help with *that* thing?"

I understood that she was talking about her attempt to uncover the truth of the Campus Creeper. She had seemed to be quite involved with the mystery surrounding it, and I was a little concerned with the possibility that my and Raven's cover could be blown, but only a *little* concerned.

"Yeah," I replied, "I remember."

"I might not need your help after all," she told me. "Truth is, I'm beginning to think it might not be worth it."

"Really?" I said, trying to look interested.

"Yeah," she said. "It's too bad, though. I was looking forward to working on this with you and that other girl. Raven, I mean."

Deep inside, I was actually really glad that it ended just like that. The thought of going on some absurd wild goose chase for the sake of protecting the club's secrecy was daunting.

"If you don't mind me asking," said Samantha, "could you tell me your birthday?"

That came out of nowhere, I thought.

"May fourth," I told her.

"Interesting," she said.

She reached into her backpack and took out a folder, from which she removed a page containing all of the Zodiac signs. As she examined it, I wondered if she always carried that with her everywhere.

"That would make you a Taurus," she said. "I'm a Cancer, and it says that both signs are compatible."

"Um, okay," I said, unsure of how to respond.

"Don't think it means I'm leaving Lawrence for you," she said. "He's a Pisces, a water sign like me. I won't give that up so easily!"

"I didn't say you would," I said.

"You're a Taurus, which is an earth sign," she explained. "The other two earth signs are Virgo and Capricorn. Do you know any Virgos or Capricorns who play important roles in your life? You may want to figure it out."

I had never paid much attention to Zodiac signs and such, but I thought I'd give it a shot. Apparently, my amulet was made from sapphire because it corresponded with my Zodiac sign, so maybe there was some credibility in all of it.

"My friend Aaron was born on the twentieth of September," I said, looking at the chart. "That would make him a Virgo, which it says is an earth sign."

"Good," said Samantha. "He must be one of your best friends, then."

Looking at the chart further, I was shocked when I looked at the birthdates for Capricorn, the other earth sign. Hayley's birthday was January fifteenth, making her a Capricorn. Samantha seemed to notice my reaction.

"Did you think of someone else?" she asked.

"My ex-girlfriend," I said flatly. "She's a Capricorn. Her birthday is the fifteenth of January."

"So you dated a fellow earth sign!" said Samantha brightly. "Too bad it didn't work out between you two. It would've been a great relationship, I bet."

"What do you know about birthstones?" I asked, just trying to get off the subject of Hayley.

"Oh, I've got a chart for that, too!" she said, opening her folder.

Another chart? I thought.

She showed me the birthstone chart, and I immediately had to make something clear.

454

"I've heard there are various charts that tell people's birthstones," I said. "Is this one based off the Zodiac?"

"Of course it is!" she replied. "I'm surprised you know that. Are you really into this kind of stuff?"

"Not really," I said modestly. "I just, uh, stumbled upon these things one day."

I glanced over the chart, curious to see what birthstones were assigned to the individual birthdates.

"Hmm, if Aaron is a Virgo, then his birthstone is carnelian. Hayley is a Capricorn, which is ruby. I'm a Taurus, so I get sapphire."

"Pretty interesting, huh?" said Samantha.

"Yup," I said, handing the charts back to her.

Jorge arrived just before the bell rang. He took the seat on the other side of me, looking more tired than I did. Now that spring break was over, it was normal for everyone's morale to slip a little. I was guilty as well, but the excitement of my approaching degree was sufficient for keeping me on my game.

While Mr. Kaiser was giving the day's lesson, I felt my phone vibrate in my pocket. Using the phone while the instructor is addressing the class is considered poor etiquette, so I waited until he was finished speaking to check it. I had received a text message from Raven, telling me to meet her in the library after class.

"Aw man," I mumbled under my breath, putting my phone in my pocket.

"Hmm?" Jorge asked. "Something wrong?"

"No, not really," I replied dully. "Just some people can really get on my nerves."

"I know what you mean," he said.

When class let out, I packed up and headed straight for the library. Before leaving the building, Aaron came out of nowhere and put his arm around me.

"Mike!" he said. "What's up, man?"

"Not much," I replied. "On my way to the library."

"The library?" he asked. "Do you have something to research?"

I didn't want to tell him that I was meeting Raven there, knowing that I wouldn't hear the end of it.

"Yeah," I told him.

"Sucks to be you," he said. "I have the rest of the day off."

"I'm *supposed* to have the rest of the day off," I said, "but these things happen, I guess."

We walked outside, and I quickly noticed how much warmer it had gotten since that morning. The sun was out, making it a great day to avoid dark libraries in exchange for something more fun. That wasn't an option for me, though.

"I just want this semester to be done with," I said. "Then I'll finally have my degree!"

"Are you going for your bachelor's degree after that?" Aaron asked. "If so, then you're only halfway done with college."

"One step at a time, Aaron," I replied. "I might go for my bachelor's. This past school year has really taken a lot out of me, so I'm still deciding on what I really want to do."

"That doesn't seem like you, dude," he told me. "When I first met you, you were pretty straightforward with what you wanted to do and how you were gonna do it. Now you're saying you wanna change plans just because college wore you out a little?"

"It's been a long year," I replied, smiling tiredly.

While Aaron and I continued walking, a buzzing sound began swirling around my head. A big bee circled us, and I really wasn't in the mood to deal with it at the moment. Clutching one of my textbooks tightly in my hands, I watched the bee closely, anticipated its flight path, then swatted it right out of the air. The bee hit the sidewalk, bounced right back up, and stung me on the right arm before zipping off into the sky.

"Damn it!" I shouted fiercely.

"Did it sting you?" Aaron asked nonchalantly.

The combination of pain and failure to eliminate my target made me too angry to answer Aaron. I shoved my textbook back into my bag, then noticed a nearby flower patch blooming in the spring sun. Realizing that they were the flowers that supposedly attracted the most bees, a fit of rage came over me.

"Stupid-ass flowers!" I yelled at the yellow and white patch. "It's all your fault!"

The petals fluttered gently in a small breeze, as if to mock me.

"Hey," said Aaron, "those are flowers. They can't hear you, dude."

"Aren't these flowers supposed to be really attractive for bees?" I grunted. "Who would plant these here if they knew that? What were they thinking?"

"Uh, that's what I hear," said Aaron. "I don't really know much about them. You aren't allergic to bees, are you?"

"No," I replied, looking at the sting, "I don't think so."

"Well, if your throat swells up, like, text me or something," he said. "That's a serious side effect of bee allergens."

"If my throat swells up, I'm calling 9-1-1!" I told him.

Aaron gave a look of agreement.

"Yeah, that might be a better course of action. I'll let you be the judge if the time comes."

"The stinger isn't stuck in me," I said. "That's good."

"I hate pulling those out," said Aaron. "Wouldn't it technically be a wasp if the stinger doesn't stay in you?"

"How would I know?"

"You're lucky it only stung you once. Does it hurt?"

"Of course it hurts," I muttered. "Bees aren't famous for making you feel good."

"You know what they say!" said Aaron. "No pain, no gain, right?"

"I'm not sure I'm gaining much from a bee sting," I replied.

Aaron laughed a loud, dumb laugh.

"Alright, I'll catch you later," he said. "Have fun being bored in the library."

"Thanks," I said.

As I walked into the library, I tried ignoring the sting. The pain was beginning to subside, but it was still irritating.

Raven was sitting in the far corner of the library, and I could easily see a mountain of papers from where I stood. Hoping for the best while expecting the worst, I walked over to her. She was looking through everything with a scornful glare in her eye.

"Hey," I said to her.

"You!" she barked, pointing her finger at me like it was cocked and loaded.

"Me?" I asked defensively.

"Look at all of this paperwork!" she said angrily. "These are all documents concerning the club's activities. Thanks to you, we need to organize everything ourselves!"

"What do you mean because of *me*?" I asked, squinting at her.

"Miss Flamingo says you're being punished for treasonous words against her and the club," Raven told me. "I'm being punished for not keeping you in line."

I groaned as I took a seat. Did this have anything to do with all of that talk concerning how badmouthing the club was dangerous? That had happened about two months ago, and I had pretty much forgotten all about it. More accurately, I had *tried* to forget.

"I can't believe this," I muttered. "Is this about that time when I said those things to everyone?"

"Bravo, Roadrunner," she said sarcastically. "You remember your crime. That whole incident is why we're stuck here to do this."

Not wanting to start an argument, I just sighed and let it go. I couldn't say that nobody had warned me.

"Why are we doing it here?" I asked. "Wouldn't it be safer to do it somewhere more private?"

"This is fine," she told me, "and I have my own reasons to do it here. I asked Miss Flamingo and she approved of it."

"How are we supposed to organize this stuff?" I asked, looking at a couple pages.

Raven was busy texting on her phone and didn't answer my question. Instead, she handed me a page containing the organization instructions. What we had to do seemed simple

458

enough, but when I took another look at the sheer volume of documents to sort through, I could see that we were in for a monumental task.

"This is going to take a while," I said grimly.

"Don't complain," said Raven, still texting. "You brought this upon us. Honestly, I think a little extra hard work will do you right. A chopped onion brings no tears to the dehydrated chef."

"Who are you calling dehydrated?" I replied, annoyed. "I'm sorry I got us in trouble, okay?"

"Stop talking about it," she said sharply. "I will silence you with the power of a thousand mute buttons!"

When Raven started spouting angry metaphors, it was the signal to leave her alone. Having little choice but to follow orders, I started sorting through the documents. Making matters worse was the fact that they were all typed by Oriole, and her unique code required me to have Raven constantly translate. This only made her more aggravated, obviously.

After a while, the mountain of papers that still needed to be sorted seemed to stop getting smaller. While this was partly due to the fact that there was an obscene number of documents, I was catching on to Raven's inability to stop texting, which was slowing down our pace. I tried letting it slide at first, but then it started getting ridiculous.

"Why don't you put the phone away for just a few minutes?" I said, getting flustered. "We've been here long enough. We'll be here all night if you keep getting distracted."

"Shut up and mind your own business," she fired back.

Since I was already expecting that she wouldn't comply, I just let her be. Trying to get into an argument against Raven with logic as my only weapon, I was sure to lose.

About another twenty minutes passed before Raven finally tossed her phone down on the table. She let out an audible groan that made people look in our direction. By default, I didn't pay much attention to what she was doing, but then she suddenly stood up.

"I'll be back in a bit," she said hastily, taking off before I could even respond.

After watching her swiftly leave the library, I just shrugged and went back to sorting through the immense quantity of information we were stuck with. The task would have been a little more relaxing with her gone, but most of Oriole's cryptic documents were still complete gibberish to me without Raven's interpretation. Nearly ten minutes had passed before I gave up trying to continue on my own.

"Come on, Raven," I sighed, rubbing my eyes with the palms of my hands.

I took out my phone to call Raven and tell her to hurry up, but I saw her phone was still sitting on the table where she tossed it down. That added to my growing frustration, so I just decided to find her and drag her back myself.

I'm not gonna be here all night! I thought angrily as I walked briskly out of the library. *Why can't that girl just sit down and work on one stupid thing? She had better not be trying to dump this all on me. We're in this together!*

I combed through the campus, keeping a lookout for Raven as I went down every hall, building to building. Hopefully, she didn't leave the college. Who knew how long it'd take for her to get back if she had driven off somewhere?

To my luck, I actually found her in the music building, which didn't surprise me much. What did surprise me was that she was talking to someone, and the conversation didn't sound pleasant. This other person was a young guy with a tanned complexion and wavy hair. As they were in the middle of their discussion, Raven had her back turned to me and was unaware that I was nearby.

Normally, I'm not an eavesdropper. For whatever reason, I found it hard to walk away from what was going on in front of me. Maybe it was because I was seeing a part of Raven that I had never seen before.

"Why won't you just talk to me?" Raven asked the other guy. She sounded slightly upset, but not in the way I was used to.

"I *have* talked to you about it," the guy replied. "We've talked about this a bunch of times!"

"That's not what I mean," said Raven.

"Then what *do* you mean?" he asked. "This isn't what I want. I've told you before. I'm not trying to be a jerk, but you just won't get the hint."

"How do you know it's not what you want?" said Raven. "You haven't even tried. You could be surprised, you know."

"I just don't think of you that way," the guy told her. "I'm sorry, Tabitha, but it won't work between us. I already tried letting you down slowly, but you keep putting yourself up just to get let back down. I'm through discussing it. Just take it easy, okay?"

The guy turned around and walked away, and Raven just stood there with her back to me. While I was in the middle of deciding what to do, she whirled around and stopped abruptly when she saw me.

Honestly, I had no idea how to respond to the situation. As the look on my face gradually grew more confused, the look on Raven's face gradually grew sourer as she stared at me. After a while, she looked as if she was sucking a lemon and I looked as if I had discovered my real name was Weasel McNutwagon.

"What's with *you*?" she asked, walking up to me. "Yes, I have boy problems, too. Don't look so surprised."

"Who was that guy?" I asked. I wasn't sure if I was being more sympathetic or more curious.

"Fredrick," she replied, walking back in the direction of the library.

"Have you known him long?" I asked, walking alongside her.

"He was a technician for our band," she told me. "It's been two years, about."

There was a short silence as we walked.

"I'm sorry it didn't work out," I told her. "I'm also sorry that I listened to your conversation."

Raven suddenly stopped walking, and I stopped and turned to face her. She pushed her bangs back and tucked them behind her ear, revealing her entire face. There was a soft look in her eyes I had never seen before. This was the first time I had ever seen her appear so fragile, and it actually pained me a little.

461

"It's funny, isn't it?" she said quietly, diverting her gaze. "Things don't always go according to plan. I guess that means plans are nothing more than just ideas...fantasies. You can spend a lifetime trying to make plans into reality, but the only thing that's real is the outcome, and outcomes sometimes have minds of their own."

I've heard a great share of deep and intuitive things come from Raven, but none resonated with me quite like that last statement. Not only did I know what she meant, but I *understood* it. I felt her words. That was when she looked at me with a small smile (also a look I had never seen on her face), and I was a little disappointed in myself. Disappointed that I was utterly shocked that such a gorgeous and delicate smile could come from Raven.

Maybe she was a little more normal than I had previously assumed.

She walked up to me slowly, making me feel slightly uncomfortable. After expecting her to do just about anything while she was that close to me, she grabbed my right arm and looked at my bee sting.

"This looks like a bug bite or something," she said.

"A bee sting," I said. "I got it on the way to the library."

"Does it hurt?" she asked.

"Not really anymore," I told her.

I should have known better than to let her get so close, because she quickly smacked the sting. When I yelped in pain, she cackled maniacally.

"This is your punishment for eavesdropping on my private conversation," she told me.

"What's with you and issuing punishment?" I asked angrily, rubbing my throbbing arm.

"Let's hurry up and finish our task," she told me, suddenly sounding like the Raven I was familiar with as she flipped her bangs back over her face.

After three hours of tedious organization, the pile of unsorted documents was almost gone. The mind-numbing and mundane task was driving me crazy, and I was happy beyond words to see that we were almost finished.

"Does Oriole typically do this herself?" I asked Raven.

"Oriole and Cormorant," she replied. "It's a job for two people, otherwise it would take all day."

"This *is* taking us all day," I said, yawning. "I'm about ready for a nap."

"You sound like an old man," said Raven. "I thought you enjoyed this kind of stuff."

"Who said that?" I muttered. "Hey, can I ask you something?"

"Maybe," she replied, looking over the page in her hand.

"What's your birthday?"

She looked at me and raised an eyebrow.

"Is there a reason for you to know?" she asked.

"Just curious," I said.

A grin spread across her face.

"It's a secret," she told me.

We completed the organization and had to separate the documents into individual piles. Using string, we bundled each pile nicely, much like stacks of newspapers getting ready to be shipped. When the bundling was finished, almost the entire table was covered with piles of papers.

"How did you bring all of this in here?" I asked Raven, taking a look at all of the documents.

"It took a while," she said. "Lots of trips to the car. They were all bundled like they are now, so they were easy to carry. I had Cormorant help out, since all of this wouldn't easily fit in my car."

"And now we have to carry this all back?" I said dully.

"You got it!" she said in a spunky tone. "Pull your car up to the closest parking spot. You're going to take them back to the cabin."

Carrying the bundles of paper out to my car didn't take nearly as long as the organization, but my back started to get sore after the first few trips. When we finally packed the last bundles into my car, I was so relieved to be finished with everything that I started to laugh. Maybe I was really was going crazy.

"Miss Flamingo said to drop them off as soon as you can," said Raven. "I let her know that you're on your way, so I'll see ya later, Roadrunner. There's something else I gotta do."

She turned and walked off. Despite me getting a peek into her love life, Raven was still Raven. Perhaps she'd make a good partner for Aaron, and I would have to tell him that I know she's available. After all, he'd be the one dealing with her, not me.

I arrived at the cabin, and the first thing I noticed was Skylark's and Kookaburra's cars parked out front. When I walked through the front door, I flipped on the light switch and looked around. The place was always quiet, but it seemed especially quiet this time. Going up the stairs, I found that the door to the meeting room was locked, so I knocked to let them know I was there. When there was no answer, I knocked again.

"Hello?" I called through the door. "Is anybody there? It's Roadrunner. I'm dropping off the, uh, paperwork."

There didn't seem to be anyone there, so I wandered back downstairs to look for somebody.

"Hello?" I called out. "Anyone here?"

I looked around for a little bit, but there was no trace of anyone. Feeling disgruntled, I figured I would have to bring the papers in by myself and wait for Miss Flamingo to come back. Raven said she informed Miss Flamingo that I was on my way, so why wasn't she around? This was very unlike our club leader at all.

When I exited the cabin to start bringing in the papers from my car, I stopped abruptly at what I saw. Sapphira was standing in the driveway, right out in the open. I hurried over to her, thinking that she'd better have a good reason to show herself around the cabin and in broad daylight.

"Sapphira!" I hissed when I approached her. "What are you doing here? I told you not to come here! Don't you know what this place is?"

"I am fully aware of the situation," she told me. "However, this is an emergency and I had to disobey your previous orders."

"An emergency?" I asked, feeling uneasy.

"I have just confirmed the presence of a very powerful demon," she said. "He is readying an attack on you and your allies who meet at this location."

My heart felt like it was going to stop for a moment.

"An attack?" I gulped. "Who is this demon?"

"His name is Eligos," said Sapphira. "He is a very high-ranking demon and is significantly more powerful than myself. In fact, he commands his own legion of demons underneath him."

"You don't say," I said wearily, feeling my throat dry up.

"As it turns out," Sapphira continued, "both Asmodeus and Valefar were part of the legion he commands. Their advances on you appear to be part of a plan formulated by Eligos. After their failures to kill or possess you, Eligos himself is beginning to make the next move."

"And you didn't know this sooner?" I squeaked.

"He used his powers to conceal his existence," said Sapphira. "This is why I was unable to speak of him. However, he has recently lifted his powers from me, allowing me to inform you of him. I believe this is so he can focus all of his power into this upcoming attack. Due to his superior rank, I am unaware of the full extent of his powers and abilities. There is much that he can do, and most of it is unknown. However, it is well known that he can cause malfunctions in machines and electronics, such as automobiles and cellular phones."

"Should we go inside the cabin?" I asked quickly, rationalizing my actions as much as possible.

"I am unable to enter that establishment," she said. "There is a magical barrier that prevents demons and spirits from entering. However, it will be ineffective against Eligos because he is too powerful. Inside, I will be unable to protect you at all."

I glanced around nervously. Where were the club members when I needed them most?

"What else is there about him?" I asked Sapphira, keeping my composure.

"He has been fixated on you for a long time," she told me. "This entire time, I have been trying my best to protect you from him. Unfortunately, I have been unsuccessful because he is much more powerful than me. It is strongly evident that Eligos is responsible for the curse that was placed on you. I also believe he is the one who had sealed my powers that one time."

A malicious feeling suddenly descended on me, making the air feel dense. My heart started beating faster as my bones were chilled by the ominous feelings rising up inside me. Sapphira looked behind me and pointed.

"He has arrived," she said.

I whirled around and came face-to-face with the demon responsible for most of my torment over the past school year. When I saw who it was, a lot of things suddenly became clearer.

~Opus 31~

"Eli!" I shouted.

Still dressed in camouflage fatigues like a soldier, Eligos stared me down with piercing eyes. His demonic powers were so great that they manifested as a visible black aura around him. My suspicions of him were finally realized, but I really didn't feel any sort of triumph for finding out.

"Michael," he said, his voice encompassing me. "Michael...Michael...Michael...Michael...."

Instinctively, I reached into my pocket, pulled out my sapphire amulet, and held it out in front of me.

"Get the hell away from me!" I yelled, brandishing the amulet.

"He is mildly repelled by your amulet," Sapphira told me. "It will not provide sufficient protection."

"What am I supposed to do?" I asked her frantically. "Isn't there *something*?"

I looked back at Eligos. His face had become frightening and distorted by his demonic aura, his eyes shining like an animal's in the darkness. I wasn't able to get a good look at this terrifying form because he quickly vanished without a trace.

"Oh no!" I exclaimed. "Where'd he go?"

When I turned to look at Sapphira, there was nobody there. Now I was all alone, and I glanced around, feeling scared out of my wits. My first thought was to get into my car and hightail it out of there, but it was probably safer by the cabin. Somebody was bound to come to my aid, right? *Right?*

A warmer sensation broke through the demonic presence that surrounded me. When I felt a hand suddenly grab my shoulder from behind, an immediate calmness overcame me. Feeling much more at ease, I turned around to face this welcoming person. There happened to be an angel, appearing as a beautiful woman with short, light brown hair. Just seeing her smile made my fears melt away.

"Hello, Michael," she said.

Her voice was gorgeous, filled with the same warmth as Lemuel's.

467

"Who are you?" I asked, wide-eyed.

"My name is Bithiah," she replied. "I have been watching over you ever since you became part of this club, just as I have watched over the others."

"A guardian angel?" I felt so relieved that I could have cried.

Bithiah put her arm around me. We both walked slowly toward the cabin.

"Right now, Sapphira and Eligos are dueling," said Bithiah. "At this rate, Sapphira will be defeated and he will come for you next."

"Why is he after me?" I demanded. "What did I do for Eligos to target me?"

"He knows you have powerful ties to all that is spiritual," she explained. "That makes you an easy target. However, you must not fret. This battle is not yours to fight."

"But what about Sapphira?" I asked.

"You mustn't worry about her," she told me. "Right now, you need to meet your friends."

"My friends?"

Bithiah pointed into the woods.

"You should find them if you go that way," she said gently. "Go now. There isn't much time to waste."

With those words, Bithiah spread her wings and took flight, disappearing into the sky at incredible speeds. The warm feeling disappeared with her, leaving me alone with the malicious feeling of Eligos' presence. Swallowing hard, I took off into the woods as fast as I could.

Where am I going? I thought as I tore through the brush. *I hate how every explanation is kept to a minimum!*

This was certainly the fastest I had ever gone through woods on foot. The branches of the trees and shrubs scratched my face and arms, cut my skin, and ripped my clothes as I forced my way forward. The bee sting on my arm began to throb, but it would take much more than that to stop me at the rate I was going.

I can't say for sure how far I ran or for how long. All I know is that it seemed to be quite some time, not knowing if or

468

when Eligos was going to come out of nowhere and attack me. During a sudden confrontation, I would be completely helpless.

At long last, the woods started to clear up. Voices could be heard ahead, and I pushed myself as fast as I could to get to them. Not much later, Skylark was visible through the leaves. Hurrying over to him, I saw that he was helping Kookaburra draw a large magic circle on the ground. The surrounding trees were covered with numerous magical inscriptions, which looked freshly carved.

"Roadrunner!" said Skylark as I staggered over to them.

"You guys!" I panted, speaking between breaths. "What a relief to see you here!"

"What are you doing out here?" Kookaburra asked firmly. "We're in the middle of something important."

"You guys gotta help me!" I gasped. "There's a demon after me! His name is Eligos, and he's crazy strong!"

"We know," said Skylark, continuing to draw the magical circle on the ground. "We're on an assignment right now to vanquish Eligos."

A rustling sound caught my attention. Fear swept over me as I saw a beast emerge from the thick brush like a ghost, and I instantly knew it was Eligos by feeling his demonic aura. He was no longer using his soldier appearance, instead taking his true demon form. Standing almost seven feet tall, he didn't seem to be fully in the physical world, his appearance being almost smoky and somewhat translucent. His muscles were scarily huge, and large, black wings protruded out from behind him.

"H-he's right there!" I shouted, pointing at him.

"You can see him?" Skylark asked, bewildered.

"I sense the demon right there," said Kookaburra gruffly, picking up the old notebook we used for the Gumball Procedure. "I'll take care of this."

"Careful," Skylark warned as he quickly worked on drawing the magic circle on the ground. "He's very powerful. I'm almost done with this, so hold him off for now."

Kookaburra quickly removed something from his pocket and gripped it tightly, which I assumed was an amulet

469

of some sort. He seemed to know what page in the spell book to flip to, opening it immediately to the spell he needed. Without wasting any time, he began reciting the incantation.

The incantation instantly affected Eligos, who seemed to be cringing from Kookaburra's voice. Becoming infuriated, Eligos charged at Kookaburra with an absolutely frightening ferocity that was far beyond anything human, possibly beyond animalistic for that matter. It was so fast that I had no time to warn Kookaburra. Expecting to see Kookaburra plowed over by Eligos, I was shocked when I saw the demon go straight through him and vanish. However, the attack caused Kookaburra to stop the incantation. He dropped the notebook and staggered to his knees. I hurried over to him to see if he was going to be alright.

"Kookaburra!" I said shakily. "Are you okay?"

He groaned loudly, holding his head.

"Ahhh! Did that bastard just attack me?"

"Yeah," I replied. "He charged right through you."

Kookaburra picked the book up and flipped back to the page he was reading from.

"So, you can see him?" he asked me with a scruffy tone. I nodded, and Kookaburra chuckled.

"That's a nifty talent," he said. "Better than what I got."

His black shirt appeared to be getting wet, and I quickly realized that he was bleeding.

"Is that blood?" I asked grimly.

He looked down at his shirt, which he pulled up. His chest had four long scratches going across it, each one looking pretty deep.

"Damn it," he grunted, pulling his shirt back down. "Skylark! Hurry up with that symbol!"

"It's almost done," Skylark replied.

Another rustling sound alerted me of Eligos. He manifested from a cloud of blackness, assuming his demonic form again.

"There he is again!" I yelled, pointing at the demon.

Kookaburra continued the incantation, making Eligos cringe again. I removed my amulet and held it out in front of me. Even if it had minimal effects, it was still better than nothing. Eligos seemed to be incapable of escaping this time, and my heart pounded with the hope that we were going to win this struggle.

"Done!" Skylark announced when the circle was complete. "Kookaburra, hold him there!"

With unprecedented swiftness, Skylark reached into his briefcase and removed a phial of clear liquid. He looked at Kookaburra, who began nodding in Eligos' direction while the demon was weakened by the incantation. I watched their actions, noticing that Kookaburra was nodding to tell Skylark where Eligos was without stopping the incantation. Skylark watched the direction Kookaburra nodded in and was able to zero in on the demon's location. Kookaburra was clutching his amulet in his other hand, moving it in cross-shaped patterns. I would've been able to just tell Skylark where Eligos was, but I didn't want to interfere with their procedure. Apparently, they had done this many times before and knew what they were doing.

As soon as Skylark was right in front of Eligos, Kookaburra winked to signify that it was the correct location. Skylark opened the phial and sprayed Eligos with the liquid in crisscrossed motions. Judging by the demon's violent reaction, it was more than likely holy water being used. Although the water went straight through the demon, it was doing its job.

"Eligos!" Skylark shouted. "I command you with the power of my voice and the power of my words! I command you to enter this magic circle!"

Skylark's words had some kind of effect on Eligos, but the demon didn't seem to be fully under control. Instead, he bellowed fiercely. Whether or not the other two could hear the horrendous demonic screams, I started shaking from fear. Eligos' evil eyes were glaring at me alone, and I could practically feel the hatred burning into me.

"Roadrunner!" Skylark told me. "The incantation and holy water should have weakened Eligos significantly. If he's as powerful as I think, you'll have to help me command the demon to get into that magic circle. We'll be able to vanquish him then!"

Skylark and I began yelling at Eligos, telling him to get into the circle while Kookaburra kept reciting. After a while, the demon began sliding across the ground toward the circle. Keeping my amulet out in front of me, I continued to help Skylark with the commanding. Ever so slowly, the demon slid closer and closer to the magic circle.

As Eligos was a couple feet away from the circle, I saw him reach his arm out in the direction of a tree branch hanging over Kookaburra. Before I could figure out what he was doing, Eligos yanked his arm down, bringing the branch down from over twenty feet away. The loud snapping of the wood alerted Kookaburra, who jumped out of the way before being crushed. However, his incantation was interrupted, causing Eligos to break free from the vocal commands Skylark and I were using.

Just when I thought all hope was lost, Sapphira dashed out of nowhere. She slammed into Eligos, forcing him into the circle before she disappeared. The magic circle seemed to act like flypaper as Eligos struggled to move his legs. He began to flicker in and out, apparently trying to disappear out of the circle, but he seemed pretty stuck.

"He's in the circle!" I shouted excitedly. "Get him, now!"

Skylark and Kookaburra scrambled over to the circle, standing on opposite sides. They immediately began reciting another incantation from memory, causing Eligos much distress.

Yes, yes, yes, YES! I thought. *This might be it!*

The magic circle suddenly burst into flames, engulfing Eligos completely. His roars were slowly drowned out by the raging fire as Skylark and Kookaburra jumped back to avoid the heat. In mere seconds, the flame was snuffed out. Eligos was nowhere to be found.

"I think he's gone," said Kookaburra, looking around. "I don't feel his aura anymore."

"That's good," said Skylark tiredly. "He was a brute, wasn't he?"

"But there's another demon nearby," Kookaburra growled, looking around. "I sensed it right before Eligos entered the circle, but it disappeared real quick."

I knew he was referring to Sapphira, but I didn't say anything.

"We need to report back," said Skylark, sounding calm and casual now. I guess it was just another job, after all.

Skylark and Kookaburra cleaned up the site before we headed back to the cabin. Now that I wasn't in a hurry, I realized just how thick the woods actually were as we made our way through them.

"We'll need to treat your wounds," Skylark told Kookaburra. "They look pretty bad. Your shirt is soaked in blood."

"It's just a scratch," Kookaburra muttered. "So, what'd ya think, Roadrunner? Still think your position in the club is lousy?"

"Uh, not so much anymore," I said meagerly.

"Can you actually see demons, then?" Skylark asked me.

"Yeah," I replied. "All kinds of spirits and stuff."

"That's incredible," said Skylark. "You really are a good addition to our club. It's too bad you're mostly stuck doing things for Raven."

When we stumbled out of the woods, I saw that everyone else's cars were parked in front of the cabin. The club wasn't supposed to meet that day, so I wondered why everyone was there. Before we made it inside, the door flew open and Miss Flamingo strode across the lawn toward us, her dirty-blonde hair flowing behind her. She was immediately followed by Cormorant, Oriole, and Raven. Miss Flamingo stopped right in front of Skylark, Kookaburra, and me, wearing a stern look.

"The assignment's done," Kookaburra told her gruffly.

Miss Flamingo didn't respond to him. Instead, she stared at me sharply.

"I take it you encountered Eligos," she told me firmly.

"Uh, I did," I replied softly.

"Would you agree that demons are very dangerous?" she asked me.

"Definitely," I told her. "I'm glad to be alive after that."

"Interesting for you to say that," she said, her hardened expression cutting into me.

"Miss Flamingo," said Skylark, raising his hand. "Kookaburra said he sensed a second demon nearby."

She looked at Kookaburra, who nodded.

"I see," she said, looking back at me. "Oriole?"

Oriole handed Miss Flamingo a piece of papyrus paper with some kind of magic inscription on it. She pressed the paper against my chest.

"Hold that there," Miss Flamingo told me.

As I held the paper to my chest, Oriole used tape to stick it onto me. Not wanting to ask, I remained silent.

"Raven?" said Miss Flamingo.

Raven slipped her backpack off and set it on the ground. Reaching inside, she pulled out the grimoire that was the center of my entire supernatural endeavor. The moment I saw it, anger immediately built up inside of me. Part of it was probably because they took it without permission. Part of it was probably because I knew the jig was up. Just as I opened my mouth to protest, Miss Flamingo quickly hushed me.

"I've been looking for this for quite some time," said Miss Flamingo as Raven handed her the grimoire.

Knowing that resistance was completely futile, I hung my head in defeat.

"How did you know I had that?" I asked glumly.

"You ask too many questions, Roadrunner," Miss Flamingo replied, flipping through the grimoire.

She stopped on one of the pages, examining it closely.

"Miss Flamingo," said Skylark, raising his hand again. "Kookaburra's hurt, so maybe we should tend to his wounds."

"Are you dying, Kookaburra?" Miss Flamingo asked.

"No," Kookaburra replied.

"Then we'll deal with this first," she replied, showing me the page she was looking at. "Roadrunner, I assume you're familiar with this spell?"

474

Just as she said, I recognized the page. It was none other than the spell that had conjured Sapphira.

"I am," I told her.

Miss Flamingo tore the page out of the book and handed it to Cormorant.

"Cormorant, I'll trust you to destroy that page," she told him.

While she returned to looking through the book, Cormorant took out a lighter and held it up to the page. The flame danced around the paper for several seconds, having no effect whatsoever.

"You know that won't work," Miss Flamingo told him without looking up from the book.

"I know." Cormorant chuckled. "I just wanted to see for myself. I'll make sure to dissolve it in acid."

Miss Flamingo stopped on another page. After looking over it, she took a couple steps back from me and beckoned for everyone else to step away from me as well. At this point, I really had to know what was going on.

"Tell me what you're doing," I said sternly.

"I'm going to sever your pact with the demon," she replied without hesitation. "It's for the best."

Everyone else looked shocked as they exchanged glances. All I could do was stand there, feeling disgraced and ashamed as Miss Flamingo began reciting a Latin-sounding passage from the grimoire. I really couldn't feel anything happening, but I doubted she was doing anything incorrectly.

Moments later, a shadow appeared on the ground about five feet away from me. The shapeless form rose up and began to take shape. Before I knew it, Sapphira was standing there in front of Miss Flamingo, Raven, and the rest of the club. They all looked at her with bewilderment, a sure sign that they could clearly see her.

When the incantation was complete, I just stared at Sapphira. She looked back at me, not saying anything. Miss Flamingo snapped the grimoire shut loudly.

"Sapphira," I said quietly.

She didn't answer me. Instead, her face suddenly became twisted and demonic. Black wings protruded from her back. Claws, fangs, horns, glowing eyes, and the whole works. She was no longer the beautiful woman who had been bound to me by contract. She was hideous. She was abhorrent. She was a demon.

Sapphira quickly lunged at me without warning, baring her fangs and claws. Miss Flamingo already predicted the attack. Using some kind of amulet she took out of her pocket, Miss Flamingo ensnared Sapphira with an invisible energy field. I looked at the demon as she attempted to claw at me, but she was trapped in place by Miss Flamingo. All in all, I truly felt almost nothing from the scene, other than a sense that I wanted to do what was right.

"Sapphira," I said straightforwardly, "it's been a lot of fun, but now I think it's time for you to go."

While Miss Flamingo kept Sapphira ensnared, Oriole and Skylark used Skylark's spell book as a guide to draw a magic circle on the ground next to Sapphira. After a quick invocation, Oriole and Skylark opened a Hell portal on the ground.

"I shall banish you back to Hell!" Miss Flamingo shouted, sounding just as scary as any demon I've ever encountered. "Begone with you, demon! You shall be banished back to the bowels of Hell, and you shall never torment anyone or anything *ever again!*"

Pushing her amulet forward, Miss Flamingo repelled Sapphira into the portal. I watched as she was swallowed up by it, being dragged down to the flaming depths before Oriole and Skylark quickly closed it up.

It was all over now, and yet I wasn't very upset about it. Watching Sapphira's banishment made me realize that I'd been looking forward to that moment when all would be set straight.

"Oriole," said Miss Flamingo dutifully, "take Kookaburra inside and treat his wounds. Skylark and Cormorant, meet me in the meeting room. Raven, you're dismissed for today."

476

Everyone else walked away, leaving Raven and me in the yard. Raven looked at me, gave me a small smile, and then walked off toward her car. Not having any idea as to what I should do next, I hurried over to Miss Flamingo before she went back inside the cabin.

"Hey," I said when I caught up to her. "What should I do now?"

Miss Flamingo pulled off the papyrus taped to my shirt.

"You still have an assignment to complete," she told me. "Come to the meeting room when it's done."

Thinking for a second, I remembered the documents in my car. Opening the car door, the mass of bundled papers stared me in the face. The first bundle I picked up felt much heavier than it did when I was at the college, and I figured it was due to all of the stress and action that I had just gone through. Upon turning around, Raven was standing behind me.

"You're still here?" I asked.

"What's the matter?" she asked snobbishly. "I guess you don't want me helping you carry all of this upstairs."

"No, please do," I said.

Apparently, I was now immune to Raven's bittersweet way of offering assistance. She seemed satisfied that I wasn't affected by this instance of sarcasm, and she snatched up one of the bundles out of the back of my car without a word.

Kookaburra was in the living room as Oriole was treating his cuts with peroxide. Raven and I carried the documents up to the meeting room and placed them on the big center table.

"How are your cuts, Roadrunner?" Oriole asked me as I walked through the living room to get more stacks of documents. "Want me to put peroxide on them?"

"No thanks," I said politely. "This is nothing."

After a few trips, Skylark and Cormorant helped Raven and me out. With four people carrying the papers, the job didn't take much time at all to finish.

"I'm done with my assignment," I told Miss Flamingo when I placed the last bundle on the table.

Miss Flamingo was sitting in her usual spot at the head of the table. She sipped her steaming mug before standing up.

"Good," she said, handing me my envelope. "That completes your club duties, Roadrunner. You are now relieved of all obligations to us."

That statement didn't sink into my head quite right. I looked at Miss Flamingo, who stared at me as she took another sip from her mug.

"What's that mean?" I asked.

"It means I won't be needing you anymore," she told me. "You're free to go."

"You don't need me anymore?" I asked, exasperated. "Why not?"

I looked at Skylark and Cormorant, but they looked away, avoiding eye contact.

"The pact you held with that demon granted you with heightened sensitivity to the supernatural," said Miss Flamingo firmly. "Now your pact has been broken. That's only one reason why I won't be needing you anymore. Everything else I needed you for has been accomplished."

"You mean you just used me!" I replied angrily. "Is that it?"

"Of course I used you," she told me. "This was your job, more or less. Bosses use their employees, and they pay their employees for the service. That's what I did."

Getting over the initial resentment of being fired from the club, I realized that I was being set free from all of the shady, mysterious business that I had been affiliated with. No longer needing to wonder about what my actions were really contributing to, my departure from the club would mean that I was, once again, able to lead a normal life. There wouldn't be any more crazy missions and supernatural experiences. In a way, Miss Flamingo was truly setting me free. Looking at it from that standpoint, it was safe to say that I didn't have much problem with it. The weight and thickness of my final paycheck envelope added to the notion that I had built a very reliable cushion of money to fall back onto for a little while.

"Alright," I said boldly. "Um…I'll be on my way, then."

"Take it easy, Roadrunner," said Cormorant. He shook my hand with a firm grip. "It's been real, man."

"Later," said Skylark. "Thanks for all you've done."

Raven gave me a delicate smile and crossed her arms.

"I had fun working with you," she told me. "Don't die before you get old, okay?"

"I'll try not to," I replied.

Miss Flamingo walked over to me and shook my hand. The smile she wore almost didn't suit her, but I gladly accepted it.

"You have a lot of potential," she told me in a soft tone totally unlike her. "Take care of yourself, Roadrunner."

"I will," I said.

When I walked downstairs, Oriole was just beginning to bandage up Kookaburra's scratches. From what I had gathered, she needed to use some kind of special ointment because the wounds were inflicted by a demon. Kookaburra was slipping his bloody shirt back on when I walked over to them.

"So," said Oriole softly, "I take it that Miss Flamingo let you go already?"

"Yup," I replied. "Looks that way."

She gave me a gentle hug as her eyes grew watery.

"It'll be different without you here," she told me.

"You'll still tutor me, right?" I asked. "I'm really gonna need help with psychology homework."

Oriole looked away, and I could tell that I wasn't going to like her answer.

"I would like to," she said, "but there's a policy about excessive interaction with ex-members."

"For some reason," I muttered, "I knew something like that would come up."

Kookaburra grabbed my hand with a strong, painful grip.

"I'll miss ya, man," he said. "Enjoy your freedom."

"If any of us are relieved of our club duties," said Oriole, "we'll be able to get together, for old time's sake. Ex-members aren't forbidden from spending time with other ex-members."

479

"Sounds good," I said. "Well, um, I guess that's it for me."

"Later," said Kookaburra.

"Bye, Roadrunner," said Oriole, sniffling.

"Oh, sorry for keeping such a big secret from everyone," I apologized. "That was some really crazy stuff that just happened!"

Kookaburra grunted a laugh.

"You thought *that* was crazy?" he chuckled. "You really didn't learn anything about this club, did ya?"

I smiled.

"No," I replied, "I guess not."

As I walked out to my car, the sadness finally hit me. I looked back at the cabin, thinking about how much it had sucked to work there. Yet, while I was driving down the long driveway for the last time, I thought about how enjoyable it was to have worked there, actually. No other job would be able to provide the kind of excitement and mystery that the club did, and a part of me was actually going to miss that.

I parked my car in front of my apartment building and let out an audible sigh. The fact was now I was jobless *again*. The saved funds in my savings account would only last so long, and I wanted to conserve as much of it as I could for the time being. When I tore open my envelope and removed five grand in cash, a grin spread across my face. Perhaps I could take it easy for a bit before searching for a new job, after all.

The apartment was dead silent when I entered. There was nobody there to greet me anymore, and that thought made me somewhat lonely. Although she was a demon, Sapphira had provided me with company at the very least. I really didn't care so much about the fact that I could get her to do whatever I wanted to her to. Just having someone simply be there was enough for me. However, solitude was exactly what I needed at the moment, so I supposed it was all good.

Going into my bedroom, I noticed something on my dresser where the grimoire had been, next to my cookbook. A small package wrapped in Christmas wrapping paper had been left there by someone, along with a card resting next to it. Flipping the card open, I read the note written inside.

Roadrunner,

I had to break into your apartment by climbing through the window again. Nothing personal, I was just following orders. Anyway, I forgot to give you your Christmas present, so here it is.

Raven

Thinking back, Raven had called me while I was at my parents' house to tell me that she wanted to drop off my present, and I had completely forgotten about that. Curious to see what on Earth my gift from Raven could possibly be, I quickly tore off the wrapping paper from my present and revealed a small box. When I opened the box, there was a CD inside labeled *Triangular Lockjaw – Final Demo.*

Smiling to myself, it was now clear that Raven truly didn't neglect any fans of her band. I immediately put the CD in my laptop and rocked out to the best local band I've ever heard, feeling lucky to have known one of the members so closely.

~Opus 32~

The old routine: get up, go to school, come home, go to bed. Such was my life again, just like in the old days. The old, boring, dull days when the predictable schedules of day-to-day events ruled just about every aspect of my livelihood. Ever since Sapphira's banishment and my expulsion from the club, I once again became a normal college kid stuck in the rut of normal college life.

Raven was the only club member I still saw from time to time, but only on campus and from a distance. She avoided every possibility of interaction with me, acting as if I never existed. There was no blaming her, though, since Miss Flamingo would probably smite her if she so much as made eye contact with me.

With the month of May gracing the calendars, it brought with it my twenty-first birthday. Despite everyone telling me differently, I insisted not to drink until the school year was over. Now that the finish line was finally in sight, my resolve was stronger than it ever had been. Playtime would have to wait until after the final exams.

However, when the final exams were completed, the ultimate reality check reached across the table and slapped me awake from the dream I'd been having since high school graduation.

The envelope that carried my reality check remained in pieces on my living room floor. My hands shook as I reread the report card over and over. No matter how much I couldn't believe it, there was no denying the sixty-nine percent grade next to the psychology class entry.

By a one percent difference, I had failed psychology.

"Don't beat yourself up over it, dude," Aaron told me later while I was drowning my sorrows in a coffee shop.

"I won't be able to graduate," I replied dismally, staring down into my coffee loaded with health-shattering amounts of sugar and cream. "I'll need to take a summer class if I want the required number of credits."

"You shouldn't have taken psychology if you knew it'd end up like this," Aaron told me flatly.

"I didn't think it would!" I shot back. "Hayley was going to help me this semester like she did the first semester...."

"But then you two broke up," said Aaron, sounding as if he had foreseen it all in a crystal ball. "Don't put so much trust into the person you date. I've seen people get screwed over bad because of stuff like that. You're damn lucky to have gotten out of it with as little damage as you did."

Although Aaron was never known for his tactful input of the hard truth, he still had a point that I couldn't deny.

"I screwed up," I muttered. "I had a lot of money saved up, and now a chunk of it's gonna go toward an extra class that I wouldn't have to take if I hadn't screwed up."

"Well, at least it's only one class," he said, taking a bite of his doughnut. "Take something simple this time so you won't, like, have to dedicate so much time and energy to it. You're used to working your ass off in school, so it shouldn't be hard to work just one class into your schedule. You can even take an online class. That'll cut out all the time needed for attendance."

"I guess," I sighed.

"It looks like that spell we performed on the camping trip was just garbage after all," said Aaron. "It was supposed to help you pass psychology, but you failed anyway."

"Oh, the irony," I mumbled incoherently.

"Hmm?" Aaron asked, finishing his doughnut. "What'd you say?"

"Just talkin' to myself," I replied.

I stared out of the coffee shop's window, watching the cars go by. Aaron continued to munch his other doughnut, making me envy his carefree take on everything. He was always better than me at shrugging off the things that don't go his way, reducing the amount of weight from the luggage we all carry through life.

"It's hard to believe that school's been out for almost a week," I said. "At times, I forget what's going on anymore."

483

"Yup," Aaron agreed with his mouth full. "Now it's time to take a step into the real world! At least for me."

"I thought we were already in the real world," I replied with a smirk.

"I think it depends on your concept of what the real world is," he said.

"What's that supposed to mean?"

"I don't know." He shrugged. "It's like each step we take gets us ready for the next step, ya know? We all have our problems to sort out before we move on. Everyone has their own demons, and it's up to us to figure out how we'll deal with them. I guess that's my take on the real world."

"You didn't take any philosophy classes, did you?" I asked sarcastically.

"Me?" he snorted. "Do I look smart enough to take philosophy?"

When we were finished at the coffee shop, Aaron told me he had to help his dad with something at home. He got into his yellow truck and headed off, leaving me with an open agenda and no clue how to fill it. I went back to my apartment to think things over for a little. Maybe something fun or interesting would turn up.

I climbed the stairs up to my apartment, thinking about how many total steps I'd climbed since I had moved in there. Thousands, was it? Possibly tens of thousands? Upon entering my apartment, I realized that it had pretty much stayed the same since day one. Moving furniture around just for the sake of change was never my style, but maybe it would do me some good to shake things up a bit once in a while.

In the back of my fridge was the ham sandwich I had received from Sapphira, still as fresh as it always was, now wrapped in cellophane just to keep the dust off. If I would ever eat it or not, I really didn't know. Maybe in an emergency situation where there was a huge food shortage. Rather, I could feed it to someone else and smile as I knew what they were really eating.

I poured myself a tall glass of orange juice. When I turned around to put the juice back in the fridge, somebody suddenly appeared right in front of me, making me jump back.

"Lemuel!" I said, catching my breath. "You scared me!"

"Sorry for that." The angel chuckled. "I see you are doing well, Michael."

"Yeah," I said, putting the juice in the fridge. "Is everything alright?"

"Of course," he replied warmly. "I was just checking up on you now that Sapphira is no longer around. Your pact has been nullified, so your ties to the spiritual world have thusly been moderated. How has this been for you?"

"Everything's good," I said. "It's all returned to normal. Seeing you is the first 'abnormal' thing that's happened since Sapphira was banished."

Lemuel smiled and walked into the living room, and I followed him. He stopped in front of the window and gazed out. I took a sip of my orange juice and waited for him to say something, but he didn't. A short silence followed before I spoke up.

"So…" I said slowly, "what's next?"

The angel turned around to face me.

"Well," he said, "that's for you to decide."

"Ah," I replied, feeling that I should've realized what his answer would be.

"There's an entire world out there waiting for you," he told me.

"I know," I said. "I'm just not sure how to go about it yet."

"That's what makes it an adventure," said Lemuel, "not knowing what awaits around the corner."

"I think I've had enough adventure for now," I said. "Maybe I'll settle for a more predictable lifestyle."

"And that's all up to you," Lemuel told me. "Do you have what it takes to achieve that?"

I nodded.

"I'm pretty sure I do," I replied. "If not now, then someday I will."

Lemuel seemed pleased by my response.

"That's good," he smiled. "This looks like goodbye, then."

"You're not coming back?" I asked.

"There's no need," he told me softly. "I've done all I've been sent here to do."

"Oh," I replied.

"Take care, Michael," he told me. "You have your whole future ahead of you. Make the best out of it."

"You're starting to sound like my father." I chuckled.

And just like that, Lemuel vanished. That was the last time I had ever seen him, any other angel, or any supernatural being for that matter.

I disconnected my tablet from its charger and used it to surf the web. My laptop was a little faster, but I figured it wouldn't hurt to use the tablet once in a while. Eventually, I found myself checking the upcoming events at the Boney Feather on their website. To my surprise, there was an event going on that night. Some local band was playing and there was no admission fee to get in.

I don't have any other plans, I thought. *Maybe I'll just check it out.*

The last time that I had spontaneously decided to check out an event at the Boney Feather, I found myself starting an unexpected journey. Although I had just told Lemuel that I would prefer a life without surprises, I thought it wouldn't hurt to throw a little spice into the works.

According to the website, the band would start playing at eight that evening. I arrived twenty minutes early, remembering how packed it was the last time. However, this event didn't draw in such a big crowd. That was all fine with me, since it meant I wouldn't feel overcrowded.

With some time to spare, I decided to get a drink from the bar. I provided my temporary ID to show the bartender that I had just turned twenty-one, and bought a random beer, not yet knowing what drinks I would prefer. For the heck of it, I started a tab. Sitting down at an empty table, I took a sip of the beer and cringed. It was just like getting the acquired taste for black coffee.

More people slowly arrived as the crew set up the stage for the band. I had no idea what kind of music they would be playing, but I really wasn't there just for the music. The idea crossed my mind that Raven would probably show up onstage and do something crazy, and I smiled at the thought.

"Hey!"

To my surprise, Miyuki had walked up to me. For some reason, I hadn't really considered the possibility of bumping into someone I knew.

"Hey, Miyuki!" I said. "What are you doing here?"

"Just getting out of the house," she replied. "What about you?"

"Same thing, I guess," I told her.

"Are you drinking?" she asked, noticing the beer in front of me.

"Yeah, I just turned twenty-one this week," I told her. "I'm still waiting for my new license to come in the mail, so I had to show the bartender my temporary license."

"Oh, cool," she said. "Is anyone else sitting here?"

"Nope," I said. "Take a seat."

As soon as she sat down, I recognized how familiar this scene was. In a sense, this was exactly how I met Hayley.

"Do you know anything about the band playing?" I asked her.

"Not really," she said. "All I know is they're some kind of lounge jazz group."

"Lounge jazz?" I took a sip of beer. "What makes the lounge part?"

"I'm not sure," she replied. "I wouldn't really consider this place a lounge, right?"

"No, I wouldn't." I chuckled.

Miyuki and I chatted for a while as the band played. The music really wasn't my thing, but I wasn't paying much attention to it. After explaining to her how I had failed psychology and would have to take a summer class, she suddenly looked excited.

487

"I'm taking a summer class, too!" she told me.

"Did you fail a class?" I asked.

"No," she said. "There was a class I didn't have time to take because of work, so I'm taking it this summer."

"Oh," I replied, feeling alone in the world of failed classes.

"Maybe we can take the same class," she said. "Have you thought about what you wanna take?"

"I haven't given it much though yet," I said, "and I kinda wanna take a little break without thinking about school at all."

"Yeah, I know how you feel," she said. She looked up at the band, then back to me. "Hey, you wanna get out of here?"

"And go where?" I asked.

"I don't know." She shrugged. "Somewhere to get away from this jazz."

I thought about it for a moment while I finished the last of my beer.

Depending on what I say, it could really affect my future, I thought. *What'll happen if I decline her offer? What'll happen if I go with her somewhere? What if I just went home after this?*

Setting my empty bottle on the table with a *clink*, I came to my conclusion without caring about the outcome.

"Alright," I told her. "We can get some dinner or something. I'm kinda hungry."

"Yeah," she replied happily, "that works for me."

"I gotta go pick up my tab first," I told her.

The two of us walked up to the bar. I reached into my pocket to remove my wallet, and my sapphire amulet accidentally slipped out and fell to the floor. Miyuki picked it up for me, looking closely at the blue gem. I didn't say anything to her as I paid for my beer. She held it up to the light and smiled.

"What is this?" she asked me. "It's beautiful."

She handed it to me, and I looked at it with a small smile of my own.

"Just a memento," I told her.

Made in the USA
Middletown, DE
30 May 2016